RELUCTANT HEROES

G. L. VERNON

DEDICATION

To my mother and father. The best parents any child could wish for.

DISCLAIMER

"Reluctant Heroes" is a work of fiction. It includes fictionalised portrayals of a variety of organisations and places. It does not depict actual persons or bodies.

In the interest of authenticity and historical perspective, the events contained within the book are loosely based on actual events that took place during the Nazi era.

For example, the bombing of Hamburg, and the chapters relating to the fictional town of Haldersdorf which reflect events that occurred in the town of Demmin in 1945.

Life as a member of the Bund Deutscher Mädel (BDM) are based upon first-hand accounts as related in the Spartacus Educational website.

The Swingjugend movement were a group of German 15 – 22 year olds from mostly middle and upper-class backgrounds that admired American and English popular music and culture. Although anti-Nazi, the authorities tolerated their existence until 1942 when Heinrich Himmler ordered a crackdown.

ACKNOWLEDGEMENTS

Writing is not easy without a lot of encouragement, moral and practical support. As always, my wife Andrea has been my biggest support, along with family and friends who urged me on. I have also been hugely encouraged by readers of my first novel **"FALLEN HERO"**. Not only have many of them posted lovely five-star reviews on Amazon and through my web-site (www.Vernonmedia.com), but also there was a clamour for me to write a sequel. **"RELUCTANT HEROES"** has been written in direct response and hopefully it will exceed expectations.

I would also like to thank Dilys Brooks who has worked extremely hard to correct my appalling grammar, punctuation and tendency to write a hundred words, when a dozen would suffice.

CONTENTS

6

"Five years!" The American looked astonished. "Let me get this straight - you haven't seen the dame in five years?"

The man nodded.

"Jesus!" He took a drag from his cigarette and shook his head. "I tell you this - my old lady wouldn't wait around five years for me. Goddammit, she wouldn't wait five days." He gave a sideways look. "You won't recognise her."

"I'm worried she won't recognise me," the man muttered, then glanced down at his tunic. "Me turning up in a Royal Navy uniform is the last thing she'll expect."

The American levered his legs up on the Jeep's dashboard and settled himself as his interest increased. "What if she's met someone else?"

The man hesitated. It was a question he'd asked himself countless times. He gave the same unconvincing answer he'd given himself. "The world's a big place. I might head home, or maybe to America."

"Home being England, right?"

"I was born in Germany."

"You're kidding me!" He flicked the butt into the road. "What's with the British uniform then?"

"Many Germans had good reasons to hate Hitler: Communists, some priests and other Catholics, Jews, of course, and people that simply didn't like living under Nazi rule."

"Well, I'll be jiggered!" The American abruptly swung his legs off the dashboard and pointed through the windscreen. "Checkpoint."

The man slowed the Jeep to a crawl. Ahead of them, a freshly painted sign announced their arrival at the border of the *Republik Österreich.* Above it, as if to remind the local population that they were a defeated nation, was a larger sign emblazoned in French, German and English. '*You are now entering the French Administered Zone – 1st Army Corp (French).*'

They flashed their identity cards and were waved through.

The American was keen to continue their conversation. "So, how come you ended up on our side?"

"It's a long story."

"Obviously."

"Let's just say the English needed German translators and made me welcome."

"You left the dame behind?"

"I had no choice." He glanced across. "Which is another reason I hated the Nazis."

"What about your friends and family?"

The man fell silent. "I'm the only one left," he muttered.

"Jeez! Sorry, pal. I didn't mean to pry."

"It's okay. Where do you want dropping off?"

"Edge of town. Allied Liaison Office in the French Regional Headquarters. It's up on the left." He reached behind him and grabbed his kitbag. "What's German for good luck?"

"Viel glück."

The American jumped out as soon as the vehicle came to a halt. He held out his hand. "Appreciate the lift, and I wish you all the veil glück in the world"

The man smiled at his clumsy German. He slipped the Jeep into gear and headed into the border city of Brandt.

Like most towns and villages he'd passed through on his long journey, the city had an uneasy atmosphere. People went about their business, doubtful about the future and uncertain whether the world was now a safer place. He passed French occupation troops standing guard outside some of the civic buildings, or wandering along the pavements, presumably off duty and seeking either a coffee shop or a Gasthaus. The locals barely acknowledged them.

Apart from a few buildings damaged by artillery fire, the city bore few obvious scars of war. But there were plenty of indicators of hard times: the half-empty shops, the bread queues, groups of bedraggled looking refugees and their families tending vegetables in the small parcels of land that surrounded their homes. The war was over but normality was on hold.

He felt similar insecurity. He ought to be excited, expectant perhaps or even euphoric, and yet all he felt was mounting trepidation. Once again the awkward question intruded - what if she had met someone else? For years, he'd batted the idea to one side. He didn't want to contemplate the possibility. She was all he had. With her gone, he really would be alone in the world. Absorbed by his dark thoughts he nearly missed the sign 'Brandtnerwald', followed by a list of villages. He swung the Jeep around, engaged low gear and began the long twisting ascent up the mountain road. In two hours, he would have his answer.

8

HAMBURG 1920 – 1936

Heinrich Heppel was drunk. He'd consumed half a bottle of Schnapps that he'd preserved throughout his wife's pregnancy, on the promise it could be consumed after the birth of his first child. He stumbled across the threshold of the Gasthaus Ochsen at the end of Bismarkgasse. A cheer greeted his entrance.

"Comrade Heinie's arrived."

"Here's the new dad. Make way, comrades."

"Leave him alone, the man's not had much sleep."

Heinrich disappeared beneath a flurry of good-natured banter, back-slapping, hair-ruffling and celebratory hugs. He did his best to respond to the leg-pulling and barrage of questions.

"Boy or girl, Heinie?"

"How's the wife?"

"How heavy?"

"What's her name, Heinie?"

"Trudy," he managed to reply, as a Schnapps was pressed into his hand and a cigar rammed into his mouth. Everyone caught the mood. Good news was in scarce supply, and the birth provided reason enough to rejoice.

The Party Secretary led the toasts: to comrade Heinie and comrade-to-be Trudy Constance Heppel, before breaking into a rousing chorus of *The Internationale*. Once started there was no stopping. The old favourites tumbled out one after another - *Einheitsfrontlied* followed by *Das Rot Flagge* and more. Lulls in the singing prompted toasts of loyalty and solidarity with the heroes of the revolution.

Heinrich peered bleary-eyed through the smoke at the ranks of beer-filled, sweat-stained comrades who linked arms and swayed as they boomed out the songs. In between ribald laughter, constant leg-pulling and coarse jokes, they roared defiance of the capitalist dogs that caused the Great War, lost the empire, and undermined the country's self-respect. In the deafening, smoke-filled chaos, Heine had never felt so euphoric or such a strong sense of belonging. A moon-like expression became fixed across his face as he tried to comprehend the stein of beer the waitress placed in front of him.

"On the house, Henie," she said, as she scooped up half a dozen empty glasses.

Heinie's eyes swivelled from her cleavage towards the handle of the mug. With luck, he might be able to steer his hand without upsetting the contents. The task became a challenge. His objective seemed to shift and blur. One minute it was close; the next out of reach. He became so fixated that the shattering of windows and the crash of doors being kicked in barely registered.

Dozens of screaming Freikorps thugs, wielding pick-axe handles, knuckle-dusters, flick-knives, crowbars and sledgehammers, fell upon the detested Communists. Heinie's comrades fought back. They threw themselves into the fight with the recklessness of men that had lost all fear and reason. Glasses, bottles, chairs and tables were hurled at the rampaging invaders. Brutal melees erupted. Anyone who lost their footing disappeared under a deluge of flying boots. Eyes were gouged, hair ripped out, ears bitten off and heads bludgeoned.

The Nazis held the advantage. They outnumbered their foes two to one, attacked without warning and were organised and sober. A few Communists fled into the street, only to be met by the crowbars of more gleeful thugs positioned in anticipation of their flight. The Nazis worked their way through the bar in an orgy of violence - yelling obscenities, smashing mirrors and lights, and sending bottles and glasses flying from the shelves. They forced their adversaries back up the stairs to the upper meeting rooms. Once trapped on the upper floors, the Communists had no escape other than to drop from the windows down to the street below and face further savagery.

Heinrich gazed in bewilderment at the mayhem. He knew he should be doing something, but his addled mind failed to connect. He watched in dazed confusion as the barmaid desperately fended off three Freikorps thugs. Her screams prompted him into action. He hauled himself unsteadily to his feet. A pick-axe handle was the last thing he saw, a split second before it smashed into the bridge of his nose.

"Thank you, I'm so grateful." Frau Heppel clutched the purse to her chest and looked at her benefactor through tear-filled eyes.

"I wish it was more. Everyone donated... Heinie was popular." The shop steward fell silent. What more could he say?

Frau Heppel nodded.

"What will you do?"

She wiped her eyes and stared hopelessly at the floor. "We'll manage," she whispered.

He shuffled awkwardly. "Let me know if there is anything you need." His empty words hardly registered. He patted her shoulder and left.

Two weeks later, she and Trudy were evicted.

For two years they moved from one neighbourhood to another: each more squalid, crime-ridden and wretched than the last. Small apartments gave way to a series of decrepit flats and hostels, until they found a tiny room amidst the slums of Hamburg. They shared the bathroom with two other families on the same floor, and the single privy with the rest of the block.

Trudy's world consisted of being looked after by a succession of 'aunts' and transient 'brothers' and 'sisters'. Meals were sporadic and insubstantial. She was constantly hungry. The overcrowded conditions meant diseases spread quickly. Someone was always ill. Trudy's earliest memories were of musty-smelling rooms with damp walls, nicotine-stained ceilings and the endless sound of wracking coughs.

Her mother receded in her memory. She became vaguely aware of some connection with the woman with the painted face, whose bed she shared. However, contact became increasingly fleeting. There was little sign of motherly affection: no cuddles, good-night stories, or concern about how days had been spent. Each evening the woman decorated herself, and smeared her lips a gaudy bright red, before disappearing into the night, leaving a whiff of cheap scent in her wake. She'd re-appear next morning, hollow-eyed and stinking of Schnapps and stale cigarettes. Trudy found herself evicted from the bed as the exhausted creature collapsed into oblivion. When she wasn't sleeping, the haggard-looking woman chain-smoked cheap cigarettes that stained her teeth and hair a rancid yellow. Trudy owed her survival beyond four years of age to Tante Bri.

Tante Bri swept up the human debris the slum struggled to absorb. Anyone cast adrift in the sea of desperation found comfort under her wing. She had a heart as big as her figure. She'd nurtured six children of her own, but her compassion embraced any child of the street. She developed a soft spot for Trudy. Perhaps she recognised that, although life was tough for everyone, it was particularly hard for the youngster. Through Bri, Trudy was washed, dressed and fed as well as any other child of the slums. Bri ensured her attendance at school, provided applause and encouragement for the small triumphs the youngster managed to achieve, and became Trudy's Madi and surrogate mother.

Life in the slum was precarious, yet, for Trudy, this was normal. She never questioned her lot or complained about the cards she'd been dealt. Fortunately, she was a fast learner. She needed to be. Only those with an instinct for survival succeeded in the slums, and only those with intelligence or good fortune escaped. For all her sharpness, it took thirteen years for the opportunity to present itself.

It was late afternoon. Despite the open window, the sour odour of boiled cabbages and cigarette smoke hung in the air. At a casual glance, the apartment appeared chaotic, and yet everything had its place. The small kitchen was festooned with pots, pans and cheap china cups hanging from nails driven into shelves, upon which mismatched plates and bowls were piled haphazardly, alongside tins of processed meats and jars of pickles and jams. A stove, with a tiny oven and a couple of hotplates, stood beside a large cracked stone sink. An ancient dresser provided storage for everything else: towels, soaps, a sink plunger, loose vegetables, candles, matches. A solid wooden table was jammed against the only window. A bench-seat on one side and a stool meant four people could be squeezed in to share a meal.

11

A large threadbare armchair dominated the rest of the room. Only Tante Bri ever sat in it. It was her throne and was surrounded by her workbasket, piles of clothes, curtains, blankets and half-finished knitting. Mending, altering and making clothes provided Tante Bri's main source of income. A bottle of cheap Schnapps, a glass and an ashtray lay on a small table within easy reach. A battered sofa occupied much of the far wall. Visitors that chose to stay would endure an uncomfortable night on its broken springs.

There were two bedrooms - one for Tante Bri, the other shared by Trudy and her mother. For all its clutter, Bri managed to keep everything and everybody clean.

"Get that inside you, young lady." Tante Bri ladled a helping of steaming cabbage and turnip soup into Trudy's bowl. "Here, dunk that in it." She tore a lump off the K Brot loaf. Trudy needed no encouragement. She wolfed the food down, saving the last morsel of bread to wipe every last trace from the bowl.

"Done your homework?"

Trudy nodded.

Tante Bri tried to look stern. "Show me what you've done."

Trudy smiled. Tante Bri always played this game: expressing false doubt that she'd neglected her schoolwork. For Trudy, that was never a possibility. It was the highlight of her day. It meant she had her Madi's undivided attention. She dropped from the table and retrieved her books from the satchel, while Bri washed the dishes.

Once the bowls and cutlery were stacked on the draining board, Tante Bri dried her hands and settled her bulk in her throne. Trudy perched on its arm and snuggled up close.

"Who's this man?" Tante Bri stabbed her finger at the ink portrait on an inside cover.

"That's Adolf Hitler, Madi," Trudy laughed. "You know who it is."

"And what does this say?" Tante Bri squinted her eyes. '*Who wants to live, has to fight.*' She shook her head. "Maybe Herr Hitler should pay a visit to this neighbourhood," she muttered. "And what's your homework task today, Schatzy?"

"To learn by heart at least one lesson from Herr Hitler. I've learnt two," Trudy said proudly.

"Go on then." Tante Bri closed the textbook and adopted an expectant pose.

'*Learn to sacrifice for your fatherland. We shall go onwards. Germany must live. In your race is your strength. You must be true, you must be daring and courageous and, with each other, form a great and wonderful comradeship.*' She looked at her aunt expectantly.

Tante Bri pretended to be unimpressed. "You said two."

'*Youth must be led by youth.*'

12

"Is that it?"

Trudy nodded. "Oh, and I had to learn my times tables, but you know I can do them already, and read the first two chapters of this." She rummaged around in her satchel and extracted a pristine textbook, *'Principles of National Socialism.'*

"And have you done that?"

"I've started."

"Well, make sure you finish it." She reached out and cradled Trudy's chin in her hand. "You're a bright girl, Trudy. Make the most of your schooling. You don't want to be living in a place like this all your life."

"I like it here, Madi. I want to live here with you forever."

Tante Bri looked serious. "No, you don't, Liebling. The only reason I'm in a place like this is because I never had no schooling. You've got a head on you. Use your wits, my girl, and you'll do better in life than me." She patted Trudy on the knee. "Well done. Now nip to the cellar and bring up the washing, there's a dear. Once you've done that, you're free to go." She raised a warning finger. "Don't get into any mischief, mind."

Trudy gave her an affectionate kiss and made for the door. Her aunt's advice, however, presented a dilemma. She intended to use her wits. But that meant getting into mischief.

Gangs were part of slum culture. Unemployment and poor education drove many towards a life of crime. By the age of seven or eight, every child knew that stealing fruit from distracted market stallholders was as easy as picking apples off a tree. It wasn't much of a stretch to graduate to shoplifting.

Trudy became adept at both. The difference, she realised quicker than most, was that stallholders happily gave away damaged fruit, and more besides, for free at the end of the market day. She also saw, at first hand, that the risks of being caught shop-lifting were high. Goods were well protected, and escape routes out of shops easily blocked. It wasn't worth it.

Pickpocketing, on the other hand, presented few downsides and offered better rewards. Plus, the pickpocketing gang had a certain cache - daring, dashing, full of bravado. Gang members took their inspiration from the American talkies. The slum kids knew how to create enough confusion within a cinema queue to gate-crash entry. For them, *Little Caesar, Scarface, City Streets* were more than escapism: they were real. Crime could pay if they learned the language, dressed the part and played it smart.

Trudy's initial request to join was met with brusque dismissal.

"You're too young."

"I'm thirteen."

13

The gang leader took a long drag from his cigarette and eyed her. "You can't run fast enough, you don't know enough to be a stall, and Tante Bri would skin you alive."

Trudy decided cute appeal was a better tactic than confrontation. She gazed at the gang leader with doe-like eyes. "I'll learn."

Yankee Franz wasn't won over. He looked into the middle distance and exhaled a steady stream of smoke, as if his mind had already turned to more weighty matters. He nipped the cigarette between his thumb and forefinger, took a last drag, flicked the butt on the pavement and ground it out with his heel.

"You're too young – babe. Get used to it," he drawled in what he thought a passable imitation of an American accent. He retrieved a comb from his inside pocket, ran it through his slicked back, brilliantine-glossed hair, before checking his reflection in Old Man Mordechai's pawn shop window. Satisfied, he shrugged to adjust his jacket, as he'd seen Edward G Robinson do in *Scarface,* and made to move off.

The other gang members smirked at her naivety. Unlike their leader, none could afford or were brave enough to dress as he did - in dark jacket and closely matching trousers that gave the impression of a suit. A fedora provided additional pizzazz to the swagger. But they took their cue from Yankee Franz in all other respects. They slouched with heads tilted back, cigarettes hanging loosely from the corner of mouths, and hands thrust in pockets with just the thumbs showing.

Trudi's career as a pickpocket seemed thwarted. Rescue came from an unexpected quarter. A teenage girl in a cheap flapper dress, with her hair cut short in Gatsby style, spoke up. "We need a spotter, Franz."

Franz's head jerked up, his eyes narrowed, and he turned slowly around to consider whether his authority was being questioned. The girl was his moll, Gabi, and that eased his mind. Gabi pushed herself off the wall, swayed to his side and caressed his arm. "Herbert's sick, and Helga's had to duck out since she got caught." She brushed some imagined dirt off his lapel. "We need a spotter, sweetie." She looked into his face and gave a long, languid blink that she knew he found enticing. "We need new blood."

Yankee Franz pursed his lips and gave a slow nod as he weighed her words. "Tante Bri will kick-up," he drawled.

"She doesn't need to know." The girl glanced at Trudy, who stood almost vibrating with nervous tension. "She'll only be a spotter; she can't get involved with any serious action."

"We can't afford to mess up. I don't want her blubbing or snitching."

"I ain't no snitch." Trudy looked outraged. That was one thing every slum child learned. "I ain't never snitched," she added, for good measure.

Yankee Franz wavered. Gabi had a point. Losing two gang members was a blow, and Helga faced a lengthy stretch having been caught twice before.

Gabi kissed him on the cheek. "I'll show her the ropes," she breathed.

Under Gabi's tutelage, Trudy became a reliable spotter and graduation to a runner quickly followed. She was eager to get closer to the real action. Her wish became reality quicker than expected.

Franz recognised her potential. Trudy's innocent, angelic face could easily distract a mark. She'd a quick mind that enabled her to blag her way out of trouble, and was a fast, agile runner able to dodge through crowded markets and tram queues, or mingle within the confusion of rush-hour travellers at the railway stations. Above all, her small hands slipped easily into unguarded pockets and open handbags. Her nimble fingers proved adept at loosening watch straps and easing bracelets off wrists. Trudy had just turned fourteen when she carried out her first 'touch'. She lifted a kid-skin purse from an old lady's pocket. No matter that it contained a wad of almost worthless Reichsmarks, she'd been blooded.

She honed her skills and, for the first time in her life, she had status and respect. A life of crime seemed seductively attractive, especially once she learnt to recognise the value of her endeavours, and the person who taught her that was Old Man Mordechai Furnstein.

AUSTRIAN HOMECOMING - 1936

Harriet screwed up her eyes against the onrushing air that sent her hair billowing. Pungent steam and coal smuts forced her to duck back inside. Unable to contain her excitement she stuck her head out again, eager to spot a familiar landmark. "I can see our mountains!" she exclaimed as she collapsed back into the compartment. "It can't be far now. Ma, what's the time?"

The engine's whistle heralded the train's approach to Brandt. Her mother consulted her watch. "Twenty to twelve. We're on time," she said, masking the fact she was equally thrilled. In ten minutes, she'd be reunited with her husband after a three-week absence. She glanced at her daughter, and her composure evaporated. "For goodness' sake, look at the state of you." She rummaged in her bag for something to clean the soot from her daughter. "You're not greeting your father looking like that!" Her search became desperate as another wail of the whistle, followed by a lurch of brakes, signalled the train's approach to Brandt.

"Here." Johan passed a large handkerchief over with the weariness of someone familiar with his sister's waywardness.

His mother gave him a grateful look before despatching Harriet to the washroom with the extra instruction, "brush your hair as well."

As the train came to a squealing, juddering halt, Harriet still hadn't returned, adding to her mother's stress.

"You jolly her along. I'll look after the luggage." Johan said. He swung the two heavy suitcases onto the platform before picking up his own and Harriet's smaller bags, his mother's hat, and the paper bags containing the remnants of their picnic. Satisfied everything was unloaded, he clambered down to be confronted by the beaming face of his father.

"Welcome home, young man." Sep Breitner swallowed up his son in an enormous bear hug.

Johan managed to hold himself in check. It wasn't manly for a seventeen-year-old to burst into tears, especially in public.

"Papa!" Harriet ducked and weaved her way through the crowd before throwing herself at her father, almost bowling him over. With her arms locked around his neck, she simultaneously sobbed into his cheek and smothered him in kisses.

"How's my beautiful girl?" Sep gently disentangled himself from her grasp.

"I've missed you. We all have." Harriet wiped her tears and reluctantly let go of his hand as her mother approached at a more dignified pace.

Susan Breitner found herself wrapped up in the cocoon of her husband's arms, and instantly felt warm, safe and secure. It was as if the noise, bustle and confusion of the station ceased to exist as she pressed her lips to his.

Johan shuffled with embarrassment. "I'll get the rest of the luggage," he muttered, and headed towards the guard's van.

Their pile of luggage was impressive. "You left with two suitcases. You returned with two suitcases, two trunks and two other bags!"

Susan looked sheepish. "You know what it's like. Family and friends are so generous. It's difficult to say no. Besides, we won't be together again for a long while."

Sep's grumbles earnt him a playful slap on the arm. He waved a porter over and arranged for their luggage to be transferred to the Brandtnerwald train, then glanced at his watch. "Time for something to eat – a special treat at the Krone. You can tell me all about England over lunch."

For Johan, the short walk to Gasthaus Krone embodied the sights, sounds and smells of his homeland. The air felt crisp with a faint odour of woodsmoke. The backdrop of pine forests and craggy snow-capped peaks to the south and east were unmistakably Austrian. To the north, lay the great blue expanse of the lake, shimmering in the autumn sunshine, and the distant peaks of the Swiss Alps stretched over the tops of the flood dykes of the River Rhein to the west.

The Krone was one of Brandt's oldest inns. It stood in the town's central square beside the offices of the diocese, and the medieval Cathedral Church of St Cuthbert's from which the square took its name. The Rathaus and civic buildings lay opposite. Shops, cafes and a few banks filled the remaining two sides.

Although the capital of Brandtnerwald, Brandt was like a dowager whose best days lay behind her. In its heyday it was vibrant and thriving, but the Great War had crushed its spirit and stunted its development. Unemployment was rife; there were pockets of poverty and an undercurrent of resentment and rebellion. Groups of shabbily dressed men sat on the park benches in the middle of the square. They looked dejected, smoked cheap cigarettes and drank from bottles. All had the grim faces of the desperate. Some carried evidence of war wounds. They watched with cold, hard eyes those fortunate to be employed or wealthy enough to indulge themselves.

Johan's father always found the sight unsettling. He looked on them as old comrades. He'd lost his leg and nearly his sanity in the Great War. Yet, by accident of birth, family inheritance, an astute business brain, an excellent marriage and a lot of good fortune, Sep ended up relatively prosperous. Nevertheless, the plight of the destitute pricked his conscience. "Good men that the country has forgotten," Sep muttered. "Fought for their country, now look at them." He squeezed his son's shoulder. "Count yourself fortunate, son. We could easily be in their position." That had been over ten years ago, and yet it seemed the same men still remained trapped in the same sorry situation.

The aroma of bouillon soup, Schnitzel, roast chicken and freshly ground coffee proved distracting. The Krone held a special place in the Breitner family's affections not just for its excellent cuisine, but because their visits tended to generate incidents that lodged in the family memory.

Johan's visit as a six-year-old was a case in point. Having tricked his distracted parents into ordering two double helpings of ice-cream, he had regurgitated it on the Gasthaus floor ten minutes later.

That was followed by the 'Harriet Event', as the family now referred to it. His sister had mastered reading and became intrigued as to where words might lead. How the soups were prepared? If potatoes were described as Dauphinoise, how this differed from them being boiled? She analysed the menu with forensic diligence that had her parents glowing with pride. Unfortunately, besotted by their daughter's precociousness, they failed to notice the menu's proximity to the table candles. The flames spread with impressive speed, causing other diners to leap to their feet ready to flee. Sep's coolness contained the situation. Only a couple of guests on the adjoining table received a soaking from a misdirected water jug, a few glasses were smashed and the ceiling did have a scorch-mark for a few weeks, but total disaster was averted.

Despite their history, the arrival of the Breitners was noted by Frau Braun, the Krone's landlady, with interest rather than trepidation. The Krone had a reputation as being the hub for all worthwhile information and tittle-tattle. That standing was built on attracting a clientele from all quarters of Brandt society, combined with Frau Braun's smooth interrogation expertise. For the moment, she was content to let the family settle at their table.

Susan flapped her napkin before laying it on her lap. "Had you been waiting long?"

Sep shook his head. "Caught the first train from Achbrugge. I'd arranged an appointment with the bank, saw the agricultural supplier, ordered one or two things for the farm, met up with Gunter for a coffee, then came to the station."

Susan looked anxious. "Everything all right?"

"Yes, accounts are signed off. We're not making money, but we're not losing it either."

"No, I meant with Gunter?"

"Oh! He's fine. Got himself another promotion. He's now Chief Inspector Schwartz. Loves his job with the Kriminipolitzei."

"And?" Susan gave her husband a meaningful look.

"No. There is no lady in his life. Not from lack of trying on his part, I assure you." Sep chuckled as he recalled his conversation with his friend. "He's a disaster when it comes to romance."

Harriet's ears picked up at the mention of romance. "It's a shame. He's such a nice man. He'll find someone sooner or later."

Susan cast a surreptitious glance to gauge her husband's reaction to Harriet's intervention. Over recent weeks, the fifteen-year-old had developed a self-assurance that appeared out of nowhere. Sep returned her look with an amused half-smile.

She shook her head at his indulgence. "And everything is okay at home?"

He nodded. "You've been missed. The Rubensteins' can't wait to see you back in the surgery. They've been rushed off their feet." He suddenly looked up. "Oh, talking of things medical." He shifted his chair around so he sat sideways to the table, then bent down and pulled his left trouser leg up over his ankle to reveal the shiny metal.

Susan looked delighted. "It arrived!"

"Two days after you left." He tapped it with his fingernail. "It's aluminium, weighs nothing, and has an adjustable spring which takes a bit of getting used to." He rolled his trouser back down. "It's marvellous what they can do with prosthetics these days."

The arrival of their meal halted further conversation. Harriet fidgeted as the waitress placed plates of piping hot goulash and thick slabs of bread in front of them.

"For goodness' sake, Harriet, sit still."

"I can't help it. My bum hurts from too much sitting."

For a second, her mother regarded her in open-mouthed horror. "Harriet Breitner! We do not use such a word."

"Which word?'

"The…the…you know very well which word."

Harriet looked confused. "What? Bum?"

Susan glanced around to see whether anyone nearby might have overheard. She lowered her voice. "That is not a word that we use in our family."

Harriet pounced on the flaw in her mother's assertion. "Yes, we do," she said with precocious certainty. "In England, every morning when we stayed with Granny Jones, she always said 'wash your hands and park your bum' before serving breakfast." Harriet looked to her brother for support. "She did, didn't she, Johan?"

Johan nodded and stayed silent. His instinct warned him this was a discussion best avoided.

Susan sat open-mouthed as Harriet seized on another example to press her case. "And she said that a posh woman, who we went to visit, had a bum like a barge's bottom."

19

It was doubtful if her mother could look more outraged. "I don't care what Granny Jones said." She squeezed the words through gritted teeth. "It's vulgar and inappropriate for a young lady to say that."

"Which word should I use?"

Her mother looked thrown by the challenge. "There's no need to refer to that part of your anatomy in polite conversation in the first place."

Harriet was unconvinced. "You can't do that. What happens if you go to the doctor's?"

"That's different."

"Why?"

"We're talking about when we're not at the doctor's."

"So, I can use bum if I'm at the doctor's but not anywhere else?" Susan cast her husband a desperate glance.

Sep shrugged his shoulders. Like his son, he'd no desire to get involved. Added to that, he couldn't immediately think of a suitable alternative. He considered 'rump' but thought that might not be helpful.

"Posterior is acceptable."

Harriet spluttered. "Posterior! Ma, that's so snobby."

"Don't be cheeky, young lady."

Johan raised his napkin to his mouth in an attempt to smother his giggles.

"I'm not." Harriet looked genuinely contrite. "I'm just asking for a polite word for bum?"

"Backside," Sep suggested.

For a second Susan looked startled, then considered the word. "Yes," she said cautiously. "That's acceptable."

"Or behind." Sep offered an alternative.

"Or arse." Johan knew as he said it that it was a mistake.

"What is the matter with you children?" Susan stared in disbelief at each of her offspring. "We will not have vulgarity in our family. Do I make myself clear?"

The arrival of Frau Braun curtailed the argument. "Sep, Susan, so good to see you. And you too, Harriet and Johan." After shaking hands, she stood back and appraised the children. "My word, you two are growing up fast. Been to England, I hear?"

"Yes. This time for three weeks." Harriet answered on behalf of the family. "It's nice to be back though," she added.

Her mother rolled her eyes at her daughter's forwardness.

"Three weeks!" Frau Braun pulled up a chair, made herself comfortable, and began her interrogation. Within minutes, she'd discovered the purpose of the visit was for Susan and the children to meet their English grandma, aunts, uncles, various cousins, and family friends and acquaintances. From that, she gleaned that Susan came from a moderately prosperous family, and was respectable, educated and well connected. Her English heritage alone would be sufficient to ensure her standing in Brandt society. It was also evident that the family had a broader perspective on the world than the Krone's usual clientele, who rarely ventured beyond Brandt and its immediate hinterland. Her observation was confirmed by Susan's opening question.

"The *London Times* reported that there has been excitement in Austria while we were away." Susan looked anxious. "Was there trouble here?"

Frau Braun lowered her voice. "A bad affair, if you ask me. Ever since Chancellor Dollfuss was assassinated, the Germans have been causing trouble." She sniffed and cast a furtive glance at the surrounding tables. "Not much trouble in Brandt though. Just Hitler Youth and SS distributing propaganda, shouting slogans and brawling with the Communists." She gestured vaguely at the unemployed men outside. "There were a few scuffles."

"The Gendarmerie quickly dealt with it, according to Gunter." Sep looked unconcerned.

"Aye, this time. But who's to say it won't happen again?" The landlady gave a meaningful look. "Many are coming around to Nazi thinking." She abruptly got to her feet as the main course arrived. "I'll let you have your meal in peace."

"I'm glad we don't live in a big town or city," Harriet said, as she started on her Schnitzel. "I can't imagine anything like that affecting a sleepy place like Doppelgau." It turned out even an isolated alpine village couldn't remain detached from the world.

DOING GOD'S WORK

Monsignor Wagner waited until the young deacon departed before he squeezed himself behind the double-pedestal mahogany desk, sank into the padded leather chair and gazed around the room, revelling in the symbols of power and authority that festooned the walls. Rows of dusty books, files, folders and indexes filled the bookshelves. Within the records, the names of every resident of the diocese could be found. After all, it was the Church's business to know everything and everyone of importance. On the frieze above the shelves, portraits of six former bishops, three cardinals, and the two saints that hailed from the diocese, gazed down with eyes that spoke of ruthlessness, plots and treachery.

He reached across the desk for the crystal decanter and poured himself a generous glass of fine Burgenlander Zweigelt, then took a leisurely draught, closed his eyes and savoured the taste. When he opened them, he found himself looking at the blank space to the left of the last bishop's portrait. Perhaps, one day, his own visage might hang there? He swirled the wine around in the glass and let the idea take hold. "Why not indeed? He was in his sixties, loyal and ambitious. He'd served the Bishop well and worked his way up the hierarchy. He was competent, reliable, trustworthy and had not caused scandal or embarrassment. As soon as the lie entered his consciousness, he inwardly winced.

He put down the glass, stood up and wandered over to the window. He'd need a clear head for the task ahead. The flock was restless, anxious and confused. They needed to be steered away from godlessness towards the path of enlightenment.

A commotion outside disturbed his concentration. He drew the lace curtain aside and peered down. A group of roughly dressed men had gathered on the street corner. More were drawn to stand beneath the red banners and placards. The group became a small crowd, and people stopped to listen to a small, animated, one-armed man. The nodding heads and bursts of applause indicated the rhetoric struck a chord.

Wagner felt his rage build. He knew what message was being preached. The Church had seen off the barbarian hordes, the pagans, the heretics, the Lutherans and Protestant polluters – now there were other, more insidious, cancers that needed to be dealt with. As if the diocese didn't have enough problems.

He snatched up a folder, extracted the draft and began reading. Then re-read it, this time with pen poised. It was good – but not good enough; the disease needed to be dealt with. It took him over an hour: furiously scribbling notes, replacing weak adjectives and phrases with more direct, powerful and pithy ones. What emerged was a plausible fiction sufficient to convince the already prejudiced and sway the undecided. It would outrage the enemy, and some misguided liberals would see straight through the distorted facts, blatant lies and contrived circumstances, but such degenerates were too few in number to cause concern.

He placed the revised text into the folder, and then reached for the bell to summon the deacon. His hand hovered. It wouldn't do to rush things. Working too fast only attracted extra work and unwanted pressure. He redirected his hand towards the decanter; plenty of time for another glass. Besides, he needed to calm down, and there were other more pleasurable matters he could linger over.

He cradled the half-filled glass in both hands, leant back in the chair, closed his eyes and released his imagination and memory. Nearly caught, but the authorities remained ignorant and he held a much more secure position now. A thin smirk spread across his lips.

Eventually the images faded, and time forced him to summon the deacon. The young clergyman's instant response triggered suspicion. The man must loiter outside the door, Wagner thought to himself. Nevertheless, he kept his expression neutral. "I've made amendments." He pushed the file across the desk.

The deacon reached for the file. Wagner's fingers remained spread, spider-like across the document. Father Thomas's eyes flicked nervously towards his superior. Wagner weighed up his assistant. The youngster had acumen and was eager to nurture it. Wagner couldn't make up his mind whether ambition was the motivation or intellectual compensation for his polio inflicted deformities. He tapped the file with his index finger. "Read it, and I mean read, and understand, Father Thomas."

"Of course, Your Reverence."

Wagner's eyes narrowed. "Do you?"

The deacon withdrew his hand and drew himself erect. He realised he was being tested. "The Church always needs to be ready to provide spiritual leadership and chart the path towards truth and enlightenment." He bowed his head and searched for the exact phrase that would impress. "It is not just a matter of what is said – but exactly how it is expressed that ensures words and ideas have maximum impact. The truth needs to be unequivocal." He risked a furtive glance towards his superior and felt relieved when a thin smile flickered across Wagner's lips.

"Indeed, my son. Never underestimate the power of words." He sighed. "But written articles aren't enough. New technologies," He gestured with his hand. "radio, for example, theatres and cinemas. We mustn't neglect them."

Thomas bowed his head in acknowledgement. "That would be a mistake."

"I'm glad you agree. Which is why I want you to make sure this text finds expression on the radio, as well as every newspaper across the diocese." He tapped his fingers on the file to give added emphasis to his words. "We are engaged in a crusade, Father Thomas. Read and learn." He pushed the file across the desk. "And make sure all originals are returned to me."

The young man turned and shuffled towards the door.

"I've not finished, Thomas."

"Your Reverence?"

Wagner gave a delicate cough. "I've been neglecting my pastoral duties."

"Do you wish me to stand in. I'm always ready to serve."

Wagner inwardly sneered at the young cleric's obsequiousness. "Not all tasks can be delegated." He leant back, steepled his hands and stared at the ceiling. "Some inspections, I think." He cocked his head to one side and eyed the deacon. "A few unannounced calls to keep our brothers and sisters on their toes." He pursed his lips and considered his approach. "A random selection. A call on the abbess to see how the good sisters are faring, I should also take in selected schools, orphanages and institutions. Oh, and one or two of our more isolated parishes. We can't neglect our country brethren."

Thomas bowed deferentially. "I'll prepare a schedule."

"Oh, and one more thing. The file we hold on that Trade Union activist, the one-armed chap – make sure it is up to date. He's wielding too much influence for his own good."

Wagner waited until the door lock clicked shut before replenishing his wineglass and drifting back towards the window. He held the glass to the light and stared through the blood-red liquid, then transferred his gaze to the scene outside. The police had dispersed the demonstration. He watched a family emerge from the Gasthaus Krone and followed their progress towards the station. They seemed familiar, especially the man. His slight limp reminded Wagner of someone.

MORDECHEI FURNSTEIN

"Good afternoon, Fraulein Heppel." The old man greeted Trudy with his usual good grace.

"Good afternoon to you, Herr Furnstein. I have some business to discuss."

The old man nodded, shut the door, flipped the sign to 'closed' and beckoned her to follow him into the back of his pawnshop. He pulled out a chair for her, then sat opposite and looked expectantly across the table.

Wordlessly, Trudy emptied the contents of her battered school bag. A small pile of rings, watches, bracelets, necklaces and bangles clattered across the table.

Mordechai donned his steel-rimmed spectacles and spread the pile with his fingers. For a couple of minutes he studied the objects, occasionally picking an item out and examining it more closely by holding it to the light or scrutinising it under a large magnifying glass. Having made his assessments, he glanced across at Trudy. It was her cue to begin the ritual the pair had established.

He watched in silence, and his face gave nothing away as she rearranged the pile according to her assessment of the value of each piece. Once satisfied, she sat back.

He stroked his snow-white goatee beard and examined her handiwork. "Very good, Fraulein Heppel. Only two mistakes, I'd suggest."

Trudy looked crestfallen.

"Both of which would have cost you a fair few Reichsmarks."

Trudy looked even more dismayed.

The old man noticed her chagrin and chuckled. "Don't be so hard on yourself, Trudy. Some experts wouldn't have spotted one of your errors.' He retrieved a small ladies watch. "This, for example. Why do you think it of average value?'

"It's silver but not hallmarked."

"Not *obviously* hallmarked." Mordechai corrected her. He produced a small tool, resembling a minute screwdriver, and prised open the back. He dangled the watch in front of Trudy. "It's English, made in London around eighteen seventy, and it's valuable." He chuckled. "The hallmarks are behind the casing which makes it unusual. Easy to miss." He placed the item at the top of the pile. "Your other error is this." He selected a gold ring with a single diamond set in a golden clasp. He reached into his pocket and pulled out an eye-glass which he wedged into his eye socket. "It's a beautiful cut. Whoever made it was interested in creating a diamond of exquisite beauty, rather than preserving its carat weight." He glanced across at her. "Do you want to pawn these or invest?"

Trudy already knew her answer. She'd no need for cash. Relieving marks of their notes was bread and butter to her. Accumulating wealth for a rainy day was her priority. "Invest."

He smiled and looked at her with respect. "You have an old head on young shoulders and a good business brain, Fraulein Heppel."

"Please." Trudy gestured towards the pile. Mordechai bowed his head in thanks and selected an item of relatively modest value as his fee.

With business concluded, Mordechai reached for a bottle of wine and poured a couple of small glasses.

"Always a pleasure doing business with you, Fraulein Heppel."

"Likewise, Herr Furnstein."

They touched glasses.

Mordechai looked fondly at her. "How old are you now, Trudy?"

"Fifteen." She returned his look. She liked Mordechai Furnstein - not only for his straight-dealing, but because he treated her as an adult.

He looked quizzical. "Do you think about your future?"

"All the time."

"And what do you see?"

"Nothing good at the moment."

"Maybe you're looking in the wrong direction?"

Trudy looked puzzled.

He chuckled. "Things often come at you from the most unexpected quarter. When they do, it pays to be prepared." He held her in a steady gaze as if he was trying to make up his mind about her.

Trudy felt uncomfortable. His next question startled her.

"Does it bother you that I'm a Jew?"

Trudy looked at him in astonishment. She knew he was Jewish; everyone in the neighbourhood knew. Why he should suddenly ask the question baffled her. He was Mordechai Furnstein, the kind, straight-dealing, pawn-broker. "No," she said, "I've never thought about it."

"But you're taught to hate Jews. We are the country's misfortune. You're supposed to despise me."

"I've no reason to hate you or any Jew. Not that I know any, apart from yourself and Frau Furnstein." She frowned. "Why do you ask?"

"Because for some people being associated, or doing business with a Jew can lead to trouble."

Trudy shrugged. "That's their problem."

He took a long sip from his glass, almost draining it, then placed it carefully back on the table. The silence grew as he appeared to mull over her response. He looked across at her. "You're a bright girl, Trudy. Brighter than your peers and, thanks to your aunt, you are blessed with an attractive personality and an independent spirit." He waved his hand to dismiss her embarrassment. "I'm not complimenting you. I'm stating facts." He stared hard at her. "You stand out." He raised his eyebrows and nodded to himself. "That's not necessarily a good thing."

"Why not?"

"We live in troubled times, Trudy. People are being taught to distrust anything and anyone that is different." He gave a wan smile. "Us Jews are despised because we look different, have a different religion, speak a different language or at least some of us do. Gypsies are different. Communists are different. Some of your old teachers wanted to teach something different, didn't they? What happened to them?"

Trudy acknowledged he had a point. In the past two years, over half the teachers had left or been removed. At the time, she hadn't thought too much about it.

"In our country only one thing matters - conform. Don't stand out in a crowd."

"You're not making much sense, Herr Furnstein. What are you suggesting? That I should conform as well?"

"No. I'm suggesting you lose yourself in the crowd, but keep your ears and eyes sharp. Watch what's going on. See the world for what it truly is. Question everything, but keep your thoughts to yourself. Do you understand me?"

Trudy looked at the old man, who'd become animated. She knew he was probably talking sense, but she found his words confusing. "I can't say I do. But I'll think about everything you've said."

Mordechai half smiled and gave her hand an affectionate pat. "I can't ask for more than that." He eased himself to his feet. It signalled the end of their meeting. Trudy stood and held out her hand. "Goodbye, Herr Furnstein."

"Farewell, Fraulein Trudy. Think on my words, eh?"

MAY 1937 – WINDS OF CHANGE

Change wasn't something that made Doppelgauers comfortable. Most adopted a perverse attitude towards it. A combination of mutual support and agricultural self-sufficiency meant the community ticked along quite nicely without it. Indeed, the villagers took pride in their belief that if something wasn't broken, nothing needed fixing. But indifference quickly turned to a sense of outraged grievance if other Brandtnerwald settlements benefited from progress ahead of them.

      The village lay at the furthest reach of the Brandtnerwald, nestled in a broad, lush, green valley, divided by the rushing torrent of the River Ach. Dense pine forests clung to the steep lower slopes of the surrounding mountains. Above the treeline, alpine meadows gave way to majestic craggy snow-topped peaks. Apart from being a natural location for a settlement, the village also provided the last refuge for travellers looking to brave the high pass that led to Innsbruck and the rest of Austria. If it hadn't been for the Breitners, the village might have been even more isolated from the world.

      Johan's great grandfather was widely recognized as the most effective Burgermeister in the history of the community. He'd pressurised and cajoled the state and local authorities to improve the roads, construct flood defences to contain the Ach, and connect the village to mains water and the sewage system. Successive Breitners ensured a single communal telephone and telegram arrived in the small post office in the late 1920's, and the electricity grid was gradually snaking its way up the valley.

      The Breitners' elections as Burgermeisters were not because they were especially popular, but for reasons of practicality. They were well travelled, educated and informed, and therefore better equipped to deal with politicians and bureaucrats, and complex procedures that most Doppelgauers happily admitted they didn't understand and had even less interest.

      This was the peaceful, comfortable, narrow-minded and predictable community that Johan and Harriet grew up in. It was their family and friends, especially the Rubensteins, who exposed them to the world beyond. Even so, neither sibling had ever considered their future, been confronted by uncertainty, been troubled by shortages or required to make their own decisions. They existed in a comfortable cocoon of family love, stability and relative wealth.

      But change was in the air. Childhood was over and innocence along with it. Discontent crept up the valley like an invisible zephyr seeping into people's thoughts. Fault lines began to open up within the village, and the herd instinct along with it. Johan and Harriet's world became less certain. A conversation in a pigsty provided the initial catalyst.

"Wait for me!" Harriet cried out, as Johan overtook her and sprinted to be first home.

"You have to be faster," Johan laughed.

Harriet was already racing as fast as she could and ran straight through the puddles in an effort to keep up. "It's not fair, Johan," she wailed. "You should give me a chance." Her appeal fell on deaf ears, and she slowed as she realised the race seemed lost.

Johan reached the back door of the Stube. He leant on the door jamb with his chest heaving and glanced back at his sister, who now plodded with exaggerated flouncing steps and bowed head. Harriet hated losing at anything. He allowed her to catch up.

"It's not fair," she said sulkily. "You're not a gentleman at all."

Johan rolled his eyes. "It's got nothing to do with being a gentleman. I'm eighteen, you're sixteen. I'm bound to be faster."

"A gentleman would have given a lady a head start," she said as she drew level with him. "It's not a proper race if someone cheats," she said, pouting.

Her brother looked indignant. "You left church before me. You had a head start."

"I didn't say you were a cheat. I said if *someone* cheats." In a flash, Harriet used Johan's distraction to rush past him, push the door open, enter the Stube and claim victory. Her ruse might have succeeded had her brother not caught her waist and held her firm. No matter how hard she tried, she couldn't wriggle free. "I win," she shrieked with laughter, as she struggled to squirm herself from his grip and cross the threshold.

"Will you two behave!" The sharp admonishment brought the siblings up short. They found themselves under the stern scrutiny of their neighbour, Tante Josey Wachter, their mother, and her friend, Frau Hannah Rubenstein.

"Get changed out of those clothes, Johan, your father wants the pigsty cleaned out, and Harriet, I'd like you to prepare three birds for dinner."

"Is Simon here?" Harriet asked Frau Rubenstein.

"He and Jurgen are outside."

Ten minutes later, Johan clattered down the stairs, hastily doing up the buttons on his shirt as he went. He found his friends had already cleared more than half the sty.

Simon Rubenstein leant on the pitchfork as Johan entered. "Good to see you, mate."

"How was Mass?" Jurgen Wachter peered up from beneath a head-dress of strands of straw.

"Your absence was noted."

"Not my fault. First chickenpox, now the mumps." He looked pained. "It's no joke getting mumps at my age."

29

"It's sweeping all of Brandtnerwald. All the Rubensteins are doing at the moment is visiting sick children," Simon said.

"You'll find yourself getting roped in." Johan grabbed a pitchfork and began spreading fresh straw.

"We all have to help when it gets busy."

"It's good practice for you. You want to be a doctor, don't you?"

Simon sighed "That's what the family expects. If you are a Rubenstein, your destiny is the medical profession. My grandfather, aunt, uncle and my parents keep dropping unsubtle hints."

Harriet arrived in time to catch the tail end of the discussion. "You have to be intelligent to be a doctor." She made a face that suggested she doubted Simon passed muster on that score.

Jurgen said. "My Pa expects me to take over the farm."

"I wouldn't mind becoming a farmer." Harriet said, masking her irritation that Simon hadn't risen to her bait.

Jurgen was dismissive. "Girls can't be farmers."

"Why not?"

He looked non-plussed. "They just can't. You need to be strong. It's hard work. You wouldn't be able to lift anything heavy."

Harriet's face flushed "Really?! You think lifting heavy things is what farming is all about?"

"It's not just about lifting things."

"So, you've never heard of a farm being run by a woman."

"Er, no." Jurgen realised both the flaw in his argument and that he was now in Harriet's crosshairs.

"What about Petra and Tara up in the high pass?"

"That's different."

"Why? They've been running their farm for years. Isn't that so, Johan?" She rounded on her brother.

Johan didn't say anything. He'd plenty of experience of his sister's temper and knew when to stay silent.

"There's no reason why women shouldn't run a farm. Only a few years ago, it was thought women couldn't become doctors. It hasn't stopped my mother and aunt." Simon's observation blunted Harriet's anger.

"Exactly." Harriet glared at Jurgen as she headed towards the hen coop.

Simon settled himself on the bench. "What about you, mate? Do you know what you'll do?"

Johan shrugged. "I've not thought about it. The one thing I do know, though, is we'll end up like England. The farmers there moan that all the youngsters moved to the towns to work in the mills or factories."

Jurgen looked surprised. "You wouldn't take over from your Pa?"

"Farming doesn't pay much. It's best to have something else. It's why my grandfather started our building company."

"There's no building work!"

"Not at the moment. But Pa reckons things will pick up sooner or later."

Harriet emerged from the coop with a plump chicken tucked under her arm. She soothed the bird, said a quiet prayer under her breath, and then wrung its neck.

"Do you have to kill it in front of its mates?" Simon gestured towards the flock, nonchalantly scratching the dust around their pen. "Animals have feelings, you know."

"Yes, alright. I wasn't thinking." She swept the dirt off the bench, sat down next to him and began to pluck the bird.

Jurgen looked thoughtful. "The trouble is this isn't England. They've got massive factories, mines, mills and steelworks. I can't think of one factory in the Brandtnerwald, and there aren't that many in Brandt."

"And most of them are shut or only half working," Simon added. He glanced at Harriet and Johan. "You two are lucky. You could go and live in England."

"What are the English like?" Jurgen asked.

Johan frowned. "No different from us."

Feathers flew from Harriet's fingers as she systematically stripped the bird. She paused for a second and considered the question. "They can be snobby." She looked across at her brother and grinned. "Tell them about Lady Grantham."

Johan closed his eyes and shook his head in mock despair as he recalled Lady Grantham. "She's a friend of our grandma and lives alone in an enormous house by herself. Our grandma feels sorry for her and calls in, to give her some company. Anyway, we were invited to meet this lady." He glanced at Harriet. "You were in trouble straightaway, weren't you?"

"What for?" Simon sat beside Harriet.

"Running!" Harriet's grin set her eyes dancing. She adopted a mock posh voice. "Young ladies who are concerned about their reputations do not run." Harriet giggled. "She didn't like me at all. She said I was frightful."

"She said you were flighty, not frightful." Her brother corrected her.

Harriet shrugged and then sneezed.

"It's as well you came back. You might have found yourself packed off to some posh English school to learn how to become a lady," Jurgen said.

Harriet looked amazed. "She suggested exactly that! She said a year at a finishing school would knock me into shape." She sneezed again before adding, "The cheek of it!"

"My cousin is heading to a school in Switzerland." Simon suddenly reached over and grabbed the now almost naked chicken from Harriet's grasp. "In case you didn't know it, you're allergic to feathers."

31

Harriet stared at him, unsure whether to argue or not. "Ma said I need to prepare three."

"Go and get the other two." He plucked the few remaining feathers. "And don't kill them in front of their mates," he called after her.

"How is it you and Harriet are half English?" Jurgen asked.

"Our parents met in the War. Pa was wounded and captured by the English. My mother was a nurse in the hospital where he was treated. Once back home he wrote to her, asking her to come to Austria." Johan rolled his eyes. "Apparently, they were madly in love, and my Ma decided to take a chance and come to Austria. After she arrived they got married." He spread the last of the straw around the sty, and the three of them admired their handiwork.

"I killed them behind the coop," Harriet announced, as she reappeared with a couple of hens dangling from her hand. She nudged Simon with her hip to encourage him to make space for her. She gave him a sideways glance. "Happy?"

Simon didn't react. "Give them to me. Otherwise you'll decorate them with snot." He began plucking. "Seriously, lads, we need to work out what we want to do. Next year we all leave the Hauptschule." He glanced at Harriet. "And I can't see you being content as a traditional Austrian hausfrau."

"Fat chance of that. I want to be like Tante Josey and become a businesswoman."

"I thought you said you wanted to be a farmer?" Jurgen looked at her in exasperation.

Simon interjected before Harriet exploded. "Farming is a business, and most farms around here could do with modernisation." He handed the plucked chicken to Harriet before starting on the third bird.

Harriet smiled her thanks. "You'd make a great doctor."

"I think I'd rather be a vet."

Harriet laughed. "How can you be a vet when you are so squeamish about killing animals?"

Their conversation would stay with Johan. He realised he was at a decision point. His secondary education ended in six months, and he had no idea what came next. Neither parent expressed a view on him taking over the family farm or the construction company. Perhaps because the farm was only ticking over, and the depression reduced demand for building work, which meant neither business offered an enticing prospect. For the first time in his life he was confronted with real uncertainty, and he found the experience unsettling, all the more so when he glanced at his sister and his friends. It could be that each might go their separate ways. Their cosy friendship might be at risk.

COMING OF AGE

Mordechai Furnstein's words lit a fire of inquisitiveness within Trudy. Initially, the flames were small and weak, but gradually her interest in the world beyond the slum developed.

The first thing she noticed was a change in the public mood. Adult conversation changed. She'd known for years money meant nothing. The price of bread and basic foods could triple in a single day. Herr Furnstein steered her towards pickpocketing anything gold or silver, and even cigarettes. Such items held their worth, he explained.

People blamed the French, the Bolsheviks, the Jews, corrupt politicians and almost anybody for the hyperinflation, the loss of German pride and national dignity, as well as for their own poverty. However, rapidly - it seemed almost overnight - the root cause of all Germany's problems became the Jews alone. Most people didn't challenge the assertion. They wanted a scapegoat and the government provided one. Get rid of the Jews, and the country would progress.

As if to prove it, grand buildings were thrown up. New highways were built - connecting the city to Berlin to the East, and the industrial Ruhr to the South. Even the derelict docks burst into activity. Streets bustled, well-dressed pedestrians crowded the pavements, and suddenly everyone had a job and money. It was as if the sun had come out and every day was a carnival. Neighbourhoods became festooned with red and black Nazi flags. Images of the Fuhrer in heroic poses, or looking at some distant horizon at a future only he could see, loomed over everyone. The down-and-outs disappeared, to be replaced with men and young boys in uniforms. It seemed the entire male population had joined some universal army.

Trudy struggled to make sense of it. Despite the obvious improvements, wealth still lay alongside poverty. For the first time, she questioned why she lived in such a desperate neighbourhood when riches seemed so tantalisingly close. Her awareness unsettled her, and she looked around for answers. School just fed her confusion. For years she'd played and socialised happily with all her schoolmates. Then some children were distanced by the teachers, shunned by their classmates, and later abruptly disappeared. She recalled the triumph in the schoolmistress's voice, during one morning assembly, when she declared the school "clean of Jewish vermin." Trudy became bemused at how quickly her class degenerated into a mean, vindictive, spiteful mob. She once questioned what was wrong with being Jewish. She was dragged in front of the class, forced to stand on a chair and ordered to recite ten times from a textbook: *'Jews have different noses, ears, lips, chins and different faces than Germans'* and *'they walk differently, have flat feet... their arms are longer, and they speak differently.'* Even as she read it, two thoughts burned into her mind. The first was the absurdity of the text. The second was Herr Furnstein's advice 'not to stand out in a crowd.'

There was no point broaching her confusion with her mother. Alcoholism gave way to opium addiction, as her looks faded as fast as her ability to attract anyone other than the most desperate clients. Trudy decided to confide in the only person who showed her love and understanding.

One overcast Sunday morning, Trudy, sitting on the bench-seat opposite Tante Bri, picked up and threaded a needle. Their 'make-do-and-mend' days became a ritual both looked forward to. The pair sat in the half-light of a battered paraffin lamp. Initially, Tante Bri insisted the occasion be used for homework. Then, as Trudy grew older, she taught the youngster how to sew, knit, patch, darn, alter and adapt clothing. As a consequence, Trudy was always well turned-out despite their poverty. Their get-togethers then evolved into an excuse for a gossip, conversation, shared confidences and the chance to laugh at their neighbours and themselves. It also provided an opportunity to share their worries and cares. To help stimulate the conversation, Tante Bri fortified herself from a small bottle of home-made Schnapps.

"Madi, why is it we are so poor?" Trudy opened their discussion with typical bluntness.

Tante Bri wasn't fazed because the same question perplexed her. "We're not poor. It's just that we ain't got as much money as other folk."

"That makes us poor then, doesn't it?"

Tante Bri continued to unpick the hem from a dress she was sure she could lengthen to accommodate Trudy's growing frame. She shrugged. "That's the way things are."

"Does that mean we'll always be poor? That doesn't sound fair."

Trudy's comment set off a tingle of concern within Tante Bri. She gave the youngster a sharp look. "Has them Communalist troublemakers been talking to you?"

Trudy laughed. "No, Madi."

"You sure? Them Communalists are nothing but trouble, putting wrong thinking into people's heads, especially them who know no better."

Trudy stretched across and gently rested her hand on Tante Bri's forearm. "No honestly, Madi. I see so many people who seem much richer than we are. I was just wondering." She gave the old lady a disarming grin. "And they're Communists, not Communalists."

Tante Bri sniffed and looked unconvinced. "Well, there's no point wondering about it. Some people is born rich. Some people gets rich by stealing from other people, and some people gets rich by having a proper job and working hard."

"We steal and it isn't making us rich."

Tante Bri shuffled uncomfortably. She was well aware of the activities of the pickpocketing gangs, and she disapproved not only of

Yankee Franz, but also of the pimps, fences and hardened criminals that exploited the youngsters' ignorance and vulnerabilities. However, necessity forced her to be flexible with her morals. She readily accepted the purses, silk handkerchiefs, gold rings, silver bracelets, expensive watches and, especially, food of any description or condition that might be snatched from market stalls. "That's different. We steals out of necessity. What I'm talking about is stealing to get rich." She frowned, filled her glass to the brim with Schnapps and took a swig before staring hard at the youngster. "What's brought on all these questions?"

Trudy expertly threaded another needle and started sewing on a button with practised ease. She remained silent for a few seconds as she considered her question. "I don't want to be poor forever. We steal but sooner or later we get caught and put into prison. Nobody on our street has a proper job like the people I see in the city. It doesn't seem right."

"It's the way it is, sweetheart. There is always people in charge at the top, the big-wigs with the money, and there is always people at the bottom without the money or the means to better themselves." She threw the dress into the air and gave it a firm flap to release the unstitched hem. "Except for you, of course."

Trudy looked surprised. "What do you mean?"

"You've got a head on you." She gave the dress another flap and held it up to assess its condition. "You're a smart girl and, if you takes the time and trouble, you can learn your way out of here."

Trudy's surprise turned to astonishment. She peered at the old lady to see if she was teasing.

Tante Bri gradually became aware of her scrutiny. She put the dress down in her lap and turned to face her favourite adopted child. "You were lucky to be born with beauty and brains, Trudy," she said seriously. "It's a gift that most people ain't got. Lord knows they both bypassed me. You're right to question your lot. You above everyone in this sorry neighbourhood. If you use your brain, you can escape this place if you're minded to." She sniffed and looked dismissive. "Or you can use your looks and end up on the game like your mother." She jerked her head toward the bedroom in which Frau Heppel lay oblivious to the world.

Trudy was glad the dim lamp-lit room concealed her blush. It turned out to be a day of surprises. For the first time, Tante Bri mentioned her mother's occupation. Even outside the apartment, no one in the neighbourhood felt it necessary to make any comment or pass any judgement. After all, Frau Heppel wasn't the only prostitute on the street. And nobody cast aspersions on Trudy for being the daughter of a lady of the night. Most people considered her to be another orphan Tante Bri had gathered under her wing. The lack of connection meant the few snide comments and sniggering, cruel jokes that were made about her mother, especially as her looks faded and drug dependency addled her brain, were often made within Trudy's hearing. Not that she was upset. Frau Heppel hardly figured in her life at all.

"You do know what your mother is?"

The blunt question further increased Trudy's embarrassment. She was old enough to know roughly what being 'on the game' meant but not the details and wasn't sure she wanted to know. She didn't trust herself to reply.

Tante Bri failed to pick up on Trudy's discomfort. She decided Trudy was old enough to be exposed to the more sordid aspects of slum life. "She sleeps with men who are prepared to pay her." Tante Bri wagged her finger in front of Trudy's face. "And keeps bad company as a result." She wrinkled her nose as if describing Frau Heppel's occupation lay beyond disgusting. "Her life's not her own no more. And you mark my words, young lady, that's where young Gabi is heading 'cos she don't know any better." She tossed her head back and her body shuddered at the thought of life as a prostitute. "And it's where you'll end up. Unless you use what the Good Lord provided you with."

Trudy maintained a look of calm interest, although inside she cringed with unease. She recognised the signs. Once Tante Bri got the wind in her sails, the topic would be endlessly dissected, analysed and pontificated upon. Usually, Trudy welcomed such diversions as it meant a quite innocuous subject might open endless tributaries of interest and tittle-tattle. On this occasion, however, it seemed wrong to be discussing her mother's misfortune, especially when she was in such close proximity. She decided Tante Bri needed to be diverted. "So how will I get out of here?"

The question had the desired effect. Tante Bri looked befuddled at the sudden change in tack. "Oh Lord, how would I know? I told you, I ain't blessed with brains. All as I do know is that them's what get learned can find a way to better themselves." She suddenly leant over and gave Trudy an affectionate peck on the cheek. "I can see a bright future for you though, girl."

The brief conversation stayed with Trudy for the rest of the day. In fact, it would return to her many times throughout her life. That evening in bed, she ran Tante Bri's comments through her mind time and again. Did Tante Bri really think her clever or was she simply being kind? Her teachers never praised her for anything. She remembered Gabi saying she was a fast learner, and Herr Furnstein's comments, but that was about it. And as for being beautiful she had no idea. She slipped out of bed, tiptoed across the room, lit several candles and arranged them in front of the only large mirror in the apartment so they cast their light on her. For several minutes she stared at herself, twisting and turning in an attempt to appraise herself from every angle. Finally, she turned back to face the mirror, placed her hands on her hips and decided, all things considered, she wasn't at all bad-looking. She'd need some help with her hair, and maybe she could dress in a more mature and modern way. She made a mental note to examine more closely what fashionable young ladies were wearing, next time she was in the city.

She blew out the candles and made a dash for the bed, leaping in and pulling the covers over her. Immediately, the residual smell of cheap scent, stale beer and cigarettes reminded her that her mother had only vacated the bed two hours earlier. The odours curtailed her good mood. She lay still and once again went over Tante Bri's conversation. She was clever and beautiful, she reminded herself, and she wasn't going to end up like her mother. On that she was determined.

AN ENGLISH ROAST

Sunday lunch represented everything the Breitners loved about family life. Every three months or so, close family friends were invited. As well as a traditional English Sunday roast, guests could expect music, singing, parlour games and lively conversation that flitted from German to English.

The Stube became drenched with the homely smells of farm and garden. Pine wood smoke and the sweet perfume of apples, cinnamon and almonds, combined with the aromas of liver stock, herb-infused soup, and sage and onion stuffed chicken and roasting potatoes that escaped from the oven, had everyone drooling.

Although the Stube was large, it felt small. The carved-pine panelled low ceiling and walls, and the bulk of the Kächelofen and the bench seats that wrapped around it, gave the room a cosy, intimate feel. Everywhere the debris of domesticity lay scattered. In one corner, half-mended curtains lay draped across a sewing machine. Rows of preserved fruits and pickles lined the shelves either side of the range, and the few remaining pans, that were not sat gurgling and hissing on the hot plates, hung from the ceiling hooks. On the wall opposite, an old pedal-organ had pride of place beside an equally ancient grandfather clock. A large crucifix, set at an angle in the top corner, loomed over everyone. Not that it held any significance: beyond attending Mass, the Breitners weren't religious. The cross hung there because of tradition - every Austrian home had one. A writing desk, with its neatly ordered pens, inkpots, blotter, clips, letter openers and assorted paperwork, stood on the far side of the room. From here Sep prepared his accounts for the farm and, in more buoyant times, ran the family building firm.

Eleven people squeezed around the table. Jurgen and his parents, Tante Josey and Oncle Stephan, were already seated along with the Rubensteins – Rudi, Hannah and their son, Simon. The head of the table was always reserved for Sep. Susan sat at the opposite end so she could keep an eye on the cooking. Harriet and Johan sat beside each other on the bench seat alongside the eleventh guest - Marie Haufmann. Tante Marie was Stephan's sister and the widow of Sep's best friend who fell in the Great War.

Their conversations reflected the cosmopolitan and outward-looking characteristics of the Breitner's circle of friends. On this particular Sunday, the impact of the economy on Josey's business was the opening topic.

"Will you have to close both factories, Josey?" Rudi Rubenstein asked.

Josey wrinkled her nose. "One, certainly, unless we win work."

"Any prospects?"

"Just one contract with the Railway company for uniforms. If we win it, it will keep us ticking over for twelve months."

Susan laid a sympathetic hand on her sister-in-law's arm. "The recession can't last forever."

"I can't see it ending," Sep said. "War reparations are crippling the country; we've got a weak government and a disorganised opposition." He gave Josey a fatalistic look. "We've got to tough it out."

Josey shrugged. "Life's not just tough at the moment, it's desperate."

Rudi pressed his lips together. "Desperate times lead to desperate measures. People are fed up waiting for their lives to get better."

"Especially when they read the propaganda about the progress happening in Germany. Even the *London Times* reported Germany's resurgence." Susan started placing bowls of steaming soup in front of each guest.

"There's constant talk about Austria becoming part of Germany," Marie said.

Hannah Rubenstein screwed up her face in disgust. "God help us if that happens. Have you heard Hitler's speeches? They're all full of hate and stupid ideas about conspiracies and international plots against Germans."

"There're plenty of people who like what he's preaching. Even in this village some people admire him."

His wife laughed. "Oh Stephan, who are you talking of?"

"The Hagspiels think Hitler is talking sense."

Josey laughed. "I doubt the Hagspiels have a clue who Hitler is, let alone what the man stands for."

Hannah didn't join in the laughter. "That's what scares me," she muttered.

Susan glanced at her friend and realised the conversation had entered territory that could blight the afternoon. She changed the topic. "Have you visited your mother-in-law recently?"

Hannah immediately brightened. "I popped in last week. Their surgery has been busy."

"Rachel would have been pleased to see you. The house must feel empty now her boys have left." Susan finished serving the soup, took off her apron and sat down.

Hannah grinned. "Empty, clean, quiet and with plenty of food in the pantry!"

"She'll miss them, though?"

"She will, but she won't be lonely for long. My niece is coming to stay for the summer."

"Oh, how nice to have another female in the house."

Sep said grace, and everyone piled in. For the next few minutes all conversation ceased, to be replaced by the sound of spoons tinkling on the crockery and contented slurping.

Sep smacked his lips and practically threw his spoon into his empty bowl. He'd reached for the flagon and started to pour himself a beer when Josey looked up and cocked her head. She frowned. Everyone looked at her.

"You alright, Josey?"

"Shh, Susan." Josey held up her hand. "You hear it?" She became animated. "Who'd be out hunting in this weather?"

Stephan looked at her, askance. "Don't be daft, love. No one in their right mind would be…" The sound of a distant shot stopped him mid-sentence.

"That's a long way off," Sep said. He turned his head to try and get a fix on the noise. Another shot rang out, followed immediately by another. "That's coming from the other side of Gau," he said confidently.

The explosions were now clearly audible and coming thick and fast at irregular intervals.

"That's an engine," Johan announced, pleased he'd solved the mystery quicker than anyone. Sure enough, beneath the detonations the sound of a straining petrol engine emerged.

"If that's in Gau, the villagers won't be happy." Josey waved her hand to still the conversation as she tried to work out where the mystery vehicle might be heading, and which family might be responsible. Sunday was a day of rest, peace and quiet. An intrusion of this magnitude would cause complaint.

"Whoever it is isn't stopping in Gau," Sep murmured.

The sound of the motor abruptly changed as the driver shifted gear for the gentle slope into Doppelgau. The adjustment resulted in a salvo of backfires, and the engine screamed as if it might separate from its mountings.

"Good Lord!" Marie exclaimed.

Outside, the cattle in the barn protested as another enormous explosion caused a ripple of panic in the small herd.

"It's coming past here," Simon said.

There was an immediate rush to the windows. Curtains were pulled back and noses pressed against the rain-dappled glass.

"Probably someone making for the pass," Sep said confidently, before glancing at the grandfather clock. "He's leaving it late if that's his intention."

A motorbike emerged through the rain. It roared towards them, swerving to avoid the larger puddles, its exhaust periodically discharging explosive bolts of black grey fumes. In its wake figures tumbled out of farms and houses to stand hands on hips in the middle of the road, staring at the retreating rider, too late to vent their irritation at the hooligan.

To everyone's dismay, the motorcyclist didn't continue towards the pass. He swerved into the farmyard and came to a halt under the shelter of the barn eaves. For a few seconds, the engine continued to splutter and spark until at last the rider killed it. Peace descended, punctuated only by the plaintive lowing of discomfited cattle.

The rider dismounted, heaved the bike back on its stand, stared at the machine for a few seconds before patting the fuel tank in a gesture that suggested either satisfaction or relief that his steed had got him this far. A brown leather helmet encased his head, and his face was concealed behind a dirty white scarf and an enormous pair of goggles so covered in rain, mud and road grit it was a wonder that he could see anything. A pair of sturdy, black knee-length boots encased his legs and a water-stained, tan-brown leather coat wrapped itself around his body. He removed his gauntlets and paused to use them to remove the excess moisture and debris from his coat. He glanced up at the row of astonished faces pressed against the window glass, gave a cheery wave and strode purposefully towards them.

"Who on earth is that?" Susan asked. "We're not expecting anyone."

Everyone's head swivelled in unison towards the Stube door. The latch rose and the door swung open to reveal the mystery man who stared back at them, although it was difficult to tell whether he could see anything as the heat of the room instantly misted up his goggles. For a few seconds, each party regarded the other in silence. The man gradually became aware not only that the Stube door remained open allowing cold air in, but also that a puddle was slowly forming around his boots as his coat dripped on to the stone floor.

"Oh, I'm terribly sorry, I seem to have bought the weather in with me," he mumbled, his words distorted behind the scarf. He swung the door shut and stared at the puddle, seemingly at a loss as to what to do about it.

"Do you mind telling us who you are?" Sep stood up and advanced towards the man, who didn't look threatening but Sep was cautious nevertheless.

"Oh?" The man realised his scarf, helmet and goggles rendered him anonymous. In a fluster, he peeled them off. "Sep, it's me!" he announced, and threw out his arms as if presenting himself for applause.

"Gunter Schwartz! What on Earth are you doing here?" Sep laughed as the pair slapped each other companionably on the back, adding to the pool at Gunter's feet.

"Only partially planned. I wasn't sure that the 'old girl' would get me here. I've just bought her. Her engine's a bit dodgy."

"We heard," Susan said in a deadpan voice. "You'd better get that wet coat off before you flood us out."

"So, what brings you here?" Sep asked, as Gunter started to unbutton his saturated coat.

"I thought I'd head up the Brandtnerwald to give the 'old girl' a bit of a run." He caught sight of Stephan, another old comrade in arms. "Stephan, mate, I didn't see you there. My God, man, you've not changed a bit." He glanced around at the other people in the room as if suddenly becoming aware of their number. "Oh, I'm not interrupting something, am I?"

"Sunday lunch," Harriet piped up.

"Indeed, Fraulein Harriet." Gunter looked uncomfortable at the news.

"Come and sit down, Gunter." Susan said, vacating her own seat. "Johan, go and fetch a chair from the cellar."

Johan disappeared off as his father did the introductions. He arrived back as Gunter announced himself.

"Gunter Schwartz. And I'm delighted to meet you all." He gave a formal bow, then glanced uncertainly at Susan, scratched his nose and looked embarrassed. "I apologise for interrupting your gathering. It was thoughtless of me."

"Nonsense, Gunter. You're always welcome in our house. You'll stop and have something to eat. I insist."

Gunter's eyes swept across the steaming, gurgling pans on the range. "Well…if there's some left." He edged closer to the table, suggesting he could be easily persuaded.

Marie retrieved the soup pan and ladle from the range as Gunter's frail defences crumbled.

"We've some chicken and roast potatoes to come," Susan said.

Gunter licked his lips. "Perhaps a small plate."

"And some vegetables and gravy?"

"Um…if it isn't too much trouble." Gunter needed no further encouragement. Discarding his coat took on a degree of urgency. Removing his boots, however, represented a challenge. Johan stepped forward to give him a hand. The left boot slid off, after a brief wrestle, to reveal a fetching chequered sock from which a large pink big toe peeped out. Removal of the other boot revealed the left big toe had a brother. Gunter was oblivious to the exposure. Everyone pretended not to notice. Harriet clapped her hand over her mouth to stifle her giggles.

Gunter sat down and, after Marie had filled his bowl, began his assault on the soup. After the first mouthful he sat back and looked at Susan. "My word, this is excellent."

"It's Josey you need to thank."

Gunter bowed his head deferentially towards Josey. "Stephan is truly a fortunate man, Frau Wachter."

Having accommodated their friend, the others recommenced their attack on the spread.

"Is there something wrong with your motorbike?" Marie asked innocently, still standing beside him, ready to top up his bowl should the need arise.

Gunter slowly turned his head towards Marie. He couldn't look her in the eye. He looked like a little boy who'd been caught scrumping apples. "Ah, yes. It is a bit on the noisy side, for which I sincerely apologise."

"It's not me you should be apologising to. It's the village, in fact the entire valley."

"There is something wrong with the engine," Gunter mumbled.

"If there is something wrong with the engine, why didn't you fix it before taking the… the thing out on the road?" Marie jerked her head back toward the farmyard and the offending machine.

Gunter's winking big toes succeeded where his verbal apology failed. The sight of two pink appendages waving about at the end of his feet undermined Marie. She struggled to keep a straight face. "There are plenty of people who mend engines," she said in a strained voice, her eyes now fixed on the two squirming toes. "Surely you know an engineer?" She transferred her gaze from Gunter's feet to look him straight in the eye. "And why have you got holes in your socks?"

Her question threw Gunter. He turned to stare at the holes for a few seconds, trying to guess whether having defective footwear represented a worse failing than owning a motorbike with a faulty engine. "I can't darn." He glanced up at Marie in some trepidation at her reaction. "I can sew buttons on and stitch seams, but I never learnt to master darning…unfortunately."

"It's the timing, Herr Schwartz," Simon said.

Everyone looked at him in confusion. None more so than Gunter who was not only thrown by the abrupt changes in the direction of conversation, but wary of uttering a response that might result in him falling even lower in the estimation of the room generally, and Marie in particular.

"The engine's timing is out," Simon said, as bafflement swept the room. "It needs adjusting."

Gunter cast Marie a furtive look. He'd convinced himself that she considered him to be little better than a buffoon, and he was loath to add to her low opinion of him by admitting he had yet more character failings. However, Simon had put him on the spot. He decided to come clean. "I'm sorry, young man, but I haven't got a clue what you are talking about."

Marie turned away to hide her giggles.

"The ignition is advanced, which means the exhaust valve remains partly open when the ignition takes place. As a result the petrol explodes in the exhaust pipe."

Gunter tried not to look vacant. "Oh, I see." He nodded sagely. "Is it easily fixed?" He looked earnestly at Simon in the hope the young man's knowledge and capability might provide some salvation to his dented standing.

To Gunter's relief, Simon looked confident. "It should be a simple matter of fine-tuning. My Pa's car had a similar problem when he first got it. I'll have a look if you like."

"Not now you won't," Susan said firmly. "This is supposed to be a family lunch. You can take a look when we've finished.

43

THE SLIPPERY POLE

Wagner felt a sense of smug satisfaction as he made the last entry in his pocketbook, before returning it to its compartment at the back of the drawer. It amazed him how easily even intelligent people could succumb to temptation. Every quarter, the parish returns, letters and diocese internal reports threw up titbits of misdemeanours of which the perpetrators were mostly either indifferent, naive or ignorant to how exposed they had left themselves.

He sighed and considered how he might exploit the latest information. The parish priest, who was clearly an alcoholic, needed to be removed. His behaviour was now attracting too many complaints. The new priest at Brandtkreuze needed to be reined-in. Wagner was all for laying down Catholic teachings, but outright opposition to the fascists was out of step with the public mood. He made a mental note to give the youngster a dressing down and encourage him to redirect his energy towards undermining the Communists. And the contractor, who was overcharging for restoration work on the cathedral, needed to be reminded that failure to honour personal agreements had consequences.

Then he turned his mind towards those wielding power and influence. It always paid to get close to such people. Top of his list was the unexpected visit of a Vatican delegation. Although it was a fleeting one day stop-over, there would be a reception and a meeting between the cardinal and the bishop. Wagner was determined to place himself at the centre of proceedings and rub shoulders with Church establishment.

He rang the bell and counted down the seconds until Father Thomas's arrival. "Father Thomas!" Wagner feigned surprise. "We are blessed by the presence of a Vatican deputation." He handed over the letter. "Make appropriate arrangements and run them past me for approval."

The priest nodded and handed back a piece of paper.

"What's this?" Wagner was immediately suspicious.

"The itinerary for your pastoral inspections."

"Ah." Wagner scan read it. "You've included Doppelgau!"

Thomas smiled. "Your old parish."

"My first parish, Father Thomas." Wagner said it as if it was a particular source of pride.

"I thought you'd appreciate a trip down memory lane."

"Who's the incumbent these days?"

"Father Haphold. By all accounts he's settled in well."

Wagner suddenly felt a shiver of concern. Not all memories were pleasant. The image of the family leaving the Krone flashed across his mind. Sep Breitner and his family. He could recall them now. Sep had a sister - he struggled to remember her name... Josey - that was it! His anxiety increased. She could be trouble. Then again, it was a long time ago.

Memories fade. He became vaguely aware that Father Thomas was still talking.

"I've left the dates open. But I understand the village is planning a memorial service soon. It might be worth considering attending."

Wagner collected himself. "Yes, excellent idea. Find out the date and let me know."

"Shall I inform Father Haphold of your attendance."

"No, that won't be necessary." Wagner waved a dismissive hand. "Focus on the Vatican delegation."

GUNTER'S MISFORTUNES

"That's what I like to see," Susan said, as she surveyed the piles of empty plates and the chicken carcases picked clean of flesh.

"It's a sign of a good meal and fine cooking, if I may say so." Gunter patted his stomach contentedly. "I haven't had such a treat since, well, I can't remember."

"Are you not married?" Marie asked.

Throughout the meal, Gunter had proved an amusing, courteous guest and a consummate conversationalist.

"You can tell by the holes in his socks he's not married." Sep laughed.

"Sep, don't be rude." Susan gave her husband a black look. "I'm sure Gunter picked up an old pair by mistake."

Gunter chuckled. "If only that were true. Sad to say, almost all my socks have holes in them. One day I'll get around to teaching myself how to darn."

"Sewing and darning is women's work." Marie said, earning herself a raised eyebrow look from Josey.

"Needs must, Frau Haufmann. In the trenches us men could knit and sew as good as any woman. Darning socks though? Well, that's a different matter. Once your socks were on, they stayed on – sometimes for months at a time until they rotted off your feet. Isn't that right, Stephan?"

Stephan gave an almost imperceptible nod and said nothing. He rarely talked about his war experience.

"You live on your own then, Gunter?" Josey asked.

"Not through choice. I'd like to get married one day. I just can't find the right woman who'll have me." He looked around at his audience. "It's not through lack of trying on my part, I can assure you."

Gunter had the women intrigued. He seemed an affable, fairly attractive man and appeared reasonably fit, despite carrying a few extra kilos. "So, what's the problem?" Susan noticed her husband's broad grin, suggesting he already knew the answer.

Gunter took a swig from his Pils and considered his reply. "Well, being in the police doesn't help." He wiped his lips with his fingers. "People feel uncomfortable with it, and the hours are irregular which makes developing a relationship difficult."

"Farming hours are irregular. It doesn't seem to be a barrier in this village." Marie sounded unsympathetic. "Are you telling us that establishing relationships is difficult just because of your job?"

Gunter shuffled in his seat, scratched his nose and looked uncomfortable. "Unfortunately, yes," he said eventually.

Susan glanced at Sep. The fact he looked to be enjoying his friend's discomfort fuelled her curiosity. "So, are you going to tell us about it? Not that I'm being nosey," she added disingenuously.

"Well, as an example," Gunter looked around the company who were now intrigued. "I did enjoy a relationship with a young lady which, I admit, I had high hopes of advancing towards a more formal arrangement."

"Had you known her long?" Josey asked.

"Just over a year. Enough, I'm sure you will agree, for both parties to get to know one another."

There was a collective nodding of heads. A serious relationship needed to be nurtured.

"Anyway, the young lady felt sufficient time had elapsed for me to be formally introduced to her family, as a necessary first step prior to…well, you know… making things more…"

"Getting engaged," Harriet piped up, keen to jolly Gunter along.

He bowed to acknowledge her assistance. "Indeed. So, I was invited to meet the family. Over Sunday lunch, as it happens." Gunter's gesture indicated the event described was not dissimilar to current circumstances. "Everything went well. Her parents were present and seemed to like me, as did her two sisters. Even their pet spaniel took a shine to me. And the regard was mutual. They were a delightful family. Anyone would have been pleased to have such in-laws." He fell silent and, for a few seconds, a far-away look came into his eye as he relived the moment.

Josey couldn't contain herself. "So, what happened?" she said with a tinge of exasperation.

The policeman's expression changed to one of sorrow. "Her brother came home. It provided a shock for them as well as me. They weren't expecting him, and the young lady had barely mentioned she had a brother."

Flickers of perplexity crossed the faces of his audience as they tried to deduce the significance of the sudden arrival.

Gunter continued. "Well, I recognised him as soon as he entered the room. We'd been after him for years. He was wanted in Austria, Germany and half of Europe for a whole host of crimes including fraud, embezzlement, racketeering, blackmail – you name it."

A collective gasp went around the Stübe. "What did you do?" Susan asked.

Gunter seemed surprised by the question. "I arrested him – after a bit of a struggle, which involved me trying to hold off the rest of the family, who understandably didn't want to see one of their number hauled off to jail." His look turned wistful. "In the fracas most of the crockery got smashed. That didn't endear me to her mother." He took another sip of beer as if to wash away the pain of the event. "So that ended that relationship."

Sep chuckled, earning a sharp rebuke from Susan. "Sep, it's not funny. It's sad." Having scolded her husband she adopted a more sympathetic tone with Gunter. "Didn't you try to patch things up with the family, after all, you were only doing your job."

"I sent some flowers. But that made matters worse."

Sep laughed, earning him another scowl from his wife. "Gunter doesn't have much luck regarding presents, do you mate? Tell them about, what was her name?... Katya."

Gunter held his hands up to his forehead and slowly shook his head as another painful memory was dragged to the surface.

"Who's Katya?" Marie asked the question on behalf of all in the room who now hung on his every word.

"Ah! If you wanted to describe a man's ideal vision of the perfect female companion, Katya would likely emerge. She had everything! A beautiful face and figure, and intelligence - she was a qualified legal assistant with a prestigious law firm in Brandt. I met her when she helped her legal team mount a prosecution against a local villain." He glanced around at his audience. "Consequently, she knew I was a detective. So, my police work wasn't a problem. She had a great sense of humour – well, up to a point. Best of all, she loved handiwork. Knitting, sewing and making clothes was her passion. I guess it provided a relief from working on endless witness statements and court notices." He grinned. "I didn't have any holes in my socks when Katya and I were stepping out."

"Did she have a brother?" Harriet asked.

"No. Her brother and father were both casualties of the Great War. She lived with her mother."

Susan looked puzzled. "What's this got to do with giving presents?"

"Ah, well, I picked up on the fact that, although Katya had everything a first-class seamstress needed, the one thing she always complained about was her reliance on flat irons to press clothes and seams prior to stitching." Gunter looked around and spotted Susan's own set lined up next to the range. "She had twice as many as you, Susan, but, as you know, they are cumbersome, difficult to get to the right temperature and are just not up to the job. So, for her birthday I bought her a new iron."

The women glanced at each other, aghast.

"You bought your girlfriend an iron for her birthday!?" Marie sounded incredulous, before bursting out in a gale of laughter.

Gunter looked affronted. "No, no, no, you misunderstand me, Frau Haufmann. I didn't buy a flat iron. I bought an electric iron. You know, the type you screw into the light."

"Was she pleased?" Josey spluttered, struggling to stifle her giggles.

Gunter pondered the question. "Difficult to say." He ran through her reaction in his head before replying. "I think she appreciated the thought and the expense. Those machines aren't cheap, I can tell you."

Harriet looked perplexed. "I don't understand. If she wasn't upset with the present why didn't you end up getting married?"

"Because of a turn of events of which I was an innocent party." He felt it necessary to fortify himself with another draught of Pils, drew a deep breath and proceeded. "A week after her birthday Katya decided to use her present. She followed the instructions to the letter. She turned off the light, removed the bulb and screwed the plug into the fitting." He gave a slow, sad shake of the head. "Unfortunately, at that precise moment, her mother entered the now darkened room and turned on the light-switch."

"Oh, my goodness!" Marie's hand flew to her mouth. "She could have been killed."

He acknowledged her observation. "Luckily, Katya survived the incident. She was only in hospital a couple of days."

"She ended up in hospital!?" Marie stared wide-eyed at Gunter.

"The shock threw the poor girl off the chair she was standing on." Gunter looked miserable. "She broke her arm as a consequence, as well as suffering a mild concussion and a chipped tooth," he added.

Only the gentle ticking of the grandfather clock could be heard as everyone pictured the tragic scene. Susan broke the silence.

"I fail to see why such an incident would terminate your relationship unless Katya was particularly hard-hearted. It was an accident, after all."

"Ah Susan, that very question has been troubling me ever since. I think sometimes I was born unlucky. You see, I wasn't made aware of the incident for over a week. Her mother didn't think it important to inform me and, not being a blood relation, the medical staff had no reason to contact me. My silence and absence betrayed an unsympathetic and uncaring side to my nature, at least as far as Katya was concerned." He gave a mournful sigh. "Added to that, one of the medical staff, a young doctor, quickly filled the vacuum my lack of attendance provided."

"Oh, Gunter," Marie said. She reached over and patted his arm.

Gunter gave her a wan smile. "You shouldn't feel sorry for me, Frau Haufmann. I believe in fate. Such things are meant to happen. In any case, it hasn't curtailed my determination to find the right person." His face gradually lit up, and he looked at each of them in turn. "I've a new lady in my life, and I have high hopes," he said with obvious enthusiasm.

In the background, Sep buried his head in his hands and groaned. He'd heard so many tales of his friend's romantic misfortunes that he felt certain that this was another affair destined to end badly.

Gunter wasn't to be deterred. There was no mistaking his fervour as he provided details. "She lives on the same street as me; the sweetest girl you could ever wish to meet. I know her family, and I'm sure they already hold me in the highest regard, but, best of all, she is genuinely interested in the work I do."

"What's her name?" Josey asked.

49

"Gertrude." Gunter beamed as if the girl's name alone was sufficient to confirm her suitability and ensure the success of his endeavours.

"Well, I wish you every success with the young lady," Susan said firmly. "Now, enough of this talk - we ought to have some music, and some singing and dancing."

The mention of dancing sent a ripple of panic through Johan. He didn't mind playing music, or singing, since he excelled at both. However, unlike his sister, he'd little sense of rhythm or timing when it came to dancing. Fortunately, salvation presented itself in the form of Gunter's motorbike. "Mama, perhaps I could help Simon fix Herr Schwartz's motorbike? It's getting late and the light's fading."

Susan wavered. She attached great importance to the Sunday family get-together. Nevertheless, her son had a point, she conceded. She thought of Gunter's explosive drive back through the village which was bound to cause real annoyance.

Simon seized the opportunity to support his friend. "It shouldn't take long, Frau Breitner," he said eagerly. "All I need is a screwdriver and a set of spanners."

"Papa, can we use your tools?" Jurgen pitched in, determined not to be left out. Singing and dancing paled to insignificance compared to the opportunity to tinker with an engine.

Stephan's grunt of consent and her husband's almost imperceptible nod swayed Susan. "Alright. But you get out of your Sunday best."

The lads bolted to avoid any last-second change of mind. As Simon predicted, correcting the engine's timing proved simplicity itself. For Johan, the smell of oil and petrol, and the throbbing power as the now tamed engine ticked over with a satisfying low rumble, seemed to run through his entire being. He felt the heat of the engine and exhaust. It was as if the machine came alive. He sat astride the seat and imagined how it might feel to speed up the valley and over the high pass. He set his heart on owning one.

"How much do you think they cost?"

Simon sat back on his heels and considered Johan's question. "I dunno. About two thousand Schilling new. Half that for an older model."

Johan had his target. Now he had to raise the money.

50

ESCAPING POVERTY

"Whatcha got, Babe?" Yankee Franz asked, as soon as Trudy and Gabi entered the cellar. The place was full of rusty and mostly broken garden tools, old bicycles with flat tyres, cheap cardboard suitcases that contained discarded clothes or moth-eaten faded material that might once have been curtains or table-cloths. A jumble of half-empty hessian sacks containing potatoes, swedes and cabbages lay in one corner, and an equally dishevelled pile of winter overcoats lay in another. Half a dozen jars of pickled Sauerkraut lined a rough timber shelf. Dust and cobwebs covered everything apart from a large wooden work-bench and four mismatched wooden chairs placed in the centre of the earthen floor. The cellar smelt of dried wood, vinegar and Yankee Franz's cigarette. This was the gang's centre of operations, and three of them gathered around the pale light of a paraffin lamp to assess the day's takings.

Yankee Franz now regarded Trudy as his star pickpocket, and even Gabi acknowledged her erstwhile pupil had graduated into an expert. She regularly delivered good quantities of quality items. Trudy tipped the contents of her school bag on the table. Several gold gentlemen's watches immediately caught Franz's attention. He gave a low whistle of admiration as he held one to the light for closer inspection.

Trudy draped herself on the chair and looked casual, as if delivering such bounty was of little consequence. "That's not the best," she said nonchalantly.

Franz was immediately suspicious. "You've got more stuff?"

Trudy inwardly smiled at his lame attempt to intimidate her. Although well aware of the punishments for anyone tempted to retain stolen goods without permission, Trudy knew that Franz was all bluster and too much of a pussycat to administer any form of retribution.

"Nah, I meant that's not the best in the heap." She gestured towards a delicate lady's watch, so small it remained half-buried under the pile of cigarettes, bracelets, wallets and purses.

Franz picked it up and ran the diamond-encrusted strap through his fingers. "Jesus, babe, this is some sparkler." The watch looked exquisite and worth a small fortune. "The cops will put the feelers out to get this back." He glanced sideways at her. "You sure you ducked out clean?"

Trudy gazed back at him with cool, confident eyes. "She didn't know I was there. Too busy giving her husband a hard time for ogling."

Gabi grinned. "Classic distraction, Franzy. I showed a bit of leg. Old man's eyes are on stalks. Wife gives him grief. Trudy does her thing. Job done."

Franz looked unconvinced. "No one clocked you?"

The two girls shook their heads.

"What you got there, Yankee boy?" The question was delivered with quiet menace.

Instinctively, Franz thrust the watch into his pocket as he spun around to confront the enquirer. "Nothing special, Lothar. Just going through Trudy's gear."

Lothar Müller slowly crept down the last of the stairs like a cat weighing up its prey. He slunk to the edge of the table. Suddenly he struck. His hand shot out and locked on Franz's wrist. "Show Lothar."

Franz winced as the grip tightened. Lothar pressed his head to Franz's ear. "I said show Lothar," he hissed, as he forced Franz's arm away from his pocket.

An air of intimidation seeped into every crevice of the cellar. Franz was all false bluster. Lothar, on the other hand, was a mean, sadistic thug. Gabi took a step back as if to disappear into the shadows. Lothar held out his hand expectantly. Franz needed no more persuading. He dropped the watch into Lothar's palm. Lothar released his captive and dangled the watch from his fingers. In the dim light, the jewel glittered as it spun.

Trudy watched Lothar with mild interest tinged with anxiety. She'd heard of Lothar Müller but had never met him. He was a man of the night, dark shadows and evil. He was a pimp, a blackmailer, a fence, a man with a hand in every crime and racket that went on in the ghetto. He was also a leech that lived off the endeavours of others. And he ruled through terror. His grotesque appearance matched his character. A long scar ran from his forehead, across the bridge of his nose and halfway down his left cheek. The result of a dockside brawl when he was set upon by half a dozen Bolsheviks, two of whom he claimed to have killed. No one disbelieved the story.

Trudy's wariness increased as she observed Franz's fear and the way Gabi shrunk from his presence

"Very nice, very pretty." Lothar grabbed a chair, swung it beside the table and made himself comfortable. He casually dropped the diamond-encrusted watch into his pocket before running his fingers through Trudy's bounty. His eyes were immediately drawn to the high-value items. He pushed them to one side until he'd divided the cache into two small piles. The room fell silent as he completed his examination.

Trudy glanced at Franz, who seemed paralysed with dread, his face covered by a gleam of sweat.

"Very, very nice." Lothar drew out the words and glanced at Trudy. "You are responsible for this?"

"She is."

"I wasn't talking to you, Yankee boy." Lothar kept his eyes on Trudy as he barked his rebuke at Franz, who reeled as if he'd been physically hit. Lothar gave Trudy a reptilian smile. "Well?"

Trudy coolly returned his gaze. She jerked her head towards Gabi. "Me and her – we work together."

"How long did it take you to turn this trick?" His eyes flicked towards the pile.

"A day."

"You deliver this each time?"

Out of the corner of her eye, Trudy noticed Franz tense. She thought fast. Lothar must be receiving a share from Franz in return for something. Trudy guessed it must be some kind of protection. Maybe Franz was short-changing him. Although she felt a tight knot of fear build inside her, she maintained her eye contact. "No. This is a good haul. We were lucky."

Lothar studied her, deliberately letting the tension build. Trudy didn't waver.

After what seemed like an eternity, he broke the silence. "Cocky little thing, aren't you?"

She stayed mute.

"Let's have a look at you."

Trudy looked non-plussed.

Lothar leant back in the chair and gestured to the table top. "Stand up. Let's see what Trudy Heppel looks like."

The use of her name threw Trudy. How did he know her name? And why would such a man make it his business to take an interest in her? Suddenly she felt her anxiety shift into a knot of fear. In one brief sentence he destroyed her carefully constructed façade of confidence. She slowly eased herself off the chair and stood up, trying not to shake.

He patted his hand on the table. "Up you get, Fraulein Trudy Heppel – if you please." His voice was soft and sinister.

She slowly climbed on the table, using the chair as a ladder, and stood in front of him.

He ran his half-slitted eyes up and down her. "Turn around," he commanded.

She slowly did as she was told until she faced Gabi, who looked terrified. Trudy felt her own courage evaporate. What was she thinking trying to stare down this monster? She felt his scrutiny and steeled herself for whatever might follow.

"How old is Fraulein Trudy Heppel?" Lothar's voice now had an almost sing-song taunting timbre to it; he was enjoying himself.

Her throat went dry. She gulped and steadied herself. Despite her internal dread, she was determined not to give him the satisfaction of knowing he scared her. "Sixteen," she said with a confidence she didn't feel.

"Oh, really." Lothar forced her to stand, stretching out the tension, deliberately prolonging her discomfort. A smirk played across his lips as he spotted the slight tremble in Trudy's fingers. He leant back further in the chair and crossed his feet up on the table. Wordlessly, he indicated with a languid finger that she should turn around again.

53

Anger replaced fear in Trudy's mind. How dare this reptile treat her as some plaything. Nevertheless, she baulked at jumping off the table to put an end to his theatre. Instead, she looked at him with contempt. It seemed to unsettle him.

"Well, Miss Trudy Heppel, I suggest you choose an item from your ill-gotten gains as a reward for your hard work."

She jumped down, turned round and considered the pile before selecting a large, gold gentlemen's pocket-watch and chain. She gave him a defiant glance, daring him to deny her choice. His eyes exuded a low cunning, and the thin smile still played across his lips. Abruptly, he got up and swept the pile of the more valuable items into his pocket, before heading out of the cellar. He cast her a departing glance. "Very smart," he said.

The release of tension was palpable.

"Bloody bastard." Franz spat the words out.

Gabi covered her eyes and wept out of sheer fright. Trudy felt her heart pounding; her throat remained constricted. She felt angry and humiliated. Nobody had the right to make her feel so fearful. Normally, she would have waited for Yankee Franz to divide the loot, followed by the usual argument over the share to be retained by Gabi and her. This time she couldn't care less. Her fury grew as she made her way back to the apartment. The words of Tante Bri rang out in her consciousness. If she was so clever why did she now feel so frustrated and powerless? Things had to get better. There had to be a way out. Unfortunately, things only got worse.

Two weeks later, Yankee Franz was beaten almost to death by a gang of Freikorp thugs. His crime, according to the gossip that swept around the slum, was for being unpatriotic and insulting the German people. Dressing and speaking like an American gangster offended the Freikorps, who believed only Germanic fashion demonstrated true patriotism. Trudy guessed the real reason was that Lothar thought he was being scammed, or maybe he hadn't been out of earshot of Yankee Frank's outburst.

Unfortunately for Trudy, Lothar became an unwelcome presence although his initial attention focused on Gabi. It started with small gifts, then he'd buy her clothes from expensive shops that were almost mystical to anyone from the slums. Trips to restaurants and up-market cafés soon followed. A visit to the theatre led to late-night cocktails at the city casino. Trudy was appalled by the ease Gabi became seduced and dismayed by the naivety of her friend as to Lothar's purpose. It seemed Gabi expected it and was resigned to her fate.

Despite her efforts, Trudy could not avoid him forever. He appeared outside the gates at the end of the school day. She was allowed first choice over the week's pickpocketed trinkets. Worst of all, he became a frequent visitor to Tante Bri's apartment. One afternoon, she left school by the back entrance to evade him. She arrived home, thinking she'd outwitted him, only to find him seated at Tante Bri's table casually smoking a cigarette.

"Ah, Trudy. What an unexpected pleasure." He said, his voice oily and tinged with sarcasm.

"You're late, girl. Where have you been?" Tante Bri's brusque question cut across Lothar's false welcome. She barged her way across the room and helped Trudy out of her coat. She turned her back on him to physically shield her girl and rolled her eyes at Trudy to signify her annoyance at his presence.

"Sorry, Madi. I had some extra homework."

"Doing well at school, are we?" Lothar took a drag from his cigarette and blew the smoke out in a long, slow breath.

"I'm doing alright."

"She's doing more than alright. She's a bright girl." There was no hiding the pride in Tante Bri's voice. She smiled broadly at Trudy and brushed the blonde curls away from her adopted daughter's face.

Trudy smiled back at her. She loved the small, unconscious gestures of affection that Tante Bri frequently delivered.

"Got ambitions, sweetheart?"

Trudy cringed. Being called sweetheart by Lothar felt loathsome.

"Course she's got ambition. Ain't you, girl?"

Lothar sneered. "What? To be a waitress or barmaid? Or follow her mother's footsteps?"

Tante Bri stiffened. Her face turned crimson. "She ain't one of your floozies, Lothar Müller, nor one of your empty-headed tarts for you to lead astray."

"Hey, I asked a reasonable question. It's a tough world out there. A girl's got to use what she's got." Lothar took another deep drag from his cigarette and let his eyes linger on Trudy.

His lecherous look was too much for Tante Bri. She grabbed the poker from the stove and loomed over Lothar, who flinched in anticipation of the blow that wasn't delivered. "You ain't welcome in my house. Now shift your arse out." She waved the poker towards the door. "Go on, before I do you a mischief."

Anger quickly replaced Lothar's initial shock. He wasn't used to anyone standing up to him, let alone threatening him with violence. For a few seconds, he glared at the formidable form that loomed over him. He decided a swaggering departure more prudent than his instinctive desire to give the old lady a slapping. This was no timid teenager that could be easily beaten and cowed. Tante Bri wielded her own power and influence in the ghetto. She could and probably would give him problems. He assumed a look of indifference and picked up his packet of cigarettes with exaggerated slowness, before easing himself out of his seat and holding his hands up to reinforce the reasonableness of his intentions.

"No offence, Brigitte. But if little Miss Smartass wants to earn some serious money I'll be happy to help."

Tante Bri crashed the poker on the table. "Earn some dirty money, you mean. Get out, you little worm."

Lothar needed no further encouragement.

The confrontation reduced Tante Bri to a heaving, gasping wreck. She leant heavily on the table, her face flushed red. Trudy was anxious. She'd heard of people having heart attacks and was convinced she was about to witness one. She helped Tante Bri shuffle into her chair, then dashed to the kitchen for the bottle of Schnapps. Tante Bri took a couple of generous swigs and gradually recovered.

"You shouldn't have done that, Madi. He'll only give us trouble, and it's bad for your heart."

Tante Bri raised her eyebrows to acknowledge the truth of Trudy's statement. "I hate that man. He's ruined more lives than I care to think about."

"You shouldn't have done it though, Madi. I can look after myself."

"Don't under-estimate him, Liebling. He'd slit his own mother's throat if he thought he'd profit from it." She suddenly took both of Trudy's hands in hers. "Promise me you won't fall for his charms."

"Charms!" Trudy laughed. "What charms? The man's a pig."

"Not charms then but his tricks." Tante Bri didn't laugh. She squeezed Trudy's hands and looked distressed. "You know what I mean."

Trudy knelt so she could look directly into her aunt's eyes. "I mean to get out. I've been thinking about it for weeks."

"Easier said than done, love."

Trudy nodded. Although her intention was clear in her mind, she hadn't a clue how to achieve it. She knew she was on borrowed time as far as working the marks was concerned. Twice she'd nearly been caught. Despite being careful to hit different locations randomly, and never work the same patch twice in the same month, the police were on to her. Gabi's good looks and her own distinctive blonde hair made them stand out, despite their precautions. With Gabi being enticed into a different world, Trudy found herself even more exposed. The mood of the people had turned as well. Apparently, bystanders had applauded as the Freikorps thugs beat up Yankee Franz. The intolerance of anything that looked, sounded or felt foreign, or was counter-cultural to the new sense of German nationalism, had taken root. As a consequence, the gang had taken fright which meant she couldn't rely on the back-up of spotters and runners.

But the main reason was, deep down, she knew being a petty criminal wasn't her. She needed something or someone to help her chart a new course. She glanced fondly at Tante Bri before planting a kiss on her cheek. She recognised, despite all her love, affection and encouragement, that that someone wasn't her beloved aunt. She'd have to use her own wits. As it happened, her exit came from an unexpected direction.

The following Saturday, at the end of lessons, the teacher held everyone back. She picked up one of the two piles of forms that lay on her desk and which had intrigued the pupils all morning. She caressed the sheaves as if they were sacred scrolls and stood until the class fell silent. Her face became flushed, her forehead glistened with a thin sheen of perspiration, and Trudy noticed the hand clutching the small bundle quivered, as if she struggled to contain an inner ecstasy.

"I have here some joyful news." The statement was delivered in a gasp of barely suppressed excitement. The teacher's beatific smile embraced the entire class. "Our dear Fuhrer wishes to include you all in his great endeavour to build a new Fatherland." She gazed around as if expecting some applause. A few picked up on the cue, exhaled a gasp of astonished wonderment and wriggled in their seats in excitement.

"You will *all* complete these forms and get your parents to sign them." The teacher moved along the ranks of pent-up children, dishing out one form to each boy in turn. "They are to be returned to me Monday morning without fail."

A hand shot up. The teacher indicated the youngster should speak. "What are they, Miss?"

"What are they? What are they indeed!" She held the forms aloft. "These are your future and your path towards helping establish the greatest nation the world has ever seen. A mighty Reich built on the vision of our Fuhrer." She continued her progress through the class. "You boys will join the Hitlerjugend where you will learn the skills of a German warrior." She suddenly spun around and addressed the sea of faces. "Who can tell me the motto of the Hitlerjugend?" Several arms strained as if the limbs might separate from the shoulders, for the honour of delivering the answer. The teacher selected a boy at random. "Blood and Honour, Miss."

"Correct – Blood and Honour. From this point forward, your blood and sweat, your body, your entire being, shall be devoted to the service of the Fatherland. The youth of Germany shall become our soldiers, our defenders, our new nobility." The teacher's eyes moistened as she continued; her voice quivering with emotion. "You will live and breathe the principles of National Socialism." She was stopped mid-flow by another raised hand. "What is it, girl?"

"What about us, Miss," the girl asked, her voice shaking as much as her raised hand.

The teacher beamed at the youngster. "Don't think our Fuhrer would leave the fair maidens of our country out of his thoughts. You girls are the future. Only women can breed the sons and daughters the Fatherland will need. Only women can provide a home and provide sustenance to keep

57

our men strong." The teacher finished doling out the boy's application forms. She swept the second pile of papers from her desk and distributed them to the girls, speaking as she went.

Trudy didn't know what to think. She'd seen the Hitler Youth strutting around the city, trying to look important. To her, they were no different from the lads in the pickpocketing gang: boys pretending to be men. They had the same swagger, the air of arrogance and false bravado. She only half-listened to the teacher's tirade, and idly picked up the form as it fell on the desk in front of her. She read the banner title — *Anmenderformula - Bund Deutscher Mädel*, and made to fold it and put it in her bag. Suddenly her ears pricked up. The teacher had moved on to the virtues of joining the Nazis' youth movement.

"You do your duty to the Fatherland and our Fuhrer, and you become a true German. The Party will train you. Boys will learn how to fight our enemies and further the cause of National Socialism. Jobs and opportunities will open up for you. Being a member of the Hitlerjugend or the BDM is your passport to success."

Trudy unfolded the form and scanned it. Her eyes lingered on the paragraphs that spoke of developing the girls' careers: undergoing training to be nurses, administrators, teachers, accountants, lawyers and more. It also mentioned teaching the skills needed to be good housewives or mothers. She couldn't believe what she read. There were sports activities, skiing, and camping trips in the countryside. All that was required was the need to wear a uniform, attend some meetings, and spend a year working on a farm or helping a family with their children. Trudy's instincts told her that this was her opportunity to escape the slums.

NEW LIFE AND OLD DEATH

Johan stirred at six o'clock. Over the gentle patter of rain, he heard his father dragging the milk pails to the water butt, followed by the sound of each bucket being scoured. He pulled off the covers and swung his legs over the side of the bed. For a few moments he paused with his hands on his knees and went through his plan one more time. Over the past few weeks, countless vague ideas had run around his head, crashing and colliding with each other and breaking into small pieces which in turn generated new trains of thought. He knew he stood at a crossroads in his life. The trouble was the absence of signposts.

His friends had mapped out their futures, but he was struggling to do so, and that concerned him. Simon had inherited the effortless genius of the Rubensteins. He intended to be a vet and just had to secure a place at a university veterinary school. Although Jurgen had the self-effacing, steady, reliable attributes of his father, he had his mother's genes when it came to ambition. His exposure to Gunter's motorbike fired his desire to become a mechanic or engineer. Sooner or later, he'd reasoned, more cars, vans and lorries would appear on the streets. Tractors would replace horses on the farm. Someone needed to know how to repair and service them.

Johan identified his own driver: independence! He wanted to be in a position where he could make his own decisions, and make something of himself on his own terms and through his own efforts. Eventually, the ideas coalesced into a plan. For the next few weeks, he carried out research, refined his thinking and marshalled his arguments.

Having washed and dressed, he joined his father. Sep had finished milking the first of the herd and had moved on to the second cow. He glanced up as his son entered. "Trouble waking up?" he said pointedly.

"Trouble getting to sleep," Johan replied. He picked up a pail and swung the stool underneath the udder of the adjoining beast.

"Something on your mind?"

Johan nodded. Over the years, an easy relationship had developed between them. Johan felt there were few matters he couldn't discuss with his father and get a sympathetic hearing. "I've been thinking about my future."

"Oh! And?"

Johan washed the cow's udders and began the gentle, rhythmic squeeze to extract the milk. "I've got a few ideas." He looked across at his Pa.

"Go on."

"I'd like to earn some money."

His father chuckled. "That's always a good start. Doing what?"

Johan took a deep breath and launched his plan. The first part proved relatively straightforward. He proposed to invest in part of the animal stock. It was how every farmer's son started out. His father suggested he begun with a breeding sow. His next suggestion, to take responsibility for running the family's stall at Achbrugge market from his mother, surprised Sep. "You'd give up your Saturdays!?"

Johan nodded. "And increase the amount and range of products."

Sep looked intently at his son. "Is there some reason behind all this?"

"I want to buy a motorbike."

"Ah!" His father laughed. "Well, I shouldn't mention that to your mother." He eased himself to his feet, grabbed the half-full milk pail and emptied the contents into the large settling vat. "You'd need to sell a lot of produce. There's not much money around at the moment." Sep glanced at his son. "Don't get your hopes up," he said, as he shoved the stool along the shed floor with his foot, towards the next cow.

"That's not all, Pa."

Sep stopped milking. "This is a morning of surprises. Are you planning to take over the world?"

"It would be a good idea if I became an electrician."

His father looked astonished. "Where did that idea come from?"

"Gunter. His story about electrocuting his girlfriend got me thinking. That, and our trip to England. Most villages in England have electricity. Once places get connected people want all sorts of electrical things, but they also need electricians to run the wires into their homes." He took his father's silence as a signal to continue. "I know we've not won any building business for a long time, but you've said the recession can't last forever, and next year the village will get electricity. Everyone will want to be connected." He glanced up at his father to gauge his reaction.

Sep's expression turned serious. "And be trained where?"

"The technical school in Achbrugge. They are offering apprenticeships." He studied his father, nervously. "I've got the application forms."

"You've thought this through." He studied Johan in silence. Although he didn't show it, he was immensely proud of his son.

A recent outsider who settled in Doppelgau was the parish priest, Father Haphold. He appeared an odd appointment for a village steeped in conservatism. Relatively young, charismatic, forward-thinking and self-effacing, he crept into village affection because he was a good man.

Sep was paying his respects to his late parents when the priest approached.

"There stands a man deep in thought."

Sep looked up, startled. "I'm sorry, Father."

"A lot to catch up on, eh?" He nodded towards the church entrance where Susan stood gossiping with Josey. Harriet and Johan loitered at their mother's side. "Are they planning another trip to England?"

"Maybe next year. We need to focus on protecting our existing business this year." Sep glanced sideways at the priest. "Talking of business, have you cajoled Herman into playing the organ?"

Father Haphold sounded triumphant. "Perseverance, Sep. It's all about perseverance."

"He's agreed?"

"His debut will be at our service of remembrance in two weeks." The priest pondered for a few seconds before adding, "I know I shouldn't speak ill of the dead, but the day Frau Lindsdorf ascended was a blessing for all music lovers."

Sep kept a straight face. "A unique talent."

Father Haphold gave a reflective sigh. "Added and omitted notes missed by the original composers."

A silence fell between the two friends as they recalled the late Frau Lindsdorf and her singular approach to music.

"You don't think it's a bit of a risk?"

Father Haphold looked quizzical. "What risk?"

"Asking Herman Paulus."

"Why – because he's deaf?"

Sep's raised eyebrows were sufficient to indicate his doubts on the matter. Father Haphold waved his hand as if the carpenter's disability was of little consequence. "Beethoven was deaf." He paused and reconsidered Sep's comment. "Maybe his hearing will recover."

"Father, you don't recover from having your eardrums blown out by an exploding breech."

The priest wasn't letting such detail curb his delight in securing Herman's services. "You never lose a gift taught from birth. I tell you, Sep, you should hear him play. It's magnificent."

Sep remained unconvinced. Father Haphold felt more reassurance was required. "I'm working on developing visual cues so he knows when to begin playing and can keep track of the order of service – that sort of thing."

"He's deaf, *and* he's not familiar with the order of service?"

Father Haphold rolled his eyes and sighed. "He's not a Catholic." He patted Sep's shoulder. "Don't worry, he'll be fine."

Wagner's unexpected arrival at the remembrance service two weeks later caused tension.

Sep collared Father Haphold as soon as he recognised Wagner's black limousine parked outside St Martin's Pffarhaus."What's he doing here?"

61

The priest looked equally dismayed. "No idea. It is an unannounced call." He shrugged.

"The man's not popular among some in this village," Sep muttered.

"I know. But let's not make a fuss. He's probably checking up on me."

Everyone felt they were being scrutinised by the sinister-looking clergyman, not just Father Haphold. The disquiet infected the choir boys who fell over themselves in their efforts to look efficient: the silver candlesticks were adjusted, the careless heap of hymn books restacked in neat columns, and the cards, indicating the sequence of hymns to the congregation, straightened - a task that revealed their stress as they succeeded in knocking them off their hooks. They scrambled to remount them in a precise line, while casting nervous eyes towards Wagner in the hope he hadn't noticed.

Wagner was quietly pleased with the tension his presence caused. He drew smug delight at the readiness of the lower orders to act with deference in the presence of their betters. His self-satisfaction improved further as he noted the queue of people who were keen to bend the knee, kiss the ring and receive his blessing. Some faces were familiar, even if he struggled to recall their names. As each devotee knelt before him, his eyes flicked around the church seeking out those that wielded power and influence. A ripple of disappointment coursed through him as he seemed to be the only dignitary present. His chagrin was fleeting, however. Absence of worthies merely heightened his own status.

With a crash, the great church doors swung shut and the church filled with the glorious sound of Bach's Fugue. In an instant the tense atmosphere was banished. St Martin's had never been filled with such majesty. A gasp swept around the congregation. The little parish church suddenly felt like a cathedral. The audience craned their necks to see who sat at the keyboard. All that could be seen was a bald head swaying to and fro as the maestro extracted maximum passion from the work.

Wagner slid into the Throne Chair and adopted a pose designed to convey saintly humility, combined with a connoisseur's appreciation of the soaring music and the words of Father Haphold that followed. His stance also enabled him to surreptitiously scan the congregation. The return to his old parish stirred his memory. Sep Breitner sat at the front, and Wagner assumed the striking fair-haired lady beside him was his wife. English, apparently, and popular for her work as a district nurse, according to his intelligence. Wagner made a mental note to introduce himself. It paid to cultivate anyone of standing. His narrowed eyes swivelled to take in others. He recognised most, but faces were older, more haggard. Despite the uplifting music, some sat hunched as if shouldering invisible burdens. Grief most likely, he assumed. He ought to have informed himself on which families had suffered losses. He silently chastised himself for the oversight, before transferring blame onto Father Thomas's inadequate briefing.

His scrutiny took in the Ansbachers, Hagspiels, Drössels and other village families, along with Herr Zinnerman, the owner of Gasthaus Adler. His eyes locked on a wizened old man, bent almost double, on the front pew to the left of the aisle. Now there sat a man of importance. Doctor Rubenstein was well known throughout the Brandterwald. A highly experienced physician, he'd served the valley communities for well over forty years. Wagner was surprised to see the old man still alive. He flicked his eyes to take in the people sitting around the old doctor. It seemed the entire Rubenstein family were present. Rudi, his youngest son, had followed in his father's footsteps and taken over the family practice, along with his sister, Rachel, who'd become an eminent medical professor. Wagner felt a wave of pleasure. Perhaps his visit to this rustic backwater wouldn't be a waste of time after all. He allowed his eyes to drift from the Rubensteins. He moved on, only to find himself staring directly into the contemptuous gaze of Josey Wachter. A feeling of guilt instantly washed through him, and he quickly looked away. Josey's expression revealed a deeper knowledge. He adjusted his stance so he faced away from her.

Father Haphold completed the initial prayers and turned towards Herman, who was waiting expectantly for the flamboyant visual cue to begin the first hymn. Once again, the church resounded to magnificent virtuosic organ playing.

Wagner resumed his surveillance but found himself unsettled. He felt Josey's eyes burning into him. As he scanned the rows of faces he noticed a transformation. Pleasure and delight replaced previous careworn expressions as the music lifted spirits. But Josey's disdainful stare remained unwavering. And there were others. It took a while to register those that seemed to resent his presence. The young woman dressed in mourning looked familiar, despite her dismissive glance. His blood froze as her name suddenly entered his memory - Marie Wachter. She lost her husband early in the war. Married for less than a year, she would grieve more than most. Yes, that was the reason for her expression. As soon as the thought entered his head, he recognised his self-deceit.

Wagner found himself bathed in a cold sweat. He could almost feel the hostility directed towards him. He beat down the knot of fear and forced himself towards a silent outrage. He was a senior churchman. These people should show courtesy, respect, honour. How many parish priests achieved the position of Monsignor, and senior chaplain to the Bishop? He pulled himself erect and replaced his sly surveillance with a haughty sweep of the audience.

The service progressed and once again glorious, soaring music lifted the mood. The congregation took inspiration from the swaying maestro. The joy of singing felt like a release, and the tone of the service gradually changed as Father Haphold intended. The community had grieved for too long. Now the atmosphere felt right to celebrate the lives of the fallen and precious memories of life before the Great War.

The uplifted ambience failed to reach Monsignor Wagner. This was a service to commemorate the dead. It should be sombre, reverential and done in the Catholic tradition. He scowled, anticipating the flock would recognise his displeasure and adopt a more obeisant behaviour. His indignation morphed into seething fury with what happened next.

The congregation reached a state of heightened expectation. So far, they'd been treated to a masterclass of organ music. The last hymn was bound to be a fitting finale. However, bewilderment swept through the congregation. Father Haphold's hymn selections were familiar and popular songs. The final hymn, No.81, was instantly recognisable but, being a Christmas carol, it seemed a strange choice. Bewilderment turned to confusion as Herman launched into a thunderous introduction of a completely different hymn.

The choirboys aligned their singing to the organist, and a choral war broke out as they sought to assert their hymn over the congregation's efforts.

A bout of pushing and shoving broke out within the choir, indicating the root of the chaos. In their effort to impress Monsignor Wagner, the choir boys had transposed the digits on the display board and now were blaming each other.

A withering look from Father Haphold quelled the rebellion. He then raised his arms and stood, Moses-like, until he had his flock's attention. He slowly lowered his arms, signalling all should fall silent. His initiative might have worked if it hadn't been for Marie, who got a fit of the giggles. Despite trying to stifle her mirth, her laughter infected those around her. Half-suppressed tittering fed on itself until uncontrolled laughter swept around the congregation. Nothing like this had ever happened before, and it was deliciously anarchic.

Herman continued with the most sublime rendition of Hymn No.18, oblivious to the chaos behind him. Eventually the laughter died, and the congregation fell under his spell and sat in relaxed contentment. As the last note faded away they broke out in spontaneous applause.

Monsignor Wagner barely contained his rage. The fact that Marie Wachter found the situation hilarious fuelled his fury. The Church had been made to look foolish. Unfortunately for him, worse was to come.

Sep made his way to the pulpit for the eulogy. He glanced at his friends and neighbours. The sombre mood that marked the start of the service was replaced by a sense of wellbeing. Sep's anxieties melted away. He knew what sentiments were appropriate.

"Neighbours, friends. We are gathered to honour the men from our village, summoned to fight for their country and who never returned. Fifty-three men from our community fought for a cause they didn't understand, against an enemy with whom they had no quarrel, and in an unfamiliar land.

All lie in graves far from their homes and the people that loved them. We honour them all. I remember my two brothers and my best friends as clearly as if they were with us today. I can hear their voices and remember what made them happy or sad, their individual characters, their sense of fun and mischief."

Sep paused and took in all the uplifted faces. Most sat with sad half-smiles as each recalled a treasured son, father or husband, and the memories of less troubled times.

"I think you all might have enjoyed this service, not just because of the outstanding capabilities of our organist, but perhaps even more for the quality of the singing."

Good-natured laughter greeted his observation. Sep gazed around his audience before adding as an aside. "No doubt it will be the main topic of conversation in the Adler for months, if not years."

The laughter and knowing nods of heads told Sep he'd caught the mood of the village. Inside, the knot of his own grief was tinged with anger at the futile losses the village had suffered.

He gathered himself and continued. "A memorial to our boys has been erected in the centre of our community and in the centre of our hearts. We will remember our fathers, uncles, husbands, sons and friends in their prime, and the good times, the fun, laughter, camaraderie and love that each brought to our lives. Amen."

He turned towards Wagner and bowed politely. Wagner could barely control himself. His bow was stiff and his smile locked in a tense half-grimace. The service was a travesty. The music should have been sombre and reverential. This was a church, The Church, his church, not a music hall. The mix-up with the hymns was bad enough, but for Breitner to introduce levity into the proceedings was totally inappropriate. Wagner shook his head to try and erase the outrage. He glared at the congregation that, in his mind, had lost its sense of decency. The light-hearted chatter faded and silence descended.

Then he launched into them. "Brothers and Sisters, we are here to commemorate heroes." His eyes swept across their faces. "Patriots. Proud Austrians, Defenders of the Empire. Soldiers of Christ." He punched each word out as if to hammer it into the consciousness of this recalcitrant flock. "They died for the honour of our country and the glory of God." His look and tone brooked no dissent. "We treasure their memory and should strive to achieve a world they fought and died for."

Sep inwardly groaned. In an instant, the celebratory atmosphere that Father Haphold had created was replaced by a tirade of religious zeal and nationalistic jingoism. He closed his eyes and blanked the words that were so inappropriate. Patriotic duty was the last thing on his brother Klaus's mind. He was a reluctant conscript: mild-mannered and creative, with a desire to hold a set of artist's brushes in his hand rather than a rifle. Obliterated by a direct hit from an artillery shell wasn't a noble sacrifice. It was murder. Sep had no idea how his younger brother died. All he knew was his section had been over-run by an infantry assault. Sep prayed he'd been shot, not butchered by a bayonet. There was also nothing 'glorious' about Marie's husband's death. Wingnut Haufmann was shot through the temple at point-blank range by an Italian soldier who, only seconds before, Wingnut had rescued from a frozen shell hole. As for his own role? He'd sent countless men to their graves through the end of a sniper's telescopic sight. He opened his eyes to see Susan staring anxiously back at him, her expression full of concern. She, more than anyone, knew what he'd been through. He gave her a reassuring smile. He dismissed Wagner from his thoughts, closed his eyes once more and ignored the sermon.

At the end, Sep observed basic courtesy and thanked the Monsignor for the service. Over Wagner's shoulder, he caught the eye of Father Haphold who gave him the briefest of nods and a cheeky wink. He knew the main service had been well received by the community. However, he'd have to absorb the wrath of his superior alone.

Sep left the two clergymen to it. He quietly thanked God for the lives of his two lost brothers and best friend, then gathered his family together and headed home.

ESTABLISHING A BUSINESS

Johan's father's advice proved prescient. But for his mother, trade might have been disastrous. Her presence on the stall attracted locals who'd benefited from her nursing services. They were always keen for a catch-up and gossip. The problem was that his competitors were Achbrugge farming families, and locals instinctively stayed loyal to their friends or neighbours. Johan realised he needed something extra on the stall to drive interest. Two unexpected incidents solved his problem.

Early one Saturday morning, as he heaved slabs of Bergkäse on to the cart and prepared to head for market, a large leather coat came running up the road. Inside was Herman. He leant on the footplate gasping for breath.

"I'm glad I caught you," he bellowed.

Johan reeled. Herman still hadn't mastered controlling his volume.

"I've a favour to ask," he shouted.

Johan waved his hands to indicate suppression was needed. Herman mouthed an apology before dropping his voice to an almost inaudible whisper. "I've a favour to ask?" he repeated, unnecessarily. His hand disappeared inside the voluminous folds of his coat and emerged clutching a small notebook. A further rummage resulted in a pencil stub being produced. He scribbled, then held up the note. "Can you sell my statues?" While Johan read the scrawl, an investigation of another quarter of the coat produced two examples of his work. One was of a young girl in a flowing gown, caught in the act of brushing her hair; the other, an eagle, frozen at the moment of launching itself from a rocky crag. Both were exquisite. The carvings captured every crease and fold of the girl's gown in minute perfection, and each feather of the bird looked individually sculpted. There were woodcarvers in Brandtnerwald, but none came close to the artistry and skill displayed by these two objects. "How much?" Johan wrote the question down.

Herman shrugged and spread out his hands, suggesting he was relaxed as to the amount.

"How many do you have?" Johan again resorted to pencil.

'Loads' came the scrawled reply.

Johan took six. The additional four were larger. Each depicted some aspect of life in the upper reaches of the valley. There was a farmer, which looked uncannily like his father, wielding a large scythe, carved in such detail it seemed the swish of the blade through the grass might be heard. Another was of a priest leaning over the pulpit, haranguing his flock. The likeness to Father Haphold was unmistakable.

The statues had an immediate impact. No sooner had Johan set up the stall than a small crowd gathered to admire the figures. By lunchtime, he'd generated more sales than he usually did in a day. But, despite shifting satisfying quantities of farm produce, no statue had been sold. He had resigned himself to transporting the figures back to Doppelgau when the second incident occurred.

A Mercedes pulled up at the edge of the market. An immaculately dressed man emerged. Not a speck of dust sullied his black military uniform: each trouser-crease was like a knife-edge, every silver button gleamed. Under his arm he carried his hat, the brim of which was decorated with gold piping. A Partieadler badge adorned his breast pocket, and gold braid festooned the collar of his jacket. A red and black swastika wrapped itself around his upper left arm.

His family trailed in his wake. His children, a girl and a boy, were mini-versions of their father – both dressed in a military style. A small, silver swastika hung on a gold chain from each infant's neck. His wife appeared to be an accessory to the rest of her family and her surroundings. She wore a floral summer dress, and her gaze passed through Johan and everyone else as if they were invisible.

The man ran his eyes across the wares as if he were inspecting some grubby soldiers. He picked up the eagle and examined it. "How much?" he said without looking at Johan; his accent harsh, guttural north German.

Johan mentally assessed the man. He looked wealthy. "One hundred and twenty," he said.

The man wrinkled his nose and examined the statue more closely. "I'll give you one hundred."

"The price is one hundred and twenty." Johan nodded towards the small statue of the girl. "That is one hundred and ten," he said levelly.

The man's eyes swivelled towards Johan. For a few seconds, the two held each other's gaze. The German broke first. "I'll take them both." He reached into his pocket and peeled off the amount from a roll of new notes. He threw the money on the stall, picked up the two statues and gave the eagle to his son and the figure of the girl to his daughter.

Johan felt his heart pounding. Two hundred and thirty schillings was more than an entire day's takings.

As the family returned to their car, a local couple stepped forward and shook the German officer's hand, made a fuss of his children and admired the statues. Emboldened by their action, a few others followed their example. By the time the family reached their limousine, they were surrounded by a dozen or so people. As the car departed, everyone in the crowd stood back and gave a stiff Nazi salute.

SHAKING THE TREE

The angry staccato of rain against the window matched Monsignor Wagner's mood. He felt cold and wet, and a black cloud enveloped his mind. The entire week had been a washout. In fact, now he came to think about it, the whole month had been a series of organisational catastrophes, administrative incompetencies and personal disappointments. He threw his briefcase beside the desk, hung his damp cape and dripping hat on the stand, poured himself a generous glass of cognac and slumped back in the chair. He leant back his head, closed his eyes and tried to calm himself. His efforts came to nothing. One after another, the disasters tumbled through his memory like a dreadful movie.

The visit by the Vatican delegation had been chaotic and left the Bishop feeling humiliated. Only half the local news and media outlets published his articles in full. The rest edited his copy and relegated the piece to obscurity in the inside pages. The visits to the convents, schools and children's homes had been unsatisfactory. Wagner drained the glass and squeezed his eyes shut in frustration. And none of this was his fault. He was surrounded by idiots. It was time to remind a few people of their obligations, he decided. It was time to shake the tree. He reached for the bell.

The instant arrival of Father Thomas further blackened Wagner's mood. The man always hovered and seemed over-anxious to please. Wagner eyed the young man as he entered. "This place is falling apart," he said flatly.

Although fleeting, Wagner caught Father Thomas's raised eyebrows and pursed lips that suggested he thought otherwise. His petulance was a mistake. Wagner laid into him: his voice low, tense and menacing. "You disappoint me, Father Thomas. I'd hoped you could be relied upon to be competent."

Thomas looked shocked, then immediately assumed a humble demeanour. "If I've failed to meet your expectations, I apologise." He bowed his head in contrition.

"The Bishop has standards, *I* have standards, and I expect them to be not only met, but exceeded!" Wagner lowered his hands until the tips of his stiffened fingers rested on the blotter. He struggled to contain himself. "I'm still dealing with the Vatican, trying to placate the Cardinal's office." His words squeezed out through clenched teeth. As the Bishop's senior chaplain, it would be Monsignor Wagner's name associated with the debacle.

"There was a failure in communication – the transport department weren't told the delegation would arrive twenty-four hours ahead of schedule."

"And whose fault was that?" Wagner didn't bother to look up.

69

"In all honesty, I think the fault lay with the Cardinal's entourage. They should have telephoned or sent a telegram."

"Oh! So, I should inform his eminence he has incompetent staff?" Wagner sneered. "Were you aware of the situation?"

"I became aware of it."

"But did nothing about it!"

"With all due respect, it's not my responsibility, Your Reverence."

Wagner slowly swivelled his head and regarded his assistant. "Not your responsibility?" He let the statement hang as he stared at his assistant with cold, unblinking eyes. "Father Thomas, it is your responsibility to use your intelligence and initiative to keep me and my office above any reproach or criticism. Your role is to maintain the highest possible standards of behaviour and competence, to act decisively to manage a crisis and to have in place contingency plans covering all eventualities. Your job depends upon protecting my position. Do I make myself clear?"

Father Thomas didn't trust himself to speak; the explicit threat to his post unnerved him.

"The visit wasn't the only failing." Wagner leant back, folded his arms and stared directly at Thomas. "None of the diocese establishments had prepared for my visits."

"But you wanted your visits to be unannounced. You gave me specific instructions," Father Thomas protested.

Wagner waved a dismissive hand. "You misheard me. I recall instructing you to arrange random visits. Our brothers and sisters must have sufficient time to ensure they are seen in the best possible light, certain arrangements for my comfort and welfare are in place, *and* I am properly briefed." He pointed his finger at the priest. "My visit to that God-forsaken village, for example. Why didn't you ensure I was provided with the names of families who'd lost sons and fathers?" His finger wagged. "Fortunately, Doppelgau was my first parish and I remembered some."

"That was an oversight." Father Thomas sensed an empathetic approach might deflect further chastisement. It seemed to work.

Father Wagner nodded as the travesty of the memorial service became resurrected in his memory. "An oversight indeed," he muttered.

Father Thomas stayed mute and watched him, trying to anticipate what further misdemeanours might be raised.

Wagner noted the silence and inwardly smiled. It paid to keep one's servants guessing. "Things will change, Father Thomas. I intend to take a close interest in all aspects of the management of this diocese and the performance of all staff, especially those holding senior positions of trust. Standards will improve." He stared hard at the priest. "Do you understand?"

Thomas gave a curt bow.

"Good. Now fetch me the personnel file of the parish priest of Doppelgau, what's his name?...Father Haphold."

Thomas bowed his head and headed for the door.

THE VISITOR

"Will you be alright by yourself?"

Johan laughed. "Ma, I'll be fine. You go off." He heaved the last cheese on to the stall.

"It's just that Rachel's down with the flu, and she needs help in the house."

"Ma, I can manage!" He turned to release Cleopatra from the traces and attach her nose-bag.

"I'll be back to help you repack."

He waved her off and set about arranging the stall. Herman's figures now took pride of place. Germanic symbols and eagles, in particular, sold well, along with figurines in German national dress. Demand coincided with the return of tourists. A few were Swiss but most were Germans keen to flaunt their wealth. Many wore uniforms, or a small swastika badge, necklace or bracelet, as if to demonstrate their allegiance to the cause responsible for their prosperity. There were times when trade became so brisk a modest queue formed.

Towards market close, his mother unexpectedly appeared looking flustered. "I've a favour to ask," she said breathlessly. "Rachel's niece is arriving on the afternoon train from Brandt. I'm looking after Rachel, her husband has been called out on a medical emergency, and Herr Rubenstein is too frail to go." She looked beseechingly at her son. "The poor girl will arrive with no-one to meet her."

Johan sighed. "What time?"

"It's due in now. You need to be quick. Take the cart – she'll have luggage, I'll pack up the stall."

Ten minutes later, he stood on the platform of Achbrugge railway terminus. Only then did it occur to him that, in her haste, his mother hadn't divulged the girl's appearance, age or name. Fortunately, the train carried few passengers. Of the females that did alight, most strode off with the purposeful confidence of those familiar with the geography of Achbrugge. Others were either already accompanied or were soon embraced by waiting family or friends. That left an anxious-looking young woman, wearing a long stylish coat and broad-brimmed hat, standing beside four suitcases that an elderly porter had unloaded and who now loitered in expectation of further instructions, a tip or maybe both. That, Johan deduced, was Rachel's niece.

She studied him warily as he approached.

"Are you waiting to be picked up?"

Her cautious look became tinged with suspicion. "Who are you?"

"Johan Breitner, I'm here to meet you," he said, and held out his hand. "And who are you?"

She ignored his hand and took a step back. "Don't you know my name? I'd have thought you'd know who you were supposed to be meeting?"

Johan looked confused. "No, I don't but I've been sent to collect you."

"I'm not about to go off with someone I don't know," she said haughtily.

"Very sensible, Miss," the porter interjected.

"But I was asked to pick you up."

"My aunt's letter stated that either she or my uncle would greet me."

"Your aunt's ill, and your uncle has been called away on an emergency."

The porter expressed his doubt as to the veracity of the statement by expressing a dismissive "Pah!"

"How do you know my aunt and uncle?"

Johan rolled his eyes at the question. He began to wish he hadn't agreed to carry out what should have been a straightforward task. "My parents are friends of theirs. We live locally."

"What's the address of my aunt?" she said quickly, as if trying to catch him off guard. A hint of annoyance entered the girl's voice as if she'd no intention of being trifled with.

"What?" The question threw Johan. He knew precisely where the Rubensteins lived, but, for the life of him, he couldn't recall the name of the street or the house number. There was no reason he should. He had no need to write them a letter. "I don't know. It's down the street." He pointed vaguely towards the market.

"So, you're local, claim to know where my aunt and uncle live, yet don't know the address."

The porter interjected. "Begging your pardon, Miss, but I've been working at this station for years. I know everybody in this town. And I must say I've never seen this young man before."

Johan cast the porter a withering look. "I live in Doppelgau. I come here every Saturday for the market."

"Well, I don't know who you are, and thank you for your offer, but I shall make my own way." She turned to the porter. "Can you arrange a taxi, please?"

The porter looked confused. "Taxi?"

"Yes, taxi."

"Good Lord, miss. This is Achbrugge. We don't have such things." He glanced nervously at the four suitcases which he'd already discovered seemed to weigh a ton each. "People walk to where they want to go or arrange for a horse and cart if they live further afield." He eyed the suitcases. "I could take your suitcases to the Gasthaus opposite the station, if that's what you want. But it will take some time." His tone suggested the prospect of carting four heavy pieces of luggage anything further than a few metres was a task to be contemplated once hell had completely frozen over.

Johan watched the girl squirm with indecision. Her eyes flicked toward him. He folded his arms and regarded her with casual indifference. He couldn't stop himself from grinning as she grappled with her dilemma.

After he judged she'd suffered enough, he offered a suggestion. "I'll take you both to your aunt's. That way, he can act as your protector. Afterwards I can run you, sir, back to the station."

They considered the suggestion.

"That sounds sensible," the girl conceded. The porter nodded.

Johan didn't allow any further discussion. He swooped on the luggage, placed the smallest suitcase under one arm and grabbed two others in each hand. "Follow me," he said, leaving the porter to carry the remaining case. He strode towards Cleopatra, tethered at the end of the platform. The girl struggled to keep up with him. The elderly porter trailed in their wake. He heaved all four suitcases into the back, before jumping on the footplate and holding his hands out to help the girl up. For a second she held back and regarded him. Johan found himself staring into dark, alluring eyes. It must be a Rubenstein trait, he thought. They were also very expressive. And, right now, Johan felt sure the girl wasn't happy with him. Nevertheless, she took his hands and allowed him to pull her up. She settled on the seat and gave a shriek of alarm when the cart lurched as the porter clambered aboard.

Five minutes later they drew up outside the Rubenstein's residence. Rachel stood waiting at the front door, in her dressing gown. Johan dropped the suitcases in the lobby as the girl was swept into her aunt's arms and bustled inside. He shouted a cheery "see you next week," received a "thank you, Johan," in return, and set off once again with the porter, who was miffed that at no point had a gratuity been forthcoming.

Johan ignored the disgruntled railwayman. His mind revolved around the girl. His impression of her wasn't good. She seemed a thoroughly spoilt brat. She hadn't even offered thanks. Her lack of manners shocked him. The Rubensteins were always polite and courteous. By the time he'd returned to his mother, standing alongside the now packed market stall, he also realised he hadn't discovered the girl's name.

PLOTS AND SCHEMES

Father Haphold's personnel file shocked Wagner. The priest was clearly highly competent and well thought of. Worse, he had been in regular contact with the Bishop. Wagner re-read the letters. There was a common theme - ideas. Father Haphold appeared to be something of a radical. His writing included initiatives to increase church attendance, improve welfare support for the unemployed and poor, and amend the school curriculum to make it more relevant to the modern world. What most troubled Wagner was that Haphold's suggestions had gained traction with the Bishop.

"Is something wrong, Your Reverence?"

"Eh?"

"You look worried, if you don't mind me saying."

"No, Father Thomas. I'm quite well." He snapped the file shut and laid it on the desk. He sat still, deep in thought.

Father Thomas fell silent. He was becoming adept at reading his superior, and it seemed the file contained unsettling information. He casually recharged Wagner's glass. It wouldn't harm to oil the wheels.

Wagner picked it up and absently nodded his thanks. "Tell me, Father Thomas, what do you know about Father Haphold?"

Thomas shrugged. "Very little. He has a reputation as a competent parish priest. He's popular with his parishioners, and I'm told he can be unconventional. Why do you ask?"

"He's causing a few ripples." Wagner took a sip of wine. "My instinct tells me to be concerned about men who cause ripples. Ripples can become waves."

"Is that bad?"

Wagner shook his head. "Not at all, providing they are channelled and wash up on the right shore."

"Would you like me to arrange an interview for Father Haphold?"

Wagner considered the suggestion. "Perhaps at some point. In the meantime, I'd like you to find out what the man is like, what type of sermons he's delivering, what company he keeps. That sort of thing." Wagner took another sip. "Oh, and I want to see all correspondence between him and the diocese."

Thomas looked surprised. "What, everything?"

Wagner frowned "Is that a problem?"

"No, not at all. It sounds a bit irregular, that's all."

"As the Bishop's Chaplain, I need to know everything that might impact His Grace." Wagner pushed the file across the desk. "Give me a weekly update, or tell me immediately if something you think I should know about crops up."

"Of course. Is there anything else?"

Wagner reached for the wine. "Yes, there is one other matter. How long is it since my last pastoral inspections?"

Father Thomas furrowed his brow. "I'm not sure."

"Never mind. Make appropriate arrangements?"

"You want me to forewarn everyone you are coming?"

"Of course." This time Wagner was determined there would be no repeat of the disappointments of his last visits.

NEW AQUAINTANCE

Johan's plans remained on track. He'd been accepted as an electrical apprentice, owning a motorcycle had moved a step closer thanks to a modest deposit in his savings account, and Sylvia, the sow his father had sold him, was pregnant.

"Life's good," he thought, as he journeyed to the market one Saturday. He gave Cleopatra a light flick of the reins, settled himself and drank in the beauty of his surroundings. Early morning was his favourite time of day. Snow-covered peaks bathed in warm, soft pink sunlight stood out against a brilliant cobalt blue sky. It promised to be a hot day. However, the warmth had yet to reach the valley, and the air was sharp and invigorating. A heavy dew covered the grass verges and dripped off the pine trees. The only sounds were the soft gurgle of the River Ach as it tumbled over the rocky shallows and the occasional cries from a pair of hawks quartering their way back up the valley.

Working stupidly hard was the flaw in his contentment. Every morning began at five-thirty, when he had to feed the animals, milk the cows and check the chicken coop. He snatched breakfast before catching the Postbus to Achbrugge for a day of college and practical work. Cheese making, preparing smoked hams and wursts, and being taught the art of distilling Schnapps were waiting for him on his return, followed by more milking and bedding the animals for the night. He'd collapse into bed around ten o'clock and fall into exhausted sleep. Running repairs to the farm buildings, drainage ditches, barns and haylofts, along with harvesting crops and maintaining farm equipment, were crammed in to the remaining nooks and crannies of his time.

The Saturday market offered a respite, and he looked forward to it. Banter with fellow market-traders and chatting with the locals provided a welcome diversion, and he'd increased his regular customers. He glanced at his watch. He could afford to relax, Achbrugge lay twenty minutes away.

As he crossed the bridge over the Ach, he noticed a young woman striding purposefully towards the town. The broad-brimmed hat swinging carelessly in her hand seemed familiar. She glanced over her shoulder as he approached. It was Rachel's niece, and she looked cross. Johan's instinct was to pass by. He'd no desire to have his morning ruined by a spoilt brat. To his surprise, she took the decision out of his hands.

"Am I glad to see you! Would you be kind enough to give me a lift?" She'd clambered up and sat beside him before he'd brought the cart to a halt, let alone replied. "I'm Sara, you're Johan Breitner, and I owe you an apology," she said brightly. "And some thanks," she added.

"Oh! Okay." Johan found himself swept away by her effusiveness and bewildered by her friendliness. He snapped the reins and Cleopatra walked on. "Has something happened? You looked upset."

"I missed the bus." She turned away from him and placed her hat on the seat beside her. "I couldn't find the bus stop in time."

Johan looked puzzled. "We don't have bus-stops. If you want the Postbus to pick you up, you wave it down. Same as if you want to get off, you just ask the driver to stop."

She gave a self-deprecating smile. "Yet another thing I need to learn about this country." She turned and faced him. "Anyway, I'm glad I bumped into you. You must have thought me a right little madam at the station."

That's an understatement, he thought to himself. "You were a bit abrupt," he said.

"And rude. I apologise. You were kind. If I've any excuse, it is that I was tired and upset that my aunt wasn't there to meet me." She looked thoughtful as she recalled the incident. "Also, it's disconcerting finding yourself alone in a strange town in a foreign country."

"Had you travelled far?"

"From Stuttgart."

"With four suitcases!"

She nodded. "No help at all in Germany, apart from an English gentleman who embarrassed a porter into carrying my bags."

Johan looked sideways at her. "Why wouldn't the porters help you?"

She looked surprised at his question. "Things are difficult in Germany at the moment." She leant back, swept her hands through her hair and took in the surrounding forests and peaks. "I'm here now." She tilted her head back and closed her eyes as the cart moved from the cool shadows into dazzling sunlight. "I love early mornings. It's my favourite time of day." She looked relaxed and content.

Johan took the opportunity to study her. She looked slightly older than Harriet. If anything, she could be the same age as him or perhaps older. She had the same dark-skinned complexion that, like her eyes, appeared to run in the Rubenstein lineage. Her hair was dark, almost jet black, swept-back on either side of her face and tied loosely in a cream ribbon. She'd dressed for walking with a knee-length flowing skirt and a lightweight loden jacket, just thick enough to keep the early morning chill at bay, worn over a white blouse. A pair of sturdy calf-length walking boots rested on the weatherboard.

He wasn't aware that she was surreptitiously watching him from the corner of her half-closed eyes. "Have you finished examining me?" she said, laughing.

"I was wondering how old you are to be travelling by yourself." He managed to sound unfazed, although inside he cringed with embarrassment.

"I'm seventeen." She gave a bitter laugh. "There are kids younger than me travelling out of Germany."

"Not on their own, surely?"

She leant forward and gave him an intense look. "Have you any idea what is happening in Germany?"

Johan felt embarrassed. "Not really." He gestured towards the centre of town which was now less than a kilometre away. "We get a few German tourists, and they are eager to boast about their country. They give themselves plenty of holidays and have money to spend – which is good for us."

He turned to face her when she didn't immediately respond. He was startled by how quickly her mood changed. "Don't be fooled by the propaganda. Germany is hell right now." She spat the words out. "My family, who have been German for generations, were stripped of their citizenship last year. Overnight, we became foreigners in our own country. They prevent us from becoming lawyers, doctors or holding any public offices. My uncle was elected Burgermeister of his town three times. Not anymore. He's banned from even standing for election." She became increasingly angry. "I have relations who work in the film industry. They went into work one Monday and were told they were sacked, no reason, no appeal, no compensation, just thrown out. And I was thrown out of school." She stared at him, her eyes on fire.

Her anger startled him. "Why?" he asked lamely.

"Because we're Jews."

Johan was genuinely shocked. "I had no idea."

"That's the trouble. Few people do." She sounded bitter. "And those that are aware do nothing."

"Is that why you're here, to escape?"

"Partly. My aunt is home tutoring me until we can sort out a school in Switzerland." She realised her anger had got the better of her. In another abrupt mood swing she suddenly grinned at him. "I'm glad to be out of Germany. Here I feel free."

"And safe. The Government banned the Nazis after the attempted coup. They cause too much trouble."

"Let's hope it stays that way."

Johan said nothing. His memory of the crowd around the Nazi officer and his family caused a shiver of concern.

He dropped her off outside the Rubenstein's. This time she did seem grateful and offered her thanks.

Setting up the stall and dealing with a steady stream of customers filled the rest of the morning. By early afternoon the temperature reached thirty degrees, and Johan felt tired and thirsty. The crowd thinned as people completed their purchases, and either drifted home or fled into the cafés and Gasthauses to escape the heat. He cleared part of the stall before clambering up and making himself comfortable in the shade, with his back propped against the iron roof support. He closed his eyes and let the tension of the morning's bartering fade away. Gradually, he dozed off.

"I've brought you some refreshments."

Johan nearly fell off the stall in surprise.

Sara stood squinting at him with one hand shading her eyes against the direct sunlight. Her walking attire had been replaced by a sleeveless summer frock and light leather sandals. The cream-coloured dress set off the darker hue of her complexion and accentuated her black hair. A bright red sash belt provided a vivid contrast. Johan found himself momentarily stunned. She looked beautifully exotic. She held a large glass jug, and a small tankard dangled from her little finger

"I thought you'd be thirsty."

"Am I glad to see you!"

She gave a delightful smile. "*That's* what I should have said when you picked me up at the station."

He slipped off the stall and relieved her of the jug and glass.

"It's lemonade," she said.

"I'd have been grateful if it was water."

Sara moved into the shade beside him, turned and leant on the edge of the stall. "Business has been good." She said it as a statement. "I came earlier, but you were wrapped up serving."

He drained the second glass. "Beaten the day's target which is just as well as there won't be many more customers today."

"Why not pack up?" She glanced around at the other traders, most of whom had either already gone or were loading their carts. "I'll give you a hand."

He poured another glass and offered it to her. "If you don't mind?"

It took less than fifteen minutes to pack away, during which they stole glances at each other in between fragmented conversations about where various items needed to go, or which perishable cheeses and delicate statues required protecting.

There was much he noticed about her. She had a slim, shapely figure that the cut of the dress accentuated. Her movements were graceful and very feminine. From the way she held up and examined the statues he deduced she appreciated art or at least its craftsmanship. She smiled easily, a rueful smile as if she was trying to suppress it. She wore no adornments except for a delicate gold bangle.

For her part, she saw in Johan a boyish charm. She knew from her aunt he was slightly older than herself. He had natural self-assurance. He'd been unfazed by the station porter and dealt with his customers with good-natured friendliness. He was well built, taller than her and obviously fit. She initially thought he was showing off when he had effortlessly swept up the suitcases that she and the porter struggled to shift. She realised farming was hard physical work. It was little wonder he had strength. And he had a pleasing countenance, with striking hazel eyes which were looking at her now as they stood facing each other in front of the empty stall.

"So, what would you like to do?" she asked.

"Well, I ought to head back home."

"I'd like to come with you."

He masked a fleeting wave of panic. He'd no idea what he might talk about to a girl that seemed a bit pushy and about whom he knew little. "You want to come to Doppelgau!?"

"Just halfway. A bit beyond the place you picked me up this morning. I can walk back from there." She bent down, removed her left sandal and shook a small stone from it before replacing it. "I fancy a walk and, with luck, that part of the valley will be in shadow by now."

His initial fear that the journey would pass in awkward silence proved wrong. God, can she talk, he thought to himself, as she answered his questions with fulsome explanations and descriptions as if she was taking an oral examination. She spoke quickly and managed to cram in so much information about herself, her relations and her hopes and ambitions that, after four kilometres, Johan felt he knew more about her than his own sister. She intended to pursue a career in some form of scientific research. Her family had found her a place at a Swiss boarding school, not far from the Austrian border, to ensure she secured the required academic grades. She was the eldest of four siblings. She loved walking, sports, dancing and music, especially the new modern music coming from America. It dawned on him that she talked fast because of nervousness.

She abruptly stopped mid-flow and cast him an embarrassed grin, confirming his suspicions. "I'm jabbering, aren't I? I always do this when I meet someone new." She nudged him gently in the ribs with her elbow. "You should have told me to shut up."

As a consequence, he then found himself doing all the talking. Gradually, their conversation relaxed. They found interest in each other. He'd finished relating details of his apprenticeship when they realised they'd travelled more than halfway to Doppelgau. Sara now faced a good hour's walk back.

"Do you want me to turn around?"

"Don't be silly, I'll enjoy the stroll." She sat back, put her hands behind her head and gazed at the surrounding mountains. "I envy you having all this in your back yard."

"You're not a city girl?"

She blew a dismissive breath. "Certainly not. I like the great outdoors: rivers, lakes, mountains and forests, where the air is fresh and clean and there aren't too many people. Cities stress people. They become short-tempered and aggressive." She pointed at the highest peak. "If I lived here I'd want to climb to the top of that mountain, and each week I'd pick another one until I'd climbed them all."

"And then what?"

She smiled. "I'd start all over again until I'd explored every corner."

"You'd need more than walking boots to climb that." He nodded towards the summit. "Climbing gear, ropes, crampons a local guide and luck with the weather."

"There must be easier routes."

"The whole area is crisscrossed with paths. Some are easy, where we drive the cattle to the high pastures; others are more tricky that only foresters and hunters know about. They're only open in the summer. In winter, everything is impassable unless you have snowshoes and skis. But winter is the best time of year. It can be wild and cold one minute, with driving blizzards, avalanches and great snowdrifts. The following day everything is transformed. No wind, blue skies, and the whole valley smothered in a blanket of pristine snow so bright it hurts your eyes."

She leant forward and looked at him intently, her elbows on her knees, her chin cradled in her hands. A half-smile played across her lips as he continued in a world of his own.

"When I was younger, I'd walk to our farm in the high alpine meadows and stay for a day or so, just to see the world immediately after a major snow fall when nothing had walked across its surface. Everything is pure white, and the mountain peaks stretch way off to the horizon," He glanced across at her. "And you should see the sunrises and sunsets."

"You're very lucky," she said, then smiled. "Can you show me?"

"Of course. It would have to be a Sunday. Every other day I'm flat out."

"Sunday's best for me. When I don't have school work I help around my aunt's house and the surgery during the week. You decide on a date." She suddenly grabbed his wrist and turned it so she could see the face of his watch. "My goodness, I need to get back." She swung herself from the footplate and looked at him with eyes he decided were nothing short of enchanting. "Johan, I've enjoyed today."

"So have I," he replied.

"I'll see you next week?"

He nodded and watched her stride purposefully down the road. She hadn't gone more than fifty metres away when she turned, smiled and waved.

He waved back and found himself grinning. He called out, "In about a hundred and twenty metres there's a path to your left. It leads to the river. Just follow it. It's a nicer walk than the road."

She waved in acknowledgement.

BECOMING HITLER

"Dagmar Greber. Come to the front," Frau Felder barked.

From the back, Dagmar slowly stepped forward. The eyes of thirty-two girls followed her nervous progress towards the Gruppenleiterin. They fell silent, not knowing what to expect. Dagmar faced the group.

Frau Felder circled her. "What's that on your face?"

Dagmar looked confused. "I don't know what you mean, Gruppenleiterin."

"What is that on your face, girl?" She stabbed a finger into Dagmar's cheek.

Dagmar winced as the nail cut into her skin. "It's a rouge," she blurted, before a hard slap across the face sent her reeling across the room.

Frau Felder turned to face the shocked assembly, ignoring the whimpering Dagmar as if she'd ceased to exist. "German girls don't wear make-up or paint their faces like whores," she barked. "German girls have pure, natural beauty. Soap and water are all that is required to keep the skin clean and healthy. Good hygiene prepares healthy bodies to breed strong German babies for the Reich. Our Fuhrer wants us pure in mind and body. Girls, take note. Katerina Mossman, come to the front."

Katerina instinctively wiped her face. She wasn't wearing cosmetics but checked just in case. Every girl scrutinised her, trying to guess what crime she'd committed. She reached Frau Felder and looked terrified. To her surprise, the Group Leader smiled and, in a kindly voice, ordered her to "Turn and face your comrades, Katerina."

Frau Felder circled the trembling girl, inspecting her as she might a prize cow. "You will study Katerina Mossman. She is a true German Fräulein. The hair is clean, brushed, plaited and styled in the German manner, face unsullied by make-up." Frau Felder continued her commentary as she orbited Katerina, using a ruler to point out each item under review. "The blouse freshly washed, clean and smart. The neckerchief properly tied and laying straight, the skirt must be this shade of dark blue and modest in length. White socks, clean and gathered at the ankle, and polished brown shoes." She ended her inspection standing behind the quivering Katerina. She placed her hands on the girl's shoulders. "Your rank badges will be neatly stitched on your uniforms exactly here." Her index finger pointed to the space above Katerina's left breast. "Girls, take note. Next week you will turn out exactly like Katerina. Is that understood?"

"Jahowl, Gruppenleiterin," they shouted in unison.

"Take the oath," Frau Felder bawled.

As one they stood to attention and yelled the words that had been drummed into them. Even the reject Dagmar pulled herself straight and joined in. "*I promise always to do my duty in the Hitler Youth, in love and loyalty to the Führer. One Reich, One people. One Fuhrer."* They thrust their right arms out in the Nazi salute "Seig heil," they shouted.

Frau Felder beamed. "Well done, girls. One final order. Pay attention." Her gaze passed over each girl. "You will keep your eyes and ears open and listen carefully to the conversations of your neighbours, parents, friends - even your brothers and sisters. If you hear anyone saying anything nasty or critical about our Fuhrer or the Party, you are to report it to me. Is that understood?"

The order barely touched Trudy's mind. As with all the girls, she responded like an automaton, "Jawohl, Gruppenleiterin."

"Dismissed. Heil Hitler."

Trudy breathed a sigh of relief. Apart from the endless saluting and shouts of Seig heil, she loved the Bund Deutscher Mädel. It was as if the BDM had been designed for her. She had a good voice and often led the singing of the German folk songs. Thanks to Tante Bri's tutelage, she was a skilled seamstress and made her own uniform. Learning other aspects of domesticity came easily to her. The cookery lessons provided an opportunity for extra rations, maintaining and cleaning a house was merely an extension of what she did at home, and she found the child-care and First-Aid lessons fascinating. She excelled at sports and easily beat the modest goals. Only in swimming did she struggle, having never swum in her life. However, the BDM instructors taught her, and within four weeks she managed the minimum 100 metres.

Swimming wasn't the only thing the BDM taught. She learnt about German history, folklore, her race and heritage, and why she ought to be proud of the Fatherland and the path the Fuhrer had mapped for the country.

They weren't false promises - Germany was on the rise. Work became plentiful. Unemployment fell, more food arrived in the shops and markets, prices stabilised and living standards improved.

But, as far as Trudy was concerned, the League offered a means to an end. The BDM would equip her with skills. All she had to do was mouth off a few meaningless slogans, sing patriotic songs, shout 'Seig heil' whenever required, and lose herself within the group. She'd seen the posters and her reflection stared back - young, athletic and clear-eyed with blonde Aryan looks. She'd found her ticket out of the ghetto.

The wife of a high-ranking Nazi needed a nanny and housekeeper. Only Aryan girls need apply. The approving look Trudy received as she entered the drawing-room convinced her that her effort to be the BDM poster girl paid off.

"You're obviously a member," the woman said, as she lit a cigarette and blew a steady stream of smoke across the desk.

"It was my patriotic duty," Trudy replied.

The woman gave a thin smile. "Too many young girls fail to see where their duty lies."

"We need to be ruthless in exposing them."

"You seem keen. The issue is whether you are competent." She tapped Trudy's application letter with a manicured fingernail. "You say in your letter that you can cook, are an excellent seamstress, and have taken courses in child-care for which you received promotion within the BDM. You have also been awarded a silver merit badge." The woman leaned back and appraised Trudy with cold, dispassionate eyes. She took another long drag from her cigarette and considered what question might throw the confident-looking young woman. "What is your attitude to discipline?" she said abruptly.

"Of children, Ma'am?"

The woman nodded.

Trudy never imagined she'd be grateful for the slogans of the rabid Frau Felder. "True German children need to be taught discipline, the importance of being the best, and to win for their own self-esteem and for the furtherance of national socialism. Fitness of the mind goes hand in hand with fitness of the body. Only through discipline can the young be shown the true path to success."

"Children are so easily influenced. How would you protect my children from the pollution of the world?"

"By rigid adherence to German values, Ma'am. German education, culture and history is the bedrock of national socialism. Anything alien is, by definition, unacceptable to the path our Fuhrer has chosen for us. If I thought for one second your children were exposed to such filth, I'd have no hesitation in removing them from its influence and reporting those responsible to the authorities."

The woman got up, adjusted some minor defect in her cuff before walking towards a large mirror that dominated the room. "My word, you are a Godsend. Almost too good to be true." After studying her reflection, she appeared to notice her swastika brooch was misaligned. Having adjusted the insignia, she stood back and admired herself. She looked every inch the perfect Nazi wife. "Can you drive?"

Panic seized Trudy. She couldn't recall the ability to drive being mentioned in the advertisement. "No, Ma'am."

"The BDM can teach you. On occasion, my husband and I wish to be taken to functions. We need to rely on you to carry out this and other minor tasks, and also run errands."

"Are you offering me the position?"

"My dear Fraulein Heppel, you are just what we are looking for." She stubbed out her cigarette. "I suppose I'd better introduce you to the children."

Trudy blinked in astonishment. In less than twenty minutes she'd become nanny housekeeper to the Hofner family.

SUMMER PLEASURE

As the clock on the Achbrugge church steeple crept towards midday, Johan peered anxiously over the heads of his customers, trying to spot Sara. She always arrived full of ideas and enthusiasm about what they might do after market close. The journey halfway to Doppelgau became a shared pleasure, no matter the weather.

They'd agreed a Sunday for the first mountain walk. Most of the village men and boys were with the cattle in the high pastures. Delivering supplies provided an excuse and a destination, but Johan planned a diversion on route. An early morning start meant Sara staying overnight at the Breitners'.

She arrived Saturday evening and found herself catapulted into the family. Harriet leapt to her feet as soon as the stube door opened. She barged her way past her brother and planted herself in front of a startled Sara. "Hello, I'm Harriet," she announced before she took a half step back, looked Sara up and down, and added, "My goodness, you are pretty. Come and sit beside me." She relieved Sara of her overnight bag, grabbed her hand and propelled her towards the table and the favoured spot beside the Kächelofen. Sara managed to call out a greeting to Susan and her cousin, Simon, as the only other people she was familiar with, before being bundled into her seat.

"Don't you think Sara might want to see her room first, Harriet?"

Harriet looked momentarily nonplussed. "I'll show her after we've eaten." She turned to Sara. "I bet you're hungry. I know I am."

The meal was a Breitner free-for-all. No one stood on ceremony and they all helped themselves readily to the fare on offer. Sara took her cue from everyone else and leant across to fill her plate with casual abandonment. Unlike Sunday dinner, informal chaos best described everyday meals in the Breitner's farmhouse. Food was placed on the table, and people arrived in accordance with the farm timetable and grabbed what they wanted. Conversations were equally chaotic. Discussions washed across the table in a continuous ebb and flow. Occasionally a topic might grab collective attention, and normal conventions of politeness would briefly apply before another subject took hold on the edge of the discourse, resulting in everyone talking across one another. The noise level rose as a consequence. It was during a brief lull that the subject of the hike was raised.

"There is a lot to take," Susan said. "Food, cigarettes, tobacco, fresh clothes, some wet weather gear, books, magazines, a few treats. It adds up."

"Ma, don't worry. We'll manage with Cleopatra's help."

Harriet's ears picked up. "Are you heading up the mountain?" She glanced at her brother. His reaction told her all she needed to know. "We'll come, won't we, Simon?'

Simon looked surprised. Clambering up a mountain hadn't figured in his plans. "I dunno," he said. "When are you going?"

"Tomorrow, first thing." Johan glanced at Sara. "We're making a day of it."

Harriet was determined not to be left out. "Oh, come on, Simon. It will do you good. I want to see Papa, Uncle Stephan and Jurgen, and I'm sure they'll be happy to see us."

Simon wasn't enthusiastic. "What time?"

"No later than five o'clock. I'm taking Sara to see The Lodge on the way."

That was the clincher as far as Harriet was concerned. "Well, I'm going even if you're not." She gave Simon a hard look.

"Five o'clock!" Simon's tone indicated five o'clock was a concept he hadn't much experience of.

"That's settled then," Harriet said.

Simon wondered at what point he'd agreed to anything. As things turned out, it was fortunate he came.

The Lodge was semi-derelict. Dense ivy covered the entire south gable end to roof level, and the creeper extended along the balcony that spanned both sides of the building. Some shutters hung askew from their hinges and sections of pine cladding were missing. At the front gable end, an overgrown green sward disguised what had once been an English-style lawn. Jackdaws had taken up residence in the chimneys, and the gravel drive had all but disappeared under a carpet of weeds. Despite the neglect, it remained largely intact. Its position provided a magnificent vista of a steep, scree-covered mountain slope and pine forests. It seemed extraordinary that such a building remained hidden. It required local knowledge just to find the entrance gates in the dense woodland.

Sara was awestruck. "What is this place?"

"A hunting lodge, built by my grandfather for an Englishman on behalf of a wealthy English banker. He used it for entertaining his rich and famous friends."

"Can we see inside?"

A magnificent, ornately carved staircase dominated the entrance hall. It divided at a half-landing, with one flight sweeping round to the left, mirrored by a second flight to the right. An ornate Kächelofen covered in highly decorated glazed tiles stood to one side.

Harriet had already climbed the stairs. "I bet they had some fantastic parties."

"Scandalous parties, apparently," Johan chuckled.

They explored each room in the dim shafts of light that stole through the slats of the blinds. The air smelt damp and musty, and the floorboards creaked. Apart from threadbare curtains, a few other Kächelofens and thousands of cobwebs, the lodge was empty.

"The taps work," a faraway voice floated from upstairs. Harriet had found one of the bathrooms. "And there're some old bedsteads."

Eventually, time caught up with them. "We need to go. We can return when we've got more time."

They would return but in quite different circumstances.

They made their way up overgrown forest paths until eventually they emerged into the open air and joined a wide gravel mountain track. The loss of tree cover exposed them to the sun's fierce rays. Jackets were soon tied around waists, socks rolled down and buttons undone. "I should have worn a lighter dress," Harriet gasped.

"You should also have brought a hat," Johan added.

"I didn't think to bring one."

The faint sound of cowbells signalled they were close to their destination. Sara stopped and gazed at the view. Snow-capped peaks stretched out to the east, west and south.

Johan caught up with her. "Worth the effort, isn't it?"

She took off her hat, shaded her eyes and traced the panorama until she had done a complete traverse. "It's breath-taking." She glanced across at him and smiled. "I'm glad you showed me this."

He leant his head beside hers and pointed at some low hills to the north. "That's Germany. And those three peaks to your left, the ones standing out above the rest? They're all in Switzerland. And on the far horizon to the south - the largest mountain, that's the border with Italy." He grinned at her. "Right now we are at the centre of Europe."

"Does anyone live up here all year?"

He jerked his chin towards the east. "About seven or eight kilometres in that direction there're some settlements. A few families live there. It's a natural plateau of high alpine meadows. Very picturesque."

She looked at him expectantly.

He laughed. "Yes, I'll take you. We know one of the families. Perhaps that's our next walk."

"Are you two coming?" Harriet called. She was already far ahead.

"I don't know where she gets the energy," Sara said.

"She needs to slow down." Johan swung the rucksack from his shoulders and extracted a flask of water. He passed it to Sara. "Here, drink."

They pressed on, passing through a herd of contented cattle that observed their passage with indifference. Soon the gentle tinkling of cowbells gave way to the sound of men singing.

"It's a custom," Johan said, to Sara's questioning look. "On Sundays, everyone up on the high pastures gets together. Father Haphold sometimes comes to conduct a service. But the real reasons are to socialise, talk politics, smoke, drink Schnapps, tell jokes and to swap stories, sing songs and exchange things like newspapers." He grinned at her. "It's a male thing. The younger boys also learn about life from their elders."

Harriet ran ahead to be swept up by her father. They were soon sitting on rough-hewn wooden benches outside a mountain hut with over a dozen men and boys, all with the ruddy complexions of people that worked under the fierce rays of the high Alps. The men fell on the saddlebags eager for the food, cigarettes, newspapers and letters.

The music and singing recommenced, and Harriet and Sara found themselves in demand. Harriet was an accomplished dancer and knew the dances for each song. Sara just loved dancing. The men's singing got louder in proportion to the amount of alcohol consumed, and they clapped and roared encouragement. Banter and jokes were thrown around. It didn't matter that everyone had heard the wisecracks hundreds of times before; the determination to have a good time, fuelled by Schnapps, ensured each witticism generated raucous laughter and a slapping of thighs.

Johan spent much of the time reassuring his father. Sep was keen to learn that his wife was well, the animals were being properly fed, watered and exercised, nobody had died or become ill, and the Breitner's farm hadn't burnt down in his absence. Half Johan's attention, however, focused on Sara. She looked a picture of happiness as she and Harriet swapped banter with the lads. Neither girl wanted for partners. The younger lads went around the back of the hut, only to reappear wearing a different hat and try to persuade the girls they were a twin brother who hadn't yet had the pleasure of a dance. The time for departure drew a collective groan of disappointment, apart from Jurgen who'd fallen into a contented drunken slumber.

Harriet skipped and spun as they made their way back down the track. "That was so much fun." She gave another twirl. "Why didn't you dance?' she said, vaguely directing her question at her brother before immediately adding, "And you didn't dance with me at all, Simon." She sounded miffed.

"How do you expect me to ask you to dance when you have such a queue of admirers?' Simon's reply seemed to please her.

Harriet's good spirits flagged as the day appeared to catch up with her. She grew silent. A slow trudge replaced her cavorting. They'd just entered the forest when she staggered, lurched to the right and, before anyone could react, fell off the edge of the track. She tumbled down the steep slope, her legs and arms flailing as she plummeted, until she collided with a tree and lay still.

Simon was already sliding down the slope after her. Johan and Sara peered down anxiously. "Is she alright?'

"She's unconscious." Simon shouted, as Johan made to join him. "It's too steep. Stay there to help pull us up."

"How bad?" Johan beat down a rising surge of panic. Already he'd assumed his sister had broken her neck.

Simon felt a similar sense of dread. Her being unconscious alarmed him. He patted her face. "Harriet, wake up!" She looked pale and drenched with sweat. He put his hand to her forehead. Her temperature seemed normal. He pressed his ear to her chest and sat up startled, then checked again to ensure he hadn't imagined what he'd heard. Her breathing was rapid and her pulse raced. He cleared his head and tried to remember what he'd learnt at his father's practice. He checked her limbs. There were no signs of broken bones. She hadn't drunk anything. But she'd been in the sun all day. And she didn't have a hat. The diagnosis suddenly presented itself. "She's either got heat exhaustion or heat stroke. We need to cool her. You need to get us up quickly."

That wasn't easy. The slope was steep, and the pair were twenty metres down. Johan thought fast. They had no rope. Cleopatra's traces might reach. He had them unclipped in seconds and threw them down.

Simon gingerly planted himself against the stump. He hauled Harriet to her feet, let her inert body crumple over his shoulder, then inched his way up the slope until he was able to grasp the reins. Johan and Sara hauled them up until, with a final heave, all four collapsed on top of one another. Johan felt a wave of terror course through him. Harriet looked dead.

"We need to drench her."

"There's a stream further down the track – about four-hundred metres," Johan said.

Simon didn't hesitate. He picked up Harriet, threw her like a sack of potatoes face down across Cleopatra's back, and set off. Johan and Sara struggled to keep up.

Once at the stream, Simon picked Harriet up and clambered over the rocks. He waded into the middle of the fast-flowing torrent and slowly submerged her into the ice-cold water. The shock had an immediate impact. Harriet's eyes flickered open. She gasped, then looked confused as Simon pushed her underwater.

"What are you doing?" Harriet spluttered as she surfaced. "You're making me wet."

"I know, sweetheart." Simon said, as Johan approached. "We've got to keep her soaked." He ripped off a section of Harriet's dress to form an improvised flannel. "Keep dousing her. She needs to cool down."

"What can I do?" Sara asked.

"Fill water bottles. She must drink."

Gradually, Harriet became aware of her surroundings. She looked bewildered at each soaking. Eventually, she decided she'd had enough and sat up in the middle of the stream, took deep breaths to steady herself, then gulped down flask after flask of water until she threw up over Simon.

"Sorry," she muttered. He sat back on his haunches and laughed. For the first time since her collapse he looked relaxed.

Johan patted his friend on the back. "You'll make a better doctor than a vet."

Sara looked at Simon in amazement. "Where did you learn that?"

"From tourists. My father dealt with two cases of heat exhaustion this summer and one of heatstroke."

Johan studied his sister. "Can you stand?"

Harriet slowly got to her feet and stood for a second with her arms stretched out by her side to steady herself. Her wet hair hung in a bedraggled tangle about her face, a large green muddy smear ran down her shredded dress, and rivulets of blood trickled down her arms and legs from grazes inflicted by her fall.

Simon stood back and appraised her. "You really ought to make a bit more of an effort with your appearance."

Harriet cast him a sarcastic look. "Trottel," she muttered weakly. "Esel," he retorted.

Despite her teasing, Simon remained concerned. "I'll go ahead with her and get my Pa to check her out." He helped Harriet mount Cleopatra and swung himself behind her.

Johan anxiously watched them disappear down the track. He glanced towards the setting sun. "Worst of the heat has gone and it'll be cool in the forest."

"She'll be fine." Sara ran her hand up his back and rested it on his shoulder. "By the time we get home, she'll be giving him grief for ruining her dress." She took his hand. "Come on, don't let it spoil the day."

"Yeah, you're right."

They set off and walked for ten minutes before they realised they were still holding hands.

For the rest of the summer, Johan found himself on an emotional roller coaster. Some days he felt on fire, alive, buzzing with energy to the point of euphoria. His world appeared vibrant, colourful, full of hopes and possibilities. Self-confidence surged through him. He imagined himself as invincible and unstoppable. Days flashed by in a blur. Every task became easy and enjoyable.

Just as quickly, his world tumbled down. He became overwhelmed by despair and despondency. Self-doubt bullied his previous self-belief into submission. Everything seemed black. The world threw up insurmountable challenges he could neither understand nor control. He felt powerless, isolated and miserable. He was in this frame of mind as he watched the last wisp of white steam drift into nothingness above the distant pine trees. The early morning train had departed Achbrugge. Sara was on board.

He couldn't understand why he felt so upset. She was only away until Christmas. She seemed equally distraught. During the short journey from her aunt's house she'd appeared tense, as if holding herself in check. She'd managed to hold it all together until the last moment as he held the carriage door open for her. "You write to me, Johan Breitner," she said, before breaking down and fleeing inside. He'd never seen her cry before.

Over the last few months, Sara had crept into his life and succeeded in tilting the axis of his world. His elation coincided with whenever she was around. Her absence diminished everything. He thought about what they'd done in a summer that had passed in the blink of an eye. Almost every weekend they'd spent in each other's company, exploring the upper reaches of the Brandtnerwald. Her overnight stays became regular. The Breitner family took her as one of their own and Sara didn't hold back. She joined in the family's Sunday celebrations; singing, dancing, playing cards and parlour games as if she'd always been included. She was teased and teased back. She helped milk the cows, clean out the sty, restock the feeding racks. She'd been present when Sylvia the sow gave birth to eighteen piglets. On several occasions, Johan recalled arriving bleary-eyed in the cowshed at sunrise to find Sara perched on the stool, happily milking a cow while engaged in earnest conversation with his father. She seemed perfect.

He smiled to himself. She wasn't that perfect. Goodness, she had a temper on her. His smile broadened at a particular memory. Sara had not found falling in the icy cold waters of the Ach amusing. He should have held her hand across all the stepping stones, he now realised. Fortunately, the water was only a metre deep, and she waded out by herself. He shouldn't have laughed, though.

He took a deep breath and slowly released it as if to banish his dark thoughts. Christmas wasn't far off. Besides, the start of his apprenticeship kept him occupied. And there were Sara's letters to look forward to.

SNAKES IN THE GRASS

"I take it the interviews went well?"

Wagner didn't look up. "Very satisfactory, Sister."

"They are good reliable girls." The Abbess appeared calm, but inside she felt taut with anxiety. "No complaints?"

Wagner looked up with a serious expression on his face. "Really, Sister. They are supposed to be confidential interviews." He returned his attention to the accounts before glancing at her and grinning. "Relax! They are young girls with wild imaginations and flights of fancy. Anything that might have been said or done can safely be ignored." He closed the ledger. "These look in order."

The Abbess gave a thin smile. "In that case, could I trouble you to sign off the laundry accounts as well."

"These are separate?!"

"Commercial activities are best kept distinct." She passed over a book already opened at the appropriate page and pointed to where he should sign.

Wagner hesitated - his pen poised as he scanned the page. "A profitable enterprise by the look of it."

"Sufficient to fund modest extras."

"For sisters who are the most deserving?"

"And priests." She raised the glass of altar wine and gave him a meaningful look.

Wagner smirked, then signed.

"And if you wouldn't mind casting your eyes over these." She handed over two large ledgers. "The top one is the refectory orders, and the bottom one is the horticultural accounts for the year."

He duly obliged, then sat back and raised his glass. "Congratulations! The Bishop will be delighted with all the good work you and the other sisters are doing here at St Catherine's."

"You'll stay?"

Wagner glanced at his watch. "I see no reason not to. I don't have any other appointments."

The Abbess smiled. "Excellent. I'm sure the sisters would welcome you leading evening prayers."

"I'd be honoured."

"And some confessions?"

"Perhaps one or two before I retire. It's been a long day." He turned in his chair so he faced the Abbess more directly. "Now, regarding other business. Is there anything else I can help you with, Sister?"

"As it happens, there is, Father." Her face turned hard. "One of the novices. I think her calling lies elsewhere."

"Causing trouble or in trouble?"

The Abbess nodded.

Wagner sighed. "There's always one."

LOVE, DEATH AND CONFRONTATION

Five weeks after Sara's departure, Johan was packing away his safety harness and hard hat into his locker. In his pocket was Sara's latest letter. He'd already read it three times but he couldn't resist reading it again, if only for its opening sentence.

'My dearest Johan. I cannot begin to tell you how much I am missing you.' He lingered over the words. She had settled in. The school was prim and proper with strict rules, but the teachers were fantastic and she was learning a lot. Most other girls were pleasant. The wealthier pupils had an air of entitlement about them that she found distasteful. But there were also plenty of 'normal' girls, and she'd made friends. There were a number of refugees from Germany which made her feel relieved that she had left when she did. He rushed through the rest of the letter until he got to the final sentence. *'Must close now as it is nearly lights-out. Each night I think about you, and hope you are thinking of me. I'm counting down the days until the Christmas holidays. Love, your Sara xx'* He carefully folded the letter, replaced it in its envelope and put it in his pocket. So far they'd exchanged two letters, and he intended to keep every one.

As he prepared to leave, a commotion further along the changing room caught his attention. Some work-mates were listening intently to an older colleague. Intrigued, Johan attached himself to the edge of the group.

"The sub-station was completely destroyed."

"What! - destroyed the transformers?"

"Yeah. Blown up."

"It's the National Socialists. Bloody terrorists," a worker sneered.

"Freedom fighters, you mean," his colleague said angrily. "They are fighting for what we all want."

"You speak for yourself," his work-mate snapped back. "As far as I'm concerned a terrorist is a terrorist. Someone could have been killed!"

"Someone has been killed," a voice piped up.

The group swung round to confront the speaker, one of the more experienced line riggers. "It's true," the man said, as he registered the looks of disbelief among his audience. "Beyond Littisau. The pylon construction team found a skeleton."

"It can't be a terrorist victim if it's a skeleton," a man said, laughing. "Who found it?"

"One of the supervisors."

"How long had it been there?"

The line-rigger shook his head. "No idea. Years maybe."

"Probably a mountaineer who got lost."

"What did you do about it? Did you pick it up?" an apprentice asked.

"You're not allowed to touch it. The gaffer sent someone off to fetch the police."

"Oh, aye. Could be a murder victim," someone said darkly.

Johan found himself drawn towards the conversation until he realised if he didn't leave soon he'd miss the Postbus, and he was keen to get home. It was Friday night and that meant beers in the Adler.

Johan, Simon and Jurgen sat at the Stammtisch alongside their fathers. As wage earners they were regarded as adults now. Johan soaked up the atmosphere. Most farmers smoked or chewed tobacco, and the aroma of cigarettes and pipes competed with smoked ham from the kitchen, the pine log fire which crackled and spat in the grate, and the earthy odour of the farmers. The paraffin lamps were lit, and the flickering flames glinted in the sharp eyes of the drinkers. Groups huddled around games of cards, dominos or the table skittles. But most came for the company, conversation and banter. The room buzzed with chat and the occasional burst of laughter and light hearted ribbing.

Simon's father broke into Johan's musing. "If I'm not mistaken, I saw you on my rounds this morning dangling from a pylon by the road to Achbrugge. Does that mean we can expect electricity to reach Doppelgau before Weinachtsfest?"

"Providing we don't get heavy snow," Johan replied.

"Not before time," a man on the adjoining table said. "Achbrugge's had electricity for over a year. Someone's been dragging their feet."

"Stop moaning." Herr Zinnerman, the landlord, wiped the table and placed the man's beer in front of him. "The point is it's on its way."

"Which buildings will be the first to be connected, Johan?" someone called out.

"The public buildings - the Post Office, Farmer's Council Offices and the Adler."

"I'm hoping we'll be connected in time for the New Year festivities," Herr Zinnerman announced to the room. "I expect you all to attend."

Heads nodded and hands waved, signifying the landlord could expect a good turnout. Seeing in the New Year was a highlight of the village social calendar.

The arrival of electricity prompted a brief discussion before conversations moved to more mundane matters on the health of livestock, the market demand for their produce and whether the hay harvest was sufficient for the coming winter. Having assured themselves that today had been much like yesterday, and tomorrow held little prospect of anything that might upset the natural rhythm of the village, the men returned to their beer and smokes.

Except on this evening contentment didn't reach all corners of the Gasthaus. Several grim-faced farmers sat around a table, their eyes averted and arms folded. A thickset man loomed over them. His head swivelled on the rolls of fat of his neckline, and his finger wagged in the faces of his audience. Will Hagspiel was in full flow. He'd been haranguing them for some time, his voice getting louder and more belligerent in proportion to the amount of Pils he consumed.

"It's a disgrace, I tell you." He stared at the table for a few seconds before raising his head, his face flushed with anger. "And a betrayal." He belched.

Johan glanced at his father, who gave a roll of his eyes and dismissive shake of his head. Every village had a Will Hagspiel. Loud, opinionated and aggressive. His tirades had become more frequent over recent months.

Will continued his rant, his eyes bulging and the veins in his temple throbbing as he counted out his grievances on his fingers. "Look what's happened. The bloody Italians, French, Czechs, Hungarians and Slovaks got everything they wanted. All at our expense. Land, resources, everything! The Hungarians were supposed to be fighting alongside us, for God's sake! The cowards stabbed us in the back. The entire world is anti-German and anti-Austrian."

From the adjoining table, Peter Ansbacher regarded Will with calm detachment. As the village elder, the village often looked to him to provide the wise council that came with age and experience. "There's no point getting worked up about it. What's done is done. We're in no position to do anything."

Will sneered at the old man. "That's wet talk. We're being treated as if we're a beaten nation - with no honour, no dignity, no self-respect, and people like you don't help with your unpatriotic, defeatist attitude."

The Gasthaus fell into shocked silence. Peter maintained his composure. He took a sip from his glass, and deliberately took his time to respond. "I'm a realist, Herr Hagspiel. Something that comes from years of dealing with politicians and hot heads." His use of the formal form of address was a rebuke.

Will knew it, along with everyone else. He found he couldn't hold Peter's penetrating look. Politeness required he ought to apologise. However, good manners weren't in him. The Hagspiels were known for gossip mongering, rabble rousing and rudeness. If they were aware of their reputation, they didn't care. As far as they were concerned, they were good, plain speaking patriots.

Fuelled by alcohol, Will continued his tirade. "The sooner we become one German nation, the better." He punched the words out and counted off each grievance on his fingers as if he was lecturing children. "We've lost two thirds of our territory, including South Tyrol, to the Italians. We just managed to stop the Hungarians taking over Burgenland.

We're paying the bloody French and Englanders billions of schillings while we've got people unemployed and starving." He banged his fist on the table and glared around. "You tell me if I'm wrong?'

No-one responded, apart from his son, Hans. He swept the room with his eyes, a look of arrogance fixed across his face as he nodded his admiration for his father's wisdom. Everyone remained silent. A fine distinction lay between friendly discussion and outright hostility, and Will had crossed the line. He took the lack of response as a license to continue. "At least we National Socialists are prepared to do our patriotic duty."

Martin Drössel, the village baker, bristled. He was a staunch supporter of the main political opposition. "Are you saying Christian Socialists aren't patriotic?"

Will adopted a mocking tone. "Of course you aren't patriotic! You aren't doing anything for the people, you're against unification with Germany, *and* you're not telling the French and English where to go."

"You want another war then, Will?" Sep asked calmly. Johan looked at his father in surprise. The last person Johan expected to get involved was his Pa.

Will's demeanour immediately changed. Sep had given Will his come-uppance many times in the past. He softened his tone. "I'm saying we need to stand up for ourselves." He gestured vaguely towards the bronze war memorial visible through the Gasthaus window. "We fought well in the Great War. We agreed to stop fighting. We weren't defeated – anywhere! We didn't fight battle after battle to be destroyed as a nation, or as a people. We…"

"We?" Stephan Wachter's intervention stopped Will in his tracks. Before the war, Stephan had been quiet and thoughtful. His shell shock had driven him further inside himself. He rarely spoke in public. Everyone was stunned.

"We?" Stephan asked again, as he calmly took a drag on his cigarette and lifted his gaze from the table to confront Will. Only the slightest of tremors as he gripped his tankard betrayed his fury. He slowly exhaled, deliberately directing the stream of smoke towards Will. "At which battle did you stand side by side with me or any other soldier from this village, or from Gau, for that matter?"

Will's face went crimson. Stephan cast Will a contemptuous look and said nothing. He didn't need to. Everyone, especially Will, knew the only man of fighting age in Doppelgau who'd avoided conscription was Will Hagspiel. His excuse was that as the single breadwinner after the premature death of his father, and with an elderly infirm mother, only he could run the family farm. Sep gave his brother-in-law a sympathetic pat on the arm. Mention of the war stirred painful memories for Stephan.

Franz Zinnerman used his authority as landlord to curtail further argument. "Change the subject," he ordered.

"I'm leaving anyway," Will muttered, as he got to his feet. He drained his glass, stubbed out his cigarette in the ashtray and scattered some coins by way of payment on the table. In a show of solidarity, Hans got up and left with him but not before delivering a derisive parting shot at the occupants of the Gasthaus in general. "You people don't realise what's coming."

The men watched them depart in silence. They tolerated Will because he was village born and bred. However, for many, his words struck a chord. Will was echoing what they'd read in the newspapers. The country was a mess. Public morale was low, the establishment were resented and politicians distrusted. A strong leader was required. Until that happened, they kept their thoughts to themselves. They were farmers, content to live a simple life. Added to that, being browbeaten sullied the atmosphere of the highlight of their week.

Jurgen succeeded in lightening the atmosphere. "So, what have you got planned for Weinachtsfest, Herr Zinnerman?"

"Usual spread, usual entertainment."

It was what everyone hoped he'd say. The mood improved further as the door swung open and Father Haphold, accompanied by Herman, entered.

"Evening all," Herman bellowed, causing everyone to clap their hands over their ears and reel theatrically as if a siren had been triggered inside the inn. Hands were waved in an apparently furious plea for him to moderate his volume. Even when Herman reduced his voice to a whispered apology the theatre continued, leaving the carpenter giving a beseeching look for guidance from Father Haphold.

"Cut it out, lads." The priest grinned, before adding his own greeting by way of an exaggerated blessing. "God bless this Gasthaus, God bless the Pils it serves, and God bless the company it keeps."

"Amen," the men responded and crossed themselves.

Father Haphold and Herman sat themselves at the Stammtisch and Herr Zinnerman placed a couple of tankards in front of them.

"We have exciting news." An expectant silence greeted the announcement. Father Haphold took a long draught from his tankard to fortify himself. "His Grace the Bishop has agreed a concert should take place in Brandt Cathedral next year to raise money for war veterans." The priest looked around confident that his audience would grasp the significance of the announcement. A sea of vacant faces stared back at him. Quite what the connection was between the Bishop, Brandt Cathedral and Doppelgau eluded them.

The priest shook his head in frustration. "It's a great honour his Grace is bestowing upon us."

Faces exchanged looks but remained uniformly blank.

"The concert is to be given by our very own organist," Father Haphold said in a slightly exasperated tone, before throwing his hands out to present Herman in a bid to provide enlightenment and hopefully some reaction.

"Ahh!" the group said as one. Herman found himself being slapped on the back, his hand shaken and being given admiring thumbs up. Having star billing in Brandt was an honour for the village, and Herman was popular.

For the next half hour, Father Haphold revealed the sequence of events culminating with the Bishop's blessing. "Handel's Messiah," he announced. "Imagine it!" He raised his head and stretched out his hand, his eyes focused on some distant object. "Brandt Cathedral choir and Herman the maestro organist." Sensing no reaction, the priest looked around the table to be confronted once again by an audience of bemused faces. "Handel's Messiah," he repeated.

"I've heard it." Simon's father said quietly, not wishing to draw attention to himself. "It's a magnificent work. We have a phonograph recording of it."

Father Haphold sighed and rolled his eyes in frustration. A phonograph perhaps represented the most sophisticated piece of technology owned by anybody in Doppelgau. "The sooner we get electricity in this village, the quicker we can all get connected to the world."

"Buy a radio," Herman suddenly roared, making everyone wince.

DEUTSCHLAND UBER ALLES

The words of Tante Bri rang in her ears as Trudy left the flat, with her coat slung over her left arm and her suitcase weighing down her right. "You take your chances, girl, and you'll be out of this slum of a neighbourhood in no time."

Trudy thought Bri might be right. She'd become indispensable to the Hofners. They'd arranged her work to be classified as official Labour Service and provided accommodation so she could be on-call, day and night. It didn't matter that it was a box-room on the top floor, with a small window that overlooked the back yards and rooftops of the adjacent street - for the first time in her life, Trudy Heppel had her own space. She'd passed her driving test and regularly relived the thrill of being behind the wheel of the big Mercedes, speeding down the new autobahn. Her heart quickened each time she passed the Berlin junction. One day, she promised herself, she'd visit the capital and the rest of Germany. So many things were falling into place that she inwardly hugged herself at her good fortune.

The BDM still figured in her life. The Hofners encouraged her to spend her free-time with the organisation. It was part of National Socialism's utopian dream, they reasoned. Unlike other girls, Trudy made her own decisions. She'd no parents that might complain about the time spent at BDM meetings, camps and activities, express moral outrage over the obsession the organisation had with preparing girls for breeding, or be concerned about the casual denouncing of anyone who expressed negative views about National Socialism.

Katerina was at the tram-stop. "I thought you weren't coming?"

"Of course I'm coming, but I need to drop these off first." She raised the suitcase and coat. "Don't worry, the house is on route," she added, catching her friend's look of frustration. "Besides, the parade doesn't start for another two hours."

"I don't want to be late and face Frau Felder's temper."

An hour later they stood at the head of the two BDM squads facing the baleful Gruppenleiterin.

"Seig heil," she bawled.

"Seig heil," they bawled back. The drill hall fell silent as Frau Felder began her inspection. She started with the novice Jungmaedel in the rear ranks. The only sound was the slow, steady click of her footsteps as each squad member was subjected to the minutest examination. Each girl's head looked forward, their eyes focused on some distant object just above the head of the girl in front. Everybody tensed, waiting for the sound of the blow that would send the girl that failed sprawling. Trudy began to sweat as the footsteps continued their slow progress. So far, no blows had been delivered. The steps got closer until Trudy felt a warm breath on the back of her neck. Like a cat contemplating exactly where to sink its teeth, the

Gruppenleiterin circled, carefully inspecting Trudy from head to toe. Trudy felt her throat constrict. She struggled to avoid lowering her eyes. What had Frau Felder spotted? What was her expression? Was she looking pleased or furious? Pleased, apparently.

Frau Felder moved on to Katerina. Trudy watched out of the corner of her eye. If Katerina passed, the entire Group passed. Frau Felder always reserved her most meticulous inspection for her favourite recruit. Katerina was frequently used as a good example. Her uniform shirt was always starch cleaned and neatly pressed. "Girls, take note." Her hair washed and tied in a tight braid or double pigtails, the favoured style of true German women. "Girls, take note." Hands were scrubbed clean with no dirt under the finger-nails. And not a hint of any make-up. "Girls, take note." Once again, Frau Felder seemed particularly pleased with her star pupil.

"Perfect, Katerina," she murmured, before making her way centre stage. She turned to address the assembly. "Well done, girls. You're a credit to yourselves, the Party and the nation." She clasped her hands behind her back and allowed her smile to settle briefly on each girl until it rested on Katerina. "But your greatest honour lies before you. The Reich needs true Aryan bred children. We need warriors who are strong in body and mind. There is no greater honour for a German woman than to bear children for the Fatherland! The Führer has ruled no family will be complete without at least four children, fathered by true patriots of unblemished German stock. Girls, take note."

An image of a cattle market ran through Trudy's mind. She'd seen the consequences of young girls becoming pregnant and giving birth to unwanted or unsupported babies, in the slum. She wouldn't wish that life on anyone. By the time her attention returned to the Gruppenleiterin, she'd moved to another topic.

"Who has Jewish friends?"

The younger girls and the new recruits cast nervous glances at their elders, looking for guidance. The question sounded so innocent, as if Frau Felder was enquiring if anyone liked chocolates. However, the group quickly learned that any question from Frau Felder tended to be loaded. Trudy kept her hands firmly by her side. She'd never reveal her friendship with Old Mordechai Furnstein and his family. Three girls cautiously raised their hands. Emboldened, another girl joined them.

"As from today, you will cut any contact with these low-lives. Jews are incompatible with being German and the ideals of National Socialism. You will not meet, speak or provide them with anything. You will not visit their homes or allow them in your presence. Is that clear?"

"Jawol, Gruppenleiterin." The group responded like a pack of Pavlov's dogs. The emboldened girl still stood with her hand aloft.

"What is it?" Frau Felder snapped.

"The Jewish family I know are friends of my parents."

101

Frau Felder's face turned to stone. "Then you have a duty to report your parents to the Party, and you should refuse to stay in their presence. Stay behind, provide me with the details and I'll ensure the proper authorities are informed." She turned to address the group. "Jews are leeches. They are filthy and care only about money. They are devious and sly, they steal off people and cannot be trusted. Girls, take note."

Trudy closed her ears, having heard all this before. Apart from the Furnsteins, she'd no idea who within the ghetto were Jews, Catholics, or atheists. Even if she did, she'd never report anyone. The non-snitching code of the slums ran deep. She willed Frau Felder to finish her tedious speech so they could focus on the main event.

"Today is special," Frau Felder eventually announced. "You will do your duty in the *Strength through Joy* pageant to celebrate the liberation of Sudentenland." She pointed to a stack of newspapers and forty swastika emblazoned collection tins arranged on a table beside the drill hall exit. "You'll distribute copies of *Der Stürmer* and raise money for the party. You will work in groups of two, spread out along the route. Untergauführerins Katerina and Trudy will be in charge. Girls, take note. There will be prizes for the team that raises the most." Her smile faded as she bawled the slogan Trudy found increasingly irritating. "Attention, Heil Hitler."

The girls responded without thought. "Heil Hitler," they yelled.

Katerina almost trembled with excitement. "This has to be the best place to watch," she said, as she grabbed Trudy's arm. "Look at the crowds!" She pointed down the street. On either side, as far as the eye could see, people were crammed eight to ten deep. Red and black flags hung from every lamp-post and window, and adorned the tops of the eagle-crested standards held by the Hitler Youth who lined the route. It seemed everyone held a swastika that they waved enthusiastically. The faint sound of a marching band drifted down the street.

"Look at all those flags. Doesn't it make you feel proud to be German," Katerina gushed.

Trudy viewed the crowd from a different perspective. She smiled to herself. What an opportunity for some serious dipping, she thought. Necks craned towards the source of the Landsnecht drums and the tremendous fanfare of trumpets, as everyone focused on the approaching parade. She could have made a small fortune. But that was a previous life.

The noise of the crowd increased. It was as if the air vibrated with energy as the head of the pageant swung into view. Ranks of black-clad Schutzstaffel goose-stepped in perfect synchronisation. The rhythmic sound of their polished jackboots crashing on the asphalt could be heard over the sound of drums, trumpets, and the wildly cheering crowd who thrust their arms out in the Nazi salute of collective solidarity. The SS looked like supermen. Each soldier stood nearly two metres tall, eyes fixed straight

102

ahead, rifles held vertically; the cold blue steel of the polished bayonets glinting in the sun. They exuded an aura of power, authority, determination and ruthlessness. Germany was on the march, everyone could see it, and almost every man, woman and child wanted to be part of it. The cheering turned to screams of delirium as the noise of the band increased. The tunes were familiar - marching songs of great sacrifices, noble battles, glorious victories that had the people singing and clapping in unison. The troops advanced with expressions of stone as if oblivious to the adoration around them. A cry of "Sieg heil" was taken up until the entire street reverberated with the call to arms.

Trudy put her hands over her ears as the band and the deafening drums passed. She glanced at Katerina, who leapt up and down cheering wildly, screaming "Seig heil" along with the masses, tears of ecstasy pouring down her face. It was impossible not to be caught up in the euphoria.

Behind the SS contingent, groups of dancers drawn from every region of the Fatherland pranced and pirouetted. Marching brass bands gave way to folk music. Magnificent floats celebrating every aspect of German life followed, including huge trailers piled high with fruit and vegetables, and others bearing models of new ships, aircraft and steam engines. Each reminded onlookers that Germany fed itself and had modern, world-beating industries.

Everywhere there were swastikas, and pictures of the Fuhrer on flags, banners, or incorporated into the displays. This was a resurgent nation, led by a powerful, uncompromising leader, and their city represented the engine room of progress. Troupes of lightly clad gymnasts, selected from the BDM, celebrated the contribution of youthful vigour. Just when the crowd thought the excitement couldn't peak further, the skies were filled with the roar of engines as squadrons from the new Luftwaffe flew low over the city. The end of the parade was marked by legions of Hitler Youth. Taking their cue from the SS, they marched shoulder to shoulder with grim expressions, eyes locked to the front, banners held high. They marched with swagger to the beat of hundreds of Landsneccht drums; the future Germanic bloodstock committed to the cause. As they made their way along the street the Hitler Youth, who'd been lining the route, fell in behind, swelling the ranks still further.

Trudy and Katerina pushed and jostled their way through the crowd. Money was thrust into the tins. Strangers happily kissed and hugged each other as the carnival atmosphere took hold. It seemed nothing and nobody would be allowed to sully the day.

Suddenly, a group of Hitler Youth broke ranks and set upon a swarthy looking man in the crowd. In seconds, their victim was on the ground, curled up in a foetal position, desperately trying to protect himself from an onslaught of savage kicks. The crowd backed off, formed a circle and egged on the young thugs. Trudy was appalled to see women and children joining in, hurling abuse and obscenities at the writhing victim. Several men left the crowd and got involved in the kicking. Soon the wretched man's face became a bloody pulp. A savage kick shattered his jaw and sent several teeth rattling across the pavement. He got no sympathy; no-one stepped forward to put a stop to the brutality.

A wave of horror swept through Trudy. Who the victim was she could only guess, as did most of the onlookers. "Bloody Commie bastard." "Probably a Jew-boy." "Dumb arsehole. What was he playing at, shouting out such insults?" Trudy allowed herself to be swept along until the scene became lost in the crowd. Suddenly, for her, the day no longer felt festive. How could people, especially what appeared to be wealthy, respectable, law-abiding citizens, be reduced to such savagery?

Her collection tins were crammed to overflowing. Just as well as she now wanted to flee the melee as quickly as possible. She picked out Katerina fifty metres ahead in the gradually thinning crowds. She looked flushed and dishevelled. "You alright?" Trudy asked anxiously.

"Yeah." Katerina found a convenient lamp-post and squatted down with her back leaning against it. She looked exhausted but then grinned. "I haven't had so much fun since... well, I can't remember." She pulled the strings on her collection tins over her head and rattled them in front of Trudy's face. "Bet I made more than you," she laughed.

"Let's get back and see how the others did."

The girls gathered round as the contents of each tin was counted and scores marked against each girl's name. Those who hadn't done well looked anxious. Failure inevitably attracted punishment from Frau Felder, for whom winning was everything. The strong deserved the accolades; the weak, humiliation.

"Right, fall in," Katerina ordered. In Frau Felder's absence it fell to her to be in command. The girls instantly obeyed.

"We've done well," Katerina said. "We deserve a reward."

The girls felt relaxed. Katerina was popular, and when she took charge there was little likelihood of anyone being cuffed.

"Who's interested in going to a party?"

The squad squealed in delight and raised their hands. For a moment they were allowed to be a bunch of over-excited teenage girls. Katerina let the sense of expectation build. "The Hitler Youth are camped in the main park. Tonight they are holding a torchlight celebration." A ripple of excitement passed through the girls. "We've been invited. We will assemble here in full uniform at seven o'clock." Katerina gave a cheeky grin and deliberately mimicked Frau Felder. "Girls, take note."

"Jawol, Untergauführerin."

Katerina dismissed the group and waited until the last of the girls departed. Then she untied her tight braids, releasing her blonde locks. She shook her head and ran her hands through her hair, deliberately roughing it into a tangled mess. "What I'd give to walk down the street like this," she said.

"And wear lip-stick, some rouge and a bit of eye-liner." Trudy laughed. "I know how you feel."

"And listen to some modern music instead of that marching stuff."

"I thought you were enjoying yourself. You looked like you were having fun this afternoon."

"Oh, don't get me wrong. I loved every minute of it. But now and then I've the urge to do something… I don't know… rebellious!" She looked around the hall to check they were alone before lowering her voice. "We've a phonograph at home and some American music. Sometimes, when I'm alone, I secretly play them and have a private dance."

Trudy looked serious. "You need to be careful. Someone might inform on you."

"I know. I close the curtains and lock the doors." Katerina suddenly looked wistful. "I can't understand why it is so wrong."

"Because it's degenerate. Only savages and black people paint their faces, and American music is wrong because it isn't German." Trudy laughed. "It's a mad world."

"Sad and mad." Katerina sighed. "Give me a hand to re-braid my hair, will you."

Trudy obliged. For no apparent reason, the image of the man being beaten up came into her mind. "Sad, mad and bad," she said quietly.

"Not tonight though." Katerina looked at her friend. "We should find some good strapping lads for a bit of fun. Judging by that parade there should be plenty to choose from."

The image of the Hitler Youth thugs flashed into Trudy's head. If that was the type of strapping lad Katerina had in mind she wanted none of it. "I can't come tonight."

Katerina looked mortified. "But you have to. I was counting on you."

Trudy shook her head. "I promised to visit my Aunt Bri this evening, and I have to be up early tomorrow. The Hofners are attending some civic function at Saint Nicolai's church." She looked apologetic. "Babysitting duty calls."

Her friend wasn't to be denied. "Oh, I'll have to have a rough and tumble with two lads, in that case," she said breezily.

WEIHNACHTSFEST UND NEUJAHR

Sara's return from Switzerland provided an excuse for another Breitner get-together. Susan combined the event with a tradition she was determined to maintain: an English Christmas dinner.

Sara arrived with old Doctor Rubenstein and her aunt just after twelve o'clock. She got out the car, and immediately her eyes sought him out. Johan was transfixed. Sara wore a long pale-blue evening gown that emphasised her dark hair and clung to her figure. A fur coat was draped across her arm. She looked poised and sophisticated, and moved with the easy confidence of an assured young woman. She stood back as Simon helped the Rubenstein family patriarch from the limousine. Again her eyes returned to Johan.

"Hand me my stick, young man. I'll manage from here." Doctor Rubenstein caught sight of Johan's father. "Ah Sep, my good man. You're looking well. I need a private word before I leave. I'm saying it now, otherwise I'll forget." He chuckled and walked unsteadily towards the Stube door, chatting happily as he went.

Johan made his way towards Sara who deliberately held back as the others filed through the door. "You look stunning," he said.

"You're not so bad yourself." She smiled broadly at him. She found herself as much surprised about the changes in him as he'd been about her. A broad-shouldered, handsome man now stood before her, although he retained the same boyish charm that first captivated her. For a second they hesitated, unsure which greeting was appropriate. Instinct took over. They embraced with a warm, close hug that neither were in a hurry to disengage from.

"I've missed you," she whispered in his ear.

"It's good you're back." He grinned.

They held each other for a few seconds, smiling at each other. They had the same thought. Throughout the summer, apart from their brief embrace at the railway station, and the occasional holding of hands as they helped each other cross streams or clamber over rocks during their long walks, they hadn't had much physical contact. Now standing in each other's arms felt natural.

Harriett stuck her head around the Stube door, abruptly curtailing their intimacy. "Ah, there you are." She rushed over to embrace Sara and then hauled her into the Stube and towards the seat beside her.

For the next thirty minutes, the room was a confusion of laughing women embracing each other, discarding hats, coats and scarves, and popping in and out of the bathroom. Bouquets were unwrapped and placed in vases, the candles were lit and the prettiness of the table setting commented upon, hairpins were adjusted and dresses admired. The lids of pans were raised, the contents stirred and the flavours breathed in. Marie squeezed into a seat beside Harriet and Sara, and the three became instantly involved in an intense conversation of their own. The men gathered in the corner, lit cigarettes, supped beer and discussed farming.

"Have we got everybody?" Susan called, to cajole everyone into their seats.

"We're waiting on Gunter," Sep replied. He glanced at his watch. "He should have been on the twelve-forty Postbus." It was already past one o'clock.

"We'll have to start; otherwise the potatoes will burn."

Nobody needed further encouragement. The release of savoury aromas from the range provided a powerful incentive. Once everyone settled, Susan placed the steaming tureen of soup in the centre of the table. The ladle was poised to serve when the sound of an approaching motorbike drifted through the windows.

Gunter swerved into the yard, leapt off the bike and sprinted towards the Stube door: an indication that he knew he was late and in trouble. He ran halfway across the yard before realising he'd left a package strapped to the pinion seat. He skidded to a halt, reversed his flight, desperately untied the cords that held a bunch of bedraggled flowers, before resuming his dash for the entrance. Johan anticipated his arrival and threw the door open, catapulting Gunter to the centre of the Stube. He stood gasping and coming to terms with the fact he was the focus of attention. He shifted his weight from one foot to the other and struggled to get his thoughts in order. He suddenly remembered his leather helmet and goggles and wrenched them off to present a picture of contrition. Susan struggled to maintain her stern expression.

At last he found the words, but in his anguish they tumbled out in a disjointed babble "Susan, Sep. Terribly sorry. Missed the bus. Sunday timetable with which I'm unfamiliar. Had to run back to get the bike." He screwed his eyes up as he recalled his panic and frustration. "I flew here. Fell off twice." He swept the rear of his coat around to reveal a long tear and an even longer streak of mud. He thrust the sad bunch of flowers towards Susan, then looked at her with puppy eyes that beseeched forgiveness.

"Gunter, it doesn't matter. You're here now. We've not yet started." Susan's expression changed to concern. "Did you hurt yourself?"

Gunter gave a vigorous shake of his head. "No – only damaged my pride. Fell off in front of Achbrugge church just as the congregation left Mass." He looked sheepish. "It's best not to have an audience."

Johan helped relieve Gunter of his helmet, goggles and coat. "I'm afraid I'll need some help with my boots again, Johan."

"Don't you dare take off those boots if you have holes in your socks." Marie gave him a steely look.

"Not to worry, Frau Haufmann. I've bought a new pair." To prove it, he waved each foot about as it emerged from its boot. He went around the table greeting each guest and took his place.

After the first course Stephan disappeared, to return a few minutes later clutching half a dozen bottles of his home-made wine. The dinner became increasingly loud and uninhibited as a consequence. To Johan's relief, the size of the table eliminated space for dancing. Singing, however, remained on the agenda, along with parlour games. Everyone was required to sing at least one song. They flitted between Austrian, British and Jewish folksongs with the same ease as the conversation moved between English and German.

Eventually, and to Gunter's delight, Susan announced it was time to play charades. "I'm a detective," he declared. "I ought to be good at this." He proved as inept as everyone else. Nevertheless, he solved the final clue. "Dudlesack," he shouted, as Harriet marched up and down with puffed out cheeks and her left elbow pumping an imaginary sheep's stomach. A cheer erupted as Harriet curtsied to acknowledge his victory.

"Bagpipes is a much better word for them," Harriet said. "It describes exactly what they are."

"Like flat irons." Josey's observation was delivered with the studied seriousness of someone on the cusp of inebriation. "Talking of which, how are you faring with your young lady, Gunter?"

Gunter's face fell and he sighed. "I tell you, Josey, I have to be the unluckiest man when it comes to matters of the heart."

"Oh no!" Marie groaned and covered her face with her hands. "What happened? You had such hopes when we last saw you."

"High hopes indeed. But I don't want to spoil today with my misfortune."

Harriet laid a sympathetic hand on Gunter's arm and looked concerned. "You should tell us, Herr Schwartz. It helps to share disappointments."

"We shouldn't pry into Gunter's private affairs, Harriet."

"No, no, Susan, Fraulein Harriet is right. Who knows, maybe you can assist me since I'm at a loss to know what to do. My self-confidence is at a low ebb." Gunter presented a picture of misery.

"So, what happened?" Marie made herself comfortable in anticipation of the tale to come.

He pursed his lips and trawled through his memory. "I think I told you the young lady's name."

"Gertrude," Harriet said helpfully. "And she works at the court, and your police work wasn't a problem for your relationship."

"Ah, yes. An expectation that proved sadly misplaced, as it turned out."

Gunter fell silent which heightened the sense of anticipation.

"So, what happened?" Josey sounded exasperated.

"Well, we'd been to the cinema in Brandt to see *Dick und Doof*." Gunter chuckled at the memory. "Have you seen them?"

Everyone looked blank.

"They are two American comedians. Or rather, one is American, the other might be English. One fat man, the other thin. They wear bowler hats."

"You mean Laurel and Hardy," Susan said. "We saw one of their films last time we were in England, do you remember?" She looked at Harriet and Johan.

Harriet's face lit up. "Oh yes! We were crying with laughter. What was the film called?"

"Never mind about that," Josey said. "We want to hear about Gertrude." She looked expectantly at Gunter and nodded encouragement for him to continue.

"After the cinema we decided to have supper at the Gasthaus Krone."

"We've been there," Harriet piped up.

"Harriet!" Josey gave her niece a sharp look.

Harriet looked suitably contrite.

"During supper we talked about our work, and we concluded that neither of us knew much about one another's job. Well, to cut a long story short, I invited Gertrude to have a private behind the scenes tour of the police station."

"Is that allowed?" Sep asked.

"Not at all. But it was after midnight and, besides, I know the Duty Sergeant well." He glanced around the table. "He and I go back many years," he said conspiratorially, before continuing. "I took her to my office, showed her the interview rooms, opened some old case files. We've had two unusual murder cases. Gertrude was fascinated and asked lots of questions, especially about how science helps to catch criminals."

Simon's interest in all things scientific was pricked. "Like what?"

"Oh, everything: photography, fingerprints, chemical analysis, telephony and telegraphy. Even radio. Did you know the first person caught as a result of using radiotelegraphy happened in 1910?"

"Yes, yes we did...probably," Josey said, clearly wanting Gunter to cut to the chase.

Gunter got the hint and steered himself back on track. "Eventually, our tour took us to the basement. That's where the holding cells, the archive, library and laboratory are located." Judging by the anguished expression that crossed his face it was also where things started to go wrong. "I'd finished giving Gertrude a tour of the cells when a voice called my name." Gunter closed his eyes as he relived the moment. "It was the desk sergeant. Apparently, three men had been admitted to Brandt hospital with stab wounds. One was a local villain who we had under surveillance.

The officers needed guidance on whether to detain him. As I was the case officer, the sergeant used his initiative and asked me to oblige."

Marie's eyes widened in excitement. "What sort of villain? Was he a murderer?"

Josey rolled her eyes and gave her an exasperated look. "Marie! If we keep interrupting, we'll never know what happened to Gertrude." Marie looked chastened.

Gunter leaned towards Marie. "Multiple allegations of assault and battery," he whispered, before quickly continuing with his tale. "I invited Gertrude to continue to have a look around as I anticipated my task wouldn't take more than a few minutes. As it happened, it took a bit longer."

"How long?" Harriet thought it safe to risk Josey's impatience as it seemed pertinent to the tale.

"About thirty minutes." Gunter furrowed his brow. "Certainly no more than forty. Anyway, when I returned she was gone! I assumed she'd taken advantage of my invitation to look around on her own, and I'd catch up with her, either in the archive, library or the laboratory. But no! She wasn't in any of these locations. Naturally, I assumed she'd retraced her steps and made her way back to my office." He looked from face to face as the gravity of the situation gradually increased. "But she wasn't there either. I went to reception, reasoning that perhaps she'd got tired of waiting and asked for a taxi. No-one had checked out, according to the desk sergeant. Since this was the only way in and out, it followed that Gertrude remained somewhere inside the building, presumably lost." Gunter leaned back in his chair, took a deep breath and blew out his cheeks. "I'd no choice but to search the entire station. It's a big place: four storeys high. It took me ages."

"Did you find her?"

Gunter shook his head. "Not a sign."

"What had happened to her?" Marie looked distressed.

"The sergeant used his powers of deduction."

Everyone looked puzzled.

"While I conducted my fruitless search the sergeant had checked in two… um…ladies of the night."

"Prostitutes!" Harriet said unnecessarily, earning herself a shocked look from her mother, who was appalled that her young daughter should know of such women.

Gunter continued. "Drunk and disorderly, according to the arresting officers. Standard procedure was to lock them in the cells, let them sober up and release them in the morning with a caution. Anyway, he does the paperwork, and the officers take the two women to the cells, lock them up, stop for a coffee and then return to their duties. Apparently, as they are about to return to their beat the sergeant casually enquires whether the…er…ladies had made any trouble? Those two, not at all, the officers reply. But the other one was in a foul mood and tried to escape. Naturally, they'd thrown her back in the cell and ordered her to behave on pain of more serious charges."

"Oh my God!" Marie shrieked. "Gertrude was in the cell!"

Gunter nodded sadly. "She was there all the time. I can only guess that, in my absence, she decided to have another look around one of the cells. At some point, either she closed the door or it swung back on its hinges. Either way, once the door closes it automatically locks and cannot be opened from the inside, for obvious reasons."

Susan looked horrified. "How long was the poor girl locked up?"

"About two hours."

"Two hours all alone in a cell!" Susan's look of horror intensified.

"She wasn't alone." Gunter looked pained. "She had the other two women as company for the last thirty minutes."

Johan didn't think it possible for his mother to look any more aghast. "You left a respectable girl locked in with a couple of drunk...of drunk..." Susan couldn't bring herself to say the word. "For *half an hour!?*"

"Bit longer, actually," Gunter muttered. "The sergeant became deliberately obstructive and insisted on completing formal release papers." He glanced shamefacedly at Susan. "He thought the situation was amusing. I didn't, of course," he added quickly, as he saw Susan about to react.

"Marie, it is not funny!" Susan admonished her friend as she caught sight of Marie trying and failing to contain her mirth that then proved infectious. Her giggles quickly developed into peals of uncontrollable laughter triggering those around her to do the same.

"Oh, Gunter." Marie wiped the tears from her eyes and squeezed his hand sympathetically. "You don't have luck on your side, do you?"

Gunter looked forlorn. "I'm jinxed."

"Why didn't you think to check the cells? Oh, never mind." Susan didn't anticipate a sensible explanation from the despondent detective. "I suggest we talk about happier events."

"Like the New Year," Harriet said. "When I'm sure, Gunter, you shall be lucky in love." Gunter's expression suggested he didn't share Harriet's optimism.

"Is everyone going to the Neujahr party at the Adler?" Josey asked.

"I'm afraid I won't be attending." Old Doctor Rubenstein said, as he struggled to his feet. "Such festivities will be too much for an old codger like me. But I'm sure you young people won't want to miss out." He waved a frail hand subtly at Sep, indicating he wanted his private word.

"Oh, we must go," said Harriet. "The Adler will be all lit up. Sara, you must stay over, then we can go together. Have you got a Dirndl?"

"Harriet, it is not for you to decide what other people must do or what they must wear. Besides, I don't recall either your father or I giving you permission to attend," Susan said sharply. As soon as she uttered those words she regretted it. Her daughter was growing up too fast, and at times Susan struggled to keep up.

Harriet's dismay quickly transformed into a look of barely contained fury. She opened her mouth to protest, but her rebellion was instantly quashed by her upbringing. She fought to contain her anger and embarrassment. She was nearly seventeen, for goodness' sake. She felt humiliated, even more so when she glanced up and saw Simon's expression. He always seemed to find her discomfiture amusing. Fortunately, Sara came to her rescue.

"I'm not certain I'll be able to attend, either." She glanced at Rachel. "My aunt and I haven't discussed it." In one smooth diplomatic statement she soothed Harriet's ruffled feathers and headed off an incident that could have spoilt the occasion. Johan could have hugged her.

Susan grasped the opportunity to get the party back on track. "Who's for some traditional English Christmas pudding and custard?" Eager hands shot up like school children desperate to catch the teacher's attention.

Johan also used the break to slip out. It was milking time, and the cows' needs came first even if it meant foregoing the treat. He ran upstairs and changed into working clothes. As he returned he caught sight, through the open door of the parlour, of his father in earnest conversation with Doctor Rubenstein. Sep stood with his head bowed, listening intently to the old man. Whatever was being discussed, Johan could tell from his father's expression it was serious. Doctor Rubenstein suddenly laid a gnarled hand on his friend's shoulder, leant forward and spoke with added intensity. Sep pursed his lips and gave a slow nod. Some acknowledgement or agreement had been reached.

Outside, the first flakes of snow drifted on the still mountain air. The sudden drop in temperature meant a heavy fall could be anticipated. The air felt crisp, and Johan had to break through the ice in the water trough to fill the bucket. He lit the paraffin lamp, set up the stool, washed the first of the udders and set to work. The pail steamed gently as the thick creamy milk, still warm from the cow, met the freezing air. Despite the cold, Johan found a cosy feeling of contentment flood through him. His thoughts immediately settled on Sara: their embrace, the delicious shock of her closeness, and her soft breath on his cheek when she'd whispered in his ear. He tried to fathom out why it seemed so natural when they fell into each other's arms.

"I'd offer to help, but I'm not really dressed for it." A voice from behind made him jump.

"Good God, Sara! You gave me such a start." His shock gave way to concern. "Don't come any closer. You don't want muck on that dress."

She laughed. "This is as close as I'm coming." She gripped the collar of the fur coat she had draped across her shoulders and pulled it close to keep out the chill.

He stopped milking and got to his feet. "We didn't have much chance to talk."

"I know. But I'm back until January the fourth. We'll have time. Besides I'm hoping we can spend time together at the Neujahrfest."

"You're going then?"

"I'm looking forward to it. I love music, singing and dancing." She grinned. "Can I expect a dance with you?"

For some reason he found himself saying. "Of course, all night, I hope."

She smiled broadly. "I've come to say goodnight." She glanced over her shoulder at the falling flakes of snow. "We need to get Grandad back to Achbrugge. He's getting anxious about the snow."

He brushed himself down and moved towards her. "I don't want to ruin that dress."

She didn't say anything. She opened her coat and wrapped him up, with her hands clasped behind his neck. Automatically his arms engulfed her waist under the fur. Their faces were inches apart. Her eyes were alight and full of fun and mischief as they gazed into his. "Every dance," she breathed, before kissing him on the cheek. "Goodnight, Johan Breitner."

He pulled her closer and returned the kiss. "Goodnight, Sara Rubenstein."

They stood grinning at each other, neither wishing to break their contact. A faint call from her aunt intruded. "Are you ready, Sara? We have to go."

Her hands reluctantly slipped from his neck. She wrapped the coat tightly around her and with a half-suppressed smile slipped out the door.

Johan quickly realised the rashness of his promise. He couldn't dance. Worse, he'd promised Sara he'd step out to each one. That commitment doubled his dilemma. He could perhaps master a waltz. But he knew from bitter experience that few people were content to stick to one form of the art but flitted from a waltz to a polka to a Ländler almost at random. He briefly contemplated a strategy of manoeuvring Sara into some country dancing. That tended to be a rough and tumble, chaotic affair where he might be able to mimic those around him, he reasoned. For a few seconds he convinced himself the idea worth pursuing, until realisation dawned that she'd quickly see through his subterfuge and might even suspect he was reneging on his promise.

For two days he wrestled with the problem. He briefly considered feigning some form of sickness before quickly dismissing it. The thought of missing the opportunity of spending time with Sara was too strong. In the end, he found himself standing outside his sister's bedroom door, steeling himself against his own embarrassment. After some hesitation he made the commitment and gave a gentle knock.

"Come in." Harriet was lying on the bed, on her stomach, reading. She looked up in surprise. "What do you want?"

"I need to ask you a big favour," he said, from the cover of the door.

Harriet's expression changed to one of wariness. "What sort of favour?"

Johan shuffled further into the room. Asking for help from his sister felt alien. For a split second he considered backing out. However, he was too far into the room. A withdrawal now would be awkward and intrigue Harriet to the point he'd be continuously harried until she forced the truth out of him. There was a common belief among the males in the village that females had an extra sense when it came to reading men. Harriet's next comment convinced Johan the belief was more than a theory.

"Does this involve Sara?"

Johan's stunned look told Harriet all she needed to know. Instantly the book closed and she sat up. "What's the problem?" Her eyes suddenly widened. "Don't tell me you're in love?"

"What? No. Don't be silly. It's not like that. We are just good friends. Besides, we only met in the summer. We hardly know one another."

Harriet's grin got broader as he stumbled over his words.

"Well, I think she's in love with you," she said, stopping him mid-flow.

"What?!"

"She couldn't keep her eyes off you during dinner. And she seemed very anxious to say goodbye to you." Harriet nodded her head as if delivering irrefutable truth to an unbeliever. "You can't hide true love, you know. It lights people up."

"Is that so?"

Harriet nodded knowingly. "You can tell Mama and Papa are in love just by looking at them together. Same with Aunt Josey and Uncle Stephan."

"You're being romantic."

She shrugged. "I don't think so. Anyway, do you want me to send Sara a love letter or something?"

"No. I want you to teach me to dance."

Harriet's mouth dropped open. "Are you serious?!"

"Well, don't be that dismissive. I can dance…a bit. It's just I need some lessons to give me a little more refinement."

"Johan, you need a new set of legs, some brain cells that can recognise rhythm and some kind of clock inside your body that can help you with timing. You are by far and away the worst dancer in the village. Everyone knows it."

"Well, thanks for the encouragement."

"You don't even like dancing."

"That's not true. It's just that I haven't seen the point of it…until now."

"Until now there hasn't been a Sara."

He looked slightly helpless. "I promised I'd dance with her at the Neujahrfest."

Harriet's face fell. "At least you'll be going."

"Oh, Ma's not given you permission."

She shook her head. "It's so unfair. Just because I'm not quite seventeen. I bet my friends will be allowed."

Johan doubted it. Seventeen was an unwritten barrier to attendance and had been for as long as he could remember. "Have you spoken to Ma and Pa?"

"We had a good talk. Ma apologised. She didn't mean to humiliate me. She was very upset." Harriet suddenly looked cheerful. "We had a lovely chat."

"But she still said you couldn't go."

"Not until next year. Until then I can go to the earlier party."

"That's for children."

"I know. Ma thinks I'm in too much of a hurry to grow up."

Johan thought for a moment. "I'll have a word if you like. It might make a difference."

Harriet looked fondly at her brother. "I need all the help I can get." After a moment's reflection she smiled. "So, when do you want to start."

"The earlier the better."

"How about now?"

"Okay."

She grinned. "Fetch the phonograph. This is going to be fun."

The locker-room was a sea of chaos. Lockers were flung open, and two dozen men were simultaneously trying to hang up their safety equipment and change out of their overalls. Everyone had been allowed to knock-off early so they could head home to prepare for the festivities. Johan pushed his way through the throng, exchanging banter and good wishes for the New Year as he made his way to the exit. He didn't want to miss the early Postbus. It had been snowing steadily, and there was a chance the road to Doppelgau might become impassable later.

Forty minutes later he entered the Breitner Stube. His mother looked up from carving slivers of ham from a joint and greeted him with a cheery, "You're back early."

Johan brushed the snow off his shoulders before taking off his jacket and hanging it to dry above the Kächelofen. "Lots to do before tonight."

115

"Like last-minute lessons from your sister?" She laughed at Johan's embarrassment. "You can't keep anything from your mother. I'm surprised you didn't crash through the floorboards."

Johan looked hurt. "Harriet told me I needed to try and float."

Susan raised an eyebrow. "You might need to practice that. Anyway, I think it is sweet of Harriet to teach her brother." She pointed her carving knife at the table where a pile of bread, pickles, wursts and sliced ham were set out. "You can start on that lot. It's only a snack as the Adler's putting on a spread."

Johan sat himself down as his father entered. "Hey, you'll eat us into poverty," Sep said. He gave his wife a peck on the lips and sat down opposite.

"How much have you saved for your motorcycle?" Susan said, as she settled herself beside her husband.

"I should have enough by late spring or early summer."

A knock on the Stübe door interrupted their conversation. Simon's head peered around the jamb. He looked nervous. "Can I come in," he said.

"Of course, dear. What a question!' Susan waved an encouraging hand.

Simon stepped in. A slice of ham destined for Johan's mouth ended suspended in mid-air as he regarded his friend with surprise. "Good grief, mate, you're dressed early. The party doesn't start for another four hours."

"I know." Simon looked uncomfortable as if he didn't know what to do with his hands and arms.

The ham remained in limbo as Johan studied his friend. Simon was usually self-confident and assured. Yet now he looked like a naughty schoolboy called out in front of the class. "What do you want, mate?'

"Actually, I want to ask you, Frau Breitner, and you, Herr Breitner, a question." Simon gave a small formal bow to each of them.

Susan and Sep exchanged perplexed looks. "What is it, dear," Susan asked gently. "Has something happened?"

"No, no, not at all." If Simon had a hat he'd have wrung it in his hands. Johan had never seen his friend looking so nervous.

Sep put down his knife and fork and turned in his seat to face the young man. "Well, fire away, son."

A sheen of sweat glistened on Simon's brow. He gulped. "I've come to ask your permission to take Harriet to the party tonight." The only sound in the room was the crackle of pine logs in the Kächelofen.

"I realise you refused her permission at the Sunday dinner, and I don't want to undermine your authority." Simon added quickly. "But I wondered if you might reconsider."

Susan cast her son a questioning glance. Johan's wide-eyed astonishment and shake of his head told her all she needed to know. "Have you spoken to Harriet about this?"

Simon looked shocked. "No, not at all. I wouldn't do such a thing without your permission."

"Well, this is a turn up for the books." Sep scratched his head as he tried to come to terms with the situation.

"She's sixteen, Simon," Susan said.

"I know it's a lot to ask. But, well, I thought it is a shame she is missing out, given Jurgen, Johan and I are going. And Sara – well, she's part of our group."

Having recovered from his own shock, Johan thought he ought to support his friend and sister's cause. "Ma, she doesn't act sixteen. You've said it yourself many times. She'll be seventeen in a few weeks, and she did put herself out to help improve my dancing."

"That's not the point," Susan said vaguely, before giving her husband a bewildered look. "What do you think?"

Sep shrugged. "I don't see why not."

"You haven't talked to Harriet about this?" She gave Simon a hard look. He shook his head.

The ham finally made it to Johan's mouth as he watched his mother wrestle with her turmoil. The fire in the Kachelöfen crackled and popped as the sap exploded, and the old grandfather clock suddenly chimed five o'clock. The dull resonance of the bells triggered a decision in Susan's mind. She abruptly got to her feet and went to the hallway door.

"Harriet," she called.

They heard the sound of the bedroom door being opened, and Harriet's voice floated down. "What is it?"

"You'd better come down here for a moment."

Harriet seemed in no rush to make her way downstairs. She entered the Stübe to be confronted by four faces staring at her. "What's up?"

"Simon has a question for you." Every head swivelled towards Simon who looked shell-shocked. He hadn't anticipated having to make his request in front of the entire Breitner clan. He pinched his nose between his finger and thumb and stared at the floor as he considered what to do. Harriet frowned and looked confused. Everyone held their breath.

Simon made up his mind. He turned to face Harriet and said in a firm voice. "I've asked your parent's permission to invite you to the New Year's Party...tonight," he added, in case Harriet had doubts as to which New Year he might be referring. The heads swivelled back to Harriet.

She reeled in surprise. She glanced at her mother, then her father for their reaction. She stumbled over her reply. "I can't...um...I can't go. My parents said I can't."

"Simon is inviting you to go with him," her father said. "We've no objection if you want to accept."

Harriet glanced suspiciously at her brother. For the second time, he deployed his wide-eyed look of astonishment.

117

"I don't know what to say," she said quietly.

Johan rolled his eyes. Didn't his sister realise what was on offer? "Don't you want to go?" he asked in exasperation.

"No!" she exclaimed.

Now Johan looked baffled. "What? No, you don't want to go, or no, that's not what you mean?"

Harriet became flustered. "I mean – no, I'd like to go," She turned to her parents, "if I have your permission."

Her father nodded. Her mother gave a tender smile; there were tears in the corners of her eyes. To Johan's surprise, Harriet didn't react the way he expected. There were no wild whoops of joy or celebratory hugs of thanks to her parents. Instead, she looked at Simon with a serious expression. "I need time to get ready," she said.

He looked equally serious. "I'll call back at nine o'clock if that is convenient."

She nodded. "Thank you." With that she turned and walked slowly back upstairs.

"Thank you, Frau Breitner, Herr Breitner." Simon gave a polite bow.

"Half-past twelve," Susan said.

Simon bowed again before turning to Johan with a relieved expression. "See you there, mate."

"Yeah, right."

"Well I never!" Sep said, as soon as the Stübe door clicked shut. Susan sank into the chair, covered her face with her hands and sobbed.

"Are you alright, sweetheart?" Sep leant forward and wrapped a consoling arm around his wife's shoulders.

"Yes, yes, of course." She wiped the tears away and looked at her husband. "Our little girl," was all she said.

"If Doppelgau has a reputation for anything, it's that its inhabitants know how to have a good time," Johan shouted in Sara's ear as they twirled once more around the dance floor. She said nothing. She didn't need to. Her reply lay in her eyes. At that moment she thought it wasn't possible to be happier. She gave an involuntary squeal as he suddenly spun her around. They hadn't stopped dancing from the off. Her dread of crushed toes and bruised ankles hadn't materialised, despite the warnings she'd received about Johan's abilities. He was actually quite good and made up for his lack of finesse with unrestrained enthusiasm. At times she found herself clinging on for dear life.

The band played and sang with increasing vigour. They knew what was expected. They teased the crowd by playing the opening bars of a popular song only to break into a different tune to howls of mock protests. They upped the tempo of the dancing in step with the amount of wine and

Pils consumed. Not that anyone felt inhibited. Everyone danced. None were left out, from the gawkiest teenager to the elderly aunt. As was the custom, everyone dressed in Brandtnerwald costumes: the women in Dirndls and the men in Lederhosen, knee-length socks and vibrant cravats. The room was a riot of colour, made all the more vivid under the new electric lights. The air became thick with the smoke of cigars, pipes and cigarettes, merging with wafts of smoke from the great bonfire outside.

Johan watched his parents and concluded his sister was right. There was an undefinable spark between them as they spun around the floor. It would take a particularly observant eye to realise his father was missing most of his left leg as he and Susan orbited the dance floor.

Harriet found herself the centre of attention. Johan now understood why it took women so long to prepare for an occasion. He realised he'd taken his sister for granted. She was Harriet: impetuous, hot-headed, impulsive, full of cheek and with a rough and ready charm. She now appeared transformed. She looked beautiful, with poise and self-assurance that reminded him of his mother. She'd had a string of young men eager to take her for a spin round the floor. Even Jurgen overcame his shyness and stepped forward. She danced once again with Simon, and he noticed another change in her. With the other lads she laughed and joked, matching their banter with effortless ease, but with Simon she acted differently. It was like watching a fledgling come back to the nest. She kept glancing at him as if unsure of what she was dealing with.

Sara followed his gaze. "I'm glad Simon asked her. She's having such a good time."

"He's a good mate. Got a heart of gold, same as Jurgen."

The band suddenly announced a break to fortify themselves for the run-up to midnight.

"I need some fresh air," Sara said.

They were about to move outside when the reception room door opened and Gunter strode in, resplendent in leather. Realising he ought to remove his jacket, helmet and boots, he retreated to re-emerge a few seconds later in a smart looking light green three-piece tweed suit. He sat down and struggled to put on a pair of shoes he'd bought specially for the occasion. He was immediately surrounded by the Breitner, Wachter and Rubenstein families and ushered into the corner they'd claimed as 'their spot.'

Johan took Sara's hand. "We'll say hello later."

Outside, the village lads were hurling snowballs at each other and throwing extra branches on the now raging bonfire. It was snowing heavily, and the flames lit up the snowflakes, giving the night an ethereal red and amber glow. They found a spot under the eaves of the Gasthaus that was close enough to the fire to provide some heat. She turned to face him, wrapped her hands behind his back and snuggled close. He pulled her tight against him. For a few moments, they were content to stand and watch the antics of the lads.

"You're nice and warm," she murmured.

He ran his hands down her back and around her waist, conscious of her curves. "Are you cold?"

"No." She snuggled in even closer and nestled her head against his chest.

"Perfect evening."

She nodded. He brushed his cheek against her hair and drew in her scent. To him, it smelt subtle, exquisite and feminine. "Are your feet intact?"

She giggled. "I'll live."

"Sorry about that. I've been practicing, you know!"

"It paid off."

He fell silent.

"What are you thinking of?"

"You," he said.

He felt her smile as she gave him a gentle hug. "Always worth thinking about."

"Couldn't get you out of my mind when you were away."

She gave another squeeze. "Same with me. Every night I'd remember everything we did together. I always went to sleep happy, no matter what had happened during the day." She lifted her head and smiled. "We're good together."

He grinned. "You didn't think that the time you fell in the river."

"Ah well, we all have our moments." She reached up and stroked his cheek with the back of her hand. "I've forgiven you."

"I'd like to ask you something."

She arched her eyebrows. "About what?"

He paused, not wishing to rush things. Then again, nothing ventured…"About something I'd like to do right this minute."

She looked intrigued. "Like what?"

"Give you a kiss."

She broke out into the half-suppressed smile he always held in his memory of her. "That might be nice."

"You don't think I'm being too forward?" he teased.

She shook her head.

"It's just that I wouldn't want to..."

"Look, get on with it." She laughed.

He cupped her face in both his hands and slowly moved towards her. His lips gently brushed against hers. He drew back to assess her reaction. In the flicker of the firelight her eyes were like pools of dark desire. They kissed again more deeply. A surge of yearning welled up as their embrace became more urgent and passionate. One kiss wasn't enough. Tongues caressed and their breathing deepened. They pressed against each other as if trying to merge into one. For both of them it seemed as if the rest of the world ceased to exist. Except the sound of the lad's snowball fight intruded and reminded them they were in a public place. They slowly and reluctantly disengaged.

"I imagined us doing that," she whispered breathlessly.

"We could think about doing it fairly regularly."

The sound of the band starting and the rush of the lads to the door invaded their privacy. Johan surprised himself. The prospect of further prancing around the dance floor now seemed very attractive.

During their absence Father Haphold and Herman had arrived to a welcoming cheer. Part of the priest's popularity was that he threw himself into community events with enthusiasm. He drew the line at actually dancing but contented himself with his own jaunty private jig on the side-lines.

The dance-floor was already full, and Johan and Sara were content sitting out the first medley. Marie waved, inviting them to join her at the annexed corner. However, any expectation she might have for some conversation was cut short. Gunter suddenly loomed over her and bowed. "My dear Frau Haufmann. I wonder whether you might consider taking a turn with me? I have my dancing socks on tonight, and I'm keen to give them a try-out." Marie's delight was compounded when it became apparent that, for a large man, Gunter proved surprisingly light on his feet. As a result, he and Marie spent the rest of the evening in each other's company.

Harriet danced again with Jurgen who appeared to have left behind his reputation as the shy retiring type. It helped that Harriet's dancing ability made him look competent. His parents exchanged looks of amazement at the transformation in their son. Their surprise turned to incredulity when, off his own volition, he approached several village girls who seemed keen to take a turn round the dance-floor with him.

Far too quickly the party came to an end, but not before the band acknowledged they were in the presence of a maestro and invited Herman to play a few tunes on the Gasthaus piano. As the flash of rockets heralding in the New Year illuminated the falling snow, and the thunderous explosions reverberated around the mountains, Herman launched into a medley of boogie-woogie tunes that had even the most exhausted revellers back on their feet.

At half-past one in the morning the Breitner, Wachter and Rubenstein families wended their unsteady way back home. Despite the snow, Gunter insisted on driving back to Brandt. "I don't want to put you to any inconvenience," he protested, until Marie put her foot down, planted herself between him and 'The Old Girl', and insisted he stay in the spare room. He could leave after breakfast. Simon took his commitment to Frau and Herr Breitner seriously. He escorted a tired-looking Harriet home and formally handed her back into the care of her parents at the Breitner's Stübe door. Jurgen disappeared. He needed to escort one or possibly two village girls back to their homes, he said, before escaping into the night.

Johan and Sara hung back, determined to enjoy one final embrace. In two days she'd return to Switzerland. This was the only time they'd have together until the summer. He fell into bed at three-thirty. He'd be up again two hours later to see to the cows. He didn't care. It had been a good start to 1938.

SPREADING OF WINGS

"You'll have to sooner or later."

"I know."

"So, what's the problem?"

"There isn't a problem."

"There must be a problem. Every girl in the squad has done it." Katerina chuckled. "Some more than once."

"I doubt every girl has done it. I suspect they're saying that so they fit in."

"You're not a lesbian, are you?" Katerina gave a mischievous grin.

Trudy looked shocked and glanced around to see whether anyone in the crowded cafe overheard the remark. "No! I'm not," she hissed.

"So, what's the problem?"

"Katerina, for the last time there isn't a problem. It's just that when I do decide I want it to be my decision and with… well… a man who is serious about me and whom I like a lot." She glanced at her friend. "It's not an issue for me. I can wait. In fact, I'd prefer to wait. Maybe I'm old fashioned."

"Well, don't wait too long. You don't want to miss out."

"I'll bear that in mind. Now change the subject."

Katerina took a sip from her coffee before leaning back in her chair and giving Trudy an appraising look. "What do you want to talk about?"

"I need to land a job."

"You've got a job." She looked at Trudy. "Or have you fallen out with the Hofners?"

"Not at all. It's just I can't see myself as a housekeeper and babysitter for the rest of my life."

Katerina grunted. "And I can't see myself working on a bloody farm for ever."

"How long have you got to go?"

"Another two months and then…" She threw her head back and mouthed, "*freedom!*"

"Is it that bad?"

"A year working knee-deep in pig shit isn't my idea of fun." She paused before continuing. "I shouldn't complain. My farm is on the city outskirts. At least I didn't end up doing National Service in some God-awful hovel with a family of inbreds, in the middle of nowhere. I get treated pretty well." She ran her finger around the edge of her cup. "Get paid a pittance though."

"That's what gets me. I work all hours for peanuts. I can't even earn enough money to escape. I'd like to go to places. To Berlin, for example, or abroad."

"Dream on, girl."

Trudy fell silent. Maybe Katerina had a point. Perhaps her expectations were unrealistic. Then again, she'd used her time with the Hofners well. She had her driving permit, she'd gained certificates in domestic duties and management, child care, and advanced First Aid. Within the BDM she'd progressed to Green Cord Leader. In the eyes of the Party, she'd completed her year's compulsory National Service and was free to seek permanent employment. The question was what sort of jobs were young women allowed to apply for?

"What exactly does Herr Hofner do?"

Trudy rolled her eyes and laughed. "Apart from eyeing me up, you mean?"

Katerina was instantly interested. "Does he?"

"Every opportunity. I swear he's even tried to watch me through the bathroom keyhole."

"Does his wife know?"

"Even if she did, she wouldn't have the guts to do anything. She's terrified of him. So are the children." She looked across the table at her friend. "She always refers to him as Herr Hofner or The Commissioner. It was two months before I discovered his Christian name – Herbert."

"Herbert the Pervert." Katerina giggled. "Perfect name."

Trudy laughed, then became serious. "He's something to do with defence planning."

"Well, there you are! Hitch your skirt up, flutter your eyelids and I'm sure he'll find you a job." Katerina lowered her voice to a sexy, husky murmur. "Become his flame and he'll make you his personal assistant or second in command."

Trudy took Katerina's advice, at least in part. That evening she took particular care over her appearance. The last time she'd deliberately used seduction distraction techniques was back in her old pickpocketing days. She smiled at the memory. Men were so strange. A little bit of ankle, the hint of décolletage and defences crumbled. She checked herself in the mirror. The sophisticated chic look was called for. Classy, not cheap, with just a suggestion of possibilities. She turned and faced her reflection. She'd pinned her hair, pulled her belt tight to emphasise her curves and left two buttons of her blouse undone as if in a moment of distraction she'd accidentally left herself exposed. That would make the old fool hot under the collar. She smiled as she imagined where his eyes might wander.

Suddenly the smile faded. The memory of a more innocent time years before, when she'd looked in a similar mirror, came flooding back. A chill ran through her as she stared hard at her reflection. Back then her beloved Tante Bri told her she was beautiful and lit a spark within her. Now what was she doing? Wearing a uniform that stifled her individuality, and dolling herself up like a cheap tart. An image of Gabi flashed across her memory. Poor Gabi who, according to Tante Bri, spent her time dockside, earning dirty money in exchange for several doses of syphilis. Almost immediately, the ghost of her drug-addled mother pricked at her consciousness.

Trudy shook her head in self-disgust. What on Earth was she playing at? Lowering herself, that's what. She was beautiful. But maybe Tante Bri meant something more. She pictured her surrogate mother with her thick arms and legs and a body so overweight that she wheezed and puffed her way around the apartment, great arcs of sweat under her armpits and the glass of Schnapps always within reach. Yet she was beautiful: in thought, spirit, courage, kindness and generosity. Nobody had a bad word to say about Tante Bri. And Trudy felt sure Bri wouldn't approve of her little bird's intentions right now.

In a second she unpinned her hair, loosened the belt and refastened the buttons. What gazed back at her was Trudy Heppel. "Never forget," she said sternly at her reflection. Out of the blue, Katerina's words came into her head. *"We've got a phonograph at home, and some American music. Sometimes, when no one's in, I secretly play them and have a private dance."* How good it must feel to do what you wanted: think freely, dress however you fancied, wear make-up and dance. She stared hard at her BDM uniform with its badges, medal ribbons and the green cord of authority. Until now she hadn't given it much thought. But it wasn't her, it had to go. It had served its purpose. But not yet. Tonight she needed to be a proper little Nazi. She grimaced and rehearsed some suitable slogans in her head. Loyalty, service, sacrifice. She raised her arm in a contemptuous salute. "Sieg heil." She sneered at her reflection. Then immediately glanced around the empty room – just in case.

Herr Hofner waited expectantly in the drawing-room. "Ah, Trudy, at last. You had me on tenterhooks." He smiled broadly. "Heil Hitler," he muttered and half raised his right arm in a lazy salute.

"Heil Hitler, Herr Hofner. I'm sorry I kept you waiting."

"Not at all, Trudy." He glanced at his watch. "In fact you're not late at all, bang on time. Can I offer you a drink?"

"No, thank you. It is a business matter I'd like to discuss."

He raised his eyebrows in surprise. "You'll not object if I indulge? A small glass of Schnapps helps concentrate the mind." He gestured toward an armchair. "Please." He poured himself a large measure from the decanter and settled himself in the chair opposite. "So, what's this all about? Kids playing up?"

Trudy smiled. The children were about the only thing in the Hofner family that approached normal, she thought. "No, I'd like your advice. I'm eighteen, and I want to do more for myself, the Party and the country."

Hofner beamed at her. "Fire away." He lit a cigarette, crossed his legs and observed her through half-closed eyes.

Trudy thought the best approach was to be open. She laid out her hopes and expectations with calm assurance, and summarised her experience, qualifications and achievements with candour. Hofner listened, seemingly intently, although behind the heavy eyelids his eyes constantly roamed her body. Trudy felt revulsion and struggled to keep her expression neutral and her voice steady.

When she'd finished he sat silently, a cigarette hanging loosely in one hand and the Schnapps glass in the other. "My dear Trudy, you make a compelling case. You're a loyal Party member. The question is whether you're prepared for even more sacrifices?" He gave a thin smile. "We're only just starting our struggle. Many challenges lie ahead. Our State is infested by enemies, degenerates, deviants and Jews. Our Fuhrer needs people that are strong, who are prepared to do whatever it takes to build a new Reich and make personal sacrifices for the good of the nation and the Party. Are you ready for it?"

"I'm ready to do my duty."

"Excellent." He took a deep drag of his cigarette and became business-like. "For some years, since the end of the Great War in fact, the nation has given scant attention to the aerial threat. Our experience in Spain demonstrated that towns and cities are vulnerable to bombing. Did you know just twenty-two aircraft decimated the town of Guernica. Imagine what a force of one hundred and twenty-two could do."

Trudy smiled nervously. She was thrown by his abrupt change of tack and demeanour. Also, she'd no idea what havoc one bomber could do, let alone a hundred, or why he talked about air raids in the first place.

"In the event of bombing, we need to prevent panic, chaos and moral collapse among the population. Professional firefighters could not extinguish the myriad firebombs that would fall through the roofs of houses, or rescue everyone trapped inside collapsed buildings. My Department is establishing self-help neighbourhood units, with each street constituting a Luftschutzgemeinschaft air defence community. Every apartment, led by a block warden, will organize a local fire brigade from among the residents." He stubbed out his cigarette and immediately reached for the packet and extracted another. He waved it at Trudy to emphasise his points. "Then there is the aftermath. How we deal with casualties, clearing bomb-damaged buildings, rehousing the homeless, feeding people." He paused to light his cigarette, then gave her an intense look. "Creating this takes effort."

Trudy's mind whirled. She struggled to make the connection between her request for advice on advancing her career and his lecture. Nevertheless, she maintained an interested look and responded with a brief, "I can imagine."

He gave her a condescending look. "I doubt it. It's not one city. Every major town and city across the Reich needs to be prepared."

126

"Surely the best thing would be to shoot down the planes before they got to the city?"

"But of course. We've people working on that as well." He suddenly remembered his Schnapps and downed it in one. "Tomorrow morning you will get the children up, washed, dressed and fed by seven-thirty. You will then drive me to the Rathaus where you'll start work."

Trudy reeled in surprise. "Doing what, Herr Hofner?"

"You'll join the Reichsluftschutzbund and help set up our air-raid precautions. You'll start as my personal assistant. That will give us both an opportunity to get to know one another better." He didn't bother to disguise his meaning. His eyes glittered.

Trudy suppressed her disgust. The man's display of naked lust suggested he held his wife in low esteem and his marriage of little consequence. Trudy risked an oblique reference to his family obligations. "What about the children?"

He waved a dismissive hand. "I'm sure there is some other respectable girl within your BDM group you can recommend to my wife. Now, perhaps you'll join me in that drink?" He leaned back, retrieved the decanter from the desk and waved it at her.

The last thing she wanted was to spend time with the oaf. However, she recognised she had little choice. He had her in his debt, and he knew it. Already her mind worked on how she might deal with him in the weeks ahead.

AN UNWELCOME INTERVIEW

For the Breitners, 1938 started with two unsettling events. The first involved Sep Breitner. He disappeared for three days. Nobody, not even Susan, knew where he went or why. He got up early one morning, packed a small suitcase and accompanied Johan on the first Postbus to Achbrugge, from where he caught the early morning train to Brandt. He came back looking serious. But apart from reassuring his anxious wife that he was in excellent health, he could not be persuaded to talk about his absence. He returned to his farm-work as if nothing had happened.

Two days later, Gunter arrived early in the morning, not on the back of the 'Old Girl' but in a police car accompanied by a uniformed officer. He knocked on the Wachter farmhouse door. Josey answered, to be confronted by Gunter holding a large briefcase in one hand and his official identity warrant in the other. It quickly became evident that this wasn't a social visit.

"Frau Wachter, I understand a Frau Marie Haufmann lives at this address."

Josey's welcoming smile died, and her face went pale. "Oh my God! What's happened?"

"I'm not at liberty to say. I need to formally interview Frau Haufmann. Is she on the premises?"

This was a different Gunter to the jovial, fun-loving character of the New Year's Eve party, and Josey found the change disconcerting.

"No, she's next door." She grabbed her coat and led the way.

Marie was sitting with Susan, enjoying a gossip over coffee at the Stübe table, when they entered. Josey's brusque introduction betrayed her discomfort. "Gunter's here in an official capacity. He needs to ask you some questions, Marie."

Marie and Susan looked bewildered. "Of course." Marie glanced nervously at the uniformed officer and smiled awkwardly at Gunter.

"I need to advise you it's an official police matter." Gunter nodded at the police officer. "My colleague will be taking notes. You'll be provided with a transcript in due course." He sat down. "You might want to consider conducting this interview in a more private location."

"Interview or interrogation, Gunt... Chief Inspector Schwartz?" Josey said sharply. "You sound very assertive, if I may say so."

Gunter's face reddened. "I apologise, Frau Wachter. I understand this is difficult for us all." His look softened as he addressed Marie. "This is official. I need to follow procedures. If you would like to be more private, I understand."

"Gunter... Inspector. You should just ask your questions. I'm happy to answer in front of my friends. I can't for one minute imagine what this is all about."

He gave a brief nod. "You are Marie Haufmann?"

Marie gave a nervous laugh. "Of course I am." Neither Gunter nor the policeman shared her amusement. They both looked grim.

"What is your maiden name?"

"Marie Wachter."

"Can you spell it for me and write it down." He passed a piece of paper and a fountain pen.

Everyone fell silent as the pen scratched its way across the paper. Gunter glanced at the scrawl. "Can you write it again, this time in block capitals."

"Is this some kind of joke?" Marie looked nervous.

"Please, Frau Haufmann. It's important."

Marie did as asked, then pushed the paper towards Gunter.

"What schools did you attend, Frau Haufmann?"

Marie stared in astonishment. She'd no idea why this was happening to her. "The local school in Doppelgau - the Volksschule and then the Hauptschule in Achbrugge."

Gunter nodded and gave a grim smile. "I'm going to show you something, Frau Haufmann. I want you to study it carefully, but on no account are you to touch it."

Marie said nothing. Her eyes looked moist. The interview was beginning to upset her. Gunter opened his briefcase, put on a pair of white linen gloves, then carefully lifted the object out of the case and placed it in front of Marie. "Look at it carefully but don't touch." Gunter said softly.

Before her was a battered, dirty leather bag. It looked like an old school satchel. Marie stared at it and seemed at a loss at what to make of it. It had no distinguishing marks. "I'm sorry. It's just an ordinary schoolbag like the ones we all had."

Gunter said nothing. He carefully turned the bag over and flicked his eyes at the object, encouraging her to take a closer look. The bag was now face up. In the top right-hand corner a faint outline of some kind of decoration could be made out. Marie examined it closely. "It's a flower...oh my God!" She suddenly jumped backwards and stared at Gunter, her eyes wide in shock. "It's mine," she said. "It's mine from when I was a child."

"Are you sure?"

"No. I can't be certain. Oh, goodness me." She looked from Josey to Susan as if pleading for help.

"What makes you think it could be yours?" Gunter's tone was neutral.

"The flower. I used to decorate all my books and bags with pictures of flowers." She sat back down. "We all did different decorations so someone didn't go home with the wrong one." She put her hand to her mouth as the memories flooded back. "I always did flowers."

"Did you mark your books and bags with anything else?"

"Well, we all had to write our names."

Gunter reached forward and gently pulled back the flap of the bag. In faint black ink the name 'Marie Wachter' was written in neat block letters that sloped backwards. Underneath was the beginning of another word. Only five letters could be read - D.O.P.P.E. .

Gunter turned the piece of paper on which Marie had written her name so that it faced her. The writing was identical. Marie gasped in astonishment. "Where did you get this?"

Gunter didn't answer but asked another question. "Marie, when was the last time you saw this bag?"

Marie looked nonplussed. "I can't remember. It was a long time ago. I recall Mama bought me a new one." She glanced back at the bag. "That isn't the new one, it's too small."

"What did you or your Mama do with the old one?"

"You gave it to Freya," Josey said. "I remember because I wanted to have it, but you insisted Freya should have it."

"Oh yes. That's right."

"Who is Freya?"

Marie's face fell. "Freya Thuller. She was a dear little thing. Her parents and brother died in a dreadful accident at the Nebelspitz. Burnt to death. Poor Freya became orphaned. To add to her troubles, she wasn't... you know... all there. She was the same age as me, thirteen or maybe a bit older, but acted as if she were five or six. I used to visit her when Father Wagner took her under his wing."

The police officer scribbled furiously, trying to keep pace with Marie's account. Gunter waited until his colleague caught up. "Father Wagner is whom?"

"Our parish priest at the time." Josey replied for Marie.

"How long did Freya stay with Father Wagner?"

"About six or seven months. She then moved to a convent near Littesau."

"When did this happen, and how old was Freya when she went to Littesau?"

Marie looked at Susan and Josey. "I was thirteen, I think. So, Freya was about the same age. That makes it 1909 or 1910 when she left."

Gunter suddenly banged the table with his fist, looked at his colleague and smiled. "We have a name and date," he said triumphantly.

"Gunter, I insist you tell us what this is all about." Josey was angry. "You're putting poor Marie through unnecessary anguish and upsetting us all."

"I apologise, Josey." Gunter returned the bag into the briefcase and removed his gloves before addressing them.

"A few weeks before Christmas, a skeleton was discovered in a remote location above the village of Littesau. That bag was found under the bones. We'd nothing to go on apart from we were fairly sure the remains were female. No name, no idea as to why she ended up there or how she died. Now at least we have something."

Marie covered her face with her hands and sounded distraught. "Poor Freya. She didn't stand a chance in life."

Josey put a comforting arm across her shoulders and looked puzzled. "How did you know the skeleton belonged to a girl?"

Gunter looked pained. "We didn't initially. But when we examined the bones we discovered there were two bodies. Whoever the young woman was, she'd either just given birth or was heavily pregnant."

Marie wailed and fled the room. Susan ran after her. Gunter looked anguished. "I'm sorry, Josey. I should have handled that better."

Josey regarded the detective for a few seconds before pulling round a chair and sitting opposite him. "You'd better prepare yourself for a lot of evidence taking, Inspector Schwartz.

FRIENDS

Katerina was in high spirits even before Trudy joined her in the café.
"We're on a roll, girl," she said.

"You got a job!"

"Blohm & Voss shipyard design office. You are looking at their
newest and smartest office assistant."

Trudy gave a small shriek of delight. "That is fantastic. Let me
give you a hug."

The girls laughed and rocked each other as they embraced, earning
themselves some amused looks from the clientele.

"When do you start? Who will you be working for?" Trudy said
excitedly. They made themselves comfortable and prepared for some
serious gossip.

"I can't tell you much. It all went in one ear and out the other. All I
know is I start Monday, the office is massive, they are working flat out and,
best of all, it's full of gorgeous looking men."

"Come on, you know more than that. We're not leaving until
you've told me everything." She looked around and beckoned the waitress.
"We should have something special."

They spent the next hour in lively conversation as Katerina went
through her interview experience. She left nothing out. The shipyard had
won a series of contracts including an order for a giant battleship and
another for over twenty submarines. The company was expanding, and her
job sounded exciting.

Trudy brought her friend up to date with her own career. She'd
passed her induction, and escaped being Hofner's P.A. after being given the
option of working in the typing pool or joining the civil defence inspection
team. She chose the latter.

Both girls felt euphoric. Entering the world of proper work felt like
a coming-of-age moment. To celebrate, they gorged themselves on
Schwartzwaldertörte. Katerina licked the last drops of cream from her
fingers before delicately wiping them with a napkin, and grinned at Trudy.
"So here we are. Two working women with the world at our feet."

"Two working women who are not well paid," Trudy replied.

Katerina waved her napkin dismissively. "It will come. What
about somewhere to live? I assume you'll move out of the Hofner's once
the new girl starts?"

Trudy rolled her eyes. "Herb the Perv wants me to stay, at least
until my replacement has learned the ropes. And he says it makes sense for
us to travel to work together."

"You might be waiting a long time if your replacement can't be
found quickly."

"Oh, that's sorted. I recommended Dagmar Greber. She's done well in the BDM, is a fanatical Party member and a perfect little Nazi Jew-hater. She'll suit the Hofners fine."

Katerina fell silent. "We should rent a place together," she said, after a bit.

"Are you serious?"

Her friend looked thoughtful as she lined up her argument, her voice increasingly enthusiastic as each bit of logic fell into place. "It makes sense. We'd only need a small apartment. I've some savings – not much but as soon as I get paid it will add up. If you did the same, we'd have enough in no time." She grabbed Trudy's hands, gave them a squeeze and looked at her expectantly, excitement written all over her face. "What do you say?"

"It's worth thinking about."

"Don't think, girl, be decisive. Imagine the fun we'll have."

Trudy laughed. "I'll think about it." She glanced at her watch and gasped. "I have to go, I'm late." She turned around in her seat and scanned the cafe for the waitress.

"I'll pay," Katerina said, and waved the girl over.

Trudy shook her head sadly. "There won't be any gallivanting around cafes when we have to pay rent."

Katerina scowled dismissively. "We'll soon be promoted. Us two - brains and beauty, we're bound to get on." She glanced at the hovering waitress. "How much, Fraulein?"

"Nothing." The girl flicked her eyes towards a smartly dressed young man sitting four tables away. "That gentleman insisted on paying."

The man had been watching them for some time. He smiled and gave a friendly nod, obviously amused at their stunned reaction. Katerina half turned her head, so as not to appear rude, and whispered, "Who is he?"

Trudy studied the man. He looked vaguely familiar. As she approached, his features triggered old memories. She broke into a broad smile. "Yankee Franz! I hardly recognised you."

"Same here. I saw you enter, and I thought - is that Trudy Heppel? It can't be." He got up and embraced her. "Long time no see, eh?"

"Years." She turned and introduced Katerina. "This is my best friend, Katerina Mossman. Katerina, this is an old friend from my childhood, Franz Kaufmann, better known as Yankee Franz."

Franz laughed good-naturedly. "I've dropped the Yankee title. Doesn't go down well in some quarters." He took Katerina's hand and kissed it, making her blush. "I'm a reformed character now – well, nearly."

"Franz, I'm sorry, I can't stop. I need to return to work." She glanced at Katerina. "You could stay though, couldn't you?"

Franz immediately pulled out a chair before Katerina had a chance to reply. "I'd be delighted if you did. One piece of Schwarzwaldtorte is never enough, is it? It will give us a chance to get to know one another." Katerina looked bemused.

"We ought to catch up," Trudy said.

Franz looked pleased. "Tomorrow's Friday. Here, seven o'clock? I'll book us a table."

"I'll look forward to it." She gave Franz a brief embrace. As she turned to leave, she cast Katerina a furtive glance, grinned and winked.

LAST DAYS

"I'll take it." Johan dismounted and leant the bike on its stand.

"You're sure?" Harriet regarded the motorcycle with the wariness of someone confronted by a young bull. The machine looked harmless enough but there was no mistaking the power hidden within. "Wouldn't it be better to wait until Simon's back? He knows everything about engines."

Johan grinned before giving his sister a knowing look. "I sometimes think you believe Simon knows everything about everything."

She tried to sound indifferent. "That's not true. It's just he does... well, you know... know about things."

"I can't afford to wait for him to get back from university. Besides, Jurgen took it for a spin yesterday and says the engine is sound." Johan stood back and admired the bike. "I'll ask Pa's opinion. I'll commit if he says it's okay."

Harriet looked thoughtfully at the machine. A sly smile crept across her lips. She took her brother's arm and glanced up at him. "Do you recall your sweet, devoted sister spending hours, if not days, teaching you to dance?"

Johan was thrown entirely. "What on earth are you talking about?"

Harriet said nothing. She slowly shifted her gaze from his face to look meaningfully at the bike, before looking back at him with puppy eyes and a beseeching expression. It took a few seconds before the penny dropped. "Alright. I'll teach you. But don't complain if you break a leg when you fall off."

Harriet grinned before giving him an affectionate peck on the cheek. Johan glanced at his watch. "We need to head home."

They'd only walked a few metres towards the centre of Achbrugge when the sound of loud drumming made them stop. "What's going on?" Harriet peered back down the road from where the racket emanated. "Is there an event today?"

Her answer came immediately as a column of thirty young men appeared from round the bend, led by a brown uniformed jackbooted officer and six Kesseltrommers. The drummers beat out the marching rhythm with an aggression that matched the youths' expressions. They marched as a determined, unstoppable force. Each boot crashed on the gravel road, sending small clouds of dust in their wake. Their uniforms of pristine white shirts, heavy brown Lederhosen and white socks reflected their unity and discipline. Each right sleeve was emblazoned with the black and red swastika. They wanted to draw attention to themselves and they succeeded. People emerged from the shops and houses to follow their progress. The market-stall holders paused their packing up to watch the spectacle. Johan and Harriet were forced to step back as the column passed.

"Who are they?" Harriet stretched up and shouted in Johan's ear.

"Hitler Youth," he shouted back, over the din of the drums. People started to clap in time with the marching; smiling and waving as the squad paraded past. Their applause encouraged the youths. Backs were straightened, chests puffed out, heads held higher and the drums were beaten with extra gusto. Some cheers broke out. A few followed their progress with indifference. One or two deliberately moved away. The officer raised the flag-staff to the vertical position as they approached the town centre. As the large Nazi flag unfurled more cheering erupted. Johan watched the expressionless faces of the youths as they passed. He recognised several Doppelgauers including, at the head of one column, Hans Hagspiel. His smirk indicated he'd seen them from the corner of his eye. Harriet spotted him at the same time. "What's he doing getting mixed up with this lot?" She sounded disgusted. Johan shrugged. They resumed their leisurely walk behind the fast-disappearing column.

"I'm sure I read the Government banned the Nazis?" Harriet said.

"They have." He nodded towards the crowd that gazed admiringly at the column. "The trouble is the Nazis have support, and it's only a matter of time before Austria joins the German Reich."

Ahead, the column chanted in time with their marching. "*Juden raus, Juden raus, Juden raus, Juden raus.*" Johan suddenly stopped walking.

"What's the matter?" Harriet looked anxiously at her brother.

A cold shock rushed through him. The Hitler Youth had started their chant as they approached the Rubenstein's house. "Nothing," he said quickly. "Let's go." He grabbed her arm and ushered her toward the market where Cleopatra and the trap were waiting. He'd made good takings on the stall, the motor-bike was exactly what he hoped for, Sara would be back for the summer holidays and he wouldn't allow a bunch of Hitler Youth to ruin his day.

136

BECOMING OSTMARK

The Desk Sergeant looked surprised as Gunter entered. "Good morning, Chief Inspector. You're very early."

Gunter slapped his colleague good-naturedly on the shoulder. "Couldn't sleep."

"The deadline bothering you?"

Gunter stopped and for a second looked confused. "No. If the Germans invade there is little you or I can do about it. What instructions have been issued?"

"The Chief ordered no resistance and full cooperation – much to everyone's relief. There's no point anyone getting hurt or killed." The Sergeant lowered his voice even though there were just the two of them in reception. "Rumour is the Chief's already been contacted by the Germans and told what to expect if there's resistance."

Gunter shrugged. "What will be will be. Sounds like now is a good time to keep heads down and focus on the day job. Which reminds me, I need a car from the pool and some snow kit."

The Sergeant picked up the phone. "What time and for how long?"

"In half an hour and I'll need it all day, possibly for two."

Forty minutes later, Gunter drove out the police car park straight into the invasion. Tanks, armoured cars, motorcycle troops and lorries laden with infantrymen poured over the border. The invaders wasted no time. Already the Rathaus, railway station and police headquarters had armed soldiers outside. Not that it was necessary. Gunter found himself part of a military column speeding down roads lined with hundreds of cheering, flag-waving residents, all happy to give the Nazi salute to each passing vehicle. Flowers were thrown, and cries of Sieg Heil reverberated around the narrow streets.

Gunter turned off at the junction for Brandtnerwald and, ninety minutes later, raced through the villages of Gau and Doppelgau. He slowed down as he approached the Breitner's Farm, half-hoping to catch sight of a familiar face. A glance at his watch persuaded him to keep going despite a strong temptation to stop for a coffee in a warm Stube. He was behind schedule, and his destination wasn't easy to reach.

The road became steeper, narrower and more treacherous as it wound its way around the escarpments and through a series of tunnels and snow shelters cut into the mountainside. The air turned ice sharp and he was soon driving through a snowy landscape. He passed the last cluster of farmhouses and the final stop for the Postbus. Now he was close to the pass summit. Only people that sought a hermit-like existence lived this high in the mountains. Two kilometres further, he slowed the car to a crawl and leant out the window looking for a large boulder, shaped like a blacksmith's forge. He'd almost driven past before he recognised it. Once parked, he opened the boot, took out the snowshoes, dug Josey's instruction from his pocket and studied them for a few minutes to orientate himself. Then he donned the snowshoes, wrapped a scarf about his face, did up his coat, pulled his hat over his head and set off. Three hours later, the smell of wood smoke and the sound of cow-bells indicated he'd reached his goal. By then he was drenched in sweat and exhausted.

The farm lay half-buried in snow. However, someone had cleared the paths around the buildings and washing was pegged out. He approached the door and collapsed on a bench that seemed to have been positioned to catch the full force of the sun and provide a weary traveller with relief. He bent over and forced oxygen into his lungs. The door opened and a woman examined him as if he was a piece of unexpected driftwood.

Gunter looked sideways at her. She was probably in her early forties with the deep nut-brown complexion that was a trait of people that lived in the high mountains. There was a wildness about her that seemed fitting, given the location.

"You must be Tara." Gunter held out his hand. "I'm…"

"I know who you are," the woman said. "You're a policeman."

Gunter sat up in surprise. "How do you know that?"

"I just know." She came out and stood in front of him with her hands on her hips. She was slim but with a robustness that suggested she was used to hard toil.

"I'm Detective Inspector Gunter Schwartz of Brandt Krimminpolitzei."

The woman looked around as if half expecting to see a squad of policemen surrounding the farmstead. "So, what?"

"I beg your pardon?"

"So, what do you want?" The woman glared.

"I was hoping you and your parents… Gregor and Petra… might help me with an enquiry."

"Who sent you?"

"Um, Josey Wachter. I'm here at her suggestion."

At the mention of Josey's name, the woman softened. "You should have said that straight away." She studied him before apparently making up her mind. "You better come in and have something to eat. You look ill."

"Who is it, Tara?" A voice boomed from inside the farm.

"A man called Gunter Schwartz, Papa," Tara called. "He's a policeman."

"What?" There was no masking the hostility in the man's voice.

"Now now, Gregor. Don't you get yourself in a fluster." A placating female voice succeeded in partially deflating the man's fury as his giant frame suddenly filled the doorway. Gunter was momentarily startled. He was a big man himself, but Gregor made him feel like a featherweight. Two angry, piercing eyes bore into Gunter from a teak brown face, framed

138

by shaggy white hair and a full and bushy beard. Gunter felt he was being assessed as lunch by an enormous and very irritable lion.

"Are you from the Diocese?"

"No, Papa. I told you. Herr Schwartz is a policeman."

"Sent by the bishop?"

"No. Josey Wachter sent me."

Gregor studied Gunter for a few seconds. "Would you like a beer?"

"That would be welcome."

"Well don't just stand there, Tara. Let the man in." Tara rolled her eyes and shook her head. By the time Gunter discarded his coat, a large pewter tankard filled with home-made beer stood waiting for him on an enormous kitchen table.

"You'll have to excuse my husband, Herr Schwartz. He has no love for the Church or the police." A frail-looking woman held out her hand. "I'm Petra, Gregor's wife."

"I'm delighted to meet you, Petra. And, before I forget, Josey and all the Breitner family send you their best wishes, as does Marie Wachter."

"You must tell me all about them this evening over dinner, once you've completed your business."

Gunter looked surprised. "Oh, I don't want to trouble you. I hope to be away before nightfall."

"Ha! Did you hear that?" Gregor laughed. "It's far too late to head back now. You'll kill yourself falling off the cliff." His great bulk landed on the chair opposite. He crashed his own tankard against Gunter's pot. "Prosit, my friend." He took an enormous swig before regarding the detective. "So, what's this all about?"

"I'd like to ask you about your investigation." Gunter noticed a wary expression enter Gregor's eyes.

"What investigation might that be?"

Gunter decided candour was the best tactic. "I'm told you were a senior clergyman within the Diocese of Brandt before you fell out of favour with the Church establishment." Gregor took a sip of his beer and said nothing. Gunter took his silence as consent to continue. "Your position was the Diocese Chief Accountant. However, your real task was to ensure that any abuse inside and outside the Church involving clergymen was discreetly dealt with, to ensure the Church's public reputation and standing was protected." Gunter maintained eye contact and continued. "Apparently, you were extremely good at your job and earned several promotions. No corruption was too widespread or scandal so large that you couldn't deal with it. You came to know every skeleton in the Diocese cupboard. Nothing shocked you. Until one day something truly appalling pricked your conscience." Gunter paused. Still, Gregor said nothing. Gunter pressed on. "That incident involved the rape of a young girl by a priest called Father

139

Wagner." At the mention of Father Wagner, Gunter noticed Gregor's grip on his tankard tighten.

"You knew Father Wagner was responsible but couldn't prove it. Your outrage was compounded by the fact that, far from wanting you to pursue the investigation, you were ordered to bury the matter. That was something your conscience wouldn't allow. You threatened to expose the rape and every other scandal to the Vatican and press. However, the Bishop turned the tables and tried to frame you for the crime. You lost your job and were forced into exile. Hence, you ended up here with the victim and her child." Gunter flicked his eyes towards a silent Petra and Tara.

"You seem to have done your homework, Inspector," Gregor muttered, after a long silence. "So why are you here if it isn't to arrest me?"

Gunter smiled. "I want your file."

"And what file is that?"

"The file you put together detailing every scandal that you'd put to bed, and your investigation into Father Wagner in particular."

"What makes you think I kept such a file?"

"Because you're not stupid. It's your insurance policy should the Church or police ever come after you." Gunter took a sip of his beer. "Also, I suspect you hoped someone like me might appear one day to put Father Wagner behind bars." Gregor pursed his lips and nodded.

It would prove to be a long afternoon and an even longer evening.

Gunter's head still pounded as he slid into the driver's seat and put the key in the ignition. He couldn't remember the last time he'd drunk so much. He rested his head on the steering wheel and tried to muster the energy to fire the motor. Despite his fragile state, he couldn't help but smile to himself. He recognised the feeling. It always occurred when pieces of an investigative jigsaw started to fall into place. It was why he loved being a detective. He knew where Gregor's file was. He chuckled at Gregor's audacity. Eventually, he steeled himself for the journey. He grabbed several lungfuls of fresh mountain air, then turned the key and set off.

Two hours later he pulled up outside Brandt central police station. The Germans hadn't wasted time. Already a huge Swastika hung outside and Wehrmacht troops stood guard. He glanced around the square. Soldiers were everywhere. An anti-tank gun had been set up as an exhibit for a crowd of excited schoolboys and Hitler Youth. Swastika flags and bunting had appeared as if by magic. A street loudspeaker played traditional Austrian folksongs. It was as if a carnival had been declared. The streets were filled with happy, smiling civilians. They applauded as more armoured cars and motorcycle troops passed through the city.

"You're wanted," the desk sergeant muttered.

"For what?" Gunter grinned.

"For being drunk and disorderly." The sergeant made a face and wafted the air in front of him. "Had a session, have we?"

"Bad as that?" Gunter looked worried, cupped his hand and tried to smell his own breath.

"You'd better scrub-up," the sergeant said. "It's a meeting with the new boss. We've all been through it." He raised his eyebrow. "First impressions, eh!?"

"What time?"

"As soon as you got here."

Gunter nodded his thanks and headed for the washroom. Despite driving all the way with the car window open, he still felt hungover. He opened his locker and congratulated himself for having had the foresight to store a washbag and spare clothes in anticipation of overtime and the occasional all-nighter. Having stripped off his shirt, doused his head under the cold-water tap, scrubbed his teeth, gargled for over five minutes and shaved - he examined himself in the mirror. He was pleased with the result. He looked functional.

The Chief of Police's office was on the top floor. Gunter felt relaxed. The Chief was an affable sort. He and Gunter had worked together for many years, and they'd rubbed along reasonably well. He knocked, entered and immediately sensed the tension. The Chief was standing and looked uncomfortable. A tall, gaunt man in a black Gestapo uniform occupied his desk.

"Heil Hitler, Chief Inspector Schwartz." The Chief raised his right hand in a smart salute. His eyes prompted Gunter to follow suit.

For a second, Gunter was thrown. Usually his boss gave a warm handshake. "Yes, of course." He raised his hand in a half-hearted Nazi salute.

The Chief turned towards the Gestapo officer, who watched Gunter enter with mild interest. "May I introduce…"

"Yes, yes, yes." The man waved his hand dismissively. "Chief Inspector Schwartz." He stared at Gunter and allowed the silence to build.

Gunter glanced at the Chief. He had an awkward grin fixed across his face. "This is Kriminaldirektor Keunsberg of the Gestapo. All city police now fall under the direct command of the Direktor, with immediate effect," the Chief explained, his voice tight with tension.

"Congratulations, Herr Direktor."

Keunsberg gave a curt nod of acknowledgement and a thin smile. "Thank you, Chief Inspector." He didn't offer Gunter a seat, although two chairs were placed in front of the desk. "You've got quite a track record?"

"Sir?" Gunter resolved not to be sucked into the man's crude effort to intimidate.

"Exemplary record in the Great War, served with distinction, awarded several medals for bravery on the front. Ended up a Leutnant, having worked your way through the ranks." Keunsberg tapped a file on the desk. "Equally impressive record as a detective. Tell me, Chief Inspector, are you a freemason?"

Gunter suppressed a smile at the attempt to throw him off balance. He glanced at the door. "If I were, I'm sure there'd be someone outside waiting to arrest me."

"Indeed." Keunsberg stood and held out his hand. "Welcome to the Gestapo." His grip was limp, like a delicate girl's. Having completed the greeting, he drifted towards the window and stared down at the street outside. "You're working on a case at the moment?"

"Unexplained death. Human remains found in the mountains. Probably happened twenty years ago."

Keunsberg turned on his heels and clasped his hands behind his back. "I thought you were a detective, Herr Schwartz, not an archaeologist. You might find yourself better deployed on more immediate priorities."

"Like what, sir?"

He pursed his lips and looked at the floor to consider the matter, before raising his head. "This is a new beginning, Chief Inspector, for Ostmark, the Reich and the Party. If we are to help our Fuhrer achieve his vision, we must focus our efforts on removing those that stand in the way of progress." He stared hard at Gunter. "Our enemies are all around us: bolsheviks, dissidents, liberals, freemasons, conscientious objectors, empty-headed students, deviants, hostile priests, gypsy scum and, of course, the Jews. These are criminals in the eyes of the state." He moved back behind what was now his desk and eased himself into the chair. "These will be your priorities for investigation and prosecution under my command. Do you understand, Chief Inspector?" There was no disguising the threat in his voice.

"Perfectly, Herr Direktor."

"Excellent. You will, of course, need to familiarise yourself with the new operating procedures that will emerge once the legal formalities and new Reich laws have been enacted."

"Forgive me, Herr Direktor, but are you ordering me to abandon my current case?"

Keunsberg gave a disparaging snigger. "I hardly think it amounts to a priority."

Gunter looked thoughtful. "Pardon me for asking, sir, but where do you call home?" Out of the corner of his eye he saw the Chief's jaw drop.

"Darmstadt."

"You live there with your wife?"

"My wife and three children."

"Aged?"

"Six, ten and fourteen."

"And, God forbid, if anything were to happen to your children – you'd expect the Darmstadt Gestapo to investigate?" Gunter coolly held Keunsberg's hostile look.

"The question's hypothetical and impertinent!"

"But relevant." Gunter glanced at the Chief, who looked as if he wanted the floor to open beneath him. "The victims are a baby and a young girl."

For a millisecond, Keunsberg's eyes betrayed him. He glanced towards the window and considered Gunter's words. "How close are you to an arrest?"

Gunter shrugged. "Couple of months maybe before I know whether I've a case that will stand up."

Keunsberg laughed. "My dear Chief Inspector, an advantage of being a Gestapo officer is you don't have to worry about any court. If you say someone is guilty, the only issue for the judge to decide is what punishment to mete out." He turned his gaze back towards Gunter. "You have my permission to complete your investigations." He waved his hand by way of dismissal.

"Thank you, sir." Gunter turned to leave.

"One more thing, Chief Inspector."

Gunter stopped.

"It would be good for your career if you join the Party."

"Of course, Herr Direktor."

Once outside, Gunter hurried towards his office, keen to start tracking down Gregor's file. He'd reached the stairs when the Chief caught up with him.

"Are you mad, Gunter?"

Gunter frowned. "I don't think so."

"Don't joke, Gunter. What were you thinking, taking the man on?" The Chief spoke in a strangled whisper that echoed around the empty staircase.

"I didn't take him on. I held my ground." He stared at the Chief and realised his boss wasn't just scared – he looked terrified. Sweat trickled down his temples, his hands trembled and a wild hunted look darted across his eyes.

"You need to be careful, Gunter. We've entered a different era. Such men are ruthless." He wiped his brow with the back of his sleeve. "You took a chance asking where he came from. And asking about his marital status!" The Chief shook his head as if he could scarcely believe what he'd witnessed.

"He had a wedding ring. I took a calculated risk."

"Well, my advice to you is don't take any more. Keep your head down and toe the line." The Chief turned to go. "And, for God's sake, learn how to salute properly."

FUN WHILE IT LASTS

"Franz, you can't say things like that, especially in a place like this," Katerina hissed.

"She's right," Trudy said. "There are informants everywhere."

Franz grinned and looked relaxed. "The Nazis don't control everything, you know."

"Bloody well seems like it," Katerina muttered.

He leant over the table and lowered his voice. "Ever heard of the Swingjugend?"

Katerina and Trudy exchanged bemused glances and shook their heads.

"Who or what are they?' Trudy asked.

"Counter culturists. They prefer to listen and dance to jazz music rather than the Nazi's awful German folk music and country jigs. The lads like to grow their hair long and copy English manners." He laughed. "They wear bowler hats and carry umbrellas. Sounds stupid, doesn't it. And it is. It's all harmless fun."

The girls looked intrigued. "What about the girls?"

"Oh, they wear what they like. Short dresses, lots of make-up and they literally let their hair down. None of this braids and pigtails nonsense." He immediately flushed in embarrassment. "Present company excepted."

Katerina hadn't taken offence. She only tied her hair in braids to fit in. Her eyes lit up. She liked the sound of the free-spirited Swingjugend. "Surely the authorities don't approve. Why don't they take action?"

Franz shrugged. "Because they keep themselves to themselves. They meet in private, out of the way dance-halls. They're not really political although they call the Hitler Youth the Homo Youth, and they are similarly rude about the BDM." He picked up his glass of wine and swirled the contents around before finishing it off. "I love going. It reminds me of my younger days." He nudged Trudy. "The days when I was Yankee Franz and you were our star pickpocket."

"Well, we're older, wiser and more careful. Remember last time when you got on the wrong side of the Nazis."

Franz mimicked an American accent. "You've got to live for the moment, babe."

"I'll go if you'll go." Katerina looked beseechingly at Trudy.

"Katerina, you've just started a new job. You don't want to put that at risk. I can't afford to be mixing with the wrong sort of people either." She glanced at Franz. "And you can't afford to be blasé."

"I work for an American company." He threw open his hands. "Ready-made excuse. I'm absorbing the culture of my employer." He smirked before adding, "And showing two dear friends exactly what degenerate culture and behaviour looks like." He waved the waiter over. "Come on, let's go and have some fun!"

"What, now?" the two girls said in unison.

Fifteen minutes later, the taxi dropped them at the end of a dimly lit street. Franz led them through a maze of back alleyways until they stood beside an innocuous-looking door to what looked like a large warehouse. Franz knocked a third time and the door opened. Trudy thought her heart would stop. A burly man in SS uniform glared at them. Franz looked unfazed. "Three of us, two guests," he murmured, and handed over some cash.

The man pocketed the money. "Some good bands tonight."

Franz patted the man on the shoulder as they passed. "Nice uniform. It suits you."

They walked along a maze of corridors before passing through a heavily padded door. The scene that greeted them looked like a movie set. Hundreds of people sat at tables, stood in groups or jived with furious abandon on the massive central dance-floor of an enormous hall. The noise was deafening. Everyone laughed, chatted, or shouted to be heard over the sound of a seven-piece band who were belting out a jazz number that, judging from the number of dancers, was particularly popular. The whole arena was lit by soft red lighting, diffused by the fug from hundreds of cigarettes, pipes and cigars.

Both girls felt instantly out of place. No-one dressed like them. The young women seemed scandalously attired. Their dresses were cut just below the knee, and among the more expert dancers a considerable amount of stockinged legs and thighs were exposed as they were thrown about by their partners. Every girl's hair was let down in thick, curled tresses that reached over shoulders and down backs in the style of American movie stars. Fingernails were painted, brows and eyes lined, and lips glossed.

The young men were similarly outlandish. A few sported the short back and sides favoured by convention, but most had thick locks quaffed and sculpted like their American idols. They wore loose baggy trousers, checked English style sports jackets, and shoes with thick crepe soles.

Everywhere there was the sound of fun. How different, Trudy thought, from the brutal, regimented, soulless atmosphere of the BDM meetings, or the stone-faced, arrogant thuggery of the Hitler Youth. Katerina was already swaying and tapping her toes to the infectious rhythm of the band. Franz led them to a table and disappeared for a moment, before reappearing with a bottle of wine in an ice-bucket and three glasses. "We ought to celebrate," he shouted over the racket. He filled their glasses, then raised his. "To us! May we have every success in our new careers and all the happiness we could wish for."

"To us!" Katerina was already in her element.

Franz's enthusiasm was infectious. He held out his hands to them both. "Come on, let's dance."

145

At two in the morning, they climbed the stairs to Katerina's small flat, exhausted after an evening of dancing, singing and drinking. For Trudy and Katerina, a joyous sense of rebellious freedom still lingered, along with the effects of one too many glasses of wine. Katerina gave a twirl as if reluctant to let the night end. "I haven't had so much fun in years," she gushed, before taking Franz's hand and leading him on an impromptu dance around the table. She stopped mid orbit, clasped her hands behind his neck and stared directly into his face with the seriousness of someone on the cusp of inebriation. "You'll take us again?"

"Of course. It will be my pleasure."

"I hoped you'd say that," Katerina said, before planting a clumsy wet kiss on his lips. Franz looked startled. For a second, Katerina appeared half shocked by her spontaneity. She broke off her contact and grabbed the kettle as if to hide her embarrassment. "Anyone fancy a coffee?"

Trudy pretended not to have noticed the encounter. "Not for me, I'm away to my bed."

Franz was still recovering from shock. "Er, no, um, I ought to head home as well."

"You don't have to go. You could sleep on the couch," Katerina said with apparent nonchalance. She had her back turned towards Franz, and Trudy recognised the unspoken hope that Franz might take up the offer.

"No, it's tempting. But I should head home," Franz said. "I'm already looking forward to taking you again – maybe next week?"

"We'll look forward to it," Trudy said. She gave Franz a warm embrace and friendly kiss on the cheek.

"I'll show you out," Katerina said.

MORAL DUTIES

Father Thomas burst into the room. "Your Reverence, a Gestapo officer is demanding to see you," he said breathlessly.

Thomas's drawn expression stopped Wagner from giving his assistant a bawling out for entering without knocking. "What sort of Gestapo officer?"

"Kriminidirektor Keunsberg. He's the new Head of Security."

"What does he want?"

"He didn't say. He said you will see him." Thomas swallowed. "I said he needed an appointment. He just laughed."

"You'd better show him in."

Two minutes later, Keunsberg entered. "Heil Hitler, Monsignor Wagner." He handed his hat, coat and gloves to Thomas with a dismissive, "you may go."

Wagner had composed himself ahead of his visitor's entrance. He looked up from his desk, pen still poised in his hand as if being disturbed from some urgent work. He examined his guest with a mild expression. "Bless you, Herr Direktor. What can I do for you?"

Keunsberg was aggressive from the outset. "I'm here to ensure that you and your Church fall into line. You've written a lot, Monsignor."

"It's part of my job."

"You incite dissent."

"I encourage people to follow the teachings of the Pontiff."

"Distributing material that attacks National Socialism."

"Such as?" Despite the calmness of his reply, Wagner already felt on the back foot.

"You issued an edict for the *Mit brenneder Sorge* to be preached from every pulpit across this Diocese. That document represented a direct attack on the principles of National Socialism." Keunsberg extracted a silver cigarette holder from his pocket.

"The edict is a Vatican encyclical, and the instruction to distribute it came directly from the Holy Father." Wagner struggled to keep his voice level. "If you had a direct order from the Fuhrer, could you ignore it?"

A flash of anger crossed Keunsberg's face. He extracted a cigarette and tapped it on the holder before lighting it. He took a long drag and slowly exhaled, closing his eyes as the nicotine hit took effect. "Don't underestimate us, Monsignor Wagner."

A sudden wave of fear washed through Wagner. Taking on the Gestapo wasn't a sensible move. He coughed and picked up the wine decanter to give him time to recover. "Herr Keunsberg, we are in danger of getting off on the wrong foot." He raised the decanter and gave the man opposite an enquiring look. Keunsberg noticed the slight quiver of the priest's hand and gave a thin smile and an almost imperceptible nod.

147

Wagner continued as he poured two generous measures. "We are often required to do things we might question. It's the obligation we carry for serving organisations and masters that have infinite power over us." He raised his glass. Keunsberg ignored the toast. He leant back, took a leisurely drag on his cigarette and studied with dead eyes the man opposite.

Wagner found the scrutiny unsettling. His throat constricted and his mouth went dry. "Personally, I've always thought that Catholicism and National Socialism have more in common than not." The Gestapo officer remained unresponsive. Wagner felt compelled to keep talking. "There are, of course, protocols that govern relations between the Church and the State to ensure proper separation of interests. I strive to ensure full compliance."

"Your writing says otherwise," Keunsberg said coldly.

A trickle of sweat ran down Wagner's temple. He inwardly cursed his fear of the man. It felt as if some poisonous reptile had slithered into his office. "You may be misinformed, Herr Direktor. For example, you will find me consistent on the threat of Bolshevism, and an abhorrence of deviants, especially homosexuals. I've written extensively in support of fascism. And don't expect a Catholic to have much sympathy for the Jews." His attempt at humour fell flat.

"You supported Dollfuss."

"Who was a fascist. He just didn't recognise the will of the people for unification with Germany." Wagner spread his hands to illustrate his helplessness. "State censorship prevented the Church, and me in particular, from expressing our true beliefs."

Once again Keunsberg fell silent. Wagner knew he was being toyed with and felt helpless. He decided to change tack. He leaned forward, glanced towards the door and lowered his voice. "Herr Keunsberg, you said your visit is to ensure proper alignment between the Church and the Reich. You only have to set out the parameters, and I'll ensure this Diocese will comply."

"I demand more than that!" Keunsberg's eyes bore into Wagner's. "My responsibility to the Fuhrer is to eliminate all enemies of the state. That is my priority. And at the moment I'm in two minds about your own status."

Wagner felt sick. Sweat covered his face. He dug out a handkerchief and mopped his brow. "You should have no doubts on that score. As I said, there is much we hold in common. And I'm more than ready to do my duty."

Keunsberg seemed pleased. He took another long drag on his cigarette and finding no ashtray, casually tapped the ash on the table. "Convince me."

Wagner suppressed his panic and thought quickly. He gestured towards the surrounding bookshelves. "Herr Direktor, the Gestapo may be masters of interrogation. We Catholics don't have to try. We have the confessional. There is very little we don't know about." He eyed Keunsberg. "I could save you a lot of time and expense."

"And save your skin in the process."

"I'm a pragmatist, Herr Direktor."

Keunsberg smiled. "I'm not after titbits. I want the full meal - leaders, leutnants, activists, financiers, and I want their wives, children, friends and supporters. I want this city picked clean of anyone who acts against any aspect of National Socialism."

Wagner felt a wave of relief. He was off the hook. Time to demonstrate eagerness and commitment. "Perhaps we might start with the Bolsheviks?"

JUNE 1938 – DOPPELGAU - OSTMARK

"What will you do?" Susan sank down into the chair.

Opposite her, Hannah Rubenstein sat with her head in her hands. "We have to leave."

"And go where?"

Hannah angrily shook her head. "I don't know. Switzerland - probably. Rudi thinks we should head for England or America."

"You can't just leave. What about the practice?"

"Susan, you don't understand. We won't have a choice. The anti-Jewish laws will apply in Austria. Sooner or later we'll be kicked out." She wiped the tears from her eyes.

"But that's just madness. Almost every family in Achbrugge, Gau and Doppelgau has benefited from this surgery at one time or another. Your family has served the community for years."

"People are fickle, Susan. Look how quickly the Nazi flags appeared in the village, and in Achbrugge a couple of nights ago Juden raus was painted on the front door of our house and surgery. Already we count for nothing." Hannah looked distraught. "Susan, we know what to expect. Our family went through it in Germany. Everyone will be encouraged to hate the Jews: the way we dress, talk, our religion, the fact we're blamed for making money." She wrapped her head up in her arms and squeezed her eyes shut. "Why do they despise us?"

"They can't shut the surgeries. That would be idiotic. Where are the doctors going to come from?"

Hannah grabbed her friend's hands. "Susan, hatred provides an excuse for everything. We'll be banned from being teachers, doctors - in fact, every profession. We won't be allowed to own vehicles, bicycles or travel on public transport. Our children will be thrown out of schools."

"What about Simon?"

"He'll be kicked out of university in Wien. His professor has already warned him, and he should know. He's a Jew as well."

Susan squeezed Hannah's hand. "We'll help. I'm not sure what we can do, but we're not abandoning our friends."

Hannah's eyes filled with tears. "Susan, you have to look after your family. People will turn against you and anyone else associated with us."

Susan looked indignant. "I'd like to see them try. I'll soon give them a piece of my mind."

"You can't afford to take the risk. We'll be forced to break our friendship."

"Only friends can break friendships."

"The Nazis can too. They break families, separate husbands from wives, children from their mothers. I know what I'm talking about, Susan. It happened in Germany. That's why Sara was sent to Switzerland."

Susan looked appalled. "So, what will you do?"

"Grandpa has called a meeting of all the family while we can still travel. He thinks we have a bit of time to make plans. It will take the Nazis a few months to get established and pass their poisonous laws."

"Maybe they'll make life difficult for you in the meantime."

Hannah gave a bitter laugh. "That's certain. Mind you, if we decide to leave they'll fall over themselves to get us out."

CAUGHT IN THE WEB

The atmosphere inside the cathedral felt like a cocktail party rather than a place of worship. Every member of Brandt society was present. Heavily made-up women, drenched in expensive perfume, eyed each other and assessed their position and that of their husbands in the social pecking order. The majority of men sported Wehrmacht, SS and Gestapo uniforms. At the centre of proceedings, surrounded by acolytes, stood the Reichgau Gauleiter deep in conversation with the Bishop and the city's business leaders.

Wagner realised, in exchanging meaningless pleasantries with some minor dignitaries and a dreadful woman from the city art museum, he'd become distanced from the power group. He quickly extracted himself and made his way towards the Bishop, only to be intercepted by Keunsberg. "Ah, Wagner. A few words." The priest found himself being steered to a secluded space behind one of the stone pillars. "Did you enjoy the concert?" Keunsberg's tone suggested he didn't care whether Wagner did or didn't. He grabbed a couple of glasses of wine from a passing waiter and forced one on Wagner.

"I did. *The Messiah* is a particular favourite of mine."

The Gestapo chief scanned the crowd and talked from the side of his mouth. "I want to congratulate you."

Immediately Wagner felt himself break out in a cold sweat. Keunsberg oozed menace. Nothing was ever straightforward. He wondered whether the man was capable of holding a normal conversation. "I'm sorry to say I had little to do with the organisation of the concert."

Keunsberg laughed. "I'm talking about your little lists."

"Oh, yes… well, I did say we have common interests." Wagner nervously glanced around and lowered his voice. "I assume the Bolsheviks were arrested?"

Keunsberg took a sip of his wine and raised his glass. "Thanks to you we bagged the lot. Your boss will be pleased." He nodded toward the Bishop.

Wagner felt ice run through his blood. The last thing he wanted was any association with the betrayals. "I'm not looking for credit."

Keunsberg chuckled. "You're too modest."

"What will happen to them?"

"You mean what *has* happened to them?" He took another sip of wine and casually swung his body around to scan the nearby guests. "Justice is what's happened, Herr Wagner. We hung the one-armed chap and other ringleaders, of course. Packed the wives, families and the rest to various camps."

"Women and children?" Wagner couldn't keep the shock from his voice.

"Of course. We need to be ruthless." He gave Wagner an amused look. "Don't worry. You just provide the names; we'll take care of the rest. Which brings me to the matter in hand." He leaned his head closer to the priest. "The Jews."

"Surely you don't need my help with them?"

"That's our arrangement."

"You must know the names and whereabouts of such people."

Keunsberg grimaced. "I'm sure we do, or at least most of them. But as I told you, Herr Wagner, I want this region sterilised." He drained his glass and gave a cold, hard stare. "I want a list. You have two weeks."

"Bastard!" Wagner muttered under his breath as the Gestapo officer made his way towards the Gauleiter. His mood turned even blacker as he noticed Father Haphold, and a man who he presumed was the maestro organist, in conversation with the Bishop and a group of the city's prominent citizens. Judging from the laughter and body language, a close rapport had developed. Haphold's wings needed clipping. He craned his neck, trying to spot Father Thomas. He'd had more than enough time to dig some dirt.

Father Thomas was already looking at him when Wagner beckoned. He immediately broke off his conversation and hurried across in a limping lurch.

"Your Reverence?"

"What progress on Father Haphold?" Wagner jerked his head towards the group gathered around the Bishop.

"There isn't much to report. He's an exemplary parish priest, popular with his parishioners and with the Bishop, as you can see. He's well thought of across the Diocese."

"For what, in particular."

Thomas shrugged. "He's an ideas man but also a good organiser. This event is a good example. The Bishop appreciates his reliability."

Wagner grunted. That wasn't what he wanted to hear. "How reliable?"

"He's regarded as a safe pair of hands. He's being considered for promotion."

"All the more reason to be thorough in your investigation. If there is the slightest hint of any flaws, we should uncover it now." Wagner gave the priest a sharp look. "Has anyone ever made a complaint against him?"

Thomas shook his head.

Wagner patted him on the shoulder. "Keep digging."

ADRENALIN

Sara shrieked as Johan threw the bike over and accelerated. "Lean into the corners," he shouted over the noise of the engine and the wind whistling around their ears. He felt her arms tighten around his chest as they approached another bend.

She leant forward and screamed in his ear, "Go faster!" Johan twisted the throttle and the bike built up speed. Sara laughed in pure enjoyment. The high pass road was almost empty of traffic, and a series of bends threw them left, right, back left again. Sara whooped as a downhill straight enabled Johan to fully open the bike up. "How fast are we going?" she yelled.

"One hundred and thirty," he shouted back. He pulled over once they reached the summit.

Sara threw her arms around his neck as soon as he'd hauled the bike back on its stand. "That was so much fun." Her eyes were full of joy. Her kiss was deep and passionate. "I feel so alive," she breathed.

"We've got the home run to come," Johan said.

"Yeah." She continued to hold him, her eyes darting around his face as if wanting to take in every last detail. They kissed again. Johan felt his head buzz from the exhilaration of the bike ride and the surging passion he felt for her. If this was love, he couldn't get enough of it.

"I love you," she said softly, as they broke off from their kiss and stood holding each other with their foreheads touching.

"I love you too." He pulled her close, revelling in their shared intimacy. Around them, the mountain peaks stretched in every direction – majestic and craggy, crowned with brilliant white snow against a clear summer sky above, and lush green meadows at their feet. And there was the absolute silence of a still alpine afternoon. It provided the perfect backdrop for them to share their feelings. For a few moments they were in a world of their own.

"I'm hungry," she said, as they reluctantly disengaged.

"Yeah. I suppose we'd better eat."

But they didn't. Another kiss wasn't enough either.

Sara giggled. "We should eat."

"Of course," he muttered, as once again their lips met.

"Johan," she said, trying to look serious and holding him at bay at the same time. "We really ought to have our picnic."

"Oh." He stared into the sky as if weighing the idea. "Okay." He untied the knapsack from the tank of the bike. He held out his hand for her.

"Where are we going?"

"There's a stream. It's the perfect place. Come on."

They sat on a grassy bank with their feet dangling in refreshing ice-cold water, and unpacked the bag. Apart from the soothing trickle of the stream there wasn't a sound. They ate and allowed the silence to swallow them. The sun beat down and the temperature rose. Johan took off his shirt, spread it over the grass and lay back with his hands behind his head. Sara lay beside him and rested her head on his chest.

"This is heaven," she murmured.

He stroked the side of her face. Throughout the day there'd been so much to preoccupy them: the anticipation as they made the picnic, the thrill of the motorcycle journey, the exquisite joy of openly revealing their feelings for one another, the frisson of their physical contact. Neither wanted to risk spoiling it all by broaching the subject they both dreaded. Both knew it couldn't be avoided. Johan took the plunge. "Do you want to talk about it?"

"No." She stayed silent for a bit. "But I suppose we have to."

"Not if it upsets you."

"It upsets us all. Simon's parents were distraught."

"Simon wasn't there, was he?"

She shook her head. "He knows he'll be kicked out of university."

"So, what was decided?"

"We leave."

Johan stopped his gentle massage of her neck.

She sensed his anxiety. "It doesn't make any difference to you and me. At least over the short term." She rolled over and rested her chin on his chest. "You'll be here and I'll be in Switzerland."

"The plan is to move to Switzerland?"

He felt her nod. He frowned. "Once you're out they won't let you back, will they?"

"Not a chance."

"So, you won't be coming back." He felt part of his life-force drain out of him.

She shook her head. "I'm hoping that a certain gorgeous man, riding a motorcycle, will appear in the middle of the night and steal me from my bed." Johan gave a sad half-smile. Sara suddenly looked sombre. "You will come for me, won't you?"

He ran his hand over her back. "I'd come for you even if you moved to New York." She glided her fingers over his arm, kissed his stomach and giggled. They fell silent.

"Maybe there'll be a change of government."

"Johan, you're clutching at straws. It's going to happen. The Nazis are here to stay."

Again they fell silent as if reluctant to continue.

"When will you go?"

"Not straight away. The first thing they'll order us to do is declare our wealth. Money in the bank, the properties we own, the furniture, any jewellery, gold, silver, anything of value, even the clothes on our back."

"What for?"

"So they know exactly how much to steal from us."

"How much do they take?"

"At least half – usually a lot more because they know we can't do anything about it. Then they'll force us to exchange our money into Swiss currency at an exorbitant rate, leaving us with a pittance."

"They rob you twice?"

"There's no way around it. Although Grandpa said he's taken steps to protect as much as he can."

"By doing what?"

"He didn't say. It's best we don't know, apparently." She suddenly levered herself up until she was lying half on top of him, her face level with his. "It won't happen quickly – so let's enjoy the time we've got." She leant forward and brushed his lips with hers.

Instantly, they became lost in each other. Their kisses grew deeper and more intense, their embrace closer and more intimate; passion overtook reason as they rolled and tumbled in the grass, their limbs entwined, their bodies crushed together. Their breathing came in gasps, and they lost track of time as their excitement soared with each hesitant exploration. Both desperately held at bay unbearable temptation.

"We can't," Sara said, almost crying with desire and frustration. "We just can't."

"I know." He closed his eyes and gritted his teeth. "God, this is so difficult." He opened his eyes and tried to take her all in. She looked wild, dishevelled and painfully desirable. She pushed herself back and sat across him with her hands on his chest. She swept the hair from her face to reveal a broad, happy smile. "One day we'll not have to stop."

He stared impishly at her. "How about next Sunday?"

She laughed, leant back, did up her buttons and tucked her blouse into her shorts. "Do you know what time it is?"

Johan glanced at his watch "Oh my God! The cows will be crossing their legs."

Their journey back was a high-speed adrenalin rush. Downhill, the bike was capable of one hundred and fifty. But the thrill for them both arose from the memory of the day's intimacies and the anticipation of where their relationship might go next.

THE NEW REICH

Nazification arrived in Doppelgau with the arrest of Martin Drössel. His crime for being a member of the Christian Democrats earned him a six-month sentence. He considered himself fortunate that he served time in Brandt prison rather than a concentration camp. Peter Ansbacher was next. He was accused of questioning the Fuhrer's wisdom in annexing the Sudetenland. His detention shocked the village but, apart from Sep, Father Haphold and Stephan Wachter, no one spoke in his defence. Their intervention enabled the village elder to be conditionally released.

The Hagspiels made no secret that they were behind the denouncements. Emboldened by his Hitler Youth uniform, Hans Hagspiel paraded around the village cajoling the young men to follow his example. Not that they or their parents needed much persuading. It wasn't long before the Breitners and Wachters were targeted.

"When are you joining, Breitner?" Hans Hagspiel leant over the wall that surrounded the Wachter's yard.

Johan didn't bother to turn around. "Join what?"

"The SS, of course."

"I won't be joining the SS." He passed a spanner to Jurgen who was helping him reassemble his motorbike after a puncture.

"You wouldn't get in anyway. They only accept true Germans."

Neither Johan nor Jurgen responded or even bothered to acknowledge Hans's presence, or that of the two other village lads standing alongside him, decked out in Hitler Youth uniforms.

"Everyone is joining. You two are setting a bad example. But then again, your families always did mix with degenerates."

Jurgen glanced at Johan through the spokes and gave an almost imperceptible shake of his head as he saw his friend tense.

"You still seeing that whore?"

Jurgen stood up quickly before Johan reacted. "I didn't realise your mother was back working the streets, Haggers."

The two Hitler Youth lads couldn't stop themselves from sniggering. Hans's face turned crimson. "I'm talking about that Jewish slag."

Jurgen's fist crashed into Hans's face, sending him sprawling across the road. For a second, Johan thought Jurgen had killed him. Hans lay still, blood pouring from his nose. Jurgen rubbed his fist and glared at the two youths. Hans slowly came round. He rolled over and managed to lever himself on to all fours. He remained still, gasping from shock and occasionally spitting blood on the gravel road. His two friends wanted no further part in the proceedings. They wandered off, casting nervous glances behind them.

Jurgen acted as if nothing had happened. He finished tightening the wheel nut and then stood back. "You should give it a spin. We might have to adjust the chain tension." Johan kick-started the engine, swung his leg over the saddle and roared off down the road. He returned two minutes later, by which time Hans had struggled to his feet.

Jurgen then appeared to notice him. "You still here, Haggers?" He went up to him and grabbed him roughly by the chin, deliberately letting his fingers dig into his adversary's cheeks. He pushed Hans's face left and right and closely examined his nose. "Looks broken, Haggers. I'd get that fixed if I were you. Doctor Rubenstein's surgery's just down the road."

Hans was too dazed to react. He turned and, without a word, staggered off towards the village. The two friends watched him for a few seconds.

"Thanks, mate." Johan patted his friend on the shoulder. "You shouldn't have done that. It might lead to trouble."

Jurgen shrugged. "Let's face it. If I hadn't done it, you would have." He glanced sideways at Johan and winked.

That night the words Juden raus were again painted across the door of Rudi and Hannah's surgery. Johan noticed it as he rode past on his way to Achbrugge. The paint was still wet. He sped back home and grabbed a cloth and a can of paraffin.

The following week, a group of Hitler Youth from Achbrugge stood outside the surgery making notes of every visitor. Only Susan Breitner was brave enough to ignore the intimidation and enter.

Despite the lack of patients, both Rubenstein surgeries remained open until October. Then the guillotine fell. Jewish doctors were confined to providing medical services to their fellow Jews and, even then, it was only allowed to be nursing care that was given.

DEAL WITH THE DEVIL

"You know - I think we've developed an excellent working relationship." Keunsberg gazed out the window at the street below. "The information you provided has proved useful. It's all very efficient." He turned around. "I'm pleased, Herr Wagner."

"Cooperation is always the best way."

Keunsberg sighed. "If only that were the case. The Jews, for example, are not what I'd call the most cooperative race."

"Forgive me, Herr Direktor, but I thought they were falling over themselves to leave."

"Not fast enough." He flicked his hand in irritation. "A Jew is like a rotten apple that refuses to fall from the tree. It hangs around looking more and more unsightly. We may need to get our friends in the SS to shake the tree a bit." Keunsberg paused to light a cigarette and took a long first drag. "But enough of my problems. Given your efforts, it's remiss of me not to offer to reciprocate?"

Wagner felt a flush of pleasure wash through him. He felt he'd finally reached something like a level playing field with the Direktor. "You are too kind. But I'm only doing my duty on behalf of the Church and the Reich."

Keunsberg laughed. "Oh come, come, Herr Wagner. You're an ambitious man. I can't believe you achieved your current position simply by playing the loyal servant. The world doesn't work like that. Something tells me beneath that benign exterior lies a ruthless man."

Wagner pursed his lips and looked thoughtful. "It's crossed my mind that we might achieve more by deepening our arrangement."

Keunsberg leant on the windowsill with his left arm folded across his stomach and his cigarette suspended in his right hand. "Go on."

"There's a priest who concerns me. His views represent a potential threat."

The Direktor smirked "To you?"

Wagner kept his face neutral. "To us." He paused as if searching for the right words. "His views are radical, liberal and unconventional. I'm concerned about what he's been preaching." His eyes flicked towards the Gestapo man. "He's the type of person that should be watched."

"His name?"

"Father Haphold. He's the parish priest for Doppelgau."

"Leave it with me." Keunsberg took another drag of his cigarette before stubbing it out in the ashtray. "Always a pleasure." He turned towards the door and put on his cap. "Heil Hitler, Monsignor Wagner."

Wagner struggled to his feet and gave a smart Nazi salute.

Keunsberg grinned. "You're learning."

PURGE OF THE UNDESIRABLES

The arrest of Father Haphold and Herman Paulus shattered any lingering doubts that might have existed in Doppelgau about Nazi malevolence. No one knew what the charges were, but the Hagspiels were quick to feed the rumour machine. Father Haphold had been arrested for expressing anti-German sentiment, they declared. While Herman's playing of banned American music sealed his fate. The fiction came supported by manufactured evidence. Surely everyone could remember Father Haphold's sermon in which he said all men were created equal in the sight of God. That was patently absurd. Jews and black people were obviously inferior, and the Slavs and Gypsies were clearly Untermensch. As for Herman, one only had to pass his house to hear him playing jazz and other degenerate music. And who could forget the playing of boogie-woogie at the New Year's celebration?

"It's an outrage." Susan paced up and down the kitchen, unable to contain her rage. "Something must be done." She glanced across at Sep. "Can't we ask Gunter to intervene."

Sep massaged his brow. "Gunter heads the serious crime division. The charges against them are unlikely to fall within his jurisdiction, but it's worth a try."

"It's getting ridiculous," Johan said. "Last week, one market trader was denounced by his neighbour for reading a banned leaflet."

"You need to be careful, Johan." His mother looked concerned. "Your friendship with Sara is bound to attract attention."

"It already has, Ma."

Susan stopped pacing and joined the rest of her family at the kitchen table. She looked at them in turn. "I don't care what the people in this village think; we will not abandon the Rubensteins."

"Of course not." Harriet was appalled that her mother should even say such a thing.

Sep reinforced the sentiment. "They've been good friends to our family for generations."

"When are they leaving?" Harriet asked.

"Tuesday," Johan said sadly. "Sara said they are just waiting for Simon to arrive from Vienna on Monday, then they'll head for Switzerland."

Harriet took her brother's hand and said sympathetically, "She'll not be far away."

"We must be able to do something." Susan clenched her fists in frustration.

"Like what?" Johan said.

"Someone should be at the station to meet Simon. I'm sure he'd appreciate a friendly face. The Rubensteins have got enough on their plate."

160

"And they can't travel without a permit," Sep said.

"I'll go," Harriet said.

Susan suddenly got up as another bout of anger consumed her. "They're leaving with nothing. Hannah told me the bloody Nazis are stealing everything they've got."

"Ma!" Harriet was shocked. She'd never heard her mother swear in her whole life.

Susan looked flustered. "Yes, sorry. It's just I'm so angry." She sank back down on her seat and ran her hand through her hair. "We still need to talk to Gunter about Father Haphold and Herman."

"I can ask him when I meet Simon," Harriet said. "I'll phone him from the Post Office and invite him for coffee in Brandt. I'm sure he'll meet me if he's not tied up with police business."

"How's your investigation progressing, Chief Inspector?"

Gunter looked up in surprise. It was rare for the Kommissioner to enter the office, let alone take any interest in the tedious details of criminal investigations.

"I need one more piece of the jigsaw to fall into place."

"That piece being what – a confession, a statement?"

"A file."

"A file?" Keunsberg looked astonished. "Has the suspect been foolish enough to leave written notes of his crime?"

"No. But everyone leaves a trail: when and where they've been, who they saw, what was discussed and what they did." Gunter eyed Keunsberg. "Crimes have a habit of catching up with the perpetrators – no matter how hard they try to cover their tracks."

"And you're confident of finding this file?"

Gunter pinched the bridge of his nose between his forefinger and thumb. "If I can get hold of it, I'll have the suspect nailed." Gunter noted Keunsberg's eyes were beginning to glaze over.

"You don't have much time." Keunsberg was already half out the door.

Gunter leaned back in his chair and stared at the ceiling.

"You alright, sir?" his colleague asked.

"Eh? Yes. Just a headache. I need some fresh air." He glanced at his watch. "Can you hold the fort. I'm meeting a friend for coffee." Gunter grabbed his hat and coat. He needed to get out. It wasn't just Keunsberg. The atmosphere within the police station had changed dramatically once the Gestapo imposed their regime and methods. Some good officers were sacked – for reasons that were never made clear. As far as Gunter was concerned, their replacements were low-grade, inexperienced and lazy. But that wasn't the only issue. Brutality and an unquestioning approach to rules and authority had become the norm. Dealing with political enemies was now more important than investigating serious criminality. Cases were forwarded for prosecution on the flimsiest of evidence, and confessions extracted through beatings and torture. There were times when he felt like throwing in the towel. The problem was that the only life he knew was police work. Perhaps he ought to become a farmer, like Sep Breitner, and marry Marie.

The thought came out of the blue and caused him to stop dead in his tracks. Why had he been so blind? The sharp blast of a bus horn forced him to leap to one side to avoid being mown down. He shook his head in disbelief. Why had he not considered the idea before? Then again he was tired, irritated and not thinking straight. He needed to slow down. He ought to have learned his lesson when it came to the opposite sex. He was too impetuous. Marie was attractive, good fun and not the sort of person he'd want to lose as a friend by being rash.

The notion preoccupied him as he entered the Krone and sat at a table overlooking the square to await Harriet. He remained seated as a demure, attractive-looking young lady, in a long dark green Loden coat, made her way up the steps of the Gasthaus and stood waiting patiently. Gunter's thoughts still revolved around Marie as he casually observed the young woman. She seemed anxious, as if she expected someone who was obviously late. With a start, Gunter suddenly realised who the guilty party was. He rushed outside.

"Harriet, I do apologise. I was occupied in a world of my own and... well." He stood back and looked Harriet up and down. "Frankly, my dear, I hardly recognised you. You look so pretty and grown-up."

"And you are such a charmer." She smiled before giving him an affectionate kiss on the cheek.

"I've a table by the window. I hope you are hungry. I know I am." In an instant, Gunter's world became a much happier place. They spent the next hour mostly in relaxed conversation. Harriet's revelation of the arrest of Father Haphold and Hermann Paulus cast the first shadow.

"If the SS arrested them they're probably being held at their facilities." Gunter's brow furrowed as he considered what enquiries he could make. "I can find out what charges they face. But as for intervening?" He gave a weak smile and left the question hanging. "It can't be serious, otherwise it would be transferred to us. I'll do my best, I promise." He reached over and squeezed her hand. "Now tell me who it is you're really meeting. You mentioned on the phone someone arriving from Vienna."

Harriet hesitated. "It's Simon."

"Oh!" Gunter looked delighted, then immediately his face fell as he realised the significance. The second shadow descended. "That is most unfortunate."

"It's not unfortunate, Herr Schwartz, it's disgraceful."

Gunter leaned forward and lowered his voice to a whisper. "Shh, Fraulein Harriet. You mustn't show your feelings on such matters, especially in a place like this."

Harriet looked around nervously. "I'm sorry. I wasn't thinking."

"When are they planning to leave?"

"Tomorrow."

Gunter covered his mouth with his napkin and lowered his voice even more. "If you ask me, they're better off out of this country. Things will only get worse."

"For them or us?"

"For all of us, I suspect. People may feel wealthy and happy to be German at the moment, but everyone is paying a price. The trouble is most people can't see beyond the good times." He glanced across the table at her. "We should change the subject, Harriet."

Harriet nodded and smiled, and Gunter thought how lucky Simon was to have such an attractive girl waiting to greet him. That in turn

163

triggered thoughts of his own love interest. "Tell me, how is everyone in Doppelgau? How's your family?"

"They're all well. And everyone sends you their love."

"Ah, that's nice. And Frau Haufmann?"

Harriet's antennae instantly activated. "Tante Marie is very well." She took a sip of her coffee and followed up with, "I'm sure she's looking forward to your next visit." She carefully observed his reaction. She felt pleased with what she saw.

Gunter felt his spirits lifting. "And what time do you need to be at the station?"

Harriet glanced at her watch. "The train is due in thirty minutes – if it's on time."

"You'll have a lot to catch up on. He's been away, what, three months?"

"Nearer four." She laughed. "No doubt we'll talk all the way home on the Postbus."

"You're taking the bus instead of the train?"

She nodded. "It's quicker now they've improved the roads through Brandtnerwald."

Ten minutes later Gunter watched her cross the square. Halfway over she turned and waved. She looked happy, almost radiant. Gunter sighed. If only he could rediscover the elixir of youth and find his own happiness. He walked slowly back to the station. His heart fell as soon as he grew near. Parked outside were four military trucks surrounded by a dozen SS troops. An officer emerged from the station holding some papers, and shouted an order. Immediately the troops scrambled into the back of the lorries. It was apparent from their banter they were in high spirits. The engines started and in a few seconds the trucks were gone.

He made his way back to his office and tried to get his mind back on his investigation but found he couldn't focus. His thoughts flitted from how he might find an excuse to visit Doppelgau and see Marie, to how he would go about finding out the whereabouts of Father Haphold and Herman, and what the next steps ought to be in his investigation of the death of Freya Thuller. Despite not really wanting one, he made himself and his colleague a coffee.

"Thanks, sir," his colleague said, as he handed him the cup. "The desk sergeant is looking for you."

"Did he say what for?"

His colleague shook his head. "He said he'd like a word as soon as you were back."

"Sounds ominous." Gunter decided to drink his coffee and try to get his thoughts in order. Eventually, he sauntered to reception. To his surprise, the desk sergeant didn't say anything as he approached. Instead he picked up the incident ledger, and flipped a couple of pages back to what looked like an order schedule that had been clipped in. He turned the ledger around so Gunter could read it. Gunter frowned and studied the papers. His face fell and he felt sick. He flicked his eyes towards the Sergeant who regarded him impassively. Gunter gave a curt nod and walked out. Once out of sight of the station he ran. The platform was empty by the time he reached it. He checked the waiting room. There was no sign of Harriet. He sped back down the platform, collaring a porter on the way. "The Wien train," he gasped. "Has it arrived?"

"Been and gone, sir." He glanced at the station clock. "Left over thirty-five minutes ago."

Gunter cursed out loud. It would have been good if the train had been late. He half-ran towards the bus station, struggling for breath all the way. There was a queue at the ticket office. Brandishing his warrant card, he barged his way to the front, roughly pushing to one side an elderly lady who was halfway through a detailed debate over which ticket she needed.

"The Postbus to Doppelgau – has it left?"

The official examined Gunter's warrant card through the glass.

"Come on, man, has the bus left?" Gunter snarled.

"Left over twenty minutes ago."

"Did a young couple get on board. Young woman about seventeen or eighteen, attractive. She'd have been with a young man, slightly taller and older."

"Wearing a long green coat?"

Gunter nodded.

"Yes, I saw them. Had a suitcase. Are they in trouble?"

Gunter had already disappeared. He ran back to the police station car park and leapt on his motorbike. Ten minutes later he sped out of Brandt and along the steep road that led to the Brandtnerwald. He scared himself by the recklessness of his driving. He threw the bike into the corners, leaning hard to extract every last bit of horsepower from the screaming engine. Several times he caused on-coming traffic to swerve as he overtook on blind bends, or dodged around slower moving cars and lorries. He cursed every time he was forced to slow down. In his haste he'd left his helmet and goggles back at the station. His eyes smarted and streamed from the cold. He wiped the tears from his face and peered ahead, hoping and praying for the back of a bright yellow Postbus to come into view. It had at least a twenty-minute start. He glanced at his speedometer which registered over ninety kilometres an hour. He ought to catch it soon.

Finally, he caught a glimpse of his quarry. He twisted the throttle and hurtled past. He suddenly realised that having got ahead of the bus didn't solve anything. He needed to come up with a plan. He accelerated hard, his mind racing as fast as the bike ate up the kilometres. Ahead lay the village of Brandtnerwald Kreuze. It formed a natural crossroads at the heart of the valley for interconnecting buses. It was also where passengers might grab a coffee whilst waiting for their own village service. Gunter raced into the village centre and parked the bike discreetly behind the main post office. He walked back to the centre and awaited the arrival of the service from Brandt. It pulled in three minutes later. The driver killed the engine, grabbed his coat and headed off. Gunter spotted Harriet and felt a wave of relief. He casually walked alongside the bus and tapped on the window next to her. For a few seconds she stared at him in confusion. Gunter raised his finger to his lips, then flicked it to indicate she should disembark.

She still looked confused as she stepped off. "Herr Schwartz, what on earth are you doing here?"

Gunter grabbed her elbow and steered her to the side of the bus stop. "Listen to me, Fraulein Harriet. Don't ask any questions, just do exactly as I say."

Anxiety replaced Harriet's confusion. "What's happened?"

"Do as I say. Please, it's vital. Is Simon on the bus?"

"Of course."

"Tell him to get off the bus and walk to the back of the post office." He nodded towards the building. "I'll meet him there."

"Gunter, you're beginning to frighten me."

"Please do as I say and everything will be alright." He gave a smile that he hoped gave reassurance. "I want you to get back on the bus and get off at Doppelgau. Go straight home. Don't talk to anyone. I'll meet you there later this evening." He glanced at his watch. "We haven't much time. Get Simon off the bus now."

Harriet looked scared. "What's happened, Gunter?"

"Something bad." He looked serious. "Please, Harriet, keep calm. Just get Simon off the bus." He left her and walked towards the post office.

Simon soon appeared, holding a battered suitcase and looking tense. "What's going on, Herr Schwartz?"

Gunter closed his eyes and mentally screamed as two SS trucks thundered through the village, heading towards Brandt.

Two hours earlier four SS trucks sped through the centre of Achbrugge, horns blaring, scattering pedestrians and vehicles from their path. From the back, the SS troops waved and cheered at the dust and mayhem left in their wake. Outside the Rubenstein's house two trucks skidded to a halt. The other two continued toward Doppelgau. The SS tumbled out, ran towards the front door, smashed it down and poured in.

Rachel was dragged out by her hair, a thin streak of blood trickling down her forehead. She screamed and kicked out, only for a trooper to deliver a blow to her stomach. They picked up her limp body and threw her in the truck. Her husband was physically hurled from the house. Blood streamed from his head into his eyes, rendering him blind and vulnerable. He staggered to his feet, only to have them kicked away from him. As he collapsed on the road, they laid into him with their boots.

166

Old Doctor Rubenstein hobbled out, encouraged along by kicks and shoves. Two men pinned him against the side of the truck, whilst a third set light to his beard. Rachel howled in horror and tried to force her way over the tailgate to rescue her father. The clubs rained down on her wrists and arms.

A small crowd gathered, attracted by the commotion. A few shouted mock encouragement as Rachel's husband tried to clamber over the tailgate, his efforts hampered by his injuries from the beating.

A cheer went up as Sara was carried bodily from the house. Screaming, twisting and writhing, she desperately tried to land blows from her thrashing legs on anyone within range. Her dress was ripped and one shoe missing. She found herself thrown into the back of the truck like a sack of refuse.

Doctor Rubenstein's torment still wasn't over. Having set him alight, they decided it would be amusing to put out the fire. Bucket after bucket of ice-cold water was thrown over him. The crowd grew, drawn by the entertainment. They laughed, clapped and cheered at each drenching. Eventually, tiring of their sport, they slung the old man into the back.

Then they pillaged the house. Windows were opened, and clothes, tables, curtains, blankets, chairs, a sewing machine and clocks were hurled into the street. The onlookers fell on the bounty.

After thirty minutes the trucks departed, with the SS men now in even higher spirits. They'd stripped the family of their money, rings and watches and were happily working their way through a dozen bottles of old Doctor Rubenstein's fine wine.

In Doppelgau, Hannah and Rudi Rubenstein suffered similar brutality. The difference was that, on hearing the commotion, Susan ran from her farmhouse and verbally laid into the troops. She yelled abuse at them in English and German. Her threats to report the officer for lack of control forced him to sheepishly order his men back into their truck. She prevented the house from being pillaged but could do nothing for Hannah and Rudi. The lorry carrying their battered bodies had already departed.

Susan was beside herself with shock, grief and fury. She turned her rage on the few villagers that turned up to watch the sport. They stood like a herd of dumb cattle until Sep turned up. A red mist descended in his mind. He seized a hayfork and physically drove them back towards the village before joining his wife in a crumpled heap of boiling wrath. He wrapped his arms around her, trying desperately to contain her wild-eyed madness.

"Bloody… barbarian… savages. Bloody vermin." She could barely get the words out. Sep continued to hold her until her fire burnt itself out, enabling Marie and Josey to gently lead her back home. Sep vented his shock and fury by aggressively hammering nails into the boarding up timbers. If any villagers were minded to loot, they would have to come past him first.

167

THE FUGITIVE

"You need to be strong, Simon." Gunter pulled the young man to his feet. "You have to survive."

Simon was in shock. His eyes were glazed, and he would have collapsed again if Gunter hadn't steadied him. "I want to kill them. I want to kill them," he muttered over and over again.

Gunter realised he needed to do something drastic to get him to function. He slapped him hard on the cheek. "Simon! Pull yourself together, otherwise we're both going to get shot."

Simon reeled; his eyes refocused and stared at Gunter. "What must I do?"

"Get on the back." Gunter lashed the suitcase to the petrol tank and kick-started the motorcycle. "Hang on."

"Where are we going?"

Gunter realised he didn't have an answer. "Somewhere safe." He shook his head and tried to think. He instinctively thought of the Breitners or Wachters before realising he couldn't put them at risk.

"The Lodge," Simon said. "I'll show you," he added, in response to Gunter's blank look.

They raced through Achbrugge, Gau and Doppelgau until they reached the turning that led to The Lodge. The sun dropped behind the mountains, throwing the track through the forest into gloom. Gunter peered ahead keeping the engine revs low to mask the sound of their progress. He daren't put on the lights in case anyone spotted them. Eventually, the dark outline of the building loomed in front of them.

Gunter killed the engine and dismounted. "You'll be safe here for tonight."

"Will they come after me?"

Gunter patted him reassuringly on the arm. "Not tonight. It will take them time to get organised." He smashed a window and levered the catch. "Make yourself comfortable. Have you any food?"

"The remains of a cheese roll." In the gathering darkness Simon managed to hide his distress. "What will happen to my family?"

Gunter swallowed hard. "The document I saw said they were to be transported to Lichtenburg and Mauthausen."

"What are they?"

"I've no idea," Gunter lied. He didn't know anything about Mauthausen, but he'd heard about Lichtenburg. The Nazis had used it as a concentration camp since the mid-1930s. It had a reputation for brutality. "You'd best try and get some sleep. We'll come up with a better hiding place for you tomorrow. It might involve a lot of travelling."

Gunter mounted the bike and pushed it to the top of the drive.

"Gunter."

"What?"

"Thank you."

Gunter said nothing. He let the bike freewheel down the track, only firing up the engine once he reached the road.

PILLAGE

Johan stepped through the front door and gazed at the devastation. The house was trashed. Looters had ripped-up floorboards looking for the Jewish treasure they were convinced must be hidden beneath. A man blocked the hall as he struggled to lever a large wardrobe through the narrow passageway. Johan angrily shoved him aside and slowly climbed the stairs. His brain failed to come to terms with what he was seeing. An image of Sara and the terror she must have endured swirled around in his mind. He pushed open a bedroom door, and almost crumpled to the floor as a wave of crushing agony and anger threatened to engulf him.

It was Sara's room. Every drawer had been opened and the contents looted. His feet crunched on the broken glass of a picture frame. The looters had even taken whatever picture might have hung within it. A small perfume bottle had rolled into the corner. He picked it up, and instantly he felt drawn to the scent of her. He put the bottle in his pocket and cast his eyes around for anything else that was hers. A man swayed into the room, his eyes full of greed. A tsunami of rage crashed through Johan. How dare such a monster invade such a sacred place? Johan battered the man out the room, down the stairs and out the door before he felt strong arms trying to restrain him. Johan became a man possessed. He lashed out at anyone careless enough to come close. They backed off and watched him warily, uncertain as to whether he was another ransacker whose greed had been thwarted, or perhaps a Jewish sympathiser. Every instinct within him wanted to exact instant revenge. Yet he knew landing further blows would only result in trouble for him and the rest of his family.

He became vaguely aware of a calming voice. "Johan, mate. You need to come home."

Johan swung round, ready to land another blow.

"Hey, mate. It's me, Jurgen."

Johan wiped his eyes on the back of his sleeve and peered at the familiar face.

Jurgen lowered his voice. "Come on, mate, leave these scumbags."

Johan found himself propelled along the road. They reached a gap in the houses that formed the edge of a small meadow. Johan sank to the grass, buried his head in his hands and wept. Jurgen crouched beside him and slung his arm over his friend's shoulder. Johan had no idea how long they remained there, almost drowning in anger and grief.

"We need to get back, mate." Jurgen said, after a while.

"Did they take Hannah, Rudi and Simon?"

"Looks like it."

Johan suddenly sat up. "Harriet is meeting Simon. Is she alright? If anything has happened to her, I swear I'll kill the bastards."

"Calm down, mate. Harriet's fine. She's back home which is where you need to be. Come on, let's get back."

It was dark when Gunter pulled into the Breitner's farmyard. Harriet ran out. "Is he alright?"

"He's fine. Keep your voice down. It's better if as few people as possible know about all this."

Sep pulled his friend over the threshold. "My God, Gunter, you've taken a risk."

"There are times when you have to do what's right. Who knows?"

"All of us."

"No one outside the family?"

"Marie, but she's family."

Gunter entered the Stube. Instantly Marie engulfed him in her arms. "You look shattered, Gunter." She stood back and looked at him seriously. "Before you do anything else you must get something inside you."

The atmosphere inside the Stube was thick with barely contained fury and unbearable anguish. Gunter sank into the chair. He felt exhausted. He hadn't realised he was running on adrenalin. Marie placed a bowl of soup in front of him.

Harriet couldn't contain herself. "Where is he? Is he alright?"

Instinctively, Gunter looked towards the door before replying in a low voice. "He's at The Lodge. He's safe there for tonight. But we'll have to think of somewhere better. If they come looking, The Lodge is an obvious refuge."

"He can't stay there by himself. Not tonight of all nights." Harriet sounded distressed.

"He'll have to." Her father laid a hand on her shoulder. "It's too dark, and we don't want to draw attention by driving up with headlights on."

Gunter suddenly looked around. "Where's Johan?"

"Upstairs. He's not coping too well," Susan said. "Jurgen's with him and I'll pop in later."

Gunter spooned the soup into his mouth and cast an appreciative glance at Marie who stood beside him, her hand resting gently on his shoulder.

"We need to keep a lid on this." Stephan said.

"What do you mean?" Susan looked outraged. "Everyone in the village saw what happened."

"That's my point, Susan. Everyone saw everything or at least will have heard about it by now. Including your efforts to stop the SS, and Johan taking a swing at the looters." Stephan glanced around at everyone. "We're

172

in the spotlight, and there's some in this village who'll be pleased to denounce us if they suspect we're harbouring Simon."

"We can't abandon him," Josey said.

"Of course not, dear. But we have to do it low key. We can't all suddenly rush to The Lodge tomorrow, for example."

"You're right," Sep said. "We've got to act as if it's business as usual. Even though it's not."

"I'll take him to Gregor and Petra," Harriet said.

Everyone looked at her. "It makes sense. You all have jobs that the village expects you to do. The farms." She nodded towards Stephan and her father. "Tante Josey, you'll be expected to travel to Achbrugge to your factories, Johan needs to get back to his electrical work, and Jurgen to his engineering course. You, Herr Schwartz, can't afford not to get back to Brandt. That leaves me. Added to that, I know the mountain route to Gregor's farm so we avoid the main road."

"And, if they do come, there's no chance they'd be able to follow the mountain route," Sep said. "That requires detailed local knowledge. It's a good idea."

"I'll leave early." Harriet stood up. "I need an early night anyway. It's been a horrible, horrible day."

"I must depart as well." Gunter pushed the empty soup bowl away from him and moved to leave. Sep embraced his friend. No words were needed.

MOUNTAIN RETREAT

"Come on, Simon. It's not far now."

Below her, Simon stopped and leant on his knees, his chest heaving. He glanced down the almost vertical cliff face and felt a wave of dizziness. The path wasn't just difficult, it was treacherous. He was exhausted physically and mentally from lack of sleep. He couldn't prevent the rage, grief and floods of tears. There were times on their ascent he felt an overwhelming urge to throw himself off. Only Harriet's constant encouragement and his burning desire for revenge kept him going.

"We'll stop at the top." Harriet adjusted the rucksack across her shoulders and resumed the ascent. Thirty minutes later they arrived at a lush alpine meadow. Harriet opened the bag and handed Simon a ham, cheese and pickle roll and a bottle of apple juice.

"Sorry, I'm so useless," Simon muttered, as he collapsed on the grass beside her.

"You're not useless. You're in shock. You of all people ought to know the signs."

He stared at the sky, grimaced and squeezed his eyes shut. "I need to pull myself together."

"You do. But don't expect too much of yourself." She draped an arm across his shoulders. "You need to focus on yourself and your survival. Starting with making sure you eat." She glanced meaningfully at the uneaten roll in his hand.

The Brandtnerwald stretched out before them. It was mid-morning and the cold air trapped some mist and clouds in the corners of the valley where the warmth of the sun hadn't yet reached.

"I've never been this far up the valley before. You can see everything."

"That's a good thing. Nobody can approach without being spotted."

"Can Gregor be trusted?"

"He can," she said firmly, and gave his arm a reassuring squeeze. "Come on, we've got another five kilometres ahead of us." She stood up and stooped to refasten the rucksack.

He placed his hand over hers to stop her. "No. I'll carry it from here. It's time I started pulling my weight."

She was pleased by the small uplift in his spirit.

Gregor was so angry Harriet thought he would explode. "What is the world coming to, unleashing such monsters on humanity?" he roared.

Petra was more fearful he'd have another heart attack or burst a blood vessel. "Gregor, calm down. For goodness' sake. You'll do yourself a mischief."

Gregor's fist crashed down on the table, making the forks rattle on the plates. "Evicting good people out of their homes – *by force!*" His great white shaggy head swivelled toward Harriet. "And only your mother stood up to them? Good for her, I say. By God, I wish I'd had a hand in the matter."

"But you didn't, dear. And I wish you'd calm down and think about what needs to be done for Simon." She grabbed his enormous fist in her tiny hand. "Please, Gregor."

He stared at her. His look of fury quickly changed to one of tenderness and contrition as he realised he'd alarmed his wife. "Yes, you're right, my sweet, as you usually are." Her dainty hand disappeared inside his, and the volcano slowly subsided. "Safest place is the summer hut."

"It needs some work."

"I don't want to be a burden," Simon said. "I'll pull my weight and help out with anything."

Gregor chuckled. "Oh, you'll work, my friend, believe me. Everyone works here. If you don't, you end up dead." He suddenly disappeared into the kitchen. He returned clutching a flagon of beer in one hand and a fistful of tankards in the other.

"Isn't it a bit early?" Petra said lightly.

"You can't make serious decisions with a dry throat." Gregor scattered the flagons across the table and filled each in turn. "The priority is making sure you are safe. So, the summer house has sorted that out. Few people know where it is, and no one can approach it without being seen." Gregor raised his tankard. "Prosit!" He took a massive swig, belched and moved to the second priority.

Harriet left them as they reached the eighth priority. "I'll come each week with some food and stuff if the weather doesn't stop me."

"You don't need to, Harriet." Simon looked embarrassed. "You've done too much already. And I don't want you taking risks on my behalf. The cliff path is dangerous."

"Simon, I've climbed that path dozens of times."

"Nevertheless."

She looked hurt "Don't you want me to visit then?"

"Of course I do."

She smiled. "Well then, that's settled." She turned and waved at Gregor and Petra who stood on the porch. Gregor had his arm wrapped around his wife's waist. She looked like a small deer in the grip of a mountain bear.

"See you then." She glanced back at Simon, as if making one last assessment of his wellbeing. He smiled and gave a brief sad nod.

175

FRIENDS AND NEIGHBOURS

"Are you sure about this?" Jurgen grabbed Johan's arm.

Johan paused, his hand already on the entrance door of the Adler. "The bloody Nazis don't run this Gasthaus"

The Hagspiels looked up with surprise as they entered. Hans leaned towards his father and whispered something in his ear. A smirk spread across Will Hagspiel's face. After removing their coats, Jurgen and Johan settled themselves at the Stammtisch. Immediately, Herr Zinnerman placed a couple of Pils in front of them. As he turned to leave, he gave Johan's shoulder a sympathetic squeeze. The atmosphere became thick with tension.

Twenty minutes later, Sep and Stephan arrived and took their seats alongside their sons. Herr Ansbacher and Herr Drössel soon followed. Stephan broke open a pack of cards and began to deal.

Another neighbour and his friend entered. They exchanged the briefest of greetings before choosing to sit alongside the Hagspiels. More locals arrived. Curt nods of greeting were exchanged, but there was no mistaking that lines of allegiance were being drawn. Eventually, over twenty men were crammed around the Hagspiels' table. Cigarettes were shared, banter exchanged, a couple of jokes told, and the men established an atmosphere of camaraderie and solidarity. The herd instinct required safety in numbers. If those on the Breitners' table wanted to be outsiders, more fool them.

Johan took care not to get drunk. He was conscious of Hans Hagspiel's smirking face and his goading comments of 'people getting what they deserved', and 'bringing trouble down on their own heads'. He took his lead from his father and the other elders who calmly smoked, played cards and supped their beer as if oblivious to the table opposite.

He decided on an early night. He walked home through a steady downpour and tried to imagine how Simon was coping, isolated with only his dark thoughts for company. He resolved to provide some moral support. He crept upstairs and tapped on Harriet's door.

"Who is it?"

"Me," he whispered, as he eased the door ajar.

Harriet sat up in bed, looking bleary-eyed. "What's up? Are you okay?"

"I'm fine. Are you seeing Simon tomorrow?"

She nodded.

I'll take you."

"I was going up with Cleopatra."

"I'll take you on my bike. Simon will appreciate seeing some familiar faces."

"We mustn't be seen."

"We'll leave before sunrise."

Simon was pleased to see them. He hugged Johan, before startling Harriet by giving her an equally warm embrace.

"How are you getting on, mate?" Johan said.

"I haven't time to stop and think. Gregor has me working from dawn till dusk." Simon smiled. "I know why he's doing it."

"To stop you from brooding," Harriet said bluntly.

"It's worked. I'm so exhausted I'm asleep in seconds."

Johan studied his friend. He'd acquired the deep mountain tan but that failed to hide the worry lines. He seemed to have grown old and no longer looked like a bookish student. Hard physical work had produced a wiry, muscular frame. As to his mental state? It was hard to tell. However, as the day progressed, Harriet's influence in that department became apparent.

Gregor's summer hut was tiny. Its thick stone walls and heavy timber roof kept out the weather. A single window allowed only limited light, and a large stone fireplace provided heat and a cooking stove. Harriet and Johan's rain-soaked coats hung in front of it. A mattress doubled as a bed and a sofa. Its size suggested it had been designed to accommodate Gregor's massive frame. A bench seat, table and single chair were the only other furniture.

Johan gazed around. "Safe and comfortable."

"We've bought some stuff." Harriet emptied the contents of their rucksacks on the small table. "I've made some bread, pickles, smoked hams and Wursts." She listed each item as they emerged from the bags. "I thought you'd like some Sauerkraut, oh, and a few eggs. I hard-boiled a couple as well. There're a few slices of Apfelkuchen, my Ma's made a Chokolade Torte, and Tante Marie's provided lunch for us all." She sat back and admired the pile that spread across the table. "Oh, and there are books and a few bottles of wine and Pils in Johan's bag, and some clothes." She glanced at Simon. "What's the matter? Oh my God, you can't eat pork, can you?"

Simon looked overcome. "No, it's not that. We were…" He stopped to gather himself. "I'm not an orthodox Jew." He gestured toward the food. "It's a bit overwhelming. It means a lot to me."

"So it should," Harriet said quickly, as she saw Simon struggle to hold his emotions at bay. "It took me a long time to make this. I'm not a great cook, you know, so you won't thank me if you get ill!"

They sat around the table. Johan opened three bottles of Pils and handed one to Simon and another to Harriet, who looked embarrassed. It wasn't done for a young woman to drink in the company of men, unless with her husband, and even then a glass of wine would be more appropriate. Johan smiled at Harriet's discomfort. "You're the best sister," he said.

177

Harriet blushed. "Even so, Johan." She looked at her bottle as if it might explode.

"I'm not drinking unless you join us," Simon said.

Harriet picked up the bottle. "Prosit!" she said, with a confident flourish. They touched bottles before taking their first swig.

Simon suddenly snatched Harriet's bottle from her grasp and half-turned his back so it was out of her reach. "That's quite enough for you, young lady."

"Hey, that's not fair!" She laughed and made a lunge to retrieve her bottle.

"See, Johan. That's what happens when young women get a taste for the beer." Simon tried to hold Harriet off as she reached desperately for the bottle. She ended up stretched halfway around his body. "You Trottel!" she said, laughing.

He gently pulled her up and handed the drink back. "Your brother's right, you know."

Johan noticed his sister look at Simon the same way as she had at the New Year's Eve party. It was with a mixture of fun, confusion and affection. It raised Simon's spirits.

They tucked into the food. Once sated, they settled back and talked. Their conversation bounced from one subject to another: their childhoods, memorable village events, Gunter's visits, and Gregor, his family and the punishing work schedule he'd imposed on Simon. But the elephant in the room could not be avoided.

"They might let them go?" Harriet said.

Simon squeezed his eyes shut as if summoning all the power of prayer he could muster. "There's always hope. It's all I've got."

"That and revenge," Johan muttered under his breath.

"And survival," Harriet added. She stroked the back of Simon's hand. "You must stay safe."

"I can't remain here forever, Harriet." He turned to look sideways at her. "Sooner or later they'll send their people here. Added to that, there must be a limit on how many trees Gregor wants felled and exactly how big a log pile he needs, not to mention the number of drainage ditches that require digging."

"Welcome to the life of an alpine farmer," Johan said. "You wait until he gets you looking after the animals."

"You don't need to decide anything straight away." Harriet gave a reassuring smile. "You need time to get your thoughts together."

"Thoughts about what?"

"The future. The Nazis haven't stolen that."

"I'll have plenty of time on my hands once the snow cuts me off from civilisation. I'll probably go mad and start talking to myself."

"We'll visit. Won't we, Johan?"

"Of course."

178

Simon seemed moved by this and muttered "Thanks."

Johan sighed. "But there comes a time when we must say goodbye. And that time is now." He drained the bottle of Pils, and glanced at his sister. "Time to move. We've got a long walk back to the bike."

"If it was winter we could ski down." She got up and smoothed her dress.

"See you, mate." Johan held his arms open. The two gave each other a bear hug.

"I'll see you next week, Simon." Harriet looked uncertain as to what form of embrace would be appropriate. Simon had no such hesitation. He wrapped her in his arms. Once again, Harriet found herself taken by surprise. For a second, she didn't seem to know what to do with her own arms. Then it seemed appropriate to return the hug. Having grasped the concept, Johan got the impression that his sister wasn't sure how to bring the matter to a conclusion.

CASE CLOSED

"What do you know about Frau Susan Breitner?"

Gunter's dealings with Kommissioner Keunsberg had taught him to mask any emotion. "From Doppelgau?"

Keunsberg nodded.

"She's the District Nurse. Everybody in the upper Brandtnerwald knows her. Why do you ask?"

"I've had a complaint. Apparently, she intervened when our Shutzstaffel friends arrested some Jews."

Gunter felt his throat tighten but he managed to sound blasé. "That's hardly surprising. It's common knowledge she worked for a Jewish doctor. And she's English and has a reputation for speaking her mind." Gunter gave a false laugh. "I bet she gave the SS an earful."

A flicker of a smile flashed across Keunsberg's face. "Sounds like an interesting person." He glanced across the table. "English, you say?"

Gunter dropped the file he'd been holding on the table. It was enough to distract Keunsberg.

"What's this?"

"The case file on my investigation into the unexplained death of the young girl and baby from Littesau. It's the reason I requested this meeting. You should read it."

"You have a suspect?"

"Yes. Which is why you should read it."

Keunsberg's attention transferred to the file. He flipped it open and scan read the contents, flicking papers back and forth as his interest took hold. "Is this watertight?" he said quietly, as he extracted a particular sheet and studied it carefully.

"All supported by evidence and witness statements."

"Well, well, well. The devious, perverted bastard." The Kommissioner replaced the paper and slowly closed the file. "Is he aware?"

Gunter shook his head. "I've not interviewed him yet. I thought I'd run it past you first, given your interest in the man."

Keunsberg gave Gunter a sharp look. "I assume I'm not mentioned."

Gunter's face remained expressionless. Inside, though, he sneered. "You'll find nothing in the file." He stretched across the table to retrieve the document.

"That won't be necessary. Leave it with me. I'll read it thoroughly when I've more time."

"Shall I bring the man in for interview?" Gunter already knew the answer.

Alarm flashed across Keunsberg's face. "No…not yet. Give me a couple of days and I'll get back to you. This needs to be handled with care."

"Of course, Herr Kommissioner." Gunter got to his feet and turned to leave. He remembered, just in time, to turn and give a passable Nazi salute.

Once outside, he made his way to a room filled with filing cabinets. It took him less than twenty minutes to find the first thing he was looking for. His second task took longer and involved a lot of telephone calls. It was late afternoon before he received answers. What he learnt threw him into despair.

REFUGE

"I can't stay, Harriet."

"Simon, listen to me." Harriet crouched down in front of him and grabbed his hands in hers. She blinked through her own tears as she stared into his face. "You mustn't do anything rash."

"I have to get revenge. I owe it to my family. For God's sake, Harriet, can't you understand that?"

His fury frightened her. But she knew she had to calm him down. "I understand. *Of course* I do. But getting yourself caught won't solve anything." She rested her head on his shoulder, not bothering to control her weeping. "We'll get revenge. But we have to be patient."

"I wish there was some kind of resistance movement."

"But there isn't, Simon, which is why you have to stay here."

The door suddenly burst open, making them both leap up in panic. Gregor's bulk filled the door frame. "I overheard you," he said. "Bastards shall pay for this." He slammed the door shut behind him and swung his shaggy head to confront Simon. "You need to be strong, young man, and not do anything stupid. A lot of people have put their heads on the block, especially that Inspector Schwartz. He could get himself hung. Do you hear me?" Gregor's no-nonsense approach succeeded where Harriet's sympathy failed. Simon wiped his eyes and looked chastened.

Gregor swept the bench seat clear and sat down. "So, what have you been told?"

"My grandfather and father are both dead." Simon struggled to get the words out. "Gunter was certain about that. My Uncle is in Mauthausen concentration camp."

"Father Haphold and Herman Paulus are in the same place," Harriet added. "And Hannah, Rachel and Sara have been transferred to Ravenbruck."

"Which is where?"

"Somewhere in north Germany, near Berlin. It's a women's prison. That's all Gunter could find out." Simon looked forlorn. "I need revenge, Gregor."

"I know, son." Gregor softened his voice. "But doing something silly won't help." He glanced at them. "Sit down, son. You too, Harriet." He shifted along the bench. He waited until they settled. He then leant forward, speaking in a low, urgent voice. "There are no resistance groups in Austria. At least, none that are effective. We need to get you over the border before winter. In Switzerland there are organisations working against these Nazi bastards. If you want revenge, lad, that's where you need to be."

"I know I can't stay here."

"Smuggling people out isn't easy. The Germans have sealed the country." Gregor held his hand up to forestall Simon's question. "We'll come up with a plan." He stared hard at him. "It might involve crossing the mountains."

"When do you think?" Harriet asked.

Gregor pursed his lips. "When everything is in place. Maybe a couple of months. Late September or early October would be best – before the snows."

"What should I do in the meantime?"

Gregor leant back and craned his neck toward the peak behind the summer farm. "Every day you climb that. You'll need to be a lot fitter than you are at the moment."

CONSCRIPTED BY THE ENEMY

"At least we'll be trained together," Johan muttered, as he and Jurgen sat morosely cradling their Pils in the Adler.

Jurgen closed his eyes in frustration. "I've spent over a year training to be an engineer so I can fix cars, hopefully earn enough money to open my own garage, maybe find a nice girl, settle down and build a good life. Since when did I agree to serve in the Austrian Army?"

Johan gave a bitter laugh. "We're conscripted into the Wehrmacht. There is no Austrian Army. In fact, there is no Austria. We now live in Ostmark remember, with German laws, German radio, German songs, German culture. Welcome to the Third Reich."

"You're half English. Why don't you appeal?"

"Because my birth certificate says I was born Austrian." He shook his head angrily. "Ma thinks we'll be sent to fight somewhere."

Jurgen looked puzzled. "The Wehrmacht aren't fighting anywhere, are they?"

"No. But my Ma thinks war is likely." He glanced at his friend. "She follows the news on the BBC and is convinced the Nazis can't be trusted."

"What's your Pa said?"

"All he said was to get the conscription over and done with. A year is nothing. We get trained, learn to march, to salute and spend the rest of the year doing whatever."

"Why can't they conscript these bloody Hitler Youth kids." Jurgen jerked his chin angrily toward Hans Hagspiel, who was drinking with his acolytes across the other side of the room. "That lot would only be too keen to prance about playing soldiers."

"Most have volunteered to join the SS."

Jurgen took a long swig from his beer, before placing his glass precisely on the table. "I feel like a traitor," he said quietly.

"Because of what's happened to the Rubensteins?"

Jurgen nodded.

"I feel the same." Johan managed to keep his voice steady as an image of Sara swam into his memory. "We're not joining the bastards," he said in a low voice. "The Wehrmacht is the army. It's not the Nazis. And we've no choice." He drained his glass, looked at Jurgen and raised his eyebrows.

Jurgen shook his head. "If I have another I won't be able to stop, and I know where it will end." He looked meaningfully towards Hans Hagspiel. "I'll only end up rearranging his face – again."

UNEXPECTED REVELATIONS

Harriet watched anxiously as a small figure in the distance ran headlong down the steep slope. Several times the runner skidded and slipped; his arms flailed as he fought to maintain balance. Only when he made it to the flatter meadow did she relax. He briefly disappeared in a shallow valley before reappearing, still running. A broad smile lit up his face as he saw her standing by the summer farm.

"Harriet, you look radiant," he spluttered, as he came to a halt and stooped with his hands on his knees, his chest heaving. "I'd give you a hug but…" He straightened and gestured at his sweat-soaked body.

"You're looking very fit."

"I should be." He waved vaguely back at the mountain. "Two hours." He struggled for breath. "First time took me over three."

"I've brought some food, fresh clothes, newspapers and stuff."

"You're a sweetheart." He glanced towards the water trough. "I'll clean myself and be with you in a moment."

He came in ten minutes later, towelling himself off. He rummaged around in a cupboard and found a shirt. He sniffed it before putting it on. "Only worn once," he said, as he noticed her disapproving look. He then surprised her by giving her a hug. "You're a kind person," he said.

"I'm slightly mad coming here, that's for sure." She grinned at him. "It's nice to see you in good spirits."

"I've a purpose, a goal and, thanks to you, a reason to live."

"You have Gregor to thank for that." She busied herself, laying out some food on the table. "We should eat the stuff that won't keep."

"I hope you've brought some good news as well?"

She stopped work and her face fell. "Not really. Both Johan and Jurgen have been conscripted."

"Oh no!" He looked dismayed. "When do they have to join?"

"September, for basic training, then twelve months service."

"Hopefully, the time will pass quickly." He gazed at the food. "Come on, let's eat. Running up and down a mountain has given me an appetite." He shifted along the bench to make room for her. "Tell me your news."

She felt pleased by the changes in him. He looked lean, fit and full of energy, and his outlook seemed so much more positive. The despair, introspection and self-pity were gone. He acted full of self-confidence, almost bubbly. She felt she nearly had the old Simon back. Nevertheless, she avoided making any reference to the fate of his family. She was surprised when he raised the topic, albeit indirectly.

"How's Johan holding up?"

She hesitated before replying. "He's angry, bitter and grief-stricken."

"She'll come back one day. God willing," he muttered. "Assuming she survives."

"Don't talk like that, Simon."

"Harriet, the camps are hell."

"You don't know that."

"I do. I met Gregor's son-in-law, Anton. He's organising my escape to Switzerland. He's already taken a few escapees over the mountains. They told him what life is really like. Prisoners are starved. They're used as slaves, and many are simply worked to death or die from disease." He looked sideways at her, his eyes full of rage. "I'm not making it up, Harriet."

"You shouldn't talk about such things, Simon. It will only make you angry and depressed."

"Harriet, I'm angry all the time." He looked forlorn, before shaking his head as if to banish his dark thoughts. "You're right. Let's talk of good, hopeful things. Sara will survive, come home, marry Johan and they'll have seven horrible kids."

"They'll be adorable."

"He's lucky to have loved and been loved in return." He gave a sad smile. "They were a pair, weren't they?"

She laughed, but soon became serious. "Haven't you someone special?" She flicked her hand. "Silly question, I expect you met lots of pretty girls in Wien." She felt an unexpected shock pass through her when he didn't immediately reply. She leant forward and tried to read his expression. "There is someone, isn't there?"

Simon looked uncomfortable and said nothing.

Harriet's shock turned to hurt. "Aren't you going to tell me?"

He pursed his lips and massaged his forehead with his fingertips.

Harriet's hurt shifted towards annoyance. "Really, Simon, as a friend, the least you can do is tell me."

He studied the table for a few seconds. "Yes, there is someone special."

Harriet shook her head in disbelief. "You are a dark horse. Come on then. Tell me about her. What's she like?"

"Are you sure you want to know?" he said quietly.

She banged her palm on the table. "Yes, I'm sure."

"I'll tell you what she's like." He paused, then looked at her. "She can be a pain. Headstrong, opinionated, always wants to win whether it's an argument or a race." He gave a wan smile. "She's a real handful."

Harriet was confused. "They don't sound like good traits. Are you sure you like this girl?"

Simon laughed. "I don't just like her, Harriet, I love her very much."

"Oh!" Harriet felt a stab of hurt. Nevertheless, her curiosity was piqued. "She must have some good points as well."

"She does and they far outweigh her bad ones."

"Like what?" She was now in two minds as to whether she wanted to know.

"She's fearless, really loyal, quite a good cook – not brilliant. Oh, and she's a wonderful dancer." He looked intently at her. "I danced with her all evening once. Well, I say all evening, but she's such a good dancer that I had to take my place in a long queue of other admirers."

"She's popular, then?"

"Very."

"Oh! And what does she look like?"

Simon stared at the ceiling and considered the question. "She's beautiful. Where shall I start? Her eyes are brown – very expressive. They light up when she's happy, but they seem to be on fire when she's angry. Her lips are warm, inviting, seductive – the kind of lips I've dreamt of kissing."

"You've never kissed her!" Harriet looked astounded. "How long have you known this girl?"

Simon waved his hand nonchalantly. "Oh – it's hard to be precise, a long time."

"You didn't meet her at university?"

"Oh, no. I've known her for years."

Harriet turned and faced him directly and became cross. "How come you've never spoken of this girl in all the time I've known you?"

"You never asked."

"Really, Simon. I thought I knew you. Does she live in the village?"

Simon nodded and adopted a resigned expression.

Harriet went silent. She held his gaze. "Apart from having kissable lips, what else makes her so attractive?" Her tone indicated that she didn't much care for this girl.

"She has long, auburn hair. Quite curly. It reaches down to her waist. Small ears, a nice neat nose similar, in fact I'd say identical, to your own. Oh, and she's allergic to feathers." Simon gazed at the ceiling and screwed his eyes as if dredging up some other details hidden in the corners of his memory. "She's slightly shorter than me. She has a lovely figure. I saw her legs once when she had heatstroke and I threw her in the river, and I…"

"Simon, you're describing me?" Harriet stared open-mouthed at him.

He didn't reply. He smiled, scratched the back of his neck and gave her a quizzical look.

"Why didn't you say?!"

Simon paused to collect his words. When he did speak, her heart melted. "I've loved you for years, Harriet. The trouble was finding the right opportunity to tell you." He grinned. "And being scared of finding out that you didn't feel the same about me." His grin broadened to a smile. "I still don't know."

She gazed at him before shaking her head in disbelief. "You Trottel."

He looked helpless. "Well - I've told you now."

She gave a rueful smile. "I've loved you too for a long time."

"Well, you're as bad as me then. Why didn't you say something?

"Because I wasn't sure whether it was true love or just a silly infatuation. And you might tease me."

"So, when did you make up your mind?'

Harriet laughed. "When you threw me in that stream."

"You didn't know much about it."

"I knew that anyone that cared that much about me must be special."

"You scared me that day." He looked serious.

"There was a spark. I remember you holding me, as we rode back down to your father's surgery, and thinking I'm safe, I get to live my life. I can't describe it but somehow I knew we had a connection."

"Fate?"

"Maybe." She smiled. "Either way, I knew our lives would be linked."

Simon looked thoughtful. "I'm not sure what to do now."

"You Trottel," she said laughing, and moved closer along the bench.

The change in their relationship left them breathless. It was as if they were desperate to make up for the years spent in suppressed denial. Harriet's excitement defined her every journey to the summer hut. Each metre she ascended increased her anticipation. She would run the last stretch, once she had broached a small rise and the building came into view. Immediately, she would seek him out. Simon would be standing by the front door, straining his eyes, trying to catch the first glimpse of her approach. When they finally embraced there was no holding back. They were startled at their passion. Hesitancy was abandoned. Their separation heightened their longing. They threw themselves at each other with the hunger of the starving. Everything was forgotten as they kissed and caressed. Throughout the day they laughed and fought with equal passion. Blazing arguments ended in them laughing at themselves at the realisation that their mutual stubbornness inevitably lay at the root of the dispute.

"We're like fire and water," Harriet said, as they lay alongside each other on the greensward by the front door.

"I'm uncertain whether we're a case of 'opposites attract'. All I know is that I feel we are so compatible." Simon turned his head towards her. "Do you think everyone feels like we do?"

"I remember telling Johan of there being a spark between him and Sara, and also between my Ma and Pa." She threw her hand above her head and let it fall to caress the hair on the top of Simon's head. "I don't want it to stop."

He fell silent.

"I know what you're thinking," Harriet said after a bit.

"We need to face it," he said.

"I know." She rolled over so she faced him. "What's been decided?"

Simon sighed. "Tara's husband says we have two options. Easy or hard. The easy option is I get taken to Brandt. There's a safe house in a village nearby which is less than five kilometres from the Swiss border. In theory, we make a dash for it and swim across the Rhein at night."

"What's the problem?"

"The Germans have set up fences, watchtowers and frequent patrols. Success is less than thirty percent."

"Don't do it," Harriet said firmly. "That means there is a seventy percent chance of getting caught."

He gave a grim laugh. "I've not told you the alternative."

"Go on."

"We head over the mountains towards the Swiss-Italian border. It's bloody tough. No safe houses. There's a small, remote hamlet. A man there regularly smuggles people and other stuff. Escapees fail, not because they were captured but because they either slipped and fell, got caught out by the weather and froze to death, or simply weren't fit enough for the climb."

"That's why Gregor got you running up and down the mountain."

He nodded and stared into her eyes. "You know what the tough decision is?"

Her lips tightened. "I just want you safe."

"I won't be able to return. Not while the Nazis are around."

"No – but I'm not restricted."

He searched her face. "You'd follow me to Switzerland?"

She gave a wan smile. "My Ma came from England to be with Pa. Travelling to Switzerland is nothing by comparison." She bent her head towards him and kissed him softly on the lips. "What other option is there?"

"We haven't got much time left together."

"When do you leave?" She closed her eyes as if dreading his answer.

"Third or fourth week in September, depending on the weather."

She squeezed her eyes tight together but tears still leaked out.

189

THE LAST HURRAH

"Do you think it suits me?" Katerina pouted at her reflection. "It's not too, you know - red. I don't want to look like a tart."

Trudy laughed. "It looks fine." She glanced at her friend in the mirror. "Honestly, it suits your personality."

"Will Franz like it?"

"I'm sure he will. He's besotted with you, with or without lipstick."

"Do you think so?"

"I know so."

Katerina looked delighted. "You ready?"

Trudy applied more blusher to her cheeks and examined herself. Even though she wore only a hint of make-up, she felt an undeniable thrill just putting it on. Alongside them, a dozen or so other young women carefully anointed themselves with eye-liner, lipstick, rouge and eye-shadow. The air became thick with the scent of cologne, cigarette smoke, excited chatter and laughter, as stockings and skirts were hitched up and wayward strands of hair carefully pinned.

The Swingjungen dance had become the highlight of the week. For Trudy, the event appealed to her sense of independence. She could let her hair down, abandon her inhibitions, and feel free. It was like a pressure release valve from the dour, brutal, conformist environment of the office, and the suffocating pervasiveness of the Party. For Katerina, it presented an opportunity for her and Franz to get ever closer. Trudy checked herself over once more and declared herself ready. The two friends linked arms and almost skipped towards the main hall.

Franz sat at a table that they'd commandeered at successive dances, such that it had become their own. The familiar bottle of wine in its ice-bucket and three glasses stood ready. Many of the lads noted their entrance. Neither girl would be short of dance partners.

They'd established a ritual. It began with each of them giving a catch-up of their week over the first glass of wine and, for Franz and Katerina, a few cigarettes. The bottle would be refreshed, and the conversation moved to any topic that took their fancy. Franz always proved good company. He had a ready wit and an extrovert nature that Trudy found endearing and Katerina utterly mesmerising. He was popular among the Swingjugen. His age, and reputation as one of the original exponents of Anglophile culture, gave him a certain cache. As a consequence, their table was a magnet for a string of his friends, acquaintances and dance partners.

The arrival of the main act signalled the start of the dancing. From then on the evening was spent in a glorious craze of jiving, jitterbugging, singing and drinking. Trudy quickly overcame her initial awkwardness that she might stand out in her conservative dress, and in being slightly older compared to most revellers. Neither mattered. She had a constant stream of young men eager to take a turn around the floor with her. The music got louder and the dance-floor more crowded. Trudy caught a fleeting glimpse of Katerina shrieking with laughter, as she was thrown around by one of the more accomplished exponents of the Jive.

"I can't remember ever having so much fun," she gasped, as she collapsed back in her chair.

Franz poured them both a large measure of wine before taking a generous swig, then waved his glass at the heaving throng of revellers. "This is what this country could be like if it wasn't for that arsehole, Hitler."

Not for the first time, Trudy admonished him. "Franz, you can't be so reckless. Even in a place like this the Party will have spies."

Franz gave her a hopeless look. "I can't help the way I feel." He suddenly became serious. "I want to get out. You know, leave, emigrate, go and live in England or America." He again waved his glass vaguely at the revellers. "That's the dream of these people. That's why they dress up. They want to look like Americans, talk like Americans, feel free like Americans."

"You will, one day."

He looked wistful. "Maybe. I'd rather be English than German right now." He glanced sideways at her and grinned. "Ready for another dance?" Trudy held out her hands and once again they joined the party.

Midway through a number, the band abruptly changed tune and a great cheer erupted as a black singer took the microphone. Trudy sensed the thrill of rebelliousness that coursed through the audience. A black jazz singer, right under the noses of the Nazis. He sang a medley of favourites that had the entire hall singing in unison.

Trudy stood on tiptoe and yelled in Franz's ear. "This is outrageous. What happens if the police decide to raid?"

He bent down, turned her head and shouted, "There are people keeping watch. We receive plenty of warning." He laughed. "In any case, many of these kid's parents are senior Nazis or rich supporters of the Party." He looked at her and grimaced. "It's a mad world we live in."

Suddenly, a change of mood affected the fringe of the crowd. Laughter died and people looked serious and concerned. News of whatever had happened swept through the hall. Groups stood around, with heads bowed, listening intently to anyone who possessed any information. On the edge of the throng, Trudy spotted a man pushing his way towards the front. She lost him for a second before he reappeared on the stage. The singer stopped and bent his head as the man reached him and spoke. Trudy felt a shiver of alarm run through her. "It must be a police raid," she thought. The band stopped playing, with a chaotic jumble of discordant notes, leaving a residue of anxious murmurs from the audience.

Trudy glanced around, frantically seeking out Katerina. If it was a raid it would be best if they were all together. She spotted her friend pushing through the crowd. She shouted to her and beckoned her over. "What's happening?" Katerina looked nervous.

"Ladies and Gentlemen, your attention, please." The speaker waited until silence descended. "At five o'clock this morning, the German army crossed the Polish border." A collective gasp swept across the hall. "We are at war with Poland." A few cheered but were instantly hushed into silence. A ripple of unease spread around the room.

"What does it mean?" Katerina looked perplexed.

"That depends on the British," Trudy said. "They've made it clear - an attack on Poland will compel them to come to their aid." She looked grim.

"Surely no one wants another war?"

"It doesn't mean war," someone butted in. "The people from West Poland are German, same as in the Sudentenland. We're just recovering what's ours."

"The Englanders don't want another war," someone else added.

Franz sighed. "Unfortunately, we have a leader who likes using military force." He grabbed their hands. "Come on. Let's head home."

WAR

"I am speaking to you from the cabinet room at 10 Downing Street. This morning, the British ambassador in Berlin handed the German Government a final note stating that, unless we heard from them by 11 o'clock that they were prepared, at once, to withdraw their troops from Poland, a state of war would exist between us. I have to tell you now that no such undertaking has been received, and that consequently this country is at war with Germany.

You can imagine what a bitter blow it is to me that all my long struggle to win peace has failed. Yet I cannot believe ..."

Susan gradually reduced the volume until the radio clicked off. She turned around to be confronted by a sea of shocked faces. "I'd a feeling it would come to this," she said.

"My God, Susan! I don't know how you can be so calm," Josey said.

Sep glanced at his wife. He knew her too well. He knew exactly what she was going through because he was experiencing it himself. His family was disintegrating. His mind seethed with anger and frustration. He forced himself to suppress his emotions.

"What will happen, Ma?" Harriet sounded anxious.

"The British will win – eventually," Susan said. "They have an empire and a large navy."

"No, Ma – I meant what will happen to us?" Harriet looked at her parents in turn. "Johan might have to fight against us. Isn't that right, Pa?"

Sep nodded.

"And what about you, Ma?" Harriet struggled to stop herself from bursting into tears. "You're British. You have a British passport."

"Susan, you'll need to apply to become German." Marie looked desperately from Susan to Sep. "That wouldn't be a problem, would it? You were married in Doppelgau. That should count for something. You've been living here for... what... twenty years now?"

"And both Harriet and Johan are Austrian," Josey added.

Susan closed her eyes and shook her head. "It's not that easy. It's the villagers." She sat down with the others at the table and buried her head in her hands. "We're already outcasts. We were friends with the Rubensteins. That's sufficient reason for many in the village to turn hostile. Imagine what they'll be like when they have a real enemy living amongst them?"

Josey snorted in disgust. "They'd be turning on us all."

"Exactly, Josey." Susan pressed her palms on the table. "They'd turn on you and your family. I can't let that happen."

"So, what will you do?"

Susan glanced across at her husband. "We haven't decided."

193

Sep noticed Susan's eyes moisten. She was close to breaking down. "We'll sleep on it. I'll try and get hold of Johan tomorrow if the post office phone is free. We'll discuss it as a family." He got to his feet. Marie and Josey recognised the signal. It was time to leave the Breitners in peace.

In reality, the family were given no choice. Four days later, Susan received a letter ordering her to report to Gestapo headquarters in Brandt for internment. Only one suitcase and her British passport were permitted. There was to be no appeal.

LITTLE BIRD FLIES

Herr Hofner was euphoric. "Isn't it splendid?" he gushed, as he folded the paper and threw it nonchalantly onto the back seat of the car. "In less than four weeks, the might of the Wehrmacht crushed the Poles."

Trudy smiled thinly. Although she loved driving, she detested the shared journey to work. It was bad enough that Hofner took every opportunity to, apparently accidentally, brush her leg with his hand, carelessly drop his pen into the footwell so he might catch a glimpse of her thigh, or casually drape his hand over the back of her seat. However, now she had to suffer his babbling adoration of Hitler, the Party and the inalienable right of the German People to unite under the Third Reich. She took comfort that she only had to endure one more week. Then she and Katerina would move into their apartment, and Hofner would become Dagmar's problem. In the meantime, she needed to keep the lecherous bastard distracted.

"Do you think the British will give us problems?"

"Pah! The British will see sense once the Poles accept their lot." He gazed out of the window and admired the avenue of red and black swastikas. "We're not threatening the British or their precious Empire. We want to unite all Germans, dispose of the Jewish problem and create our own destiny." He laughed. "If they keep bombing us with leaflets we've nothing to fear."

Trudy smiled, but inside she remained unconvinced. The leaflet raid had happened at night. No-one had known about it until the following day. A few sirens had gone off, and hardly anyone rushed to the shelters.

She parked and followed Hofner into the office, past the heel-clicking, saluting police and up the stairs. They passed through the typing pool. As usual, the girls stood and raised their arms as the boss strode through to a chorus of Heil Hitler. That morning the girls were especially enthusiastic and shouted the greeting with particular bright-eyed passion. The fall of Warsaw featured on every front page, and it was a good day to be German. The exceptions were the timid looking recruit who was yet to find her feet, and Frau Tolheim, the office supervisor, who ruled the pool with a rod of iron and was the only woman Hofner appeared to be scared of.

It was thanks to Frau Tolheim that Trudy escaped a life of drudgery typing out endless reports, orders, procedure notes, committee minutes, letters, bulletins, schedules, witness statements, prosecutions and Lord knew what else. Her intervention also distanced Trudy from the unwanted advances of Commissioner Hofner.

"Trudy Heppel is too bright to be stuck in the typing pool," Frau Tolheim informed Hofner. "She has a head on her, and would be better deployed in a more demanding position".

As a consequence, Trudy found herself attached to the Luftschutzgemeinschaft, with responsibility for inspections of the air raid preparedness across the city. She was grateful for Frau Tolheim's intervention. For the first time she felt her intellect was being recognised, and was eager to demonstrate her organisational capabilities. It also distanced her from Hofner's naked lechery and furtive groping. However, as she quickly found out, she couldn't totally escape his malign influence, and even Frau Tolheim's favour came at a price.

"So, what are you suggesting, Fraulein Heppel?' Hofner's aggressiveness initially threw Trudy. She'd expected to deliver a situation report, not recommendations on how to improve the organisation. However, she recognised that, since she had established herself in her new role, Hofner had resorted to crude bullying tactics as payback for her resisting his advances. She quickly recovered her poise.

"In what respect, sir?"

Hofner gave a thin smile, adjusted his glasses, and looked down at her report. "You say that the street and block wardens are functioning reasonably well." He flipped a page over and stabbed his finger down. "And here on page three, you mention twice that fire-fighting capability is variable." He traced his finger across the page. "And, towards the end, you mention that there is a lack of awareness in many of the air-raid protection communities of the need to treat casualties." He peered at her over his glasses. "Be specific, Fraulein Heppel. In what way is our organisation deficient?"

Tension rose within the room. Every head turned towards her. She was on dicey ground and everyone knew it. Criticising the organisation was tantamount to criticising the Party, and especially Hofner as the Head of Civil Defence. She risked a glance at Frau Tolheim, who gave her an almost imperceptible nod of support.

Trudy took encouragement. If Frau Tolheim wasn't cowed, she be damned if she would be. She knew the concerns but took a few more seconds to marshal her thoughts. "The fire-fighting issue is a matter of training and equipment. Incendiary bombs are light and tend to lodge in roofs. We're issuing stirrup pumps but, according to the fire brigade, the hoses are too short. Also, people are not keeping buckets of water full at all times." She glanced at Hofner to assess his reaction.

He stared back down the table. His bland expression gave nothing away. "And the problem with the street and block wardens?" he snapped.

Trudy took a deep breath. "They're too complacent," she said in a firm voice.

The room was absolutely silent. Either the committee members were admiring her bravery or cringing at her stupidity. Trudy pressed on. "Because there have been no serious air raids, many assume that they won't happen. They believe the Luftwaffe and the anti-aircraft guns will shoot the British down."

"And you don't agree?" Hofner's question was loaded with menace.

"I'm not a military expert, sir. My job is to plan for the possibility of buildings being destroyed - either directly by bombs, or by aircraft loaded with bombs being shot down and crashing on our city."

Hofner gave a reptilian smile. "A good reply, Fraulein. Hopefully, you can provide an equally convincing response to our inability to treat casualties."

"Few people have even basic First Aid training, and..."

"And what do you suggest we do about that?" Hofner cut in, deliberately trying to unsettle her.

"Use the BDM," Trudy retorted. "Make it a requirement for all BDM girls to become air-raid wardens. They have First Aid training."

Hofner found himself thrown by Trudy's instant response. "You'd put them in harm's way?"

She feigned surprise at his question. "The BDM exist to serve."

"I hope you are noting all this, Fraulein Fesling."

Trudy recognised the timid looking girl from the typing pool, frantically scribbling shorthand. For a second, it crossed Trudy's mind that she must be an excellent minute-taker to have been promoted so quickly. However, the girl's mumbled response and the fear on her face suggested Hofner had already crushed her. It also reminded Trudy that she was still on dangerous ground.

"Thank you, Fraulein Heppel."

Trudy felt a wave of relief as the boss sought out someone else to intimidate. She caught the eye of Frau Tolheim who mouthed, "Well done." Suddenly Trudy felt on top of the world.

SUCH SWEET SORROW

Simon spread out everything across the bed. Anton's instructions were precise: travel light taking essential clothing only, make sure boots were broken in and waterproof clothing was in pristine condition, and dress for severe weather conditions. The journey would be no casual hike. They would be climbing rock faces, crossing scree fields and, once above the tree line, there would be ice as well as early winter snow to contend with.

Outside, the rain squall blasted against the small window, making the shutter rattle. Suddenly Simon felt nervous. Although it was only a shower, in the mountains poor weather conditions quickly escalated. What it must be like being caught in a full-scale blizzard he could only imagine. He peered through the rain-splattered glass and was astounded to see someone approaching. Whoever it was struggled against the gusts with body bent double and head held low. Simon scanned the surrounding ground. The figure appeared to be alone. Nevertheless, he reached up to a beam and took down Gregor's hunting rifle. He aimed it at the figure and peered through the sight. It was Harriet. Instantly, he ran out the door and dragged her across the threshold.

"For God's sake, Harriet, what are you playing at?" He threw logs on the fire as Harriet huddled, shivering uncontrollably. She said nothing but sat unprotesting as he roughly pulled the drenched coat and boots off her. "Are you trying to get yourself killed?" He found a blanket and wrapped her up before massaging her feet to get her circulation going. He stopped briefly to fill a pan with water and hung it over the fire. Outside, the gusts increased and the rain now lashed down. "If you'd been caught in that you'd have been in big trouble," he said angrily.

"I had to see you," she whispered through chattering teeth.

He was about to really lose his temper when her expression brought him up short. "What's happened, Schatz," he said gently.

"They've broken up our family. Ma's been arrested, Pa's beside himself, Johan's probably going to end up fighting somewhere." She gazed at him as tears flowed down her cheeks. "And I'm losing you." She bent over and sobbed. "I've never felt so miserable in my life." Her body trembled with her distress, cold and shock.

Simon engulfed her, and vigorously rubbed her back to get some heat into her core as fast as possible. "Okay, it's okay, relax." He glanced around looking for any food to hand.

"There's some bread and stuff in the bag," she mumbled into his chest.

He found the food and thrust it into her hand. "Just eat. I'll get us a hot drink." He pulled her closer to the fire. "Get yourself warm. Then we'll talk."

Gradually Harriet recovered. Hot rum-laced tea succeeded in quelling her shivers. Simon removed her thick woollen socks and massaged her toes and feet. "How are you feeling now?"

She took a big gulp of the Jaeger tea. "I'm warming up."

He grabbed a spare log and propped her feet on it, facing the fire. He leant back on his heels and regarded her. "How did you get here in this weather? Don't tell me you walked up the cliff!"

"No, I rode Johan's bike. I left it near Gregor's place and walked the rest." She gave a tired smile and looked sheepish. "The weather wasn't bad when I set out."

"Why take such a risk?"

"Because I had to see you. Everything is falling apart. For your family and mine." Her face fell. "What have we done to deserve this?" She glanced at him. "The British and French have declared war on the Germans."

"Gregor told me. He suggested I contact the British once I get to Switzerland. He thinks they might be able to use me."

Harriet looked dismayed. "Oh no, Simon, I don't want you to become a soldier."

"I will strike back, Harriet. I owe it to my family and to you."

"But what about us?"

He took her hands. "The only way this war will end is if either the British win or, God forbid, the Germans do," he said fiercely.

"That may take years!"

He nodded. "We need to be strong. I'll come back for you, I promise." He leant forward and kissed her. "It will be hard for us. I've dreaded the thought. I won't even be able to write to you."

"Why not?" She looked dismayed.

"Because letters will be intercepted. It wouldn't take them long to work out who helped me escape."

She stared at him in disbelief. "It can't be so. I'll go mad with worry if I don't know you're safe."

"I'll come for you. I promise with all my heart." He fought back his tears. "As will your Ma, and hopefully Sara and what remains of my family."

Harriet wept as another wave of despair engulfed her. "Every which way we turn the bloody Nazis are ripping our lives to shreds."

"We still have each other, and it won't be long." The sudden crash of the window shutter blown by the wind startled them. He got up and secured it before throwing another log on the fire. "You'll have to stay. It's getting wild out there. You did tell your Pa you were coming here?"

She nodded and wiped the tears from her face.

He sat down and wrapped his arm around her. "We need to stay strong, think about a better future, look for positive things that are happening."

"Like what?"

"Well, the British and French are standing up to the Nazis. At long last someone is prepared to fight back." He gave her a squeeze. "And we should talk about us. Nobody can take our dreams away."

They talked and gradually fought off their demons. A shared meal raised their spirits, and their conversation moved to their hopes and rekindled their feelings for each other. They barely noticed that the weather had developed into a raging storm. By the time fatigue caught up with them, the wind had become a continuous howl, and the rain had turned to sleet that battered the door and shutters. They lay on the bed. Inevitably, conversation gave way to kisses and soft caresses until silence and darkness enveloped them. They lay quiet both trying to hold at bay their rising passion. Then Harriet got up. Simon heard rustling in the pitch black. She climbed back under the covers and snuggled up to him. He felt a bolt of shock as he touched her skin.

"Harriet, you're naked!"

She pressed her head into his neck "I want us to," she whispered. "Please, it may be the only chance we get."

It turned out that chance presented itself often enough. All night and most of the following day they embraced the novelty of it all with unbridled enthusiasm. A seductive glance, the briefest touch, or just a surge of longing, was all it took to ignite the fires. They'd little concept of time as they lost themselves in each other. Initial shyness quickly gave way to reckless abandonment. Nervousness disappeared as they discovered the thrill of unfamiliar pleasure and the desperate need to make the most of the little time they had.

"I don't know why we're even bothering to put our clothes back on." Simon gasped as they lay back, exhausted from their latest entanglement. She looked at him mischievously.

It took the impending deadline of Harriet's departure to curtail their lovemaking. They reluctantly got dressed, their euphoria replaced by mounting despair.

"You can't leave it any later, Harriet." Simon sounded anxious. He opened the window and swung back the blind. Late afternoon sunlight flooded the room. "At least the rain's stopped." He turned to find Harriet sat on the bed, her head buried in her hands. "Hey, come on. We need to be strong." He slowly pulled her to her feet and gently prised her hands away until he cradled her face. "I *will* come back for you, Schatz." He grinned. "Assuming you'll still want me."

She threw her arms around his neck. "Please don't do anything stupid."

He watched her slowly make her way down the track until, with a forlorn wave, she disappeared from view. He'd never felt so desolate.

Two days later, Anton arrived. It was time to depart.

"Wait. I'll make sure it's safe."

Simon barely had the energy to nod. He found a convenient rock and sank down on it. Almost immediately his eyelids grew heavy. He'd never felt so exhausted. He was thankful Gregor's foresight in forcing him to run up and down the mountain. The trek to the border had been brutal. Four days of walking along paths only mountain goats might recognise; stumbling on jagged rocks that twisted ankles, cracked shins, and tortured muscles; crossing treacherous scree slopes so steep that one false move would result in a headlong plummet to certain death; traversing ice fields worn to a glass-like smoothness and so dense that even the ice-pick struggled to make an impression. And all the time the relentless arctic wind cut through his clothing, burned his face and stole all feeling from his fingers and toes. It had been soul-destroying. As they conquered one mountain ridge, another would appear as if taunting them. Their overnight stays in the crude stone alpine mountain shelters offered only limited protection from the wind, and none at all from the sub-zero temperatures.

He forced himself to stay awake. Anton returned just before sunset.

"We need to camp out."

Simon felt his morale drain away. "What's the problem?"

"Mountain troops. Either on exercise or someone's given them a tip-off."

"What about our guide?"

"He'll meet us here first thing tomorrow morning." They gathered branches and bracken for a makeshift shelter. Simon didn't remember falling on the mossy bower, he was unconscious in seconds.

He woke to the sound of approaching boots. He froze. The boots stopped. Simon risked turning his head towards Anton, who lay still and stared back. He slowly raised a finger to his lips. In their shelter they'd be difficult to spot. The boots moved closer, then stopped again. A low whistle of an alpine melody drifted through the trees. Anton smiled and got to his feet, indicating Simon should remain hidden.

After a muffled conversation, he returned. "Your guide's here. I'll head back." He held out his hand. "Do exactly as he says. Good luck." Their brief handshake seemed so inadequate.

Simon emerged to be confronted by a thin, wiry man with a face so creased and weather-beaten he could have been anything from thirty to eighty years old. His clothes spoke of a man that spent his life in the wild. A dark, heavily patched green-brown leather coat, britches and a hat made him look as if he might have emerged from the very soil of the mountains.

"You ready?"

201

Simon nodded. "Which way are we heading?"

The man pointed to a snow-capped peak towering in the distance, its summit bathed by the sun's first rays. "That's the border." He jerked his chin towards a second peak, not as high. "You cross between the two." He gazed at the overcast sky. "We need to move fast."

"What about the soldiers?"

The man shifted his gaze from the sky to the surrounding mountains. "Let's hope they're occupied on other things." He pointed to the forest that wrapped itself around the lower slopes. "We follow the treeline. Where the forest stops, we traverse the open ground and climb to the snow line. From there it's straight up." He looked back at the sky. "With luck we should get some cloud cover later in the day."

They set off and made it to the edge of the forest in just over two hours. The guide paused and surveyed the route ahead. Without tree cover, the hamlet lay clearly visible nestled at the head of the valley. On the single access road two military trucks were parked. "We need to move quickly. If we can see them, they can see us." He glanced at his watch. "Hopefully, they will still be having their breakfast." He gave Simon an up and down look as if assessing his condition for the trial ahead. "You okay?"

Simon nodded. Although he hadn't had much sleep, he felt surprisingly refreshed. The guide led them across at a diagonal so they would reach the snow line quicker. After thirty minutes, Simon's hips protested at the awkward gait and he began to fall behind. The guide allowed him to catch up. "Another two hundred metres and we'll lead with the other leg. It'll spread the load. Zigzagging gives us height and..."

The sound of falling rocks and stones cut his sentence short. The clatter quickly developed into a rumble as larger boulders became dislodged, until a full-scale landslide roared down the mountain. Although over five hundred metres away, Simon instinctively crouched as the thunderous sound reverberated around the valley.

"*Sheisse!*" Simon found himself forced to the ground. The guide threw himself beside him "Keep absolutely still."

They lay until the landslide abated. Simon moved as if to get up. "Stay down," the guide snarled. Minutes passed. The valley fell silent. "*Sheisse, sheisse, sheisse.* The bastards have spotted us." He rolled over so he faced Simon. "That's bad luck. The rock fall made the entire squad stare at the mountain. We need to split up."

Simon felt a surge of panic. "Why?"

"To divide them." He looked at the slope. "We go straight up. Once we hit the snow line, you keep going. Straight, mind, no deviation. You'll be heading directly for the border."

"What about you?"

"I'll head south. Unless they know these mountains, they'll go after me as it will look to them as if they could easily cut me off." He grinned. "What they can't see is a ravine between them and me." He dragged Simon to his feet. "Come on."

Climbing straight up meant crawling on all fours, grabbing tufts of the tough mountain grass and sedges, clambering over half-buried rocks, and scaling slippery mud walls where the vegetation had eroded. Simon blanked his mind to the consequences of losing his grip. He focused on following the boots of the guide above him. The higher they went, the more difficult it became. The dew soaked into his jacket and trousers, weighing him down. It quickly turned to ice as they grew closer to the snow-line. They crawled through half-frozen bogs and drifts of snow that remained in hollows hidden from the sun. Eventually they were surrounded by ice-encrusted snow. The guide stood still and looked back down the slope. Simon hauled himself to his feet and leant on his knees, trying to force oxygen into his lungs.

"*Sheisse*, these guys are good," the guide muttered.

Simon craned his torso around so he could survey the slopes back towards the hamlet. His stomach suddenly felt as if it was caught in a vice. Dozens of soldiers were scrambling towards them like a swarm of small green ants. It wasn't just the numbers that terrified him, it was the speed they were climbing.

"These guys are seriously fit." The guide didn't disguise his anxiety. "Get going. Straight up, don't stop." With that he headed off.

Simon heard a belated, "Good luck." He quickly abandoned his desperate scrabbling on the frozen surface in favour of a slow, relentless clamber. He fought off a rising surge of panic, banished the image of the advancing mountain troops and concentrated on climbing, step by step, metre by metre.

A sudden shout, followed by a rifle shot, spurred him on. He risked a furtive glance back under his arm. The soldiers could be heard but not seen. He prayed they'd fallen for the guide's ruse. Another rifle shot rang out. A surge of adrenalin coursed through his veins. He wouldn't become a victim: not until he'd had his revenge. The ground flattened, and he got to his feet and progressed in a clumsy stumbling run. Mist descended and his hopes soared as it morphed into a dense cloud. Fine specks of snow grazed his face. Then everything turned white. There was no up or down, no horizon, no reference point. He navigated by feel and instinct. The shouts behind were close. One came from his left, another to his right as the troops moved to cut off lines of escape. He bulldozed his way through the deepening snow. Panic threatened to consume him as he realised he was leaving an obvious trail, and by packing the snow he made it easy for his pursuers. The snowfall increased, blowing into his eyes and freezing his eyelids. Then the cloud got brighter and the sun broke through. Ahead, he had a brief glimpse of a blinding white snow ridge set against a bright blue sky, before the cloud cover returned. He must be close to the summit. He sucked in great lungfuls of thin air and gathered himself for one final push.

To his horror, the sound of metal clinking on metal indicated his pursuers were only metres behind.

Suddenly the ground gave way and he plummeted. For a second he was in freefall. He hit the snow, cartwheeling and tumbling. He put his arms out, trying to stem his fall. He felt his wrist smash against something solid. He collided into a wall of snow so hard it drove the air from his lungs. He lay paralysed with shock, desperately gasping for breath. It felt as if a great weight pressed on his chest, and gradually the world went grey.

He came to, staring at a bright blue sky. White cotton wool clouds drifted overhead. His body felt numb but he was breathing and alive. He'd no idea how long he'd lain there. The threat of the pursuing troops washed through him in a tidal wave of despair. He was helpless. Nowhere to run even if he could get to his feet. He squeezed his eyes shut and prayed for forgiveness from his God, his family and, above all, Harriet. He opened his eyes to be confronted by a grim-faced soldier. Without a word, he dug Simon out and hauled him to his feet. Simon stood swaying groggily. "Händes auf den kopf," the soldier ordered. He dusted the snow off and searched Simon's pockets. "Juden?"

Simon hadn't the energy to deny it.

FRAGMENTATION

Johan and Jurgen were given leave from military training to come home for Christmas. The Breitner family seized upon their unexpected visit as a reason to celebrate. However, the events of the year cast a long shadow, and the atmosphere within the household was subdued. It took a letter from Susan to raise spirits to something approaching those of previous years.

"She's being held in a place near the Dutch border."

"Is she alright? Is she being treated properly?" Johan couldn't hide his impatience.

Sep flipped the Red Cross letter over. "She says there are about a hundred of them, and they are being treated well. They have regular meals, and the guards keep reminding them they are abiding by the Geneva Convention."

"Guards!" Harriet sounded worried. "It's supposed to be an internment camp!"

Sep scanned the rest of the letter. "They get Red Cross food parcels and an allowance from the British Government."

"That's something then." Johan sounded sarcastic.

"Some internees have also found work outside the camp." Sep glanced at Harriet. "I don't think they'd allow that if it were a prison."

"The main thing is she's safe." Josey was determined to be upbeat.

"She says she's missing us all dreadfully. Johan, you must stay safe, and Harriet, you have to…" Sep stopped, put the letter on the table and abruptly left the room. He found a quiet corner in the cow byre. His chest felt so tight he could hardly breathe. Until now, he hadn't realised how much stress he was under. Ever since her arrest he'd kept the worry and fears at bay. But he hadn't been sleeping well, and the absence of letters created a vacuum that his imagination filled with terrifying thoughts and images. The arrival of the innocuous-looking Red Cross letter had released his suppressed emotions. He leant against the wall, bent forward and held his head in his hands. He had never felt such loneliness and grief.

"You okay, Pa?" He felt Harriet's hand caress his head.

He suddenly felt ashamed and embarrassed. He nodded and, under cover of his hands, tried to wipe away his tears.

"It's alright, Pa." Harriet gave him a cuddle. "It's been so hard for you."

"It's a bit overwhelming," Sep muttered. "It must be dreadful for her."

"Now we know where she is, we can all write and send her parcels full of food, presents and reminders of home."

Sep nodded. "Bloody bastard Nazis," he swore fiercely.

"We need to look after each other, especially Johan. Imagine what it's like for him. His Ma's being held by the people he's supposed to go out

205

and fight for. The same people that murdered his girlfriend." Harriet's face was wet with tears.

"We've all suffered." Sep stood and enveloped his daughter in his arms. "Let's pray Simon is safe."

The mention of Simon opened the floodgates. Harriet sobbed into her father's chest. It took all her willpower to banish the dark thoughts of his fate. The only news she had was no news. Tara's husband could only tell her that the guide had evaded capture, and the last anyone saw of Simon was him heading for the border. Like her father, her imagination was filled with despair. What hope existed was like the fragile flicker of a candle flame caught in a draught.

"We need to look after each other." She felt her father give her an affectionate squeeze. "Come on, let's get back inside."

Inside the Stube the atmosphere was subdued. It was supposed to be Christmas but, despite everyone doing their best to celebrate, the conversation kept veering towards the war.

"Hopefully, this time next year peace will have been declared, and Susan and Simon will be back." Josey said.

"I hope you're right. Otherwise, Johan and I will probably find ourselves camped in a trench on the French border." Jurgen said.

"Have they said where you'll be posted?" Gunter helped himself to another of Harriet's mince pies, earning a disapproving look from Marie.

Johan put down his mother's letter. "Rumour is Poland or somewhere near the French border."

"Wherever you get sent, fill your pockets with food. Eat every chance you get and never volunteer for anything," Stephan said. Everyone looked at him, surprised he could bring himself to talk about anything to do with war. "And watch out for glory-hunters. They'll sacrifice anyone for a medal," Stephan continued, his voice getting more animated. "And always have an escape plan. Officers think only of attack, they don't spend much time considering how to defend or retreat. And get in the habit of looking for cover, even if it's just a rest break – something solid...."

"Pa, we'll be fine." Jurgen recognised his father was getting agitated.

"We'll go out together and we'll make sure we come back together," Johan said.

"You make sure you do, lads," Stephan said, his eyes watering.

Silence engulfed the Stube until Josey piped up, "This is all getting too sombre. Why don't you men go to the Adler for a drink? Us women want to be left alone for a girl chat."

"Of course, if you think that would be a good idea," Sep said. He and the rest of the men were already rising from the table.

"Can you drop these around to Frau Ansbacher's on your way," Harriet said, handing over a basket of traditional Weinachstküchen as they filed out the Stube door. "And wish her and her family a Happy New Year."

She turned around to be confronted by her two aunts regarding her. Both looked serious. "What's the matter?" Harriet blanched.

"We need to talk about your condition," Josey said.

Harriet felt the blood drain from her face. She slowly sat down. "Is it obvious?"

"Let's put it this way," Marie said. "You can't pretend it's too many mince pies."

A FRIEND DEPARTS

"I knew it was you!" Tante Bri shrieked with delight, as she did every time Trudy dropped in to see her. "My, just look at you." She stood back and examined her 'little bird'. "You're quite the young lady about town." Instantly, the coffee percolator was on the stove, the bottle of Schnapps moved within arm's reach of her favourite armchair, and the heap of half-mended clothes swept from the other chair to allow Trudy to sit.

"I'll make it, Madi." Trudy dropped her small suitcase beside the table.

"You stoppin'?"

"If it's okay."

"Course it's okay! What a question." Bri dropped her bulk into her seat and gasped in relief. The effort of opening the door exhausted her. "To what do I owe the pleasure?"

"I want to make sure you're looking after yourself and not overindulging." Trudy picked up the Schnapps bottle, gave her aunt a quizzical look, and moved it back to the dresser shelf.

Bri pretended not to notice. "And the real reason?"

"Franz got his call-up on Tuesday."

"Oh!" Bri looked crestfallen. "What does he feel about it?"

Trudy sighed. "Not happy. Turned up drunk and in tears on our doorstep in the early hours of Wednesday morning. He says he'll surrender to the British at the first opportunity."

"That ain't good talk."

"No. But there's nothing to be done. It's either join voluntarily, face being forced into it, or worse."

"Some can't wait to join. They think it will be over before they have a chance to be heroes. Take that Lothar Müller, for example."

Trudy snorted in derision. "Madi, Lothar Müller wouldn't join to be a hero. He joined up early to get into a flash uniform so he can become an official Nazi thug. He'll wheedle his way to some cushy job well away from the front-line."

Tante Bri nodded. "He was parading around the other week, all done up in his SS uniform. Claims he's off to Poland to carry out special assignments."

"Taking charge of the stores or the catering most likely. Anywhere where he can siphon off goods for the black market. It won't be anything dangerous."

"Didn't sound like it. He's part of... oh, he did say... do you know my memory isn't what it was... it'll come to me. I'm glad to see the back of him. He's a nasty piece of work, always was and always will be." She took the mug of Ersatz coffee Trudy proffered. "Anyway, enough of that little worm. How's my girl been getting on?"

208

"I'm doing well. I got a pay rise. So…" She reached into her handbag and extracted a small roll of notes. "I can give you a little bit more each month."

Bri immediately pushed Trudy's hand away. "Trudy, Liebling, you mustn't keep doing this. What's an old biddy like me going to spend such money on, eh?"

"Food, little luxuries, something special, anything." Trudy bent over and kissed her aunt on the top of her head. In doing so, she pushed the money into Bri's apron pocket. "Anything that will make you happy." She sank into the chair opposite and cradled her mug in her hands.

"Seeing my little bird flying free is my greatest happiness." Bri lent over and patted Trudy's knee.

Trudy felt the same thrill she remembered feeling as a little girl whenever her Madi praised her. "I'm hoping to move on, either through promotion or maybe a change of job. I've put my name forward to become part of the Reichsluftschutzbund. Katerina and I need to earn more to stay ahead of the rent."

"Oh, how's that lovely friend of yours?"

"She's landed on her feet as well. Settled in at the shipyard. She's loving being independent. And, of course, she and Franz are hitting it off."

"So that's why you're here, eh?" Bri gave Trudy a knowing glance.

"Yeah, well, I thought the two of them might welcome some private time, given Franz's news." Trudy put her mug down and stretched her arms above her head, looking relaxed. "I don't fancy being the gooseberry."

Bri looked exasperated. "When are you going to find a young man of your own, Trudy Heppel?"

"When he comes along."

Bri struggled to her feet and wagged her finger. "An attractive young lady like you ought to have a whole string of admirers. You can afford to pick and choose. Beauty and brains. I've told you before, you're quite a catch."

Trudy laughed. "Don't you worry about that. I've been treated to lots of dates - with some attractive men, I might add."

"But not Mr Right?" Bri reached the dresser, grabbed a small bowl of sugar and dropped half a teaspoon into her cup.

Trudy shook her head. "Not so far." She looked thoughtful. "I'm not sure I want a serious relationship, with so many men being called up."

"Very sensible, I'm sure." Bri wheezed and puffed her way back to her chair and collapsed into it. Trudy smiled to herself and pretended not to notice that the Schnapps bottle had magically reappeared in its familiar position.

"So, what's this Reichsluftschutzbund business all about?' Bri vigorously stirred her cup to ensure every last granule of sugar was thoroughly dissolved, then lit a cigarette.

"It's part of the air defence section. The powers that be were impressed by my organising ability. I'll be working with the searchlight team, with responsibility for coordinating recruitment and deployment of crews for the Luftwaffe."

Bri looked anxious. "Does that mean you'll be out in the open when them bombers come flying over, cos you mark my words, gal, them bombers will come sooner or later."

"Madi, don't worry. I'm organising recruitment – women aren't allowed to operate the lights, at least not yet. Besides, most of the searchlights are outside the city to catch the planes as they approach. And those that are within the city are well protected."

Bri breathed out a stream of smoke. "You'll be away from that Hofner fellow?"

"He's got another poor girl in his sights. Trouble is she's young and scared of him."

"Bloody Nazis."

Her outburst alarmed Trudy. "Madi, you must be careful what you say. There are informers everywhere."

"Don't I know it." She mimed a spit to emphasise her disgust at anything Nazi. She suddenly chuckled. "Old Man Mordechai managed to get out."

Trudy nearly spilt her drink in surprise. "He's gone!?"

"Yep, and good for him, I say. He shuts his shop last Friday as normal. Next thing, a bunch of them Nazi thugs arrive Saturday night, smash his windows, breaks down the door, only to find Old Man Mordechai and his missus gone and the shop empty." Bri's chuckle developed into a wheezy, cough-wracked laugh. "What I'd give to see them stormtrooper's faces. They didn't even find a Pfennig."

"Where's he gone?"

After another bout of coughing, Bri shrugged. "No one knows. A van took all his stuff, and another vehicle came and whisked him and his missus to the docks. Maybe he's said something in that letter." She waved a hand towards the mantlepiece. "It was pushed through my door. Go on, open it. It's addressed to you."

Trudy put down her cup and retrieved the envelope. '*T. Heppel, Private and Confidential.*' was written in neat handwriting on the front. She broke the seal and extracted a tiny sliver of paper with a single line of writing. '*Handelsbank, Flüssemühle Str, Zurich, Schweiz 23041922/09*'. She flipped the sheet over to make sure nothing else was written.

While Trudy had been distracted, Bri took a surreptitious swig from the Schnapps bottle. She hastily recorked the bottle and eyed Trudy. "Well?"

210

"Nothing much." Trudy looked thoughtful. "He's settled my account, I think."

"He's a good man. Both him and his wife were so kind. There's plenty in this neighbourhood who've got a lot to thank them for."

"Not enough to protect them, though." Trudy sank slowly back into her chair.

Bri extracted the last drag from her cigarette, before taking another quick puff to ensure not one fibre of tobacco remained, and then she stubbed it out. She sighed and gave Trudy a serious look. "Good people like them forced to leave, while them Nazi bastards steal their property and feather their own nests."

Trudy folded the paper and put it in her pocket. Bri's comment unsettled her. Earlier that day she'd heard Frau Tolheim whisper under her breath, "*God help them,*" as she went through Trudy's list of 'undesirables'.

"Einsatzgruppe!" Tante Bri said out of the blue.

"What?"

"Einsatzgruppe. That's what that worm Lothar has joined. It's just come back to me."

"Oh, right." She'd no idea who or what Einsatzgruppe were, and right now she wasn't interested. The fate of Old Man Mordechai, his wife, and the other so-called undesirables played on her mind.

CONFESSION

Harriet stood at her bedroom window and watched her father enter the milking parlour. She was dismayed at the changes in him. He seemed to be withdrawing further into himself with each passing day. Every action now seemed ponderous, his shoulders were hunched and his head bowed. She was also concerned about his state of mind. Apart from the Ansbachers and Drössels, the rest of the village treated the family as pariahs. Her father still visited the Adler with Stephan, but they never stayed long. The fates of Susan, Johan and Jurgen weighed heavily, and now she was about to add to his burden.

She pressed her hands down on her blouse. Her pregnancy could no longer be concealed beneath its loose folds. Time had run out. She knew if she didn't face her responsibility, Aunt Josey would take it upon herself to break the news. She steeled herself, then went downstairs.

Sep slowly looked up as she entered. "You're looking anxious," he said, then ran his hand through his hair and sighed. "Has something happened?" The resigned way he said it almost undermined Harriet's resolve. Blubbing like a silly schoolgirl was the last thing she intended. She needed to be confident and in control. There was no way she was going to allow her situation to further wear down her father's already low spirits. "I've something important to tell you, Pa."

Sep gave a tired smile. "When's it due?"

Harriet looked stunned. "What!"

He slowly shook his head. "Harriet, your mother and I have had the joy of creating two beautiful children. I know how pregnancy changes a woman's behaviour, I spent hours comforting your mother as the morning sickness reduced her to a wreck and, no matter how hard you try, babies to tend to reveal their presence." He glanced meaningfully at her stomach.

"You know!"

"Your face gave me the first clue." He sat down on the wooden bench and patted it to encourage her to sit beside him. "You look exactly like your mother did when she announced your presence." Harriet sank down beside him, completely thrown by his revelation.

"I take it Simon is the father?"

She nodded.

He grabbed her hand. "Then we must pray very hard."

"I'm not sorry, Pa."

"Nor should you be." He squeezed her hand.

Harriet used the silence that opened up to get her thoughts back in order. "I won't be a burden on you, Pa," she said quietly. "It's my responsibility and I'll work to support the child when it's born. Tante Josey said I can work in her factory. I'll have to start at the bottom and work my way up. It's what I want to do anyway, become a businesswoman like

Josey. So, it's a good way for me to learn. I can still be here to help you around the farm and look after you. And the factory is in Achbrugge, so I won't be an embarrassment to you in the village."

"An embarrassment!?"

"People will gossip, Pa. You know…."

Sep didn't allow her to finish. "What makes you think I give a damn about what this village thinks," he growled. "This village turned its back on the Breitner family. They can all go and hang for all I care."

"Pa." She turned to face him. "Please. I meant I just don't want to add to our problems. Things are difficult enough. I'll fend for myself." She looked at him with pleading eyes.

Sep calmed down. "Bloody Nazis," he muttered under his breath. "Bloody wars." He suddenly glanced at her. "What about your mother?"

"I've written to her and to Johan."

"You've told them Simon is the father?"

She shook her head. "I've not mentioned his name." She stared at him. "It's too risky. But they'll know from what I've written."

"He might not come back, sweetheart," he said gently.

Harriet couldn't prevent the tears welling up. She quickly wiped them away, determined not to break down. "I have to hope, Pa. We were in love for a long time. It's just that we didn't know it." She looked wistful. "Nothing is what we planned. We didn't plan anything. We never had the chance." She gave a grim smile. "One thing about starting with nothing is that things can't get worse."

"That's not true."

"Oh, Pa! Don't say that. We have to believe things will get better, otherwise what's the point?"

"I meant that you aren't starting with nothing." He leant over and gave his daughter an affectionate kiss on the cheek. "A baby is about *the* most important thing in the world."

Harriet really struggled to stop herself from bursting into tears.

"And you have a family that will support you. There're many not so fortunate. And you have your own place to live."

"Pa - I intend to stand on my own two feet."

Sep shook his head. "You misunderstand me, Harriet." He patted her hand. "We own the Rubenstein's property. Or to be more accurate, we hold the Rubenstein's property in trust. I'm sure Simon would want you to have it."

"I don't understand?"

He gave her a sideways look. "You remember when I disappeared for a few days?" Old Doctor Rubenstein saw what was coming. He took steps to protect as much of the Rubenstein's wealth as he could. He asked me to buy their house and surgery in Doppelgau, on the understanding that, once the Nazis had gone, he or one of his family could recover it. I went with Doctor Rubenstein to see a lawyer in Innsbruck who arranged the

213

whole thing – set up the Trust, finance and registration. Technically, we own the house."

Harriet looked appalled. "He knew that the family might be murdered?"

"Good God, no! He assumed they would be forced to live in exile for a few years until the Nazis were removed from power."

"So, when Simon returns, he can claim it back."

"That's the idea. Either Simon or any of the Rubensteins."

"Does Simon know?"

Sep shook his head. "The only people with the knowledge are Doctor Rubenstein, me, your Ma, the Innsbruck lawyer and now you." He looked hard at her. "It's best we keep it that way."

"What happens if the Nazis try to take it over? That's what happened to the Rubenstein's house in Achbrugge."

"The Doppelgau property register will show that I've owned the property for the past five years and received a nominal rent from the Rubensteins." He grinned. "The lawyer was thorough."

"Even so, I wouldn't want to move in. It doesn't seem right."

"I'm not throwing you out," he said, patting her stomach, "or my granddaughter."

She smiled. "It could be a boy."

"Not a chance."

CONFRONTATION

"What am I supposed to say? – 'Forgive me, Father, for I have sinned?'"

Father Thomas smiled. "Only if you are of the true faith and have something to confess."

Gunter snorted. "I've little faith in anything."

"This is where I'm supposed to say – 'Ah! But God moves in mysterious ways.' And 'His will, will be done.'"

"Well, whatever your faith says about forgiveness, it has a serious challenge on its hands if it wants to welcome this particular sinner back into the fold." He opened his briefcase, extracted a thick file and dropped it on the pew between them.

"Is that the prosecution file?"

Gunter gave a bitter laugh. "No, Father Thomas. That sits in Kommissioner Keunsberg's office, probably in a safe or in his fire grate. Either way, it is unlikely to see the light of day."

Father Thomas glanced at the file and frowned. "It's a large file."

"It contains everything: your records, the papers you retrieved from the Diocese archive, and my investigations - witness and evidence statements, criminal and common law charge sheets, all cross-referenced."

The priest lowered his voice. "Just for one man!?"

Gunter gazed around the cathedral that stood empty apart from them, and a few of the faithful kneeling in silent prayer. "Father Thomas - Wagner isn't the only person who should be sweating." Gunter gave the priest a meaningful look.

Thomas paled. "Should I be concerned? I thought I helped your investigation."

"You did. And now I'm returning the favour." Gunter looked up at the great vaulted ceiling. "Would you like to know what my investigation uncovered?"

Thomas gave a mute nod.

Gunter bent forward and rested his hands on his knees. "Let's start with Monsignor Wagner. The man is a serial paedophile, praying on vulnerable young girls. He selects victims who can't defend themselves because of their age and circumstances: orphans, children in care, young novices and youngsters of particularly devout parents who are easily intimidated. Thanks to the file you recovered, I discovered Monsignor Wagner began his attacks over thirty-five years ago. I secured written statements from four of his victims. However, they are the tip of the iceberg. He probably abused scores of young girls, and his crimes continue."

The young priest looked horrified. "I had no idea."

Gunter ignored the outburst. "In addition, our saintly Monsignor has been siphoning off Church funds and property for decades, for personal gain. The amount is impossible to quantify since the Church never investigated, and it's of little interest to the Gestapo. However, the detective in me can't help following leads.

"I can understand."

"Then there is the matter of Monsignor's relationship with Kommissioner Keunsberg. Wagner has provided details of over a hundred so-called 'enemies of the state' to the Kommissioner." Gunter glanced sideways at Father Thomas.

"Surely there's nothing illegal about that?" The young priest shifted uncomfortably on the pew.

"There is, when the names provided are of entirely innocent people on trumped-up charges, or whose only crime is standing in the way of Monsignor Wagner's ambitions."

"That would be difficult to prove."

Gunter ignored the observation and moved on. "Then there is the question of people who are accessories. The Abbess of St Catherine's, for example, is guilty not only of being fully aware of Wagner's deviancy, but of actively providing access to vulnerable novices and the means and locations for offences to take place. She is also working with him to defraud the Church by diverting Church funds. The sums are considerable - something perhaps the Church ought to look at. You agree, Father Thomas?"

He nodded. Gunter noticed the sheen of sweat on the young man's face. His voice became hard. "And would you also agree that those who aided in denouncing innocent people, knowing that they were likely to be tortured and sent to concentration camps for further mistreatment and death, should face justice?"

"I hope you're not suggesting that I knew anything about that."

Gunter sat back, spread his arms along the back of the pew and looked nonchalant. "In which case you have a clear conscience and have nothing to fear from a final reckoning by your maker, your employer, or maybe an open court, should this country ever find its way back to civilisation."

Father Thomas wiped his brow on the back of his sleeve. "Honestly, Detective, I didn't know. They were just a list of names."

Gunter looked disgusted. "Just a list, eh? A piece of paper that could be easily disposed of and forgotten about."

"I don't mean it like that. It's just that I didn't give them a second thought," he blurted, then buried his head in his hands as he realised what he'd just said.

Gunter raised his eyebrows. "It's not me you'd have to convince, is it?"

"For God's sake, Herr Schwartz, I didn't know. What can I do?"

Gunter let the young man sweat. When he judged he'd suffered enough, he adopted a more conciliatory tone. "Fortunately, Father Thomas,

216

there is a way forward from this sorry mess, *if…*" he raised his finger to emphasise the condition, "you are prepared to do the right thing."

"Of course."

"There are three files, besides Keunsberg's."

Thomas looked confused. Gunter gave a thin smile. "This is file one." He nodded at the papers on the pew. "Naturally, I have a duplicate - just in case. The third file is here." He reached across and gently tapped Father Thomas's head. "You now know your boss and the Abbess are criminals. The question is whether or not you can live with that knowledge. My investigation has hit the buffers. The case will only progress if Kommisioner Keunsberg wants it to. That will only happen if Wagner's usefulness and credibility become eroded, or he becomes a liability." Gunter stared hard at Thomas. "Or you do the right thing." He eased himself to his feet. "Oh, just so you're aware." He turned to face the priest. "Three people know that these files exist. You, me and one other. We live in dangerous times, Father Thomas. It pays to take out insurance." He held out his hand. Initially, Gunter took grim satisfaction that the priest's palm felt sweaty. Then he was consumed by a feeling of self-loathing as he recognised how quickly the insidious, corrosive effect of Gestapo methods had seeped into his own character.

Father Thomas waited until the detective had left the cathedral, then dropped to his knees and prayed. He found himself ensnared by his conscience. Ever since joining the Priesthood, he'd been obsessed with power and admired those, like Monsignor Wagner, who seized their opportunities to increase their status and influence. Although he found the man repugnant, he couldn't help but admire his ruthlessness, cynical opportunism, lack of morality and willingness to tread on anyone and anything that obstructed his self-interests. If that's what it took to climb the Church hierarchy, then Father Thomas was a willing apprentice.

Or he was, until now. He eyed the thick file and wondered what to do. The easy option would be to take it directly to the Bishop and wash his hands of it. As soon as the thought entered his head he recognised his naivety. A full enquiry was a certainty. Questions would be asked about how the file came to exist, who had access to the Diocese archive and had provided confidential information, and who had broken Church ranks and proved disloyal. Fingers would point directly towards him, and God forbid if Wagner was tipped off in advance. He'd be excommunicated. With no references and his disability, finding another job would be almost impossible.

His problems didn't end there. If Keunsberg acted, he could be in the spotlight of a full-blown Gestapo interrogation and Vatican investigation. It wouldn't just be fingers pointing at him. He cursed Detective Inspector Schwartz for handing him a ticking time bomb. He knew he had to do something, but what? He buried his head in his hands and prayed for guidance.

217

As each month passed, the matter receded in his consciousness until another odious task from his boss forcibly reminded him of his weakness. Having helped eliminate the local Jews, Bolsheviks and most freemasons, Keunsberg had demanded intelligence on Jehovah's Witnesses and the rumoured O5 resistance group that had distributed anti-Nazi leaflets in Wien and Saltzburg. Keunsberg was determined that such outrage wouldn't pollute Brandtnerwald. In Wagner, Keunsberg had a willing and able poodle.

"Ah, Father Thomas, I've received an interesting proposition from one of our more forward-thinking priests."

"Forward-thinking in what regard?" Thomas barely got the words out, his throat felt so dry.

"Improving working relations with our new masters." Wagner flipped the letter over. "His suggestions make a lot of sense."

"Such as?"

"Well, for example, he's suggesting that we instruct all priests to encourage their flock to adapt the slogan '*One People – One Reich – One Fuhrer – One God.*'" Wagner looked up at Thomas and grinned. "Quite catchy, don't you think? And another idea." He shuffled the papers until he found the relevant paragraph. "People of no obvious faith, disruptive and divisive doctrines, or beliefs incompatible with Catholic teachings, ought to be drawn to the attention of the authorities."

"With what in mind?"

"To help ensure good social order." Wagner looked thoughtful. "It would help deal with a lot of our parishioner's complaints against gypsies, for example." He waved the letter at Father Thomas. "There're a lot of good ideas here. Here are some more." He stabbed his finger at the page. "Using convict labour to maintain Church lands."

"Convict labour!"

Wagner chuckled. "Don't look so appalled. Think of it as a chance to offer these people redemption." Thomas said nothing. There was no such thing as convict labour. It was slave labour. Everyone knew it.

Wagner placed the letter down. "Arrange an appointment for this priest to come and see me, and also I'd like you to do some research."

"On what topic?"

"Find other like-minded priests." Wagner smirked. "And whilst you're at it, find out the names of those priests who are… how can I put it?… out of step with current circumstances."

"Catholics expressing opposition to National Socialism?"

Wagner frowned. "Exactly, Father Thomas. Our Nazi friends arrested several hundred misguided Catholics in Wien, and Cardinal Innitzer's residence was ransacked by Hitler Youth. We don't want any of that nonsense happening here. Preaching views likely to cause public anxiety is to be avoided." He picked up a pen. "I'd like you to start with these."

In Wagner's mind, denouncement of fellow clergymen was a logical progression, almost immediately followed by betrayal of anyone within the Church schools and institutions that expressed criticism or opposition to Nazi ideology. Lay preachers, teachers, social workers and volunteers found their names included on Father Wagner's lists. Kommisioner Keunsberg arranged disposal, and Father Thomas writhed in silent self-loathing. But there was one treachery that sickened Thomas above all others.

"Pay attention, Father Thomas?"

The rebuke wrenched his mind back to what he knew was coming. "I apologise, Your Reverence. You were saying?"

"It's time for my visit to the good Abbess and the sisters of St Catherine's. I want you to make appropriate arrangements."

Father Thomas felt he would explode, as a cauldron of emotions boiled within him. His outrage in standing by and allowing the monster loose on more innocent victims was matched by his lack of backbone to do anything about it. His wretchedness and disgust were amplified as he heard himself mutter a pathetic, "Of course."

It took over twelve months before a chance remark forced the issue.

"I'm afraid Monsignor Wagner is running a little late, Herr Kommissioner. He has an audience with the Bishop which appears to have overrun."

"That's inconvenient and unsatisfactory." Keunsberg angrily slapped his gloves on the table.

"I apologise for the discourtesy." Thomas quickly grabbed Keunsberg's coat and hat and hung them on the stand. He gave a strained smile and gestured the Kommissioner towards Wagner's office. ""Can I get you some refreshments?"

"Coffee - black, no sugar," Keunsberg snapped. "So, what's your Bishop and Monsignor Wagner discussing that so important?"

"Collaboration."

Keunsberg looked unimpressed.

"Monsignor Wagner is keen to explore every opportunity for the Church and the State to work in greater harmony to promote shared objectives and promote the Reich's interests."

"Such as?" Keunsberg extracted his cigarette case and lit up.

"Monsignor Wagner is exploring His Grace's attitude towards allowing Church premises to fly the National Socialist flag from diocese properties, including churches."

"He's sticking his neck out. I can't imagine the Bishop approving such an idea."

Thomas gave a strained laugh. "His Grace has complete faith in his chaplain. I'm sure you appreciate Monsignor Wagner is highly experienced in the way the Church operates. He will have taken appropriate precautions."

Keunsberg stiffened. "Precautions?"

For a second, Thomas looked thrown. He rubbed his nose in embarrassment. "Precautions is perhaps too strong a word. He's naturally cautious and doesn't act hastily." He cast Keunsberg an awkward grin. "He's renowned in the diocese for making detailed notes, recording every conversation - who said what, when and to whom. It's why he's so valued and trusted."

Keunsberg exhaled a stream of smoke. "He's a cautious man?"

"He's meticulous. Some put his ability to remember even quite obscure conversations and events down to some kind of photographic memory." He chuckled. "It's nothing of the sort. He maintains a journal in his notebooks."

Thomas missed the ice-cold expression that flashed across Keunsberg's face. "I do beg your pardon, Kommissioner, I must see whether Monsignor Wagner can be released from his appointment with his Grace, and fetch your coffee."

Although Thomas didn't realise it, his dilemma had just been resolved.

220

GUNTER'S DECISION

Even if he had been aware of the mental anguish he'd caused Father
Thomas, it would have barely troubled Gunter's conscience. As far as he
was concerned the clergyman deserved to suffer. In any event, his own
mind was in turmoil as a consequence of the case. Having endured nights of
disturbed sleep - constantly persuading himself that he was taking the right
course of action, only to have cold feet at the last moment, and imagining
the chaos and disruption his action would bring to his well-ordered life - he
finally made the decision. Gunter Schwartz resigned. Despite his trepidation
the world continued to spin. Nobody stared at him, crossed the street to
avoid him, or muttered darkly about the man who'd given up a well-paid
job.

Once he'd taken the plunge, the whole business was concluded
with business-like efficiency. Negotiations were quickly completed, and
Chief Inspector Schwartz of the Gestapo became Senior Sergeant Schwartz
of the Stadtpolitzei. After some compulsory training to become familiar
with procedures, his area of responsibility would be the upper
Brandtnerwald. The first piece of the jigsaw of his new life had fallen into
place. He felt extraordinarily elated and eager to share his news.

Marie was pegging out the washing when Gunter pulled into the
Breitner's farm. She stopped and watched his approach, her hand shading
her face from the early morning sun, the half-empty basket perched on her
hip. She looked pleased to see him. "I can tell from your face that you're
feeling on top of the world this morning, Gunter. Sep and Stephan aren't
here if it's them you're after. They're up in the top fields."

"No, Marie, it's you I've come to see. That is if I've not come at
an inconvenient time."

"You'd better come in." She led the way into the Wachter's Stube.
"So, what's all this about?" She put the washing basket down and took off
her apron.

Gunter threw his arms out. "I've started a new job, and a great
weight has been lifted from my shoulders."

Marie beamed at him. "Oh, Gunter, I'm so pleased for you. That
job was not right for you at all." She sat down and indicated he should do
the same. "So, what are your plans now?" She rested her chin on her hands
and looked expectant.

"Ah, well then. Yes, indeed." Gunter's fingers drummed the table
nervously. "There were lots of things to consider." He stared across at her
with an uncertain smile.

"Well, are you going to tell me exactly what conclusions you've
come to?"

"Yes, of course." He cleared his throat. "I'm determined to carve
out a new life for myself - leave behind all the things that caused me stress,

anxiety, or that were turning me into something I despised. In other words, make a clean break."

"Sounds like a very positive beginning."

"It is," he agreed. "And in doing so, I intend to focus on aspects of my life that provide me with the most happiness and joy – starting with you."

Marie jerked back in surprise. "Me!"

Gunter nodded. "Yes, Marie, you." He raised his fingers off the table-top to forestall her response. "Please, hear me out." He looked earnestly at her. He needn't have paused as he already had her full attention. "You will recall that I'm really quite hopeless regarding affairs of the heart."

She looked sympathetic. "You've been unlucky, that's all."

"You're just being kind. The fact is, I'm simply no good at it. Something awful always seems to happen."

"Hospitals and injuries do seem to feature quite a lot," she conceded.

"Exactly." Gunter banged his hand on the table. "Derails the whole process. I start with the very best of intentions, only to find myself all the way back at square one."

"It must be demoralising."

"It is, Marie, believe me."

"But such things happen. It's no reason to give up."

"No, Marie, don't misunderstand me. I don't intend to give up. It's just I feel a different approach is called for." His smile underpinned his confidence that his strategy was already bound for success.

"I'm afraid you've lost me."

"Well, I thought that if I told you right from the outset that I would really like to marry you, you could say yes or no straight away. If the idea is of interest to you then any mishaps along the way would be just that – mishaps. It wouldn't upset the applecart, so to speak. We could sort things out, smooth things over." He looked at her expectantly. "Obviously, if you don't like the idea at all, then – well, I would be heartbroken of course, but I wouldn't cause you the distress of unwanted attention – I couldn't bear the thought of that."

Marie looked stunned. She slowly shook her head and rubbed her forehead. "Let me get this straight. You are asking me to marry you – what, right now?"

"Oh no, I'm merely telling you my intentions. I wouldn't want us to miss out on all the other things, like dancing, walks, perhaps travelling to Brandt for a trip on the lake, having romantic meals in a Gasthaus somewhere. You know, all the things we might do to get to know one another better." He frowned as he thought through the process. "To do all that would take time."

"There is a name for such a process, you know."

222

Gunter looked blank.

"It's called an engagement."

"Ah."

Marie studied him. Her amused expression slowly developed into a barely suppressed giggle. "How long have you thought about this idea?"

"Oh, most days. I can't be precise, Certainly a long time." His look turned more serious. "Of course, if you don't like the idea, you must say. The last thing I want is to cause you any upset."

Marie laughed. "Gunter, I think it a very sensible idea and very sweet of you. And if I do end up getting injured we won't let it stop us, eh?" She got up and gave him an affectionate kiss on the top of his head. "Now, what shall we have for lunch?"

A NEW BEGINNING

"For goodness' sake, Marie, concentrate!" Josey gave her friend a stern look.

"Sorry!" Marie forced her gaze from the window and focused on the task at hand. "It looks too weak to me," she said as she stirred the raspberry leaves around the pan.

Harriet wrinkled up her nose. "It smells disgusting."

Josey waved her hand dismissively. "It doesn't matter what it smells like. Doing the job is what counts."

"I think I'd prefer the castor oil."

"Well, you don't have a choice. Even the Apotheke in Achbrugge has run out of supplies, thanks to the war." Josey leaned over Marie's shoulder and examined the brew. "You're right, it looks a bit weak." She glanced around for the jar of leaves.

"My grandma swore that spicy foods did the trick. Things like goulash or strong, seasoned Wurst," Marie said absently, as once again her gaze returned to the Stube window.

"That's the next thing we'll try if your waters haven't broken in the next couple of days." Josey gave Harriet an encouraging smile.

"He's here!" Marie said excitedly. Before Josey or Harriet could react she'd removed her apron and disappeared out of the Stube. The sound of her footsteps running up the stairs was followed by the frantic opening and closing of cupboards and drawers. Josey and Harriet's bemused looks changed to knowing ones as the sound of an approaching motorbike drifted into the room.

Gunter swept in like a breeze. "Good morning Josey and... my goodness, Fraulein Harriet, you are looking fit to burst," he said as he swept off his helmet.

"If only!" Harriet laughed.

"When's it due?" Gunter bent over and studied Harriet's massive bump as if it was some kind of egg that might crack open at any moment.

"Now."

"Goodness me." Gunter looked alarmed and took a step backwards.

Josey rolled her eyes at the extent of general male ignorance when it came to pregnancies. "She's two weeks overdue."

"Is that good or bad?"

"Neither. It's normal for a firstborn."

"Right." Gunter's look of relief brightened to one of delight as Marie entered. "Ah, my dear Marie. I see you are all prepared."

Marie blushed, and brushed an imaginary smudge of dirt from her pristinely pressed trousers. "I thought this would serve as appropriate attire."

"You would be in the proper attire if you had chosen to wear a ball gown." Gunter took her hand and kissed it as a knight might his lady.

Josey looked appalled. "Marie! Am I to understand you intend to go out on the back of Gunter's motorcycle?"

"Gunter is taking me out for a spin, yes." She gazed up at Gunter before giving both Harriet and Josey a beaming smile. "It's going to be an adventure."

"Marie, you can't be serious." Josey immediately confronted Gunter. "And you should know better. Honestly, I don't know what to say."

Harriet giggled. "Well, I think it's a great idea. Good for you, Aunt Marie."

"Thank you, Harriet." Marie shot Josey a defiant look before grabbing Gunter's arm and leading him towards the door. Josey and Harriet rushed to the window to watch the couple depart.

"What is she thinking of? At her age!" Josey muttered.

"What do you mean? You make her sound like an old maid. She's only forty-four, and a very young forty-four at that." Harriet laughed as she recalled her own thrill of riding Johan's motorbike. "You're in danger of turning into an old fuddy-duddy, Aunt Josey."

Josey managed to suppress a smile as the pair disappeared down the road. "I suppose you're right. She's acted like a teenager these last few months."

"She's in love, and Gunter is clearly besotted with her." Harriet's look turned wistful. "They shouldn't let the grass grow under their feet. Especially now. They should get married or just move in together."

Josey's silence suggested she didn't disagree. "We live in strange times." She suddenly leaned over and gave her niece a kiss on the cheek. "We must learn to take our chances and pray that things will improve, eh?"

Harriet lingered at the window, lost in thought. Then an idea took hold and she reached for Josey's hand. "Come on." She grabbed her coat as she led Josey out into the yard.

"Harriet, what are you doing?"

"Helping nature take its course. I'm fed up with this pregnancy." Harriet unlocked the barn door and squeezed her bulk through the gap.

Josey cautiously followed her inside and immediately recognised Harriet's intention. "Oh no, Harriet. You can't be serious."

"Josey! The castor oil isn't working and I'm sick of drinking disgusting raspberry leaf tea. It's worth trying something else." She pulled Johan's motorcycle upright and kicked back its stand with her foot. "Come on, help me wheel it out."

"I'm not having anything to do with this." Josey folded her arms to reinforce her intent. Harriet pretended not to have heard the comment. She put her weight behind the handlebars and succeeded in inching the bike forward a few metres.

"I'm not helping," Josey said firmly. Harriet ignored her and continued straining. She added a couple of gasps and some grunting for dramatic effect. Out of the corner of her eye she saw Josey's resolve begin to crumble.

"Oh, for goodness' sake, you'll do yourself an injury." Josey brushed Harriet to one side and took over the task until the bike stood in the yard. "And exactly how do you think you are going to get on this machine in your condition?" Josey said with arched eyebrows and hands-on-hips, confident in her own mind that she had found the obstacle that would put an end to the venture. She nearly had a point until Harriet waddled purposefully off towards the milking parlour, emerging a few seconds later with the stool. It took a few attempts and a lot of giggling but eventually Harriet succeeded. She looked very pleased with herself as she sat astride the bike, her distended stomach resting on the petrol tank. She levered herself up on the kick start, and the motorcycle spluttered into life at the first attempt. She looked triumphant. "Are you coming, then?"

Josey wavered. Good sense dictated that she ought to put an immediate stop to this madness. Then again, it was a sunny day and there was something deliciously irresistible about a motorbike. And, she admitted to herself, Harriet's comment about her turning into a fuddy-duddy had stung a bit. "Oh, why not?" She hitched up her skirt and, after several attempts from different angles and urging Harriet to move up a bit, finally managed to perch on the pillion seat. "Not too fast," she shrieked, as Harriet engaged the gear and they shot out into the road. "Where shall we go?" she shouted in Harriet's ear.

"Somewhere bumpy. Up to The Lodge."

Despite their intention, the thrill of the ride took them right up to the head of the pass. Only on the return journey did they take the almost concealed turn for The Lodge. Their progress was marked by continuous howls of laughter, screams and yells as the bike bucked and bounced its way up the rocky track. Several times, Josey screeched and desperately grabbed Harriet's waist as the lurching machine threatened to tip her off the back.

"Stop!" Josey shouted, as Harriet accelerated down the last fifty metres of the drive just for the thrill of coming to a skidding halt outside The Lodge.

"I expect the whole of Brandtnerwald could hear you two," Marie laughed, as she appeared from around the corner of the building, a glass of wine in her hand.

Harriet looked shamefaced. "Oh, we're not intruding, are we?"

"Not at all." She waved her glass unsteadily. "Gunter had arranged a surprise picnic on the lawn. You might as well join us."

"Easier said than done," Harriet mumbled. Getting on the bike had been a challenge, dismounting could well prove impossible.

226

"You'll have to slide yourself off the back," Josey said, after watching Harriet firstly try to swing her leg over the saddle, and then to lean backwards and lift her leg over the petrol tank. Both attempts met with no success.

"Honestly, it's like watching Humpty Dumpty," Josey muttered, as Harriet's latest attempt failed. Marie started to laugh.

"I'm stuck!" Harriet joined Marie in a fit of giggles, which proved to be infectious as Josey started laughing too.

Their mirth prompted Gunter's curiosity. He drained his glass of wine and heaved himself to his feet. "What's going on?" he said, as he emerged from around the corner. He was met by the sight of Harriet draped like a beached whale over the fuel tank, Marie leaning on the pillion seat crying with laughter, and Josey doubled up as the hilarity of Harriet's predicament took her breath away. Josey managed to compose herself enough to point at Harriet. "Gunter, you'll have to lift her off."

"Oh. Are you sure?" He eyed Harriet. She was enormously pregnant and, despite his faith in his own strength, a flicker of doubt flashed across his mind that he wouldn't be able to easily lift her. Nevertheless, he stepped up to the task. He gathered Harriet's legs under his arm as she held on to his neck. In a second, he placed her gently on the ground just as Harriet whispered, "Oh my God." Her dress was wet.

Josey immediately looked concerned. "Your waters have broken. We need to get you back to the farm."

"I've only just got her off." Gunter sounded a little hurt that his efforts counted for so little.

"Well, you'll just have to get her back on again." Marie gave him an exasperated look.

Harriet sank down on the step and cradled her stomach. "I'm not going anywhere right now." She winced and groaned.

"Are you all right?" Gunter sounded alarmed.

Marie took another sip from her wine before giving him a light cuff on his head. "She's having contractions. It's perfectly normal." Gunter's nod of understanding disguised the fact that he hadn't a clue what contractions were, let alone their role in pregnancy.

Josey knelt beside a slightly panicky Harriet. "We need to get you back to the farm, sweetheart."

Harriet shook her head. "I think it may be too late for that."

"In that case we need to get organised." Gunter sounded authoritative. The three women gazed at Gunter in silence, waiting for his idea of what getting organised might involve. It fell to Josey to fill the vacuum with military efficiency.

"We need some water."

"The Lodge's taps still work," Harriet said.

"Something to tie the cord."

"These will do." Marie untied the ribbons that held her hair in place.

"A pan to boil the water."

"There are some old cast iron pots in the kitchen." Harriet winced as she became gripped by another contraction.

"A blanket?"

"We've got a picnic sheet," Marie said.

"Some cloth to make up wadding."

"We can cut off strips from my dress," Harriet said.

"A sharp knife and scissors." The women looked at Gunter who seemed bewildered at the speed with which Josey had 'got things organised'.

"Ah yes, some scissors." He screwed up his face as he considered the problem.

"Come on, Gunter, all men carry pocket knives."

"Er, um, well, farmers might but it isn't something we policemen tend to have about our persons."

Marie rolled her eyes. "Gunter, you have that thing for opening wine bottles."

"You mean my waiter's friend? It's not a pair of scissors."

"It has a sharp blade, doesn't it?"

"Yes. A very small blade."

"I'm sure it will serve our purpose," Josey said. "Now we ought to get you comfortable." She and Marie started fussing over Harriet, leaving Gunter on the sidelines. "Is there anything I can do?" he asked hesitantly.

"Make up a fire, get some water boiling. We could be here for some time." Josey said brusquely. "Once you've done that you can head back to the farm and fetch Sep. We'll need the pony and trap."

"Right." Gunter wandered off to do Josey's bidding. Having lit a fire and set a large pan of water to boil with what he thought was impressive skill, he announced to an unresponsive audience that he would set off for the farm. Only once he'd started up his motorbike did Marie break off from tending to Harriet to give him a warm kiss on the lips. "Isn't it exciting?" she breathed. All of a sudden Gunter felt a lot better and roared off down the track in high spirits.

Sep was in the S tube looking slightly bemused by everyone's absence.

"Ah, Gunter! At least someone is around. I thought I'd have nobody to share my news." He waved two letters, one in each hand. "A letter from Susan and another from Johan, both arrived today."

"I take it from your expression they contain good tidings."

Sep pursed his lips. "Everything is relative. Susan is missing us all dreadfully but she's making the best of things." Sep scanned the writing.

228

"She says they are being treated well. Best news is that the Red Cross are trying to arrange some kind of swap between German internees held by the British, and the English internees."

"Oh! That would mean Susan heading to England?"

"Hopefully."

"And Johan's news?" Gunter made himself comfortable at the table.

"He and Jurgen are both okay and are in Northern France. He says they hope to be given leave to visit Paris."

"Does he mention the fighting?"

"Only briefly." Sep turned the letter over to find the relevant paragraph. "He says the French fought well but were easily outmanoeuvred. The British were determined but their equipment was poor."

"The main thing is that they are both safe and well."

"Amen to that, mate." Sep went to the cupboard and extracted a bottle of Schnapps. "I think a drink is called for." He raised the bottle and gave Gunter an enquiring look.

"Just a small one."

"I suspect Josey and Stephan will have received a similar letter from Jurgen."

"Might be a good idea to give them some warning." Gunter raised his glass. "It wasn't all plain sailing. I understand a couple of lads from Achbrugge were killed in Poland and another very badly injured near Dunkirk."

Sep gave a grim nod of acknowledgement. "The post doesn't always bring glad tidings." He sat down opposite and made himself comfortable. "Prosit, my friend. Here's hoping for an early end to this bloody war." They touched glasses.

Sep glanced around the room in puzzlement. "Where is everyone?"

"Oh, Josey, Marie and Harriet are up at The Lodge. I don't know where Stephan is, though."

"What's happening at The Lodge?'

Gunter took another sip of Schnapps and sounded relaxed. "Harriet's gone into labour. Marie and Josey are giving her a hand."

"Harriet's in labour!" Sep spluttered.

"Yes. I was sent to fetch you. They want you to bring the trap."

Sep was already on his feet. "Why didn't you say so straight away?!"

Gunter looked perplexed. "There's no rush. Josey said they'd be preoccupied for some time."

Sep was already out of the door.

By the time they reached The Lodge, an exhausted Harriet was propped up against the wall. She held a bundle made from Marie's picnic blanket. From within its folds a small, pink, wizened head peeped out. "Say hello to your Opi, Simone."

Sep got to his knees and peered at his new granddaughter. He then beamed at Harriet. "See, I told you it would be a girl."

VICTORY, PAYBACK AND DEFEAT

The bombers came in May 1940. This time they dropped bombs, not leaflets. For three nights, oil refineries on the outskirts of the city were attacked. There was none of the predicted panic among the citizens. Damage was slight, no buildings were hit, and casualties were minimal. Over the next four months there were more sporadic raids. Most bombs fell in open countryside. If this represented the best the British could throw at them, it was no contest.

Everywhere, Germany reigned supreme. Denmark, Norway, Holland, Belgium and France had fallen within weeks. The British had suffered a humiliating defeat at Dunkirk. The mood in the city was euphoric. The war would soon be over, and today Katerina and Trudy would witness another example of German might.

"Trudy... Trudy... It's time to get up."

Trudy gradually emerged into consciousness. For a few minutes, she lay luxuriating in the cosy warmth of the bed and the fuzzy dream world of half-sleep.

"Come on, get up," Katerina said sternly. "You'll be late." She pulled the heavy duvet off the bed by way of encouragement

Trudy rolled out of bed and staggered to the bathroom. "What time is it leaving?" she called.

"Just before ten o'clock. So, get a move on." Katerina stood in front of the mirror, making adjustments to a wide-brimmed, brilliant red hat.

Two hours later, the girls stood with hundreds of other onlookers on the banks of the Elbe. They craned their necks, hoping to be the first to see the tops of the masts over the roofs of the warehouses that lined the river.

"Here she comes," a voice shouted.

Slowly, the great battleship hove into view, towed by tugs that looked like toys against the towering grey hull of the warship.

Katerina jumped up and down in excitement as the convoy approached, and the majestic lines of the pride of the Kriegsmarine could be appreciated. "Isn't she tremendous?" Katerina gushed. "We built that!" she added proudly.

The ship looked magnificent with her graceful lines, the great sweeping bow designed to cut through the most savage of seas, and the amount of weaponry she carried. There were four massive turrets - each housing two enormous guns, dozens of smaller calibre naval weapons, anti-aircraft pieces, torpedo tubes, and seaplanes ready to launch off their catapults. She looked invincible.

"Where is Franz?"

Katerina stood still and studied the ship. "He mans an anti-aircraft gun just behind the bridge." She pointed vaguely towards the ship.

Her directions meant nothing to Trudy. She could see the heads of hundreds of sailors in their steel helmets. "We'll never spot him."

"Doesn't matter. He'll see us." Katerina took off her bright red hat and waved it frantically above her head. "Keep your eyes sharp. He's bound to wave back."

"Katerina, all the sailors will be waving back."

"We'll see him." Katerina said in a fierce voice that startled Trudy. She mentally cursed herself for failing to recognise the seriousness of the moment. Someone special was going to war, with a chance he wouldn't return. Suddenly the most important thing in the world was for Katerina and Franz to spot each other. Trudy redoubled her efforts. Somewhere in the lines of grey helmeted sailors Franz stood. He probably felt alone, miserable and frightened - the most reluctant sailor among a crew of over two thousand.

Others around them urgently sought out their husbands, sons and relations. The crowd waved and shouted out the names of their loved ones. The noise increased as the ship drew level with the wharf. Katerina desperately waved her hat and screamed Franz's name. Her face was drenched in tears. She was frantic not to miss her beloved. Trudy found herself joining her friend, trying to draw as much attention to themselves as possible. If only she'd thought to wear something equally distinctive or to have made a makeshift flag or banner.

The tug had already passed them and the massive grey armoured hull of the battleship glided by.

"Franz, where are you? Show yourself," Trudy silently pleaded. Every sailor looked the same, rendered anonymous by their steel helmets and dark blue uniforms. To make matters worse, many had their faces tilted towards the sky, guarding against a surprise British attack.

Trudy spotted him at last. A lone sailor, half standing on the guard rail of his anti-aircraft gun, furiously waving. He'd seen Katerina's bright red hat and was determined to attract her attention.

"I see him, I see him!" Trudy screamed and pulled her friend towards her.

"Where? Where?" Katerina's wild eyes darted across the ship.

"See the forward mast. Trace it down, slightly to the left."

"Where? Where? Oh, Franz, where are you?" Katerina could hardly see anything through her tears. "I see him," she shrieked. "Franz, Franz," she yelled. Her voice was swallowed by the bedlam of the crowd, who were shouting their own farewells to friends and relatives.

Franz removed his helmet and waved it in one hand. With his other, he furiously blew kisses in Katrina's direction.

"Franz, I love you, I love you, I love you." Katerina was beside herself with tortured emotion. Trudy couldn't stop herself from crying. The whole scene appeared magnificent and tragic at the same time. She silently prayed for Franz's safe return.

Suddenly Franz turned. It appeared he was being reprimanded by an officer. With a final desperate wave, he dropped from the guard-rail and disappeared.

Katerina stared in wide-eyed dismay at the empty space before turning and collapsing into Trudy's arms. Her whole body was wracked with great heaving sobs. "I won't see him again. I know it. I won't see him again."

Trudy did her best to comfort her. "That's just silly, Kat." She stroked her friend's hair. "Look at the size of that ship. Nothing can sink her."

Katerina wasn't to be comforted. She buried her face into Trudy's neck and sobbed. Over her shoulder, Trudy watched the graceful lines of the ship slide by. She made out her proud nameplate, '*Bismark.*'

Nine months passed without Katerina receiving any news from her beloved.

"I've left you some bread," she said, as Trudy stumbled exhausted through the door of the apartment. "You look shattered."

Trudy threw off her helmet and eased herself out of her greatcoat. "It was a long night."

Her friend wasn't sympathetic. "Tell me about it. I spent over four hours sharing a grotty shelter with around fifty others who, judging by the stench, hadn't bathed in weeks."

"That might be true. The water-mains are broken in some parts of the city." Trudy slumped into the chair at the tiny kitchen table.

Katerina stood in front of the mirror and made tiny adjustments to her hair. "It sounded like a heavy raid."

"Probably over a hundred bombers."

"So much for the Party bulletins that claim it's only a matter of time before the British will be begging for peace. Apparently, the British are bombing all our cities, including Berlin."

Trudy looked startled. "Where did you hear that?"

Katerina glanced towards the radio.

Trudy became alarmed. "Have you been listening to the BBC?"

Katerina wrinkled her nose and assumed a casual air. "Don't worry. I had it turned down."

"Kat, it doesn't matter. You could get us into serious trouble. Just having a radio set tuned in wrongly can lead to a prison sentence."

"Trudy, relax. I only listen to the news now and then." She swept her coat over her shoulders, signalling the end of the conversation, at least on that subject. "Do you have to go in?"

Trudy gave a tired smile. "Work doesn't stop because of an air raid."

"I don't know how you do it. I haven't your energy."

"It pays the rent." She sighed. "Although you're right. We're working too hard."

"Onwards to victory. Right, I'm off." She gave Trudy an affectionate kiss. "I'll see you – well, whenever."

Trudy listened to her friend's footsteps clatter down the stairs and smiled as Katerina started humming a popular song, before the street door slammed shut, leaving her with her own thoughts and fatigue.

She felt pleased that Katerina's spirits had recovered following Franz's departure. Most people were buoyed up by the way the war was going. Victories were announced by over-excited radio announcers. Cinemas were filled to capacity as the population drank in endless films of Wehrmacht troops marching confidently into the latest city to fall. And casualties had been light, if the broadcasts were to be believed. Yet something niggled at the edges of Trudy's mind. Everything seemed too good to be true.

She eyed the radio. She knew the State Radio distorted the news. Party reports of bombings routinely understated the number of aircraft involved, exaggerated the number of bombers shot down and claimed little or no damage had been inflicted. She wondered how the British were reporting the war.

She cast her eyes nervously around the room, went downstairs, locked the front door and drew the blackout curtain. Once back upstairs, she closed every door and made sure all the windows were shut. Only then did she switch the radio on, having turned the volume down. Millimetre by millimetre she nudged the tuning dial until a faint hiss of static could be heard. She squatted and pressed her ear to the loudspeaker. The set picked up the thin sound of mellow music. The clipped voice of the presenter confirmed she was listening to the BBC. She glanced around the room, half expecting a Gestapo agent to leap out from behind the couch. For twenty minutes, she sat and revelled in the songs and tunes that reminded her of the Swingjugend dances. The music gave way to the familiar sound of the Westminster chimes and the dull resonance of Big Ben.

"This is the BBC German Service transmitting from London. Here is the nine o'clock news. This morning the War Office reported that the Battlecruiser HMS Hood has been sunk. Early reports indicate the warship engaged the German Battleship Bismark, when, at approximately 0600 hours, she exploded and sank within minutes."

Trudy's astonishment instantly evaporated as the sound of heavy blows on the front door threw her into a wild panic. She turned the radio off and twisted the tuning dial. The blows were heavy and persistent. Trudy felt her heart thumping. How on earth had the Gestapo found her so quickly?

Maybe they had some kind of tracking device? She leapt up and made her way to the top of the stairs, half expecting to see the door being kicked in.

"Trudy, open the door." The half-muffled voice of Katerina floated up the stairwell.

Trudy breathed a sigh of relief. She flew down the flight and let her friend in.

Katerina wasn't even through the door before she burst out excitedly, "Have you heard? The Bismark has sunk a British battleship!" She rushed up the stairs. "Everyone is talking about it. It's on the radio now." She ran into the room and switched the radio on, then threw off her coat. Her words tumbled into each other in her excitement. "I had to turn back to listen. Isn't it wonderful news?! I hope Franz is safe. Everyone at the tram-stop was cheering. Oh, come on." She struck the radio a gentle blow to encourage it to work.

"I changed the station." Trudy looked apologetic.

"Oh, Trudy!" Katerina said irritably. She knelt to retune the set and, in seconds, the voice of a hysterical German announcer filled the room.

"The Hood, the pride of the British Navy, their largest, fastest and most modern battleship, was blown out of the water in less than three minutes. Both the Bismark and her escort suffered no damage in the engagement. Today is another great day for the German people. The Fuhrer has sent a message of congratulations to Admiral Lütjens and Captain Lindemann and his gallant crew. Another British warship was heavily damaged in the…"

"Do you think they'll head back home now?" Katerina's eyes gleamed before she squeezed them tight and added, "Imagine the celebrations!"

"I just hope Franz gets home safely." Trudy smiled at her friend's excitement. "I have to go. We'll catch up this evening," she said as she grabbed her coat and headed for the stairs.

Katerina waved a dismissive arm and bent her head towards the loudspeaker. She didn't want to miss a single snippet of information, even if it did mean she'd be late for work.

Trudy left the apartment and headed towards the Rathaus. It took longer than expected. Twice she was diverted. Almost every street had bomb damage. Gaps opened up where individual buildings had been destroyed. Massive timber props, supporting facades distorted by blasts, straddled the pavements. In several locations water and sewage gushed from fractured pipes, and everything was covered in fine grey-black dust.

Despite the damage, the streets were busy. The tram wires were quickly repaired, most routes were operating, traffic flowed and shops were open. The pavements thronged with people still buzzing with the news of the sinking of the Hood. More news trickled in. Greece was about to fall,

German paratroops had landed in Crete, and the British were clearly on the back foot. Victory lay around the corner, and all thanks to the Fuhrer and the Party.

Trudy had just entered the Rathaus when a voice called out. "Ah, Fraulein Heppel. A word if I may."

Trudy turned to see Frau Tolheim beckoning her.

"I hoped I'd catch you."

"Sorry I'm late. Some streets were blocked."

Frau Tolheim waved a dismissive hand. "Yes, yes, I understand. Please follow me."

Frau Tolheim seemed keen to reach her office as quickly as possible. Her pace didn't let up once she'd entered. "Hang your coat up and take a seat," she said breezily, as she took her own place behind the desk. Trudy hadn't even sat down before Frau Tolheim fired a question at her.

"You know of Fraulein Fesling?"

Trudy looked blank.

"Fraulein Fesling, the young typist who works for that... for Commissioner Hofner."

"I know of her, but not personally."

"Well, the girl's pregnant."

"Oh!"

"She pregnant and Hofner has instructed me to dispose of her."

"Why?!"

Frau Tolheim looked exasperated. "Why do you think?" She stared hard at Trudy. "It's damaging for a senior Nazi to have his reputation sullied. He's the model Commissioner and Frau Hofner is supposed to be the dutiful wife."

Trudy was shocked. "Frau Tolheim!"

"Yes, yes, I know. I should watch my tongue. However, I'm sick of having to sort out his mess." As she glanced across the desk, Trudy saw a woman both angry and scared. As if to confirm it, Frau Tolheim continued, "I'm taking a risk, talking to you like this. However, I hope I'm a good judge of character. You've never struck me as stupid."

"I hope I'm not."

"You know you're not. You're bright. You've proved that time and time again. I hear you are doing as well in your current position as you did in your last."

"I've been promoted."

"That's as far as you'll get." Frau Tolheim said bluntly.

Trudy bristled. "Are you threatening me?"

"Not at all." She sighed. "It's as far as you'll get for three reasons. First, I have no influence at the next tier of management. Second, all appointments at the next level require the candidates to be party members. Third, you're a woman."

"It hasn't stopped you."

236

"I've made myself useful, some might say indispensable, to certain senior men. It's taken years. Something which is not on your side."

Trudy felt a flush of anger. "That's a shame, as I'd hoped to talk to you about my career."

"By all means." A flicker of a smile played across Frau Tolheim's lips as she noted Trudy's annoyance. "You have a lot going for you. You're a bit of a free thinker. Prepared to take the odd risk or two." Frau Tolheim suddenly looked menacing. "Known to enjoy the odd night out with the so-called degenerates."

Trudy felt the blood drain from her face.

Frau Tolheim abruptly softened. "Don't worry, my dear. You'll be surprised to learn you have danced several times with my son." She gave a half-smile. "Believe me, I'm not trying to scare or blackmail you. I need your help."

"My help?"

"You help me and I might be able to help you. But first things first. I'm damned if little Fraulein Fesling ends up like the last one."

Trudy thought she'd been hit by a brick. "The last one! This isn't the first time?"

Frau Tolheim's laugh was bitter. "Your predecessor in the P.A. position fell into the same condition." She leant across the table with a hard look. "Why did you think you got the P.A. job so easily. You happened to be in the right place at the right time. Trouble was you proved resistant to Hofner's advances."

"You helped me escape."

"I thought you could do with some support." Frau Tolheim looked grim-faced. "There are times when women need to stick together."

Trudy felt alarm bells go off in her head. "I've not agreed to anything yet."

Frau Tolheim suddenly grinned. "Very shrewd. You prove my point, Trudy, you've got a brain on you. However, I'm fairly sure you will agree to my proposal." She leant back in her chair "Ask me what happened to your predecessor?"

Trudy shrugged. "So, what happened?"

"She was ordered to have an abortion. When she refused, she disappeared." Frau Tolheim selected a pencil from the desk and nervously tapped it on the ink-blotter. "Even her family can't find out where she was sent."

"I don't understand."

"Someone added her to the list of undesirables." She stared directly into Trudy's eyes. "Once that happens…puff…you disappear." The pencil now tapped furiously on the blotter.

"I thought undesirables were resettled in the east somewhere."

"Pah!" Frau Tolheim spat the word out. "Resettled permanently. Particularly if you're a Jew."

Trudy cast a nervous glance towards the door. "Frau Tolheim, I don't think you should be telling me this."

"Why not? In your previous job, didn't it ever cross your mind what happened to all those people your street the block wardens so diligently betrayed?"

Trudy stayed silent.

"So now you know. And Fraulein Fesling will go the same way unless we do something about it." She slammed the pencil on the table. They'd reached the nub of the conversation.

"We?"

"Yes, we!" Frau Tolheim fixed her gaze on Trudy. "I need Fraulein Fesling assigned to some other duties, preferably located somewhere in the far south of the city and as close to the village of Buchholz as possible. She has family there."

"There's a searchlight team in that area. She'll need training."

"Believe me, she'll be a quick learner. I've already put the fear of God in her."

"What about Hofner?"

"All he'll know is I made his problem disappear." Frau Tolheim continued to stare unblinkingly at Trudy. "I've no intention of having my name added to some list."

Trudy held the gaze of the woman opposite. "What makes you think I'll agree to this?"

She looked resigned. "If I'm wrong, I'm as good as dead."

"Where I come from we have a code of silence."

The office fell silent as the two women regarded each other.

"When do you want her out?" Trudy said quietly.

"Right now, immediately."

Trudy thought fast. She reached over the desk, picked up the pencil and ripped a corner off the blotter. "Order her to report here at four o'clock this afternoon." She scribbled the address. "She'll be a general admin dogsbody to start off with. She'll be trained on the job." Trudy glanced across at Frau Tolheim, who looked tense. "I hope this doesn't become a regular event," she said, and moved to leave.

Frau Holheim gave Trudy a steady, meaningful look. "That depends if you can see the world for what it is and recognise right from wrong. Believe me, right will win out in the end."

Once again, alarm bells sounded in Trudy's head. And yet she found herself intrigued by the woman opposite. She sank back into her chair. "This isn't the only person you've helped, is it?"

"I've tried my best to keep as many young women as possible from the clutches of Commissioner Hofner."

"I didn't just mean Hofner and the staff in this office."

Frau Tolheim said nothing.

"How many of the names on the lists do you actually forward to the Gestapo?"

The older woman grimaced. "Hardly any. Most were tittle-tattle. The authorities wouldn't want to waste time on them." She stared hard at Trudy, then sat back, folded her arms and lowered her voice. "The names generate files, and the subsequent investigations frequently involve brutal interrogations. Then follows a court case, run by a Party lawyer or Judge who ensures an unfair hearing, which results in an entirely innocent man, woman or, in some cases, child being hung, shot or resettled." She studied Trudy for a few seconds. "I'm as patriotic as any German, but I am also a Christian. The more serious ones I reported. But frankly, the idea that an elderly, bigoted street warden could spot a British spy or a Soviet terrorist living in plain sight in the middle of Hamburg is fanciful, to say the least."

"What about the Jews or the so-called degenerates?"

"Those receive special consideration."

Trudy studied the woman opposite. "By who?"

Frau Tolheim felt she'd said enough. "Let's talk about your future."

The conversation with Frau Tolheim played on Trudy's mind. There was something deeply unpleasant about the Nazis. She couldn't put her finger on it but somehow her previous membership of the BDM made her feel contaminated.

Her mind was still in turmoil three days later, when she arrived home. She realised part of the problem was exhaustion. She really needed to catch up on her sleep. Unfortunately, events over a thousand kilometres away meant she wouldn't sleep at all for another twenty-four hours.

The sound of splashing water and singing meant that Katerina was having a bath. "I'll leave the water in for you," she called, as Trudy entered the apartment. "I'll be five minutes."

"It was my turn to be first," Trudy called back.

Katerina was unapologetic. "You should have made sure you got home early." Despite being unrepentant, Katerina did have the good grace to vacate the bath several minutes later. "I've not taken all the hot water," she said, as she emerged into the tiny living room with a towel wrapped around her and another encasing her hair.

A long relaxing soak might clear her mind, Trudy hoped. It didn't turn out that way. No matter how hard she tried to unwind, her mind kept returning to her conversation with Frau Tolheim, which in turn triggered other thoughts and images. The Nazi thugs beating Franz up, the incident at the Strength through Joy pageant and the revelation of the fate of the undesirables, forced her to re-evaluate the world around her. She was so naïve. The realisation upset her. Her determination to take charge of her own destiny was an illusion. She was just a pawn. She began to understand

Frau Tolheim and admire her stance. What it meant for Trudy Heppel, she couldn't fathom. Eventually, she half-submerged herself in the warm water, relaxed and nodded off.

A piercing scream from the front room cut into her snooze. In an instant she was out of the bath. She grabbed a towel and ran down the hall, flinging open the living room door to find Katerina in a state of shock, kneeling in the middle of the room with both her hands clamped over her mouth.

"What's happened?" She glanced around half expecting to see an intruder, a mouse, or something on fire. Gradually, she became aware that her friend was staring in mute horror at the radio. "What's happened, Kat?"

The radio announcer provided the answer. His voice was sombre. Trudy turned the volume up a notch. It was the BBC Service. *"Here is the main news again. This evening the Admiralty issued the following communiqué 'At 10.45 this morning, the Commander in Chief, Home Fleet, signalled that the German Battleship, Bismark, has been sunk. German casualties are substantial. Royal Navy ships have picked up survivors, and other neutral ships in the area are assisting with the recovery. A full list of all German sailors known to have been rescued will be transmitted on the BBC German service at 19.00 hours GMT tomorrow evening...'*

Katerina turned her head slowly towards Trudy. She mouthed some words but no sound emerged. Her eyes looked glazed. Trudy instinctively knelt and engulfed her friend in her arms. She had no idea for exactly how long they stayed locked in a gently rocking embrace. At some point, she led Katerina to her bed, tucked her in, then lay beside her and stroked her forehead until some survival process within Katerina kicked in and she fell into a fitful sleep.

Sleep didn't come for Trudy. The fate of Franz just added to her turmoil. The odds on him surviving were pitifully small. However, she resolved to hold out hope, if only for Katerina's sake. She wept silent tears as she recalled his larger than life character, his flamboyance and determination to have fun and make the most of life. The contrast between the value of Franz's life compared with that of the odious Hofner fuelled a sense of bitterness that only increased when she turned the radio on, with the volume down so as not to disturb Katerina. The German broadcast made no mention of the sinking. Only that the Bismark's valiant crew were fighting off determined British attacks.

The sound of Katerina's sobbing indicated she was awake. "He's gone," she whispered, between bouts of weeping.

"You don't know that, Kat."

"I just know it. I said when he left that I wouldn't see him again."

"We mustn't give up hope. The British said they have captured survivors." She glanced at the bedside clock. "You should stay off work today."

"I can't. I have to go in."

"Kat, you can't go in your state. People will ask questions."

Katerina looked blank.

Trudy grabbed her friend's hand. "If you say you're upset because you've heard the Bismark has been sunk, they'll know straight away you've been listening to the BBC."

"I can't stay here alone. I'll go mad."

"I'll finish early."

Katerina still looked haggard when Trudy returned to the apartment.

"I've made some soup," Katerina muttered. Her eyes were bloodshot and her voice flat.

They ate in silence, willing the hours to pass. They managed to kill time by aimlessly walking around the block.

"I hope he was blown up," Katerina said out of the blue, as they approached the apartment's street door. "I mean, I hope he didn't drown. It must be an awful way to go."

"Don't talk like that, Kat." Trudy turned and stood directly in front of her, gripped her by the shoulders and stared hard into her eyes. "We don't give up hope, you hear me. Not until we know for sure."

Kat met Trudy's eyes. "I can't stand the idea of him suffering."

Trudy buried her friend in an embrace. "Just pray." She glanced over Katerina's shoulder to see the block warden slip back behind the doorway. "We're being watched," she whispered into Katerina's ear.

The evening dragged as the clock slowly ground its way towards seven o'clock. Three times they listened to the Reich Broadcast news. It boasted of further advances in Greece and Crete, and Luftwaffe successes against the RAF. Bismark was mentioned as a footnote. The gallant crew were engaged in a fierce battle against the might of the Royal Navy.

"Why can't they tell us the truth?" Katerina wailed.

"They won't be able to deny it after seven."

"What else aren't they telling us?"

"Anything that's bad news." Trudy made another couple of mugs of Ersatz coffee. It helped kill more time and kept her awake. It seemed the hands of the clock deliberately slowed as if to increase their torture.

At last, Trudy went downstairs, locked the front door and closed the curtains. "Put the radio on," she said, as she shut the living room door. Trudy knelt beside Katerina as she turned the set on and adjusted the tuning dial. The faint sound of music emerged from the crackle and hiss of static. The BBC was broadcasting sombre Beethoven instead of the usual dance numbers. The girls waited until the familiar Westminster chimes heralded the seven o'clock news. Katerina grabbed Trudy's hand.

"...the Bismark sank after receiving multiple hits from the guns of Royal Naval units and was despatched by torpedoes. Naval units remained

241

on scene to rescue survivors. We will shortly read out the names and ranks
of those German sailors that are known to have been rescued. Before that
..."

"Oh, for God's sake." Katerina squeezed her eyes tightly shut in anguish. "Please, just get on with it."

Trudy squeezed her hand and said nothing. She felt sick. After what seemed like hours, the names started to be read.

"In alphabetical order, here are the names and ranks of one hundred and thirteen known survivors.
Lothar Balthar – Leutnant.
Helmut Benke – Matrose..."

The sombre tone of the announcer cut through the silence of the apartment. Katerina turned the volume up another notch. She didn't care if the neighbours heard. She bent her head towards the loudspeaker, not wishing to miss a single syllable. The announcer continued on at a slow, steady pace, pausing after each name as if in silent tribute to the man's survival.

"Werner Hager – Matrosengefreiter.
Franz Halker – Matrosengefreiter..."

Katerina gave an involuntary shriek as the name Franz came from the loudspeaker.

"Heinz Jungnat – Machineobergefreiter..."

"I can't bear it." Katerina shook with tension. She squeezed her eyes shut and held her fists to her face in a desperate silent prayer. "Please God, please God, please God," she whispered.

The BBC announcer continued with his relentless, metronomic roll-call.

"Wilhelm Kaselitz – Matrose.
Franz Kaufmann – Matrose..."

Katerina shrieked. "That's him! He's alive, he's alive!" She stared at Trudy with wide hysterical eyes, her face contorted, on the edge of a complete breakdown. "He's alive, Trudy, he's alive!" Katerina wrapped her hands around her head and crumpled forward, burying her face into the rug. "He's alive," she kept repeating, her shoulders heaving with great wracking sobs.

Trudy felt numb, her face damp with tears, her throat tight as if she was half holding her breath, and her body trembled. She bent down and wrapped an arm across Katerina's prone form. The pair of them held each other; both were laughing and crying.

"What will happen to him?" Katerina sat up and wiped the residual tears from her eyes.

Trudy shrugged. "Presumably he'll be a prisoner of war."

Katerina's joy spread across her face. "He's alive, Trudy, he's safe, I can't believe it!" She dabbed her eyes again. "Can you write to prisoners of war?"

Trudy laughed. "I've no idea."

"Oh, Trudy, isn't this the best news?"

Trudy felt emotionally and physically drained. Franz's survival prompted a massive release of stress. She felt light-headed. She gave Katerina an affectionate kiss on the cheek. "I hope this means we can both get a good night's sleep."

ADVANCE EAST

Johan sat with his back against the tree, being careful not to spill the contents of his mess can. "This looks serious." He nodded towards the line of hundreds of horses, who were tethered under cover of the woods to the right of the road.

Jurgen followed his gaze. "Everything points to an attack. The fodder and ammunition trucks are fully loaded. It doesn't feel like an exercise."

"The canteen sergeant thinks we're being prepared to take over all of Poland." Johan blew over his meat stew to cool it.

Jurgen glanced over to where the rest of the regiment was spread out along the roadside. Hundreds of soldiers stretched themselves out along the verge, eating rations, smoking and chatting as they took advantage of the one-hour rest break. "Have you written home?"

Johann nodded. "You stuffed your pockets?"

"Traded in my cigarettes. How about you?"

"The same." Johan wiped his mess tin clean. "Maybe we'll be lucky again?"

"Let's hope so." Jurgen stared at the sky. "I liked France. At least it was over and done with, nice and quick."

"The fact we hardly fired a shot had a lot to do with it." Johan lowered his voice. "There are plenty desperate to see some action. They think the war will be over before they get their chance to do their bit."

"They're welcome to jump ahead of me."

Shouted orders were relayed down the road. The infantry pulled themselves to their feet and formed into ranks. In front of them, the artillerymen hitched the horses to their limbers.

"Here we go." Jurgen methodically checked through his equipment before picking up his rifle. "Two-hour march, ten kilometres. I reckon that'll put us right up against the Russians."

"Onwards to victory," Johan muttered.

"We're attacking in platoon formation. This is our start line." The platoon leader stabbed his finger on the map. "These ditches." He raised his head over the dust-dry bank and pointed. "You can see them running across the field." He smiled. "I know what you're thinking. Don't worry, the village will be attacked by Stukas. We'll advance during the bombing when Ivan has his head down." He glanced around at the soldiers. "I want us in position as soon as our Luftwaffe friends have finished. Then we go in, hard and fast. Squads three and four will take the right, one and two the left. The attack will be initiated by the two central squads with the flanks providing covering fire."

"What's the ultimate objective?" a squad leader asked.

"Take the whole village. Go straight through it. House to house. No prisoners." He laid the map on the ground and smoothed it flat. "Third platoon will sweep around the rear to cut off escape routes."

"What back up do we have?" Johan asked.

"Panzers will follow you in. However, they've been ordered to press on. They won't appreciate being held up." The officer gave Johan a hard look. "We get Ivan on the back-foot and keep him there, all the way to Moscow."

Johan kept his face expressionless. He returned to his squad, his mind focused on how his comrades might maximise success and minimise casualties. It was a standard infantry attack. His men were experienced enough to know exactly what was expected of them. It was the house to house fighting that concerned him.

"Well?' Jurgen asked.

"Daylight attack." Johan glanced at his watch. "In about ninety minutes. Tell the men to double-up on grenades."

An hour later, the black, gull-winged Stukas appeared high in the western sky. The squad watched as one by one they gracefully rolled and dived.

"Run!" Johan shouted. The squad sprinted across the open ground just as the increasing wail of the aircraft siren struck terror into the enemy. The Russians didn't have a chance to open fire as the first of the bombs exploded in the centre of the village. Johan threw himself into the ditch. The two-man machine-gun crew tumbled in alongside him and immediately set up the MG34. The rest of the squad had already spread themselves out along the ditch. In front of them, the village continued to be hit as one aircraft after another swooped down, their engines roaring and sirens screaming.

A bomb hurtled into a farm building, reducing it to shredded timber. Smoke and fire shot skyward as another bomb detonated. Johan watched the final two aircraft lining up to attack.

He raised his arm and shouted, "Ready, lads!" As soon as the bomb left the rack, he leapt from the ditch and sprinted towards the village. "Covering fire, coming through," he yelled. On either side of him the squad's machine guns opened up. Twenty comrades ran with him, firing as they went. They entered the village just as the final aircraft's bomb exploded.

Already Johan had a stick grenade in his hand. He picked a building and ran towards it, targeting the downstairs window beside the front door. Speed mattered. He had to reach the cover of the wall before any defenders felt brave enough to stick their heads out and open fire. He dived under the window sill, reached up, smashed the glass and pulled the fuse cord on the grenade. He counted two seconds before hurling the weapon through the shattered window. Two seconds later, the blast blew open the

245

door, shattered the windows and sent shards of glass flying across the street. His comrade was instantly through the door, spraying the inside with automatic fire.

Johan was already running towards the next building. His squad's experience clicked into gear. One man provided cover as his comrade moved towards the next objective. The troops moved like a single machine, systematically clearing buildings with bewildering speed. Johan had reached the centre of the village before he caught a glimpse of the enemy. A Russian soldier tumbled from a building, took one look at Johan, and fled. Two of his comrades joined him, zig-zagging to evade Johan's burst of fire. A Panzer suddenly roared down the street, throwing up clouds of dust and diesel fumes in its wake. It was immediately followed by three others. To his left, the rattle of a Russian machine gun indicated more spirited resistance had been encountered. Johan didn't dwell on it. He pressed on. Adrenalin heightened his senses. He scanned every window, door entrance, rooftop, for signs of enemy strongpoints or snipers. All the time he hurled grenades into buildings, outhouses and barns until he exhausted his supply. Another member of his squad took over and together they made it to the far side of the village. Johan followed the grenade into the last house. He clambered over smashed crockery and broken furniture, room by room. His heart pounded as he threw open doors, forced open cupboards and overturned tables, always expecting to be confronted by a Russian soldier. He finally made it to the upstairs bedroom. He peered out the window. In the distance, on either side of the road, a rag-bag group of Russian peasants and soldiers scattered across the open steppe in terror as the panzers bore down on them. Johan was drenched in sweat, breathing hard and shaking with fear. The whole assault lasted less than forty minutes. He'd survived another bout of combat.

He spotted Jurgen emerging from a building across the street. "Get the lads to set up defensive positions," he shouted. Jurgen nodded. He turned to the other squad members who'd launched the grenade attack with him. "You lads work back through the buildings. Make sure they are clear. I don't want any nasty surprises." The men moved off. "And watch out for booby traps," he shouted after them. Elsewhere in the village, sporadic gunfire indicated that some resistance continued.

Johan took deep breaths and allowed his tension to subside. He then turned his attention to personal survival. He scoured the house for anything useful - food, warm clothing, matches, flints, medicines… anything. He found nothing. The Russians had stripped the place bare.

Thirty minutes later he assembled his squad.

"Good job, lads. Anything to report - casualties?"

The squad looked at one another. Apart from two soldiers with some shrapnel wounds, they were intact.

"Wells are poisoned, grain store has been burned, and don't be tempted to drink from any bottles," Jurgen said.

"We need to go in with more grenades, either that or we use a Panzerfaust if we ever have to do this again," another said. "Sounds like the other squads had a worse time of it."

The arrival of the platoon leader interrupted their debrief. "Well done, lads. You've earned the easy job." He waved his hand at the half-destroyed village. "I want this razed to the ground by nightfall. Then get yourselves fed and resupplied. We need to keep up with the panzers."

The squad waited until the officer departed and was out of earshot. "Wonder why the other squad had a hard time of it? Could it be something to do with who was leading?" one soldier muttered.

"He's a bloody liability."

"He's working for his Iron Cross," another murmured.

Johan felt the need to intervene. "Put a lid on it. Count yourselves lucky. He could have ordered us on that duty." He nodded towards the distance where Russian survivors had been lined-up by the roadside. After a short time, a prolonged burst of machine-gun fire erupted.

Later, the squad marched past the bodies - old men, boys and a few Russian soldiers. There was no sign of the women and girls. Johan couldn't bring himself to look. He shut his mind to the barbarity he was caught up in. Behind them the flames reduced what remained of the village to ash. In front, the horizon of a pale blue evening sky gradually became stained a dirty brown from the dust kicked up by the advancing panzers.

JANUARY 1942 – HAMBURG

Frau Tolheim was arrested. At eleven o'clock, four Gestapo, in heavy black leather overcoats, strode purposefully up the town-hall steps, vaguely waved their identity cards at the two Stormtrooper guards and, without stopping, marched into Frau Tolheim's office. Seconds later she was frogmarched out, her arms pinned behind her back. At the centre of the foyer, she lifted her head, and her eyes met Trudy's with a look of despair and unfathomable sadness.

At that time of the morning the Rathaus entrance was crowded with members of the public on their way to appointments, secretaries running errands, and various officials either arriving or leaving. But it seemed Frau Tolheim had become invisible. People turned away, buried their faces in newspapers or files that suddenly contained vital information and required their full attention.

"What's she done?" Trudy asked a passing official whom she vaguely knew.

He looked disinterested. "Could be anything."

Within the week, a rumour circulated that Frau Tolheim had helped a young Jewish girl board a Swedish freighter. She and the girl had both been executed.

Trudy's sense of dread threatened to overwhelm her. She convinced herself that it was only a matter of time before the Gestapo came for her. As each day passed, an impotent rage gradually replaced her fear. Terror was used against anyone that failed to tow the Party line and dis-information became blatantly obvious. Yet the population adopted a bovine acquiescence. Outwardly, Trudy maintained a façade of the loyal diligent civil servant. Inside, she seethed. She wondered if the day would ever come when she could strike at least one blow in revenge for Frau Tolheim.

AIR RAID

"He's in England." Katerina thrust the postcard into Trudy's face even before she had wholly entered the room. "Go on, read it. Franz is in England, in Yorkshire, wherever that is. He's uninjured and is being treated well by the prison guards. His one complaint is that the prison hut is cold and damp. He doesn't like the English weather."

"Shall I bother reading this?" Trudy waved the small card and laughed. "Does he say you can write back?"

Katerina looked non-plussed. "I never thought of that." She frowned. "How do you go about writing a letter to an address in a country we're at war with?"

"Ask at the Post Office." Trudy flipped the card over. "When was this sent?" She answered her own question when she spotted the postmark. "It's taken over twenty weeks to get here!" She handed the postcard back. "You'd better start writing if you want him to get it before Christmas." She took off her coat and hung it on the hook on the door. "If you write it tonight, I'll drop by the Post Office tomorrow afternoon and ask how to send it."

"Are you still stuck with administration work?"

"Not for much longer. I've been accepted for Luftwaffe training on operating searchlights."

"I thought our Fuhrer expressly forbids women to do any type of war-like activities."

"The powers that be are prepared to allow women to operate searchlights, under the supervision of a man, of course." Trudy sounded bitter. "They are recruiting young lads of fourteen to operate flak guns. It's ridiculous. Makes you wonder why so many women continue to support Hitler." She held her hand up as she saw Katerina's warning look. "I know."

Trudy embraced her new job within the Flakgruppen Regiment with enthusiasm and thrived as a consequence. Within weeks she found herself in charge of a searchlight crew and, in less than six months, she gained promotion to Regimental Supervisor of a new 200 cm master light on the city outskirts.

Searchlight squads were usually led by men who were too old to be called up, but hers was the first to be all-female. Perhaps because they were local girls, or it was something to do with operating after dark, the women felt able to speak to each other more openly.

"It was a mistake."

"How can you say that?! Stalin hoped the Fuhrer *would* invade England. Then, while our boys were fighting their way towards London, he'd stab us in the back. It's better we attacked first."

"That's just talk put about by the Party to justify the invasion. You mark my words - attitudes will change if the Russian's hit back and we start taking casualties."

"Don't say that! My son's out there somewhere."

"And mine," another woman piped up. "And I don't like this defeatist talk. We should be supporting our boys."

"I'm not defeatist. I'm just saying it's a mistake, especially since the Americans joined in. Why can't the Fuhrer sit down with Stalin and agree a peace deal?"

"It's gone too far for that," another muttered darkly. "My husband sent some pictures back. Terrible pictures of our soldiers shooting Russian villagers, burning their houses."

"Terrorists, you mean. Our boys only shoot terrorists... and Jews, of course," she added as an afterthought.

"These were old men, women and children."

"They probably deserved it. My husband and young lad are both at the front. They say they burn the villages to stop Russian terrorists using them as a base to hide and attack our boys."

The wail of the sirens cut short their discussion. "Here they come!" the comms operator shouted.

Trudy glanced at her watch. It was ten past midnight and her last shift before a two-day break. She couldn't help thinking she was part of some mad fairy-tale. The day had been idyllic - the sun beat down, the temperature soared into the high twenties, they were surrounded by peaceful parkland, and sheep and cows wandered around the meadows. Earlier, the girls had taken advantage of the late evening sunshine to hitch up their skirts and sunbathe. It felt like a summer camp. But they talked of the killings on the eastern front as if they were an everyday event. And soon the clear night sky would be filled with bombers bent on death and destruction.

A low menacing rumble now heralded their approach, getting ever louder until the air reverberated with the roar of hundreds of engines. The girls donned their steel helmets, fired up the generator and became soldiers.

"Multiple aircraft - two hundred and sixty-four degrees, altitude seven thousand seven hundred, sixty-two degrees elevation."

All chat ceased, there were only instructions and orders now. Their training kicked in as each dropped into their role. The crew moved as one, confident and assured, eager to do their bit and not let each other down.

The horizontal and vertical cranks adjusted the searchlight skyward. Trudy swung the entire light assembly on the target heading. The beam stabbed out and all eyes strained as every girl prayed for a target to appear, to earn the honour of being the first crew to fix an aircraft. Tonight they were in with a good chance. The armada would directly overfly their position.

Almost immediately they got lucky. A bomber was flying lower than expected, its position given away by a streak of flames from one of its engines. Trudy called for more power and pulled the focus lever. The beam brightened and narrowed. The bomber stood out against the clear night sky. It made no attempt to take evasive action. Maybe the pilot was already dead, or so blinded by the lights that coned his aircraft that he had become disorientated, or possibly the plane's controls had locked up. Perhaps he was insanely brave, and determined to achieve his objective. Either way, the plane continued on its route, marked by the trail of flames. The gunners quickly got the range, and the aircraft became momentarily lost inside a barrage of tracer-fire and explosions. It emerged unscathed. Flak peppered the aircraft, its progress tracked by a constant stream of detonations. And still it continued as if living a charmed life. More searchlights locked on as it passed directly overhead. The girls instinctively ducked as a piece of shrapnel clattered on to the generator. The air around the plane became thick with tracer-fire. It seemed impossible it could survive.

The girls continued to track it as it headed towards a skyline already lit by hundreds of flashes as the bombs rained down. By the time the dull thuds of explosions reached the searchlight emplacement, great sheets of flame shot into the night sky.

The noise was deafening: the throaty snarl of aircraft engines, the constant firing of hundreds of anti-aircraft guns, the crackling ripple of exploding shells, and the continual rumble of bombs and incendiaries detonating over eight kilometres away. A massive, silent explosion on the skyline momentarily distracted everyone.

Unlike previous raids, the British formations were packed tighter together this time, making detection easier. The crew picked up another plane. This pilot and crew didn't have the good fortune of their comrades. Within seconds, the bomber was coned and obliterated. Immediately, Trudy swung the beam, seeking out another victim. Another searchlight crew had been lucky. Trudy turned the light round to seal the trap. More lights locked on to the target. No matter how hard the pilot banked and dived his fate was sealed. The lights weren't letting go.

The sound of the engines faded, the flak guns fell silent and, one by one, the searchlights turned off. The girls switched off the generator. The abrupt extinguishing of the beam made the night suddenly seem darker. A few lit cigarettes.

A voice came from the darkness. "Holy Mother of God. Look at that!" The whole of the northern horizon was ablaze.

"That's not the docks or the industrial areas," someone else observed.

Trudy glanced at her watch. The entire raid had lasted thirty-five minutes and yet it looked as if the entire city was on fire.

"That was a lot of bombers," the radar operator said. "Far more than previous raids."

"According to Goebbels, it will be a small force of forty to fifty aircraft, of which eighty were shot down."

No one laughed. The distant flames held a morbid fascination.

Trudy felt a knot of trepidation seize her stomach. She guessed over three hundred bombers had been involved. It was obvious that large parts of the city had been hit. Her thoughts turned to Katerina and Tante Bri.

The women sensed her concern. "You'd best get going," one of them said.

"I'll wait until the all-clear," Trudy said. "In any case, I imagine that the roads will be blocked."

JOINING THE FOLD

"You are too kind, Kommissioner."

Keunsberg waved a dismissive hand. "It's nothing. I wanted to show my appreciation for your cooperation over the past three years." He smiled. "I recall, that at our first meeting, you said there was much that the Church and the Party hold in common."

"And so it has proved."

"It's not just about cooperation. I have to say your initiative to promote National Socialist ideas from the pulpit was inspired."

Wagner bowed his head to acknowledge the compliment. "The flock must be guided towards truth and enlightenment."

"Although it puzzles me that apparently there are so few priests with opposing views."

"We are ever watchful," Wagner muttered. He turned the invitation card over. "Pardon me for asking, Kommissioner, but is accommodation included?"

"Naturally." Keunsberg paused to light a cigarette. "All you need is an overnight bag, and be ready to be picked up at eight-thirty. It's a six-hour journey to Lienz. You're expected to get there between two and three o'clock." Keunsberg blew out a steady stream of smoke. "No doubt you will want to stop for lunch and stretch your legs at some point on the way."

"And the dress code?"

Keunsberg suppressed a laugh. "My dear Wagner, this is an opportunity for you to relax and enjoy yourself. I suggest that your ecclesiastical robes will help other guests recognise your calling."

"I'll make sure I'm ready, Herr Kommissioner." Wagner turned just before he went out the door. "Thank you once again." He raised his right arm. "Heil Hitler."

Keunsberg smiled. "Enjoy your trip."

Once outside, Wagner felt triumphant. He almost skipped down the corridor, his mind already focussed on how his new standing with Keunsberg might be exploited with other prominent Party members who, he was sure, would be attending the reception.

He entered his office still in an ebullient mood, poured a generous glass of his favourite wine, silently toasted himself, and then spent a lot of time studying and writing up his note book. He reviewed every politician, Nazi official, senior cleric and business leader that figured in his records. It would be important to demonstrate how well connected and informed he was if he was to impress other guests at the reception. The benefits of National Socialism were firmly etched into his mind and he was glad he'd advised the Bishop to adopt a cooperative stance, or at least not openly work against the Nazis. He then turned his mind to what he ought to pack.

THE EASTERN FRONT

The lines of helmets, balanced on crude wooden crosses, sucked the morale from the platoon. Johan did a quick calculation as the men trudged past. By his reckoning, over four hundred soldiers lay buried on this stretch of road. The continuous rattle of machine guns, thump of mortar rounds, whistling of artillery and tank fire, and, occasionally, the shriek of the feared Kaytusha rockets, indicated the violence that awaited the troops. The sound intensified as they marched into a city shrouded in thick grey smoke. The stench of rotting flesh, from the dozens of horses that lay either side of the road, became overpowering. A man broke ranks to be violently sick. Johan suspected it was more a result of fear than the sight and smell of the dead animals.

The column came to a halt inside a derelict factory. Little remained of the corrugated asbestos roof, glass from the windows crunched under their boots, and the far gabled wall no longer existed. Remnants of smashed workbenches, flung on top of each other by some enormous explosion, lay in tangled heaps.

"Gather round." The Commander waved his arms, urging the troops not to loiter. He clambered on a workbench. "Attention," he shouted. Despite their fatigue, the platoon instantly responded. "At ease." The officer gazed around. "Men, a great honour awaits us." The men's eyes instantly glazed over. "For over four weeks, our Panzergrenadier comrades have held this position against overwhelming Bolshevik forces, who have relentlessly attacked but found themselves broken by German superiority. Our orders are to relieve our brothers and sweep the Untermensch from the battlefield. Tonight we move to our forward positions. Before we do, pay attention to the following briefing from the Panzergrenadier Stabsfeldwebel.

A dishevelled, exhausted-looking soldier stepped forward, his uniform so filthy from mud and dust it was impossible to establish his regiment or rank. His boots were scuffed and the knees on his trousers spoke of hours spent crawling on all-fours. Johan noticed the barrel of his machine gun was stripped to bare metal, and twice the standard issue of medical pouches hung from his belt. Even from where he was standing Johan could see the man's eyes were bloodshot, and he swayed slightly as if drunk.

"Listen hard, learn quickly, or you'll be dead in short order." The soldier's hollow eyes swept around the platoon. "Anyone wearing rank insignia, remove them now. You will watch your front, flanks and rear at all times. Ivan attacks at any moment and from any direction, including underground. They know the drainage and sewer systems so never assume you've cleared a building. Russian snipers are everywhere. You fail to be undercover, even for a second, you'll get a bullet. Never remove your helmet. Never take prisoners, they don't." He let the words sink in.

"Assume everyone is an Ivan. They use young kids and women. Shoot first, don't hesitate. Our opponents are fanatical, barbaric, will not give ground and will fight to the death. Even when you think you've killed them more appear, hundreds more. You'll survive only by being smart, eating anything you can get hold of, staying warm and dry, and being extremely careful every second - day and night."

"*Sheisse*, I don't like the sound of this," Jurgen muttered.

"Oh, and one other thing." The soldier scanned the platoon. "Write your letters now. At least half of you won't be going home."

Every member of the platoon felt sick with trepidation. This wasn't what they'd come to expect. So far, all engagements with the enemy had resulted in a rout for the opposition. The Stukas bombed, the artillery and tanks put down a barrage, the infantry followed with overwhelming fire and aggression, and the Russians ran away. Now this rag-tag infantryman scared them into believing the enemy was capable of putting up a fight.

All doubts were erased by the time they reached their forward position. Their base lay just over a kilometre into the city. It took three hours of crawling along sewers, scrambling over rubble and dodging through smashed buildings to reach it. Out in the open they were under constant fire. Bullets ricocheted off bricks and stone, mortar bombs and grenades showered down, and men, who thought they were safely undercover, crumpled as the snipers' bullets found their mark.

Half-way to their objective, Johan cowered in the debris of a basement, as artillery shells decimated ground already reduced to a wasteland from previous bombardments. Russians seemed to be everywhere. There was no front line. They found themselves hurled into a bear pit of violence and death. Throughout this terror, Johan clung to the heels of the Stabsfeldwebel. The Sergeant Major knew where he was going and how to survive.

The base turned out to be the remains of a grain storage facility. The platoon dispersed into the wreckage, finding cover wherever they could. Johan did a quick roll call. They'd started off with fifty-two men and had already lost eight, with four seriously wounded.

It marked the start of five months of hell. Each day, terror and fear ratcheted up. They endured constant fire. Attacks were mounted just to keep the Russians at bay, rather than take any objectives. Even when they succeeded in inflicting casualties and forcing the enemy to retreat, the respite was short-lived. Within hours, the Russians counter-attacked, used snipers to pick them off or infiltrated their lines, emerging like subterranean monsters to decimate the rear positions.

Ammunition ran short. Grenade supplies dried up. Artillery support became restricted to ten shots a day, and that was almost immediately reduced to only five. The squad seized any weapon, Russian or

255

German, that fell into their hands. At times the combatants were less than twenty-five metres apart. Savage hand-to-hand fighting became frequent with trenching tools and spades being the weapons of choice. And each day the temperature dropped as the brutal Russian winter turned the mud iron-hard, froze the firing mechanisms on the machine guns, and further reduced the men's shattered morale. Fingers, toes and noses turned black with frostbite. Each morning, Johan added those who'd frozen to death to the platoon's casualty list.

"This can't go on," Jurgen muttered through chattering teeth. "Doesn't the high command realise?" He handed Johan half the carcase he'd been roasting on a stick over a shaded flame.

"The high command has been told, by the Fuhrer himself, that General Manstein's Army Group Don will relieve us in a matter of days."

"Is that true?"

They both ducked and covered their heads as a couple of mortar bombs exploded less than twenty metres from their shelter. Johan waited for the dust to clear. He blew the debris from the skewered meat before eating it. "We're almost surrounded. The chances of them breaking through lie somewhere between minimal and non-existent." He chewed the meat and bones to extract every bit of nourishment before swallowing. "That tasted alright. What was it?"

"Cat."

Johan raised an appreciative eyebrow. "Not at all bad. Better than horseflesh." He dug a nodule of hard bread from his pocket and handed it to Jurgen.

Jurgen didn't hesitate, he wolfed it down. "Have you kept your last bread ration?"

Johan nodded. "Tomorrow it gets reduced to fifty grams. We need to conserve everything." They ducked again as another mortar bombardment showered them with dust and shards of masonry.

They seized every opportunity to plunder and scavenge anything that helped them survive. Clothing, especially boots, socks, gloves, woollen hats and balaclavas were stripped from the dead and dying, along with medical kits, ammunition, pistols, machine guns and, most essential of all, food. Even horsemeat became a distant memory. Anything living found itself despatched and consumed - dogs, cats, rats, mice, even birds. Rumours circulated of cannibalism. Johan had no reason to disbelieve them. Men were being driven to insanity. The Heimatschuss offered a desperate way out. Men blew-off their own hands, feet and arms in the hope of a medical evacuation. More often than not they found themselves patched up, then sent to the punishment battalion and certain death.

"We need to get out," Jurgen said quietly, as he huddled closer to the tiny flame. "Have you looked at yourself."

Johan regarded his friend. He doubted Aunt Josey or Uncle Stephan would recognise their son. Jurgen looked a skeletal wreck. His face was so thin and drawn that his eye sockets stood out. His eyes were bloodshot from lack of sleep, and his shredded nerves had produced a nervous tic. And he reeked. Terror of snipers forced them to use their positions as latrines. For over six weeks neither had washed. Thanks to scavenging, they wore layers of clothing that made them look like two elderly tramps rather than soldiers. But neither succumbed to frostbite and, compared to many of their comrades, they'd kept themselves warm, fed, disease-free - and alive. Johan slowly shook his head. "When I look like you, I'll get concerned."

"I'm serious, mate." He looked nervously around. "This whole thing is pointless. We're living on borrowed time."

They had to shout as the Russians turned on their latest weapon. Loudspeakers blared constant propaganda, interspersed with seductive offers of good treatment, hot meals, and a comfortable incarceration in a warm prison camp. A white flag was all it took.

"We're trapped, Jurgen!" Johan shouted. "Surrender and the Russians will shoot us. Go AWOL and we'll be shot or sent to the punishment battalion. Our best bet is to focus on surviving." He managed an exhausted grin. "We left home together, and we'll get back together."

"The sooner the bloody better."

Another enormous explosion showered them with bricks, snow and frozen earth. As they dug themselves out, both instinctively reached for their weapons as they sensed someone approaching.

"Don't shoot, lads. It's me." A body landed heavily on top of them. It was the Stabsfeldwebel. "Sorry lads," he said breathlessly, as he dusted himself down. "Get ready to move out."

Johan looked startled. "When?"

"Tonight."

"Where are we heading?"

"West." He looked intently at them both. "Manheim's lot aren't coming. There's talk of surrender. Frankly, I'd rather take my chances breaking out than being butchered by the Russians. It's your choice."

Johan glanced at Jurgen. "I'm in. What about you?"

Jurgen nodded.

The soldier patted Johan on the shoulder. "Eleven o'clock."

Only fifteen of the original platoon remained alive to make the attempt. They were joined by two artillerymen who'd been pressed into joining the infantry when their ammunition ran out, and four other soldiers whose units no longer existed.

Neither Johan nor Jurgen remembered much about the escape. They just ran, blinded by snow, illuminated by Russian tracer bullets and star shells. They ducked and dived through shattered buildings and scrambled over piles of ice-covered masonry that concealed hidden obstacles and trip hazards: steel girders that cracked bones, bricks and timbers that skinned the flesh from their legs, or holes that swallowed men up as they dropped into hidden basements. They stopped for nothing and no-one. It was a wild headlong dash, continuously chased by mortars and machine gun fire. In the darkness, they ran into Soviet patrols. Even they didn't slow them down. They fired and hurled grenades as they ran, every man rendered reckless by overwhelming terror and desperate determination to escape. Amid the confusion, friend fired on friend. By first light they'd reached open countryside. The snow became a blizzard, reducing visibility to almost nothing. The Stabfeldwebel shouted to them. Only seven members of the platoon responded. They gathered in a huddle; their backs turned against the howling wind.

"We need to keep going. Tie belts together. Don't let go." They began a slow, methodical trudge, heads bent against the driving blizzard. At the head of the crocodile, Johan navigated using the tiny compass from his survival pack. They staggered on for three hours before the first man collapsed. Johan had no idea who he was. The cold had finally seeped into the man's bones. They managed to force his fingers around the trigger of his rifle before they left him to his fate. An hour later, the group ran into a Panzer buried to its turret in its snow-filled berm. The tank crew panicked and opened fire with their machine gun. Frantic yelling persuaded the crew to cease fire, but by then the six escapees were reduced to five - the Stabsfeldwebel lay on his back, his glazed eyes slowly being covered by snow.

LIENZ - OSTMARK

Wagner gazed at the passing scenery and felt at peace with the world. He counted himself blessed that he lived in a country so spectacularly beautiful. The journey through the Tyrol was breath-taking. The snowy mountain crags soared up on either side of the valley, their majesty seemed to celebrate God's creative genius. In Wagner's mind it represented heaven on Earth. Gradually, the mountains gave way to gentler slopes until the fertile valley of the River Danube came into view. He sat for the entire journey in the warm, luxurious comfort of Keunsberg's official limousine. The only thing that marred his experience was the attitude of the two SS soldiers assigned as his escort.

He leant forward. "How far now?" he asked.

Neither the driver nor his companion turned around. "Less than an hour."

Wagner frowned. He would have to have words with Keunsberg, when he returned, about the serious lack of manners of these two. Then again, they were just SS foot soldiers with limited intelligence and little concept of social graces or etiquette. He dismissed them from his thoughts and returned to admiring the views.

The journey skirted around the outskirts of Lienz and along the banks of the Danube. Ten minutes later, they turned left and the road wound its way through a forest. Suddenly a large, stone-built structure loomed in front. To the left, an imposing round building, and to the right, an equally intimidating rectangular tower topped with searchlights and, to Wagner's dismay, what looked like machine guns. A substantial stone wall, decorated with a majestic, stylised eagle standing on a swastika emblem, linked the two fortresses. Directly underneath, two massive timber gates, with sentry posts either side, swung open as their car approached.

Wagner craned his neck, trying to take everything in. A feeling of trepidation seized his heart. Barbed wire fences seemed to be everywhere. The outer fence posts were fitted with heavy-duty electrical insulators. A line of wooden huts stretched off into the distance. Gaunt, emaciated figures with bowed heads were being marched and harangued by uniformed guards. A man cowered as a large Doberman strained on its leash. The frozen vapour from its snarls drifted into the man's terrified face. The handler appeared to find the sport amusing. A few ragged men risked a furtive glance towards the passing limousine, their eyes hollow and desperate.

"Is this the right place?" Wagner asked querulously, and he broke into a cold sweat. The soldiers said nothing.

"Where are we?" Wagner's nervousness turned to fear. He peered through the rear windscreen. The gates had already swung shut. The car drew up alongside a small group of four men: two uniformed SS officers, stamping their feet against the penetrating winter cold, and a couple of haggard, shivering scarecrow-like creatures - one with a bent back that suggested great age or some kind of deformity.

As soon as the car came to a halt, the two SS men got out, casually moved to the back door and peered through the window at the now terrified priest. It was if they wished to stretch out his terror. The door was thrown open, Wagner dragged out and hurled to the ground. Then the beating started. Through his petrified wails, Wagner was vaguely aware of a deluge of confused, shouted orders and swearing - to pick himself up, salute in the presence of a senior officer, and to strip off his clothes. All the time blows and kicks rained down.

One of the officers glanced at the two scarecrows, who stood as if oblivious to the savagery in front of them. He jerked his head towards the gates. Immediately, the two shuffled off in a painful, limping stagger. The gates opened and they stumbled through.

Behind them, Wagner's wails turned to screams.

Neither man looked back as the gates closed behind them.

Two hundred and fifty kilometres away, Father Thomas watched as the Abbess of St Catherine's was bundled into the back of an SS truck. He tucked the last of the ledgers into his briefcase and averted his eyes as the lorry's tyres crunched along the gravel path. He had no idea how long the journey was from Littesau to Ravensbruck. All he was sure of was that, in the freezing weather, it would be an extremely uncomfortable trip.

As for what happened to Monsignor Wagner, Father Thomas was happy to accept the Bishop's explanation that his chaplain had been summoned to the Vatican on confidential business. Even the instruction to undertake an immediate audit of every establishment under Wagner's jurisdiction, and to arrange an immediate meeting with Kommissioner Keunesberg, he deliberately obliterated from his curiosity. He would just report the facts and feign complete ignorance. In fact, from now on, he was determined to supress any inquisitiveness on the inner workings of the Church.

He was just grateful that Wagner was no longer his concern, relieved that his conscience was clear, and grateful to still have his job and his sanity.

FAMILIAR STRANGERS

Father Haphold and Herman Paulus slipped quietly back into the village. It was days before anyone knew of their presence. The pinewood smoke drifting from Herman's house provided the first indication. But no villagers knocked on the door. No one wanted to be contaminated. The pair had fallen foul of the Party. Their guilt, therefore, was obvious.

In the Breitner household, Marie was the first to mention that Herman's house appeared occupied.

"Are you sure?" Sep was already taking down his hunting rifle.

Marie became alarmed. "Don't do anything silly, Sep."

"Whoever it is, they have no right to enter someone else's property. These bloody Nazis think they can steal anything they want."

Marie's concern increased. "Sep, if it's the Nazis there's nothing you can do!"

Sep knew she was right. The Rubenstein's residence and surgery in Achbrugge was now occupied by a Nazi sympathiser and his family. Nevertheless, he felt he ought to make some effort to protect his friend's property. Minutes later, he hammered on Herman's front door and tried to push it open. It was bolted – heightening Sep's suspicions. No Doppelgauer locked doors. He stepped back and prepared to kick the door down.

The bolt slid back, and the door part-opened. An ancient, white-haired man peered nervously through the crack. "Ah, Sep. It's good to see you." The door was thrown open, and a thin hand beckoned him inside.

Sep was thrown by Father Haphold's appearance. He embraced his old friend and received another shock. The man was just skin and bone. "It's good to see you back." He turned to find Herman staring at him. Both men looked like they'd aged twenty years. Sep took in the sparse Stube, the bare table and the empty range. "When did you two last eat?"

"We get by." The priest smiled.

"Get your coats, you're coming back with me."

"Sep, we don't want to cause you any bother."

"It's no bother. You need to be fed."

"I meant with the village."

"Sod the village – begging your pardon, Father."

Josey and Marie took one look at the emaciated pair and sprang into action.

"What on earth happened to you?" Josey was already peeling potatoes as Marie placed a large kettle on the hob. "Harriet, can you come down and give a hand," she called.

"Three years in Mauthausen is what happened." He and Herman eased themselves painfully onto the bench seat.

Josey froze. "We heard about Old Doctor Rubenstein and Rudi."

Father Haphold crossed himself. "May God have mercy on their souls."

"What about the rest of the family?" Josey whispered. "Have you heard anything about Hannah, Rachel and Sara?"

Father Haphold gave a sad nod. "Before Rudi died, he was told Rachel had been shot at Lichtenberg, allegedly for incitement. Hannah and Sara were sent to Ravenbruck. I don't know for sure, but people transferred to Mauthausen from there talked about thousands of deaths from disease." The priest rubbed his chin and looked grief-stricken. "The Jews are being separated and transported further east. Everyone knows they're being sent to their deaths."

Marie flung her hands to her face and wailed. Josey angrily threw the pan down and stood clutching the range to steady herself. "Just for being Jews!? What crime had they committed?" Josey struggled to comprehend the news. Marie sank down into a chair, her face ashen. Father Haphold's words barely registered.

"Josey, all sorts of people, especially Jews, are being exterminated. Prisoners of War, Poles, Russians and anyone else who opposes the Nazis, are being worked to death, starved, beaten, shot, or killed by being thrown on electrified fences." Father Haphold swept an almost translucent hand through his hair. "In Mauthausen they throw prisoners off cliffs. I never thought I'd witness such barbarity."

"But you're a Catholic priest and Herman is a carpenter, what crimes had you committed?"

Father Haphold looked bleak. "Josey - we were accused of being homosexual."

A shocked silence engulfed the Stube. No one knew how to react.

Eventually Josey spoke, her voice strained, "Can you return to your parish duties?"

Father Haphold sighed. "That might be difficult."

"What will you do? How will you survive?" Marie asked.

"At the moment we are scraping by. On charity and whatever. Something will turn up." He gave a weak smile. "As we priests are fond of saying – the Good Lord will provide."

"Well, the Good Lord won't have anything to provide for if you don't recover your strength. You need building up, the pair of you." Josey returned to her potato peeling. "Harriet, we could do with your help," she shouted towards the stairs again.

"I could help." Sep forced his mind away from his dark thoughts and sat down. "I've got some building work and I need a carpenter, and with Johan away I'm a bit short around the farm."

The priest's eyes lit up.

"I can't pay you much but we can feed you."

Father Haphold leaned forward and grabbed Sep's wrists. "You're a good man, Sep Breitner. Ah, and who is this delightful young woman?"

He brightened as Harriet entered the Stube carrying a sleeping Simone. "My word, can this be the girl who used to race her brother down the street from the church?"

Harriet smiled. "It's good to see you, Father, and you, Herr Paulus."

"And who is this little fellow?" Father Haphold peered at the infant.

Harriet found herself blushing. Up until now, she'd explained away her pregnancy to those outside the family through the creation of a fictitious husband, who was away fighting at the front. Whether or not outsiders believed her counted for little. The Breitners were ostracised anyway. Somehow, lying to a priest, and to Father Haphold in particular, felt wrong.

Her father came to her rescue. "This little fellow is Simone."

"Oh, a little Mädchen. I beg your pardon." The priest chuckled. "We've missed so much. It seems Herman and I have a lot of catching up to do. Anyway, many congratulations, Harriet, and of course to your husband."

An awkward silence descended.

"Ah, I sense that I am intruding into sensitive territory, for which I apologise."

"You don't have to apologise, Father," Harriet said. "It's just that Simone's Pa is away and I'm... we aren't able to contact..." Harriet felt tears start to well up.

"The clue is in Simone's name, Father." Sep stood up, put a comforting arm around Harriet and tickled his granddaughter's chin.

Father Haphold looked blank until a light of understanding crossed his face. "Ah, we live in very trying times, do we not?"

263

FIRESTORM

"You can't go through."

"What do you mean I can't go through? I need to get home."

"Orders. Only fire crews, police and clearance teams are authorised." The guard's expression told Trudy that no amount of pleading would change his mind. To reinforce the point, he unslung his rifle. "I've been ordered to shoot anyone who disobeys."

"What parts were hit?"

"The centre, west and north-west mostly. There's a lot of damage. Fires are still burning."

Trudy felt a wave of relief. Her apartment was in the east of the city centre, and Tante Bri's even further away. There was nothing for it but to turn back and try another route. She arrived at Tante Bri's two hours later, having picked her way through rubble-strewn streets.

Apart from two blocks damaged by earlier raids, the slum was unscathed and Tante Bri was overjoyed to see her. She burst into tears and almost suffocated Trudy in an enormous bear hug of a cuddle. "Oh, thank goodness you're safe! I was in such a state of worry." She disengaged and held Trudy at arms-length so she could examine her from head to foot. "You are all right, aren't you? No damage? My word, what is the world a-coming to? What an air raid!"

"Madi, I'm fine." Trudy laughed and gave her aunt another kiss. "I'm more concerned about you."

Tante Bri fanned the air with her hands as if swatting a swarm of flies. "We've not been bothered. Nearest bomb dropped three streets away. Didn't half make the building shake though."

Trudy's face fell. "What were you doing in the apartment?" She gave Bri a stern look. I've told you before. You must go to the shelter."

"Yeah, yeah, I know. Easier said than done though with my hips." As if to emphasise her point Tante Bri waddled awkwardly towards the stove. "By the time I make it the shelter, them bomber-boys will have flown over, dropped their bombs and landed back in England." She banged the kettle on the stove to signal the end of the matter. "You'll stop for a coffee, or what passes for coffee these days?"

"Always got time for a gossip with my Madi." Trudy cleared a pile of clothes off the armchair and sat down. "These for mending?"

Bri looked over her shoulder. "Yep. Get yer needle and thread out, girl. Just like old times, eh?" Three minutes later, she placed the piping hot drinks on the side table and collapsed her bulk into the chair opposite. She selected an item from the pile and held it up, before deciding to choose another, when suddenly the siren went off.

Trudy immediately put down her coffee and leapt to her feet. "Come on, Madi." She stretched out her arms to help the old lady out of her seat.

Tante Bri gave her a tired look. "It's no use, Trudy dear. You can see my problem. Once I'm sitting it takes forever to get me up again."

"I'll help you." Trudy made to grab Bri's arm.

"You ain't strong enough, girl. You'll only do yourself a mischief." She batted Trudy's hand away. "You go. No point us both being blown up."

"I'm not leaving you!"

"Look, my love, I'm nearly seventy years old. I've done well to get this far. When it's time to go, it's time to go. I'd prefer to die here in my apartment sitting in my chair, hopefully not knowing a thing, rather than being killed on the street among a bunch of strangers." She looked at Trudy with sad eyes. She reached over and stroked her hair. "You are young and beautiful with your whole life in front of you. You owe it to yourself and me to live." She stared at her for a second before breaking out in a broad smile. "Now get yourself to that shelter and leave me in peace. No!" she held up an admonishing finger as she saw Trudy about to protest.

Trudy sank back in her chair. "I'm not leaving you, Madi. No!" She held up her own finger. "No argument."

They returned to their sewing, waiting for the sound of approaching bombs that never came. It must have been a false alarm or a couple of fast bombers on a nuisance raid.

Katerina was in a buoyant mood. She'd received the latest Red Cross postcard from Franz. She jumped on the couch, tucked her legs underneath her and read the brief message aloud for Trudy's benefit.

"My darling Kat,

I hope you are missing me as much as I am you. I'm well, although I shall never get used to this English weather. We live in a large hut with nothing but a thin iron roof to protect us. Despite a single stove, the place is cold and damp. We are being fed the same rations as the British so we can't complain, although some do. The guards are very correct. Not friendly, but not unfriendly. We play football and also have a plot where we grow vegetables. A few of us have been allowed to work on a nearby farm. I enjoyed that very much. Perhaps I'll become a farmer one day. We've been allowed to convert one of the huts into a chapel, gym and small theatre. Some of the lads are actors and musicians and have put on some entertainment. We invited some local villagers to attend a church service and a show. They seemed to enjoy it.

Send my best wishes to Trudy. Just enough space left to say that I love you dearly, and am missing you desperately. I live to receive your letters and look forward to a time when we are reunited.

> *Your loving Franz."*

She kissed the card, then clasped it to her breast as if it was a piece of Franz. "Isn't that lovely?"

"Sounds like he's landed on his feet." Trudy glanced across at her friend. "You should send him a photograph."

"Is that allowed?"

Trudy shrugged. "Can't see why not."

Katerina looked around the room, trying to remember where a photograph of her might be found. "I have one in the family album. But that's with my parents."

"I can have a word with the photographer we use for identity cards. I'm sure he'd do me a favour. I'm seeing him tonight."

Katerina immediately sat up. "You've got a date?" Her eyes gleamed. "You didn't tell me. Is he handsome?"

Trudy laughed. "It's not a date. It's a colleague's birthday. We're meeting at a Gasthaus for a few drinks."

"But he asked you?"

"Not strictly speaking."

"I knew it! He did ask you. Oh, Trudy, stop being such a mystery girl. What's his name? Come on." Katerina made herself comfortable and looked expectant. "Well?"

"He asked if I was going, that's all."

"He asked if you were going!? Trudy, that's as good as a proposal, girl." Katerina suddenly looked serious. "He isn't married, is he?"

"No. Not as far as I know."

Kat clapped her hands in delight. "Perfect. So, what are you wearing?"

Trudy looked bemused and glanced at her dress. "I'm going like this."

"No, no, no!" Katerina looked at her friend in exasperation. "Think, girl, be decisive. You can't go like that. You need to… you know… spice yourself up a bit."

"Kat, it's a work's do, not a debutante's ball." She held a hand up to stop Katerina in her tracks. "I'm going like this. That's final." She got up. "You write your letter to Franz. That'll keep you occupied."

Trudy found an excuse to leave the celebrations early. The whole event seemed to her to be a desperate attempt to have fun, no matter what. Apart from a few close friends of the birthday girl, there was no spark or energy among the other guests. People were tired, and the conversations inevitably drifted towards the increasing hardships almost everyone was experiencing. Food supplies were becoming erratic, some had been bombed out and were living in refugee shelters, and everyone had a tale to tell about relatives on the Russian front. The guests drank heavily, whether out of boredom or as stress relief or both. Trudy didn't stay to find out.

It was another clear, balmy summer night. Although the blackout was in force, the moon bathed the streets in a ghostly pale light. The Gasthaus was six tram stops from the apartment, and Trudy amused herself by playing a game of chance. She'd catch a tram if she happened to be near a stop as it approached. Despite the hour, there were plenty of people out for a stroll under the stars.

She'd walked for fifteen minutes when a searchlight suddenly stabbed into the sky, followed immediately by the wail of an air raid siren. Within seconds all the sirens activated. Trudy anxiously glanced around. She was in an unfamiliar neighbourhood with no idea where the nearest public shelter was. She took her cue from the other pedestrians.

No one seemed anxious to get off the street. People had become blasé. Most bombings were ineffective, and the British rarely attacked two nights in a row. Chances were that the planes would overfly on their way to bomb Kiel or some other city. Being killed or injured would happen to someone else, not to them. They took cover in basements, and under stairwells and kitchen tables, rather than inconvenience themselves by rushing to official shelters.

Only when the throb of approaching bombers became audible, the entire western horizon became crisscrossed by hundreds of searchlights, and thousands of flashes from exploding flak shells lit the sky, did people realise this was another major attack.

Suddenly, everyone ran. Trudy was caught up in the panic. The mob converged on an apartment block, pushing and shoving each other aside as they fought their way through the main door to gain access to the basement. Trudy forced herself to stop and think. Hysteria would get her killed. She remembered the adjacent neighbourhood from her days in the civil defence. There was a shelter there if she could find it. She quickly orientated herself. The main city lay to the north; she was in the southern outskirts. She needed to head east.

Above, the roar of the aircraft made the air vibrate. Detonations of the flak guns merged into one continuous wall of sound. Trudy suppressed a rising wave of terror. She'd left it too late. She was caught in the open, alone and vulnerable. A surge of adrenalin coursed through her and she sprinted, desperately seeking out some familiar landmark.

The thud of an enormous explosion made the ground shake. Instinctively, she covered her head as every window on the block opposite blew out, sending shards of glass scything across the road. The ground heaved as dozens of bombs landed simultaneously. The night sky seemed to bleed as an inferno of orange and red flames obliterated the stars.

Trudy stumbled blindly along the middle of the road. An overriding thought grasped her mind - survive, survive, survive.

Searing white flames from an incendiary burst from a roof-top, illuminating the entire road as if in daylight. Suddenly she knew where she was. The shelter lay a hundred metres away. Her relief was short-lived though. The frontage of an apartment block behind her collapsed, filling the air with thick, choking dust. In the same instant, a ripple of bombs shattered the building two blocks away. A violent blast hurled her into a stone wall. She lay still, desperately trying to draw breath into her lungs. All she inhaled was dirt, hot cinders and the smell of cordite. Another stick of bombs danced their way down another street. Every sound assaulted her hearing: whistling shrieks as more bombs rained down, the relentless crash of collapsing buildings and more explosions, and the sound of someone whimpering. Trudy wondered who, until she realised it was her.

Jagged shards of twisted metal shrapnel fell on the roads. Instinctively, she screwed herself into a ball and wrapped her head in her arms. She felt a wave of hysteria build inside her: certain death was coming.

The entire façade of an office toppled. It hit the tarmac with a noise like a thunderclap. A wall of thick dust, mixed with office papers, raced along the street like a great, rolling, boiling tsunami. The threat of choking forced her to her feet. She ran in blind panic, oblivious to the falling shrapnel. Brilliant white phosphorous flames from the incendiaries lit a scene from hell.

Trudy was lost. The street had become unrecognisable. Heaps of rubble, smashed furniture, filing cabinets, cracked window frames and burning beams of timber lay strewn across the road. A burst main spewed out a fountain of water, and Trudy could smell gas. It was impossible to know where the shelter was. A great thud obliterated her hearing.

She pushed her hands to her ears, closed her eyes and screamed in terror. Her feet left the ground, she felt weightless. There was a vague awareness of someone kicking down a door and then she fell, landing heavily. She saw a bright orange light and the outline of a figure desperately trying to beat out flames, then the top of the doorway suddenly crumpled, and the lights went out.

For a few seconds, panic consumed Trudy. Her eyes were open but nothing registered in the pitch blackness. Her hearing felt muzzy and her head swam. She lay still and allowed her befuddled mind to make sense of the world. Gradually, she made out the sound of the crackle and howling gusts of flames, the occasional rumble of falling masonry, and the steady trickle of water. The smell of damp, sewage and smoke was overpowering. Her eyes adjusted to the dark. Above her, through the smashed debris, the orange flicker of flames half-illuminated a steep iron ladder.

A wave of relief washed through her. She lay in a cellar and was alive, but in what condition? She couldn't feel anything. She gingerly moved her left arm. Instantly, a bolt of agony shot through it, making her retch. It was obviously broken. Her right arm and both legs seemed intact. Congealed blood ran down her thigh and from what felt like another cut above her left eye, and she had a large swelling to the back of her head. She considered trying to get to her feet but energy deserted her. Her First Aid training came flooding back. Lie still and allow the body to recover.

The sound of a passing fire-engine klaxon, followed by muffled voices, drifted from above. Trudy cried out but no one answered. Half heard barked orders and a petrol-driven pump starting up, followed by the splash of cascading water, indicated a rescue effort was underway. Trudy allowed herself to hope. They'd find her soon enough. The light from the cracks in the smashed doorway got brighter. It must be late morning or early afternoon. The voices sounded close. They weren't German. A curt shout and the street fell silent. They were looking for survivors. Trudy yelled. Almost immediately, the shadow of a figure blocked the light passing through the cracks in the debris-filled doorway.

A voice called, "Who's there?"

"Help me!" Trudy shouted back.

"I'll get some help." The shadow disappeared.

Trudy offered a silent prayer of thanks. Her gratitude was ignored. God must be taunting her, she thought as the lazy drone of the air-raid sirens wound up to a screaming wail. She fought to contain her terror. It must be a false alarm or a nuisance raid. The British never attacked in daylight. Her confidence evaporated as the snarl of the enemy squadrons increased. This was another big raid. Panicked screams urged people to move under cover. Already the dull thuds of explosions reverberated distantly around her. Maybe the docks or oil refineries were being hit. Trudy drew her legs up, leant her head on her knees and squeezed her eyes shut.

No bombs came close. Other neighbourhoods had been hit. But the attack unnerved the city. Three heavy raids in succession had never happened before. Worse was to come.

The bombings continued for another six days and nights. In her tomb, Trudy desperately held on to her sanity, waiting for the lazy whistle of falling bombs that would signal her death. But it seemed the enemy was teasing her as other suburbs were reduced to rubble.

The respite between raids provided little comfort or hope. No voices, nor sound of passing footsteps or vehicles – just the constant crackle of burning and the occasional rumble of falling masonry.

The wail of sirens heralded yet another attack and sapped her morale. Trudy slumped against the wall, staring at nothing in the blackness, resigned to her fate and hoping for a quick, painless end. The flak batteries opened up. Within seconds, hundreds of guns joined in. A deafening sound gradually built up as thousands of explosive shells merged into a thunderous wall of violence. Above it all, as if immune to the mayhem, the

269

rumble of aircraft engines morphed into a tremendous throbbing roar. Then the bombs fell. This time targeted at her.

Terror seized her heart. She was young and didn't want to die. She screamed as the mocking whistles suddenly got louder. The whole building shook, a tremendous blast blew apart the walls above her cellar and sent the roof timbers crashing down. The air became thick with choking coal dust. A series of explosions across the street was followed by the crash and rumble of tumbling bricks, roof tiles and timbers. The sides of the cellar seemed to bow and flex as the ground heaved. It felt like every bomb was aimed at her shelter.

An enormous explosion stole her hearing once again. Shockwaves shook the entire cellar, and waves of heat rushed down the iron ladder. She buried her head in her hands and arms, as if trying to wrap herself in her own cocoon. She lost track of time as the relentless explosions reverberated above her head.

And then they were gone, and silence returned.

Trudy couldn't believe she was still alive. She lay still and allowed her senses to recover. The sound of bombers faded, chased by the faint crack of anti-aircraft fire. She felt a wave of relief. She'd survived.

Her relief was premature. Her torment wasn't over. A new sound drifted through the gaps in the rubble. It started as a steady, low, distant moan as if the soul of the city itself writhed in agony. It grew louder until it became a roaring, seething, boiling sound as if the doors of a blast furnace had been opened. Trudy struggled to her feet and stood at the foot of the ladder. She could see the orange light of flames dancing through the chinks in the rubble. A featherlight movement of air brushed her cheeks. In minutes, the zephyr developed into a draught, swirling through the cracks in the smashed bricks and timbers.

The breeze morphed into a howling gale, bowling burning embers, red-hot dust, ash and office detritus along the street. The howls turned to shrieks as savage gusts picked up any loose debris: doors, metal sheets, burning rags, blinds and shop awnings. Shop signs ripped from their mountings and items of furniture were sucked into a maelstrom of destruction. The firestorm took hold. It was as if a gigantic blow torch had been lit.

The heat of the inferno penetrated the cellar. Every now and then the gusts vacuumed the air from inside her shelter. Trudy felt her vision fade and her head spin. The air rushed back in - oven hot, thick with soot and the smell of burnt tarmac, wood, and roasted flesh. Her mouth, nose, eyes and ears became caked in coal dust, and she struggled to breathe. She pressed her face into the floor and tried to create a small cage of air with her hands.

Trudy had no idea how long she lay there. Several times she passed out as the air was sucked away. Images flashed across her mind: Katerina, Franz, Herr Hofner and, time and time again, Tante Bri telling her she was beautiful and bright. Death felt close and yet each time the images returned as if keeping it at bay.

Suddenly, she felt a sensation of being lifted. A bright light seared into her eyes, followed immediately by a cold wet cloth that smothered her face and blocked her vision. She lashed out, convinced she was being drowned. Strong hands picked her up, and she felt as if she was floating. She heard strange foreign-sounding voices and the sounds of klaxons, bells and engines. A dog furiously barking, someone shouting, and the splash as a vehicle passed through a large puddle. The overpowering smell of acrid smoke made her retch. Something sharp stabbed her arm, and the world went black.

"Come on, young lady, time to wake up."

Trudy felt someone patting her hand.

"Come on, girl. Stop messing about."

She opened her eyes and stared in confusion at the face of an elderly woman. "Tante Bri?"

"No, I'm the Krankenschwester, but Tante Bri will do if it gets you awake."

Trudy blinked and tried to orientate herself.

"You're in the Refugee Centre hospital," the woman said, her tone brusque as if she had better things to do than sit and chat. "I need to know your name and address."

"What?" Trudy croaked, and glanced about her. She lay in bed, staring at a high iron and glass ceiling.

The woman shook her head and looked exasperated. "I said - your name and address. Come on, I haven't all day!" She held a clipboard in front of Trudy's face, before lowering it and glowering at her.

"Trudy...Trudy Heppel, I live at Velsen Gasse." Her voice was a hoarse rasp, her throat felt like sandpaper, and her tongue was swollen and dry.

"Number?"

"Um ... six. Top floor apartment."

"District?"

"Borgefelde."

The nurse shook her head and grimaced in disbelief. "You were picked up outside the City centre, in the suburbs."

"I was with friends." Trudy struggled to talk. She was desperate for water.

The Krankenswester stared at her for a few seconds before recording the information and hanging the board on the end of the bed. "A doctor will be around in due course." With that, she abruptly departed. Trudy instantly fell back to sleep.

Later, she woke and listened to what was happening around her. Wherever she was, it was full of people. There was the constant murmur of low, earnest conversation, the occasional plaintive wail of someone in pain or in receipt of upsetting news, the crash and rattle of steel trolleys, and an overpowering smell of antiseptic.

Trudy cautiously checked herself out. Her left arm and her head were swathed in tight-fitting bandages, a dull throbbing ache coursed through her right leg, she had a blinding headache, and her chest hurt every time she breathed. Her self-assessment complete, she allowed exhaustion to consume her, and she fell asleep again.

'Due course' proved to be nearly twenty-four hours later. An elderly, harassed-looking man suddenly loomed over her and, without any introduction or warning, threw the sheet off and peered at her heavily bandaged leg. Seemingly satisfied, he turned his attention to her head. Nodding to himself, he shone a light in both her eyes and gruffly ordered her to follow his fingers. He snatched the clipboard from the end of the bed and began writing, whilst giving her a simultaneous diagnosis.

"You've a broken left arm, and nasty lacerations to the back of your head and to your right thigh which, hopefully, we've managed to stop becoming infected. You have mild concussion and, most probably, some lung damage as a result of smoke and dust inhalation." He threw the clipboard back on its hook. "How are you feeling?"

"Thirsty and hungry. I've not eaten for days." Trudy's voice sounded dry and husky.

He nodded wearily. "I'll get some food sorted." He turned to depart, then stopped. "Your clothes are under your bed," he said as an afterthought. With that, he left.

Trudy felt strong enough to prop herself up and survey her surroundings. Her bed was on a raised platform, allowing her to see the length of the building. What she saw shocked her. It was enormous. She guessed either a warehouse, or an old tram or railway terminus. Great iron girders arched over a glazed roof, the far end of which was shattered from an earlier bomb attack. In between the serried ranks of rusting columns, many hundreds or perhaps thousands of injured civilians lay in row after row of makeshift cots, hammocks, and beds. Small groups of people, with scared and bewildered expressions, gathered around some of the beds. Some held their heads in their hands and rocked gently backwards and forwards as if trying to come to terms with their circumstances or obliterate memories. Uniformed nurses, doctors and officious-looking orderlies and BDM girls scurried around on urgent errands, bringing blankets, bandages and trays of medicines, A few groups of white-coated staff bent anxiously over individual beds, working on some critical casualty. The entire building hummed with confused chatter interspersed with barked orders. At the far end, a series of queues formed behind a line of desks at which officials sat filling out forms.

272

Trudy spotted the elderly doctor pushing and jostling his way through the crowd. He didn't get far. Someone grabbed him and physically dragged him towards an injured family member or friend. He managed to break free, shaking his head and waving his hands and arms, signalling that other higher priority cases demanded his attention.

She realised the prospect of food and water were disappearing as fast as his retreating form. Salvation came in the form of a rotund, serious-looking BDM girl who, oblivious to the chaos around her, made her way along the rows of beds, dispensing cups of water from bottles clipped to her belt. Trudy prayed her water supply didn't run out before she reached her. The closer the girl got, the more pathetic she looked, as if she was operating like an automaton. She could only be about eleven or twelve years old.

"Do you want some water?" She offered a bottle.

Trudy drained five cups but still felt thirsty. "Could you fetch me some food?'

"They only have soup and black bread."

"Anything you can lay your hands on will be fine."

The girl muttered a half-hearted, "Sieg heil," and threaded her way back through the crowd.

Trudy slumped back and considered her circumstances and the fate of Tante Bri and Katerina. Katerina would have been at home. There was a basement air-raid shelter. But Tante Bri!? Trudy felt her throat constrict as she imagined the old lady sitting immobile in her chair as the bombs rained down. Maybe the raids sounded worse than they were. Perhaps her street had been spared?

She eased herself up to a sitting position and gave herself a dressing down. Lying in bed solved nothing. She'd discharge herself as quickly as possible. The medical staff were clearly overwhelmed. She'd need to rely on her own resourcefulness and wits. She swung her legs over the side of the bed and almost fainted with the effort. She really needed to recover first. As if on cue, the BDM girl reappeared holding a canteen in one hand and a stick of bread in the other.

For two weeks she built her strength on bread and soup. She searched among the casualties for Katerina and Bri, and hobbled painfully backwards and forwards to the banks of scribbled messages that festooned the far wall of the makeshift hospital. Each was an appeal to a lost mother, father, brother, sister, wife, husband, friend, neighbour – or anyone. Trudy posted her own amidst them.

THE FIRST CRACKS

A change seeped into Doppelgau. Sep was slow to see it. Apart from the Ansbachers, Drossels and Herr Zinnerman, he'd little to do with the rest of the community or they with him. Ordinarily, he would have passed the man standing outside the Adler, staring at the sky, without a second glance. He was, therefore, surprised when he found himself addressed and even more startled by the man's words.

"We can't win."

"What?!"

The man jerked his chin towards the sky. "There must be hundreds of them."

Sep lifted his eyes skyward. Between the clouds, the vapour trails of enemy bombers traced their way north.

"Third time this month," the man muttered. "I reckon they're heading for Friedrichshafen this time. We're losing in the air as well as on land."

"You shouldn't talk like that."

The man lowered his head and gave Sep a hard, bitter look. "I lost my son last month. I'll say what I bloody well want."

For a second, Sep was dumbstruck. "I'm sorry for your loss." His words sounded inadequate.

The man nodded, then trudged away. Sep paused to watch his slow, mournful progress. The village had lost six young men so far, and a further two were missing in action. He shut his eyes and said a silent prayer for Johan and Jurgen.

Stephan was already seated at the Stammtisch, along with Father Haphold and Herman. Sep was pleasantly surprised. "Good to see you both," he said, as he shook hands.

"They're celebrating!" Stephan grinned.

Sep nodded his thanks to the landlord as a glass of Pils was placed in front of him. "Celebrating what?"

"My reinstatement as a priest!" Father Haphold couldn't hide his pleasure.

"About time too. I hope it came with an apology and some compensation."

"Sep – I'm just happy to return to my vocation."

Sep felt outraged. "What! - they didn't see fit to acknowledge what you two have been through?"

Father Haphold placed his hand on Sep's arm. "The past is the past, Sep. It's time to move on," he said quietly.

"It's time for some kind of justice."

"That will come, along with forgiveness."

"Forgiveness!"

"That's not all," Stephan said quickly, as he saw Sep was about to explode. "Tell him which parish you'll be taking on, Father."

The priest took a leisurely sip, seemingly enjoying Sep's irritation. "The Parish of Doppelgau and Gau," he announced, after smacking his lips in appreciation of his Pils.

"You can't be serious!" Sep sat back in astonishment. "The bastards... begging your pardon, Father... the people that betrayed you still live in this village. How can either of you serve such people? How can they dare to look you in the eye, let alone seek confession?"

Herman scribbled something on a piece of paper and handed it to Sep. Sep read the scrawl, '*If you managed it – so can we.*'

"How are Susan and Johan?" Father Haphold said gently.

Sep found himself thrown. "Er...Susan is fine. She's back in England, in Yorkshire with her mother and sister. The Red Cross organised a swap."

"And Johan?"

"Last letter we received was from Jurgen. Both boys are okay," Stephan said.

"They'll all need to return to face the community and difficult times, one day. I hope I'll be ready to help them."

Sep shook his head in admiration. "All I can say, Father, is that you're a better man than me."

The entrance of Gunter curtailed further discussion. He burst in, looking dishevelled. "I'm in need of a drink," he announced.

"What's happened, mate?" Stephan sounded concerned.

"Shopping is what happened. Have you ever been shopping with a woman?" It was a sign of Gunter's agitation that he addressed his question to Father Haphold.

The priest screwed up his face as he considered the matter. "Not that I can recall."

"Well, count yourself lucky." Gunter slumped down and took a generous swig of his Pils.

"Not a happy experience, then?" Sep tried to sound sympathetic.

"Do you know how many dress shops there are in Brandt? Eight!" Gunter answered his own question. "And I've visited every single one – several times."

"On the same day?"

"In some cases in the same hour."

"I take it you were shopping with Marie?"

Gunter nodded. "Never again." He took another fortifying glug before leaning forward and regarding each of his friends in turn. "She wanted a dress. How difficult can it be to buy an item of clothing?"

Stephan and Sep exchanged knowing looks.

"You know what colour you want, what style, and you ought to know your size?"

His audience couldn't fault his logic.

"First shop, she selects a lovely green dress. It fits perfectly, and she asks my opinion. Perfect, I say. You look gorgeous, which was true – she looked an absolute picture. You're just saying that, she says. So, off to shop number two. This time it's a red dress. Which do I prefer? That one, I say. What was wrong with the green one, then? Nothing, says I. So why did I say it was perfect, if it wasn't? Because it suits her better. Well, she didn't like it as red isn't really her colour." Gunter rolled his eyes. "Off to shop number three. This dress is another greenish sort of colour, with a pretty lacy collar and trim. What do I think? I'm now wary of saying anything. Do you like it? I say. I'm asking you! she replies." Gunter threw his hands open to emphasise his dilemma. "So, I said, I'm happy, if you are." Gunter shook his head at the memory. "That wasn't the answer she wanted. This goes on at every shop. After *five* hours we've visited *every* shop, three of them twice, and guess what she decides?" Gunter slapped his hand down on the table.

"The green one." Stephan and Sep say in unison.

Gunter looked astonished at his friends' insight into female logic. "Exactly!"

"So, the prospect of married life with Marie is paling?" Stephan asked.

"Oh goodness me, no. She's the light of my life. I love her more each day." Gunter then looked thoughtful. "Besides, I need looking after."

"You intend to fix a date then?" Father Haphold raised an eyebrow.

"I suppose I ought to."

"She'll want to buy a wedding dress." Sep dropped in the observation without a hint of mischief in his voice.

"Well, that shouldn't present a problem. You can't go wrong with white, can you?"

His friends shook their heads sadly.

AUGUST 1943 - HAMBURG

Trudy tried to spot anything that might provide a hint she was looking at Tante Bri's apartment. Only the half-melted wrought iron sign from Mordechai's pawnbrokers indicated she stood on the street where she once lived.

In hospital, she'd hoped descriptions of the havoc were exaggerated. Now she confronted reality. Entire neighbourhoods were reduced to a moonscape of desolation. Great blackened heaps of rubble made it impossible to recognise any street or familiar feature. Here and there the embers still burned, leaching plumes of thin, brown smoke from broken piles of bricks. Parts of the walls of some of the more substantial buildings still stood like ancient cathedral ruins against the skyline: their roofs gone and empty gaps where the windows used to be. It was as if the skeleton of the city was exposed. The interiors of what were once cosy havens of domesticity were revealed. A bed, still made up with its heavy counterpane and with a picture above the headboard, hung precariously on the edge of what remained of the broken floor. A bath dangled by its pipes, halfway down the cliff of a gable wall, leaning at an angle as if the faintest puff of wind would send it crashing to the ground.

Earlier, she'd stood at the end of Velsen Gasse and been confronted by a similar scene of devastation. Her apartment was obliterated and, as far as she knew, Katerina along with it. She prayed both Katerina and Tante Bri died quickly and painlessly.

Suddenly her mental defences collapsed. She crumpled to her knees, bent over and howled her grief into the melted tarmac. Her prayers for her aunt and friend became diatribes of hatred towards a God who could allow such cruelty and horror to be unleashed on the innocent. Careless of who might hear her, she screamed obscenities at the Party, the Schutzstaffel and, above all, the Fuhrer for waging a pointless war. Her hysteria mounted as the extent of her loneliness grew ever more apparent in her mind. She thought her head would explode with the depth of her despair. She felt herself teetering on the edge of insanity. She was vaguely aware of people picking over the bomb-damaged buildings, but no one cast her a second glance or stopped to help. She wondered if she'd already ceased to exist.

She willed death to come and take her. But there was no easy way out. She picked up her crutch and forced herself to her feet. She had no idea where she was heading. A tram stop shelter provided an opportunity to sit and recover. Her outburst had drained her but, slowly, she forced herself to think. There were two locations where Katerina might gravitate if alive: the Hofner's residence or the Rathaus. If Katerina was at neither, she'd have to come up with... she didn't know what. She took a few deep breaths to steady herself, then set off with a vague sense of purpose.

Long before reaching the Hofner's house it became obvious her journey was futile. Not a single building remained. It was a street of craters. She was about to turn back when a young woman wrapped in a long coat, standing in front of the pile of debris, caught her eye. A small suitcase lay on the road by her feet.

Trudy felt her heart leap. "Katerina!"

The woman turned in surprise.

Trudy's spirits fell. It was Dagmar Greber.

"Trudy? You survived." She rushed forward and wrapped her in a tight embrace. "I thought everyone was gone."

Trudy hid the wave of guilt that swept through her. She ought to feel grateful. At least Dagmar was a familiar face. Trudy nodded towards her crutch and raised her bandaged right arm. "By the skin of my teeth." She jerked her chin towards the heap of rubble. "Did the Hofners survive?"

Dagmar shrugged.

"You're left high and dry?"

Dagmar sighed wistfully and gave the suitcase a gentle kick. "I came here to see if I could salvage some of my things before I head off."

"Where are you going?"

"To my grandparents in the east. Haldersdorf, my home town. My parents returned there a year back when the Jewish terror raids started getting serious. They said at the time I was mad to remain. Seems they were right." She fumbled in her coat pocket, extracted a pack of cigarettes and offered Trudy one.

"I don't smoke."

"Sounds like you do." Dagmar gave her a rueful smile before lighting up and taking a deep drag. "What about you?"

"I'm going to check if anyone survived at work."

Dagmar breathed out smoke and shook her head. "The Rathaus has gone, Saint Nikolia's Church no longer exists, the main police station and the telephone exchange have all been flattened. There's nothing left. Everyone is leaving." She took another deep draw on her cigarette. "You should evacuate while you have the chance."

"I've nowhere to go. Hamburg is where I was born and raised. My Aunt and Katerina…" She gave Dagmar a questioning look. "You remember her?"

"She was a decent sort."

Trudy masked her grief. "I don't think they survived." She took a deep breath to steady herself. "I've got nothing except the clothes I'm wearing, and they're filthy."

"You might as well come with me." Dagmar flicked the ash from her cigarette. "Get away from all this. The British aren't likely to bomb Haldersdorf. We'll find something useful to do for the war effort. Besides, it sounds as if some country air might clear those lungs of yours."

"I'm with the Luftwaffe. I need to report for duty."

278

Dagmar took a long drag from her cigarette before dropping it on the ground and grinding it out with the toe of her shoe. "Well, the offer's there if you need it." She dug a small diary out of her pocket and scribbled an address before tearing the page out and handing it over. She eyed Trudy's ragged, soot-smeared dress. "The Party collection centres can sort some new clothes for you, courtesy of the Jewish scum." She bent over to pick up her suitcase. "There's nothing keeping me here. I might as well go."

APRIL 1944 – DOPPELGAU - OSTMARK

Gunter and Marie's wedding marked another turning point for Doppelgau. Although official guests were limited to immediate family and friends, St Martin's was almost full as villagers seized the opportunity to celebrate the event. They even lined the road as the wedding party made the traditional parade from the church to the Gasthaus reception.

"It was a lovely service, Father," Sep said, as he watched a beaming Gunter dance with his equally happy wife.

"It was, wasn't it. It's a particular delight when two people eventually find love."

Sep laughed. "I'm just pleased that Marie managed to survive the courtship without injury, given Gunter's track record." His good humour faded as he caught sight of Harriet, looking wistfully at the newly-weds. "My only wish is that Harriet could find similar happiness."

"I understand there has been no news of Simon's fate?"

Sep shook his head. "Absolutely nothing. Gregor's son-in-law, Anton, has made what enquiries he can. The guide is fairly sure Simon made it to the border. No one saw the mountain troops return with any prisoners but, apparently, on the Swiss side there isn't any news." He turned towards the priest and lowered his voice. "Personally, I think they shot and left him."

"Don't think that, Sep. No news is good news – and Harriet must have hope."

"She's coping really well on the outside. But inside…?" He left the statement hanging. He watched his daughter with a forlorn expression on his face. "She's thrown herself into work, but I think she needs something more."

"Something to raise her spirits?"

Sep nodded. "The one thing that brings her joy every day is in her arms right now."

"Little Simone?"

"Let's face it – children tend to bring out the best in us."

"In which case, I've a proposal that might be of interest." He raised one eyebrow at Sep and, satisfied he'd piqued his interest, he continued, "The Rubenstein's house and surgery are owned by you?"

"In a Trust."

"The diocese is beginning to be flooded with refugees fleeing the allied bombing."

Sep bristled. "I'm not housing any Nazis or sympathisers. Sorry, Father, but if they've been bombed out of their homes then I'm sorry, but they're on their own. Added to that, it would be totally disrespectful to the Rubensteins." Sep's outburst was quelled by the gentle pressure of the priest's hand on his shoulder.

"That's not what I'm proposing."

Sep composed himself. "I apologise."

"I'm suggesting a home for orphans."

"Oh!"

"A safe, secure, loving home, run by decent, honourable and uncorrupted people." He glanced meaningfully at Harriet.

Sep fell silent.

"I think the Rubensteins would approve, and Harriet's a good mother."

"Harriet might be interested, but not full-time. She's determined to learn from her aunt so she can become a businesswoman in her own right. You'd have to ask her." Sep suddenly raised his hand as a fresh idea took hold. "But I know someone, two people in fact, who would almost certainly be interested."

"And they are?"

Sep jerked his head towards Gunter and Marie. "I know for a fact Marie's biggest regret is that she wasn't able to have children.'

"There's still time."

"Not likely though is it, Father, she's in her forties. It's a tragedy. If anyone was born to be a mother, it's Marie."

Father Haphold pursed his lips as he considered the suggestion. "It's a good idea." He chuckled. "God moves in mysterious ways. Eh, Sep?"

Sep grunted. "Yeah. Just like the people of this village. I don't know how some of them had the nerve to show their faces."

"You're in danger of becoming a bitter man, Sep," he said gently. "You need to show your compassion."

"Compassion!" Sep was outraged. "After what they did? – to the Rubensteins, to you and Herman, and let's not forget others they denounced."

"People are easily led, Sep. Right now, over twenty families have lost relatives. That's a heavy price. Many have come to realise the folly of believing in Hitler. I know, I take their confessions. They want to find a way back and are turning to the Church. They need good men to guide them." He laid a hand on Sep's shoulder. "Men like you, my friend."

"I've said it before, Father. You're a better man than me."

"I don't think so. What's more, a lot of people in this community don't think so either."

Sep glanced up in genuine surprise.

"I mean it, Sep. You're above reproach. Your son's fighting at the front. You've been forcibly separated from your wife. You stayed loyal to your friends, and you've held your head high. People admire your integrity."

"They've a strange way of showing it."

Father Haphold patted him gently on the shoulder. "Give them a chance, Sep. Now do you want to broach the subject with Harriet, or shall I?"

Sep gave a resigned grin. "It's best you do it. You seem to have an ability to persuade."

Four months later, Josey stood with her hands on her hips and surveyed the room. Cobwebs drifted from the oil lamp and everything was covered in a thin layer of dust. "How old are the infants?"

Marie consulted the letter from the diocese. "The boy is one and his sister, two."

"Brother and sister?"

Marie nodded. "Poor little mites lost both parents. We should keep them together."

"It's the least we can do. What a start in life," Josey muttered. "We're going to need a couple of cots."

"Herman's already started making them, along with a whole lot of toys," Harriet said.

"He's a good man." Josey turned to open a cupboard, and briskly fanned the air as a cloud of dust enveloped her. "We'll need a lot more sheets and blankets."

"The village has organised a collection – or rather Frau Ansbacher is organising the village to make donations."

Josey snorted derisively. "Fat chance of anyone helping out."

"That's not true, Josey." Marie said. "Apparently a lot of people have come forward to help."

The three women looked at one another. They all had the same thought. Were the offers out of genuine concern for the plight of the orphans or a way to ease guilty consciences.

"I'm sorry, but I find it difficult to accept help from people who stood by and did nothing to stop what happened in this house," Harriet said, her voice tight. Her comment stirred unwanted memories, made all the more painful as they regarded the room. Like the rest of the house, nothing had been touched since Sep boarded up the premises. Perfume bottles and an open powder puff rested on the dressing table. Rudi's shirt still hung on the back of the chair, and Hannah's dressing gown was spread across the bed. Harriet still hadn't plucked up the courage to enter Simon's old bedroom.

"I know how you feel." Josey put her arm around her niece. "But we need to rise above it."

"We must focus on the children," Marie said. "Right now, we'll need a lot of help just to get this place up and running." She waved the letter. "The two infants and six others - four girls and two boys. None of them have much clothing, and we need to sort out food, cooking and washing arrangements."

"And their schooling," Josey added. "We need all the help we can get."

"How will they be looked after?" Harriet looked confused. "I mean, it's a big house."

"Gunter and I will take the first floor. The girls will have the big room on the top floor. Your Pa's converting the surgery so the boys will have their space and a bathroom, and there will be a big playroom."

"You can't look after all these children by yourself. Gunter will be at work. It's too much, Marie."

"Harriet, Gunter can't wait. Also, Frau Ansbacher and a couple of other village women have volunteered to help." Marie gave Harriet a look to forestall her outburst. "I know, it sticks in the craw, but we have to move on."

Harriet looked unconvinced. "Not the Hagspiels, I hope."

"No love. Even I draw the line at their involvement," Marie said firmly.

OUT OF THE FIRE

Trudy regretted her decision to accept accommodation with the Grebers. Since her arrival, she'd endured an almost continuous diatribe of propaganda. She knew Dagmar was a Nazi, but her fanaticism paled to insignificance compared to that of her family, and Herr Greber in particular.

"That man is a genius," he gushed, pointing to the photograph of the Fuhrer that took pride of place amongst the Greber family portraits, lining the dresser in the front room. "He spotted the root cause of all our troubles and had the courage to speak out. Bloody Jews." Herr Greber swung his head round to confront Trudy. "Do you know how many Jewish filth there were in this town when the Fuhrer passed the what's-its-name law? The law to get rid of the scum?" He closed his eyes and shook his head in a search for the answer to his own question. "The Nuremberg Law?" he said triumphantly.

Trudy inwardly groaned. It seemed she'd have to endure yet another tirade. "I've no idea, Herr Greber."

"Two hundred and twenty-six!" He stared at her with incredulous eyes. "Two hundred and twenty-six! Less than five percent of the town population. And yet they owned nearly a quarter of all the businesses and shops." He raised his forefinger in the air and shook it to emphasise his fury. "Charging exorbitant prices, stealing from the people, feeding their own greed." He paused to wipe the spittle that ran from the corners of his mouth. "Well, I made sure they got their comeuppance. Guess how many we've got in our town now?

Trudy's mind focused on a quick escape. "I've no idea, Herr Greber," she said absently.

"None!" He swung his head round to embrace the rest of his audience.

"Thanks mostly to you, my dear." Frau Greber beamed at her husband before tapping her hand on Trudy's arm and pointing an admiring finger towards her husband. "He made it his civic duty to ensure every Jew in the town was identified to the Party. It's largely thanks to Herr Greber that Haldersdorf is a clean town."

"I did my duty for the good of the Fatherland." Herr Greber crisply acknowledged the compliment, before selecting a photograph of a young man in an SS dress uniform from the dresser. "And my boy is carrying on the good work."

Frau Greber leant forward and spoke in a hushed, reverential voice into Trudy's ear. "He's been promoted twice already, and he's won the Iron Cross," she whispered proudly.

Trudy managed to keep the disgust off her face. She knew exactly what 'good work' the Greber's son had been engaged with in Poland and Russia. Dagmar was only too keen to provide the gruesome details and share the snap-shots her brother sent back home to be developed in the local Apotheke.

She closed her ears and let husband and wife drone on in their Fuhrer worshipping echo chamber. For the Grebers, reality retreated. The destruction of Hamburg was airily dismissed as a futile Jewish terror raid. The mounting casualty lists that filled whole columns of the press were exaggerated. Ultimate victory was a matter of time. The Fuhrer promised new wonder weapons. They deliberately blotted any bad news from their minds. Having crushed the Afrika Korps, the allies landed in Italy and were pushing their way relentlessly north. On the Eastern Front, the Russians were pushing back the Wehrmacht, and the Americans and British were pouring troops, tanks and aircraft into France. None of this was happening in the universe occupied by the Grebers. For them, the Fuhrer would defeat all enemies and the Reich would ultimately prevail.

The only solace for Trudy was that having transferred to the Ostern Flakgruppen Regiment her searchlight roster meant she spent minimal time in the Grebers' company. She'd already planted the seed that, despite their kind offer for her to stay indefinitely, she'd look for a place of her own as soon as possible.

Eventually, she could endure the drivel no longer. She gulped down her Ersatz coffee and reached for her coat. "Let's hope he comes home safely." She waved vaguely towards the Greber's son's photograph. "I must go, I'm running late," she lied, and was through the door before either Herr or Frau Greber could respond.

Outside, she threw back her head and drew in great lungfuls of clear, rural air as she passed along a street that, on the surface, was untouched by war. Bombs didn't fall on Haldersdorf because, apart from the bridge, there wasn't anything in the town worth targeting. The only military establishments were a small clearing hospital that treated the increasing number of casualties arriving from the Eastern Front and a Luftwaffe training airfield five kilometres outside the town. However, the air was country fresh and for that Trudy was grateful.

Trudy's shift didn't begin for another two hours, and she resolved to spend her free time addressing a problem that was increasingly depressing her. Despite living in the town for over six months, she was desperately lonely. She'd been made to feel welcome in the Luftwaffe Flakgruppe community but welcome was a long way from friendship. Almost all the searchlight crews were women and yet they treated her warily. She was an urban Hamburg girl and they were rural Saxons. They spoke a different dialect. Most had husbands, sons and brothers who were away serving on the Russian front. They had concerns and experiences she couldn't relate to. When the shift finished they went home to a family and a warm bed.

She'd make her own luck. Somewhere in this town there had to be a café, a church or some community group where she could meet a soul-

285

mate. She smiled to herself as she heard the ghostly voice of Katerina, *"Think, girl, be decisive."* As soon as the memory entered her head, her spirits plummeted. She'd written to Franz to break the news his sweetheart was dead. She tried to imagine his devastation. She suddenly realised that Franz was the only friend she had in the world, and maybe she was his only friend. Two people who needed each other, separated by a war neither wanted to be part of. She resolved to write to him again and composed the letter in her head as she strolled along the main street.

It was late afternoon, the pavements were deserted and the shops empty. Her letter needed to provide Franz with hope for the future, she decided. He needed to know there was someone who cared about him. And he'd need to have somewhere he could call home or at least a destination. The thought brought her up short. It wasn't just him that needed a haven. Where was she heading? Not Haldersdorf! That much was certain. Hamburg was out of the question. Maybe she should head south to Austria. Then again, Franz always wanted to go to America. She smiled to herself as she recalled his dreadful American accent. America probably wouldn't be German friendly after the war. She'd suggest Austria. She'd give herself another three or four months in Haldersdorf. If things hadn't improved for her by then, she'd head south.

The sound of Dagmar's voice interrupted her thoughts.

"Trudy, wait."

She dragged herself to a halt and slowly turned around to see Dagmar approaching.

"I thought it was you. Where are you going?"

"Exploring the town before I go on shift."

Oh, I can help you with that. There isn't a corner of the place I don't know. For example, that's where I went to school." Dagmar pointed excitedly at a decrepit building. "It's being used as a food distribution centre now." She grabbed Trudy's arm and steered her towards the single bridge that spanned the river and divided Haldersdorf. "I used to walk this route every day when I was a girl. Nothing has changed." She skipped happily as her childhood memories flooded back. "This used to be a sleepy little town before the Party won the election, got rid of the Communists and degenerates, and transformed the place. Now, look at it!"

Trudy failed to see anything remarkable. Then again, perhaps Haldersdorf had never been anything other than a sleepy, anonymous sort of place. So far, apart from a few Gasthauses, she hadn't spotted any place of amusement or entertainment.

Dagmar sensed Trudy's train of thought. "You should join the BDM choir," she said. "You've got a great singing voice, I seem to remember."

Trudy groaned. "Dagmar, I'm too old the be re-joining the BDM."

"Nonsense! There are plenty of young women joining up to do their bit."

"Doing what exactly?"

"Raising money for the Party, arranging clothes collections for our boys. Or you could become a volunteer and work at the concentration camps. It'll do you good to meet like-minded people."

Trudy winced at the thought of meeting a bunch of Dagmar clones. "Dagmar, I have a job with the Luftwaffe. That keeps me fully occupied doing my bit for the Fatherland."

Dagmar frowned. "We can always do more for the Fuhrer." She turned to face Trudy directly. "The BDM needs older women who are committed to the cause, to inspire the next generation and who have practical skills. You could be a driver. You've got a license, haven't you?"

Trudy looked incredulous "Drive who, where?!"

"The BDM and Hitler Youth to the front. The clothes need to be distributed, and the girls and boys love singing and dancing for the troops. The soldiers *really* appreciate that. Helps build morale."

Trudy rolled her eyes. "The front's over a hundred kilometres away. And I seriously doubt the Wehrmacht allows a bunch of kids anywhere near the fighting. Besides, I can't take time off to take a bunch of teenagers on a jolly."

Dagmar suddenly looked angry. "They don't go to the actual front-line; they go to the rest and recuperation centres. And it's not a jolly, Trudy. It's vital war work. Honestly, sometimes I think you couldn't care less whether we win this war."

"At least you got that right," Trudy thought.

"You need to set an example," Dagmar continued. "You, of all people – a former senior BDM officer, and now in a Luftwaffe uniform. The girls need role models."

"I'll mull it over when I'm on duty tonight," Trudy said, for no other reason than she wanted the conversation to stop or at least move to some other topic.

That night, just after three o'clock in the morning, as she sat cold, wet and miserable beside the searchlight, waiting for bombers that never arrived, Trudy reviewed her circumstances for the hundredth time and came to the same conclusion. She was in a deep rut emotionally, psychologically, socially and professionally. Maybe she should accede to Dagmar's request. At least it offered a change of scene. The moment she made her decision a distant grumble rolled over the eastern horizon. For the first time, the menacing sound of Russian artillery could be heard.

Six weeks after Dagmar's cajoling, Trudy found herself behind the wheel of an ancient, three-ton truck. In the back were piles of warm clothing, some food parcels, and a dozen excited BDM and Hitler Youth youngsters already singing a medley of German folk songs and Party anthems. They were off to the front to distribute the aid and encourage

287

morale. And morale needed boosting. After a series of assaults and counter-attacks, the Russians had advanced to less than fifty kilometres from Haldersdorf.

"They'll be exhausted with all that singing," Trudy muttered.

"It's inspiring that the youth have such belief." Dagmar threw back her head and laughed. "Last time I made this trip we had trouble getting some of the boys back on the truck. They wanted to stay and fight alongside the troops. Some of the girls too, for that matter." She pointed through the windscreen. "I mean, look at the example this bunch of cowards are setting."

Trudy slowed the truck to steer through the cowards Dagmar referred to. Groups of haggard, dazed-looking civilians formed columns heading west to escape the Russians. Most were on foot, their bodies weighed down by the burdens on their back, or bent double by pushing overloaded wheel-barrows and handcarts. Some were on horseback, and a lucky few sat on top of their few possessions, stacked precariously in the back of old farm wagons. They glanced up as the truck went by. Their eyes spoke of chaos and horror. While those of the elderly men were glazed, the children stared with wide-eyed bewilderment. But the expressions of the women and girls sent a shiver along Trudy's spine. They walked with the eyes of the dead.

Dagmar looked at the rabble in disgust. "They shouldn't be allowed to run away. It's total war we're fighting. Look!" She stabbed her finger towards an older man carrying an elderly woman on his back. "If he can carry that sort of weight, carrying a rifle ought to be no bother."

Trudy stayed silent. In the wing mirror, she caught sight of the dispossessed spitting their disdain at the truck as it passed.

The closer to the front they got, the greater the number of refugees. The last five kilometres took them over an hour to cover. Eventually, a military checkpoint directed them to the small hamlet being used as a rest and recuperation centre.

"You ought to come," Dagmar hissed in Trudy's ear.

Trudy had had enough of Dagmar's constant nagging. "I told you, Dagmar. I'm happy to give up some of my free time to drive, but I'm not taking part in any singing or dancing." Her voice brooked no further discussion.

Dagmar muttered something about excuses and disloyalty under her breath before slamming the truck door shut and barking out orders to the youngsters, who formed ranks in front of three Wehrmacht soldiers assigned to be their escorts.

Trudy watched them march off, every head held high and each holding a parcel. Dagmar and another BDM supervisor brought up the rear. She lent on the steering wheel and took in her surroundings. The hamlet was full of troops. Heavy camouflage made them difficult to spot. All looked gaunt, tired and haggard. Some appeared tense and edgy. They held their rifles and machine guns close at hand as if expecting an attack. A few squatted by the roadside, their heads bent forward to rest on tired arms as if already resigned to their fate. Some surrendered to fatigue and lay slumped in exhausted slumber under hedges or in the back of trucks. Others sat and stared with glassy eyes at nothing. A line formed by a field kitchen. It inched forward as an elderly veteran dished out ladles of thin-looking soup into each man's canteen.

The R&R centre lay some kilometres to the rear of the front-line, and yet the hamlet was heavily fortified. A tank was almost hidden in a berm, only its turret visible. She recognised the familiar outline of eighty-eight millimetre flack guns dispersed in the forest; their use changed from anti-aircraft to direct artillery support. Every now and then a truck passed, heading west. Pale bandaged faces stared out through the rear opening. If this was an R&R centre, Trudy could hardly bare to imagine what the front line must be like. Of the hamlet's civilian population, there was no sign.

MAY 1945 - EASTERN FRONT

"What's your verdict?" Jurgen peered at the map.

"What have you got?"

"Seven panzers - two of which are immobile, and none have more than ten rounds. Plus, five anti-tank rifles, a single tank-destroyer, and about three hundred infantry, made up of a core of just over two hundred trained soldiers. The rest are Luftwaffe, construction workers, catering staff and a few Volksturm men and boys."

"And virtually no cover." Johan shook his head. "You don't stand a chance."

"Thanks!"

"You know that's the truth."

Jurgen smoothed out the map with his hand. "Your sector's not much better."

Johan glanced around to ensure they couldn't be overheard. "These are the orders of a mad man. The best we can hope for is to hold them up. Talk of mounting an attack is fantasy."

"So, what do you think?"

"Remember your old man's piece of advice before we left Doppelgau?"

"Which one of many?" Jurgen half-smiled at the memory.

"About always having an escape plan."

"You think we should prepare the lads to make for these." He stabbed his finger at two marked roads that led west out of their salient.

Johan shook his head. "Everyone will be heading in that direction once the Soviets break through. It's too obvious. Ivan will already have it targeted." He bent closer to the map and pointed to a position. "I suggest we aim for here."

"The airfield." Jurgen sounded surprised.

"Chances are the Russians will want to capture it intact, and the river alongside is both an escape route and an obstacle."

Jurgen weighed up the idea as he studied the map. "Okay. If, or rather when, either of our sectors starts to collapse, we withdraw to here," He circled an area on the sheet. "Combine what remains of our forces and conduct a fighting retreat towards the airfield."

"You got a good radio man?"

Jurgen nodded.

"'Doppelgau', when it becomes inevitable."

The two friends looked at each other. Both knew this was the end.

"We get each other out."

Johan gave a tired smile. "It's served us well so far." He folded the map.

Jurgen held out his hand. "Good luck, mate."

A feeling of dread swept through Johan's mind as he watched his best friend leave. He couldn't shake off a premonition. For over four years, he and Jurgen had been continually reacting to events. Now they knew exactly what to expect. The Russians would attack with a devastating bombardment, followed by an overwhelming tank assault and swarms of battle-hardened infantrymen bent on revenge, looting and rape. He pleaded with God to keep them both safe, then set off to try and motivate his demoralised soldiers to resist as best they could.

The Russians attacked at three in the morning the following day. The shelling lasted three hours. Their tanks were already overrunning the German positions before the barrage lifted.

Johan watched through his binoculars as Jurgen's sector became overwhelmed by thousands of Red Army soldiers. They leapt off the tanks and closed in on the fragile defences. Occasionally, a soviet tank erupted in flames as a Panzer or anti-tank round found its target. But that was only a flea-bite. The disabled tank was quickly replaced by two or three others. Johan had little time to dwell on the scene. The Russians swung round towards his sector. Four tanks raced towards his position.

"Hold your fire," Johan yelled at the anti-tank gunners. "Two hundred metres."

The gunner waved his acknowledgement. Every shot had to count. Soviet soldiers desperately hung on to the turret of the lead tank as it bounced and careered across the ground, its exhaust spewing out thick grey fumes, and its track throwing great clods of earth into the air behind it as it bore down. The roar of its engine briefly blotted out the rattle of machine guns and the crash of tank fire. When almost on top of them, it erupted as a shell exploded inside, hurling the turret high into the air. The remains of the Russian soldiers rained down.

Already the anti-tank crew had reloaded and taken out the second tank. The Soviet soldiers threw themselves off the turrets and charged into devastating machine-gun fire. None dived for cover. They ran yelling straight towards the hated enemy, oblivious to their comrades being scythed down on either side. Behind them, more tanks and infantry rushed into the fight, swerving to avoid the burning hulks.

The anti-tank crew dropped into a frenetic routine of fire, reload, fire, reload. Their targets were so close they couldn't miss. But still more armour appeared. It was only a matter of time before they were overrun.

Johan waited until the gunner fired, then yelled, "Fall back!" The crew needed no encouragement. They manhandled the gun off its blocks and desperately raced back through their defensive line, hauling the gun behind them. The second line anti-tank crew took over, firing over their heads.

Johan joined the race. Diving for cover before turning and spraying the advancing infantry with machinegun fire. Dozens of enemy soldiers fell, but by now the whole of the assault force had caught up. The air became thick with the buzz and whirr of bullets. T34 tanks crashed over the German forward positions, driving across the trenches, crushing the dead and wounded beneath their tracks. As they advanced, they ran into crossfire from German defences. T34's were hit from all sides, and for the first time the Soviet infantry faltered.

Johan took advantage of the brief lull to sprint back to the main defensive line. His soldiers peered through the slits in their foxholes at the advancing Russians, fear etched on every sweat-drenched face. The sheer numbers of enemy troops and armour made it obvious they couldn't hold out for long. He scrambled along the trench to the makeshift bunker that served as the command centre. "What's the score?"

"We're holding but the left-hand flank is being over-run." The radio operator increased the volume as mortars rained down.

"Any air-support?"

The operator gave a cynical laugh. "Only if you're Russian." The radio crackled to life. Immediately, he became serious and bent over the set. He donned the headphones, adjusted the dial, and screwed up his eyes in concentration. He looked at Johan in confusion. "*Doppelgau*, repeat *Doppelgau*."

"Confirm," Johan instructed. "Then order a fighting retreat." He waited until the message was sent and received before he dived out the bunker back to the trench lines.

"Prepare for withdrawal," he shouted. The men instantly looked relieved. No one wanted to stand in a trench and await hand-to-hand combat with an enemy that heavily outnumbered them. They waited for Johan's signal. As soon as the soviets were less than a hundred metres from them, Johan gave the order. Every other man stood and emptied their full magazine, scything down those too slow to hurl themselves to the ground. Once the final bullet had been discharged, the second man repeated the action allowing their comrades to fall back, reload and form another defensive line. They leapfrogged their way back, gradually increasing the distance between themselves and the enemy. The tactic could only succeed for so long before the Russians regrouped and lined themselves up behind the cover of the advancing tanks. But it bought Johan's men time, blunted the onslaught and reduced the perimeter, making it easier to defend.

They'd made it to the river and the outskirts of the airfield before Johan spotted Jurgen, frantically directing anti-tank fire at a squadron of advancing armour.

"Dig in on the far bank," Johan shouted, as his men waded across the river, holding their rifles above their heads. He spotted the radio operator manfully holding his bulky load out of the water. "Radio for artillery cover once you get the set working." He turned his attention back to Jurgen. He and the anti-tank crew were fleeing, having exhausted their ammunition. He watched until they scrambled down the river bank and disappeared from view. He cast a glance back towards the Russians. To his surprise, they appeared to have lost interest in the fight. The tanks suddenly swung west. Perhaps the Soviet commanders decided second wave troops would be sufficient to mop up the few Germans stranded near the airfield. Johan stepped into the ice-cold water and waded across. Jurgen waited on the far bank, his right sleeve saturated with blood.

"You caught one?"

He nodded. "Patched up. Hurts like hell."

"I don't know if we've got any medics left."

Jurgen sank to his haunches. He looked drained. "Lost at least three-quarters of my men." He looked at Johan "Where do we go from here?"

"Wait for nightfall and try an escape downriver." He broke open his first aid kit and did his best to strap up Jurgen's smashed arm. "You need to get to a casualty station." He hauled Jurgen to his feet. "Are you okay?"

Jurgen masked his pain by throwing himself into action. "I'll check out the men, organise a defensive perimeter and make contact with Division."

The radio operator had the set working by the time they caught up with him.

"Any joy?" Johan asked.

"I've made contact with Divisional HQ."

"And?"

"Nothing - apart from them asking how many we are. Difficult to hear. They're at the limit of the set's range."

Johan patted him on the back. "Get some rest. I'll raise them." Johan sat himself down and wound the charging crank with little expectation of success. When he finally did get through, the message stunned him.

"I don't believe it." He looked at Jurgen in amazement. "They're flying in reinforcements."

"Bloody hell. Are they serious? We're all but surrounded."

"We're to stay put and expect relief. Fresh SS troops will counter-attack from someplace called Haldersdorf and link up with us."

"When?" Jurgen asked, as Johan spread out the map.

"Reinforcements by first light if the weather holds." He ran his finger over the map until he located Haldersdorf. "That's at least twenty kilometres away."

"Fat chance of any counter-attack getting here anytime soon then!" Jurgen winced, then looked disgusted. "Unless they intend to fly in an entire battalion, reality has gone out the window."

"Which is exactly what we've come to expect," Johan said dryly. "Get the wounded organised. You can be flown out with them."

"We stay together," Jurgen said fiercely.

"Mate, that arm needs surgery, and you've lost a lot of blood." He grinned. "And I'm the senior Leutnant so I can order your evacuation."

Next morning the reinforcements arrived. Ten three-engine transport aircraft swooped towards the landing strip. Johan and Jurgen watched each plane with mounting trepidation. The first three had the element of surprise on their side and touched down unscathed. The aircraft following on were forced to run a gauntlet of withering flak and small arms fire from a now alerted enemy. The pilots came in low, weaving their unwieldy aircraft in a desperate attempt to evade fire.

"This is suicide," Johan muttered. His observation proved prophetic as first one aircraft, then a second, was hit. To the cheers of Russian soldiers, both crashed into the ground, sending balls of bright orange and red flames and a pall of thick black smoke rolling into the atmosphere.

The pilots on the ground didn't hang around. They kept the engines running as the reinforcement troops poured out and ran for cover. As soon as the last soldier fell from the door the wounded were thrown in as if they were sacks of potatoes. The engines revved-up and the aircraft began its take-off run even before the doors were slammed shut. The speed of turn around accelerated as mortars peppered the airfield.

"Let's get our lot aboard," Johan shouted, as the next aircraft landed and sped towards them. They had four stretcher cases and eight walking wounded, including an unhappy-looking Jurgen.

None of them heard the mortar. For a millisecond, Johan felt himself being hurled sideways, sparks flashed in front of his eyes and then, nothing.

DESCENT INTO CHAOS

The Russians arrived at the outskirts of Haldersdorf in early May. The distant rumble of gunfire was replaced by the whistling sound of incoming shells and rockets that peppered the outskirts of the town. Mounting terror seeped into the sinews of the population. No one doubted their fate once the enemy broke through.

So many refugees swamped the town that the Feldgendarmarie used force to keep the bridge free for essential military traffic. For two nights, Trudy's sleep was interrupted by the constant sound of refugees travelling west and armoured reinforcements heading east.

"We need to hold our nerve," Frau Greber declared at breakfast.

"We need to hold the bridge," her husband said. "If we hold that, we hold the river. That'll stop the Russians in their tracks. Then we can counterattack. Did you see the reinforcements arrive?" He thrust his chest out in obvious pride. "SS crack troops. Magnificent!"

"The Burgermeister has organised the townsfolk to help dig trenches and tank traps all around the east of the town. Every true German is prepared to defend the town and do their duty to support our lads." Dagmar gave Trudy a meaningful look.

Trudy felt too tired to respond to the bait. She felt like a fly caught in a web. She longed to escape their corrosive influence, and sever her reliance on them for food and shelter. The price of having to listen to their idiocy was now too high.

"You won't let me down?" Dagmar deliberately pushed Trudy into a corner.

"No, I won't," Trudy said wearily. "But I expect you to find another supervisor because I'm only doing it as a one-off."

"You've lost your supervisor?" Frau Greber directed a questioning look towards her daughter. "What's happened to her?"

"She's run off. She and her entire family have fled."

"And gone where?"

"I don't know, and I don't care. All I will say is if they ever show their face around this town again, I'll make it my business to have them all sent to the camps."

"Spoken like a true German." Her father looked adoringly at his daughter.

Dagmar's expression towards Trudy conveyed the message, See - you could receive compliments like that if you embraced the cause with more enthusiasm.

Trudy bit her tongue. She committed herself to the task. The quicker it was over and done with, the better.

As it turned out, singing folk songs to the troops turned out to be more pleasant than Trudy anticipated, at least initially. The soldiers came from all corners of the Reich. Each man had a repertoire of songs that reminded him of home, and they competed with each other to have their favourites sung. The emotional attachment was strong, reinforced by the hardships they'd endured and because they were separated from loved ones, who many hadn't seen for years. They joined in, singing their hearts out, tears streaming down their faces as a particular melody brought back memories of a wife, sweetheart or a family gathered in the warmth of a Stübe or snuggled around the Kächelofen. Trudy found herself affected by their singing. They sang well, and the songs held a certain charm. Despite her tiredness, she found herself happily joining in.

The soldiers adored the youngsters and indulged them outrageously. In the breaks between the singing and dancing they shared their rations with the children and allowed them to handle the weaponry, sit in driver's cabs, listen in to the field radios, and clamber over tanks and artillery pieces.

Most soldiers treated both Dagmar and Trudy like they were their sisters. A few attempted clumsy chat-up lines, earning ribald put-down comments from their comrades. Occasionally some lewd or suggestive comment crossed the line. The perpetrators were instantly silenced.

Throughout the day, they travelled almost the entire eastern outskirts of the town, moving from one unit to another. By late-afternoon, fatigue among the children forced a halt.

"One last song!" the soldiers cried.

"One more, and then we must stop." Dagmar laughed good-naturedly. "We have to get the youngsters back."

"Don't worry about that. We'll take them back," a tall, muscular soldier, leaning against a tree trunk, called out. A shock of bleach-white hair further enhanced his distinctive presence. His lack of familiarity with the other troops, along with a smart, clean uniform, indicated he formed part of the reinforcements. His sleeves were rolled up, revealing the deaths-head tattoos of the Waffen SS. A single pip insignia gave his rank as a Scharfuhrer squad leader. He wielded his authority with casual arrogance. "They've sung well and deserve a treat." He called directly to the children, "How would you like to ride home in a tank?" He pointed to a parked armoured personnel carrier.

The wildly enthusiastic cheer was exactly the response he expected. "One last song – perhaps the *Horst Wessel* anthem."

The children duly obliged, then rushed to clamber over the vehicle.

The SS man pushed himself off the tree and approached Dagmar. "You've done well, Fraulein. I assume you are the Gruppenleiterin for these little warriors." In one easy move he'd grasped Dagmar's hand and raised it to his lips.

Dagmar blushed like a schoolgirl. "I'm not a Gruppenleiterin, but I'm in charge."

"You should be proud of yourself… " He raised a questioning eyebrow.

Dagmar giggled as she took the cue. "Dagmar… Dagmar Greber."

"And your Luftwaffe friend is?" He turned towards Trudy.

Trudy immediately dropped into military protocol. She snapped to attention and gave a smart salute. "Trudy Heppel of the Luftwaffe Flakgruppe, Herr Scharfurher."

"Doing extra duties in your free time?"

"Yes, sir."

"Very commendable. I congratulate the pair of you." He smiled, revealing a row of white, gleaming teeth. The man was attractive, and he knew it.

Dagmar was smitten.

"I'd like to invite you to my unit. We've taken our positions in this town, and have had the good fortune to have liberated a few cases of wine from our Russian friends. I'm sure you ladies would welcome the opportunity to join us for a glass or two." He glanced towards the children, who were swarming over the personnel carrier. "The children are being rewarded; it is only right that their supervisors should be equally recognised."

Trudy felt her heart sink. The last thing she wanted was to have to socialise and exchange meaningless small talk. "I'm grateful for the offer, sir, but must decline. I'm on duty tonight."

"Oh, Trudy, I'm sure you could manage to stay for a short while."

Trudy managed to muster a sweet smile, although inside she could have killed Dagmar. "Duty calls and I have my orders."

He frowned his disappointment. "Really, Fraulein Heppel! I hoped the pair of you might sing a few songs for my men and maybe have a dance or two." He gently lifted Dagmar's hand and twirled her around, making her laugh. "Our billet is only five minutes up there." He indicated the track the personnel carrier had driven down.

"Oh, come on, Trudy!" Dagmar pleaded. "I'm sure we could stay for an hour or so."

The sound of the personnel carrier's engine starting interrupted the conversation. Trudy used the distraction of the noisy children, who were laughing and screaming as the vehicle lurched forward and threatened to topple them off, to think fast.

"Why don't you go while I fetch the truck. You can enjoy the Scharfuhrer's hospitality and sing a few songs. I'll join you as soon as I can. That way we can leave promptly, and I won't miss my shift." She turned to the SS man before Dagmar could respond. "How far is your billet, sir?"

"Four hundred metres up the road. There's a farm with a large barn. You can't miss it."

Trudy seized her chance. She gave a broad smile, saluted and headed briskly off. Once out of sight, she slowed. The longer it took to walk back to the truck, the less time she'd have to spend partying.

The light was fading as the barn hove into view. Trudy killed the engine and allowed the truck to roll gently to a halt. She could hear the sound of raucous laughter and cheering drifting from the barn. She glanced at her watch. She'd only needed to endure forty minutes before making her excuses. She paused for a minute, opened the door, eased herself out the cab and made her way towards the party. Another cheer erupted and a martial song started. It seemed that, unlike the exhausted soldiers they'd entertained during the day, these troops were fresh, in high spirits, and from the sound of their boisterousness, had made an early start on their looted wine. She reached the slightly open barn door and took a deep breath to prepare herself.

She was about to enter when a piercing scream froze her hand. Another strangled cry was stifled. Men cheered. Trudy felt a wave of terror engulf her. She risked a peek around the door. A naked soldier lay spread over the writhing form of Dagmar, pinned down by four laughing soldiers. A line of half-undressed SS men formed a drunken line, cheering their comrade on, urging him to be quick so they could have their turn. The Scharfuhrer viewed the bucking soldier with cold indifference. He held a bottle of wine in one hand and a cigar in the other. An amused expression spread across his face as Dagmar's desperate shrieks were stifled. Someone shouted something at him. He waved his hand and laughed. "I prefer to wait for the main course," he replied before taking a casual swig from the bottle, then waving it vaguely towards the barn door. "She should be here by now." He jerked his chin at a couple of soldiers who were putting their uniforms back on. "You two, you've had your fun. Go and welcome her."

For a few seconds, Trudy found herself unable to move. The shock of the rape froze her to the spot. It took the sight of the two soldiers, lumbering unsteadily towards her refuge, to fire her into action. She fled in blind panic. Behind her, she heard the crash of the barn door being swung open, followed by another scream, a shout and then an excited whoop. "There she is. Come on, let's get her." Terror lifted her. Her legs pounded so fast she felt she was floating. A muzzy throb filled her head. She ran in desperation, with no idea where she was heading. She glanced about looking for somewhere to flee. Dense hedges lined both sides of the road. A fresh wave of fear crashed over her. She could hear the sound of running boots gradually catching up with her. A surge of adrenalin kicked in.

A building loomed ahead and with it, hope. If she could reach people, they would protect her. She could hear her pursuers' gasping breaths. A plaintive wail escaped her as she anticipated the thuggish hands that would take her down. She felt a tug on her coat. She swerved to break the contact. It was enough. The soldier was caught off balance. She caught his obscenity as he crashed and tumbled on the sharp gravel. She'd bought herself a brief respite.

More buildings passed. She'd reached the village outskirts but no one was on the street. The second soldier was right behind her. She spotted a gap running between two houses; maybe a path, she didn't know. She'd have to chance it. Her pursuer was inches away. She dived right down it, catching him by surprise. The narrow path delayed the two soldiers as they fell over each other, trying to squeeze through together. Trudy willed herself to run faster. The path split. She took the left-hand branch. Before her, a large orchard opened up. She ducked and weaved through the trees. She heard the soldier's curses as the low branches caught their heads. A flight of stone steps led to the door of a house. She spotted a light. Someone was in. She flew up the steps and burst through the door. She found herself in a spacious hallway. She glanced around in panic. In front of her was a broad flight of stairs. Instinctively, she raced upwards. Behind her, the front door crashed open as the two soldiers hurtled in pursuit. She fled along the corridor and picked a door at random. She slammed the door shut and frantically looked for something, anything, to barricade it. She grabbed a chair from in front of a small dressing table and tried to wedge it under the door handle. She was too late. The combined weight of the soldiers forced the door open, sending her and the chair flying across the room. In an instant, the two of them were on her. Strong hands grabbed her arm. She threw the other arm protectively over her head, screamed, kicked, scratched, and sank her teeth into the wrist of the arm trying to restrain her.

"What's the meaning of this?" an angry voice roared. "I said, what is the meaning of this?" The voice raised several decibels. Unbridled fury replaced annoyance.

The soldiers froze.

"Who the hell authorised you to enter these premises? Stand to attention when I speak to you, you vermin."

Trudy looked up from underneath her arm. A half-dressed man stood framed by the doorway - his crumpled military trousers held up by braces that crossed a bare, hairy chest. His face was half-covered by shaving cream, and his bloodshot eyes glared with boiling outrage at the two SS men. He stooped and unholstered a pistol from the belt that had fallen from the back of the chair. He cocked the weapon and pointed it directly at the head of the nearest soldier. "In case you haven't noticed, there is a large sign on the front door *Nur für Offiziere* – you can read, can't you?" he roared.

The pair looked confused, unsure as to what rank the half-dressed man held, or how to respond to his belligerence.

The officer made up their mind for them. "Get out before I have you arrested," he bellowed.

The men didn't need any encouragement. They fled.

"Bloody SS," The officer muttered, as he threw the pistol on the dressing table and returned to the bathroom to complete his shaving.

"Are you all right?" he asked.

Trudy felt traumatised and couldn't answer.

"I said, are you all right?" He sounded irritable.

"Yes," she said, her voice a quavering whisper.

He reappeared, wiping his face with a towel. "Well, you don't look it and you certainly don't sound it. Stand up."

Trudy slowly got to her feet. To her dismay, she found she shook uncontrollably. She felt cold and clammy, and her head was spinning.

He looked straight in her eyes. "Are you feeling faint?"

"What?"

He led her to the bed and sat her down, before picking up her wrist.

"Your pulse is racing, you're very pale and you're having difficulty breathing. You're in shock. Lie down. It's okay," he added quickly, as he saw the panic in Trudy's eyes. "Nothing will happen." He eased her back, placed a pillow under her ankles and threw a blanket over her. "Take deep breaths and try to relax," he said brusquely. "In fact, try and sleep. God knows, I need to." He turned to leave.

Immediately, Trudy panicked. She sat bolt upright. "Where are you going? Please don't leave me." The fear in her voice and eyes brought the officer up short.

"It's okay. They're not coming back." He sounded irritated.

"They raped Dagmar." Trudy looked at him, her eyes wide with fear and shock.

"They being the SS?"

Trudy didn't trust herself to speak. She squeezed her eyes shut but couldn't prevent the tears from flooding down her cheeks. In her mind, she could hear Dagmar's screams and picture her writhing body.

"But they didn't rape you?" he said, as if she was making a fuss about nothing.

"She shook her head.

"You've nothing to worry about here." He managed a weak smile. "I'll be in the next room if you need anything. Now get some sleep. We'll sort everything out in the morning."

"What about Dagmar?" she whispered.

Again he looked irritated. "What's done is done." He got up and headed for the door. "Now, rest. I'll be next door."

But for Trudy, sleep didn't come easily. The night was full of horrors. The screams and images kept bullying their way into her consciousness. The dull thuds of artillery bombardments, the rattle of distant machine guns and, early in the morning, the sound of dozens of tank engines starting and the metallic grind of their tracks as they advanced towards the enemy, impinged on her dreams. Even in the brief moments of calm, she imagined every creak of the old house was the sound of SS soldiers creeping up the stairs. Eventually, sheer exhaustion and the gentle snores of the doctor next door rendered her unconscious.

"How are you feeling?"

Trudy looked bleary-eyed at the doctor looming over her. "Better, I think."

"You need some food inside you. Get yourself up. The bathroom's through there." He nodded towards the door. "I'll see you downstairs."

Trudy took his terse suggestion as an order. She joined him twenty minutes later.

The doctor waved a coffee percolator at her. "It's real coffee. No sugar though. Sit yourself down." He poured her a coffee, lit his cigarette, then sat back and studied her. "So, tell me what happened."

He listened intently as she relived the violation, leaving nothing out. To her dismay, he was unsympathetic. "What on earth were you two playing at?!" He shook his head in disbelief. "Have you no concept of how evil those SS bastards are? Not only did you walk into their billet, but you chose a unit that is about to spearhead this morning's counterattack. Talk about stupidity."

Trudy felt outraged. "I'm not stupid. I was exhausted. We'd been with our troops all day. We'd had no problems."

"Wehrmacht troops are not the SS. Jesus! The Russians might spare Wehrmacht soldiers, SS ones they shoot out of hand." He tapped the ash from his cigarette. "Anyway, the point is…" He stopped and looked at her. "Did you tell me your name?"

"Trudy."

He gave an apologetic half smile, stubbed out his cigarette and immediately lit another. He closed his eyes and took a deep drag before exhaling in a long breath, as if fortifying himself ahead of delivering his brutal analysis. "You need to come to terms with the probability that your friend didn't survive her ordeal."

Trudy felt as if she had been hit with a hammer. "What?"

"It's the SS way. Dead victims can't talk. They've been raping and murdering since they were formed. It's embedded in their twisted culture."

Trudy sat open-mouthed at his harshness. She took a moment to examine the man opposite her. He didn't strike her as a callous, uncaring type. He could have been anything from early thirties to late sixties. His face was deeply lined, his eyes were sunken and, despite having slept, still bloodshot. She noticed his hands constantly trembled, so much so that he had to hold his cup with both hands to avoid spillage. He looked a wreck. If he was aware of her scrutiny, he gave no sign. He continued speaking as if to himself, his tone bitter and cynical. "There's little point in informing the Feldgendarmarie. So many have been raped. Besides, they are now spending their time rounding up anyone capable of fighting. Young boys of eight or nine are being sent to the front line, carrying anti-tank rockets that are bigger than themselves. And old men who can barely hold their bladder, let alone a rifle." He took another drag from his cigarette. "The war's over, we've lost, and yet nobody can stop the madness." He glanced across at her. "I've lost all my nurses. Those we didn't evacuate, fled. They knew their fate if they stayed. That's what you and your friend should have done."

Heavy knocking on the front door interrupted his diatribe and made Trudy jump.

"Come in," he shouted.

The door opened to reveal a short, fat corporal, bent double with his hands on his knees, his whole frame reeling as he desperately tried to force air into his lungs.

"Take your time, Schultze."

"More casualties, Doctor Voight," Schultze gasped.

Voight rolled his eyes. "Where? How many?"

"The airfield. They're being flown in. Don't know how many, sir. I've sorted transport."

"*Scheisse!*" He stubbed out his cigarette, grabbed his jacket and downed his coffee. "Let's go." He moved towards the door.

Trudy felt a surge of panic. Despite her uncertainty about the man, the prospect of being left alone terrified her. "Wait, I'll come with you."

He looked at her askance. "To do what exactly?"

"I can help, I've done First Aid." She saw him start to laugh. "You said you've lost your nurses. I'm sure I can be of use."

His laugh died as he considered her offer. "I suppose you're better than nothing. Don't cause me any problems."

She grabbed her coat and followed him out the door.

He leant towards Trudy and shouted in her ear over the noise of the truck engine, as they bounced and lurched their way towards the airfield. "If they are yelling and screaming there's not a lot wrong with them. It's the ones that are unconscious or heavily bleeding that are the priority - so long as they are breathing. Leave the noisy ones to waste their energy."

She nodded.

"You need to be ruthless."

By the time they reached the airfield a couple of three-engine transport planes had already landed; a third was making its final approach. One of its engines was out, and it was clear from the way the aircraft sank and weaved that the pilot was having trouble controlling it.

"You take that one." He pointed at the corkscrewing aircraft. "Get the wounded off, do an assessment and prioritise. We'll join you as soon as we can. Don't mess about. The Russians are bound to be alerted by all this activity."

"You'll need this." The corporal handed her a canvas satchel. "And this." He stripped off his Red Cross armband and gave it to her. Trudy snatched it from him and jumped from the truck.

The stricken plane lurched and landed heavily on the grass. Almost immediately, Russian shells exploded on the edge of the airfield, providing an incentive not to hang about.

Trudy looked around. Her concern that there wouldn't be any staff to help her, evaporated. As soon as the plane swung around and the pilot cut the engines and allowed the aircraft to roll to a halt, three Luftwaffe ground crew heaved the doors open. The walking wounded were only too keen to disembark. They tumbled out, the more able turning to help their badly injured comrades.

"Where do you want them?" a crew member asked.

Trudy turned around in surprise. Her armband provided instant authority. She thought fast. "Move the able-bodied under cover." She pointed to the nearest aircraft hangar.

She dodged out the way as another man tumbled from the door and sank to the ground. He cradled the remains of his right arm; the entire sleeve was saturated with blood. Trudy dragged her First-Aid training from the depth of her memory. "Cut his shirt off. He'll need a tourniquet," she ordered one of the ground staff. She clambered inside the fuselage and fought to stop herself from retching. The stench of kerosene and vomit was overpowering. The plane was badly shot up, and the floor slippery with blood, oil and hydraulic fluid. A soldier lay slumped as if asleep. She pulled back his head and reeled at the sight of his smashed chest. He was beyond help. Two stretcher cases had been thrown across each other by the force of the landing. Both men were still alive. "Get these two off," she yelled. "Put them under cover by that water tank. These are priorities."

The Russian shells crept ever closer, thudding into the ground, blasting columns of brown earth skyward.

At the back of the plane, a soldier bent over the prone form of his comrade. She pushed the man off his friend.

"He's a priority," the soldier said firmly, his voice distorted by a dirty makeshift bandage that encased his head.

Trudy ignored him and bent over to examine his buddy.

"He's lost his arm and has a severe head injury. Lost a lot of blood, but he's breathing." The man looked at her with hard, determined eyes.

"And you?"

"Concussion, smashed arm, broken jaw." He lifted his good arm to reveal a blood-soaked shirt. "And some Russian scrap-iron in my arm and guts." He glanced back at his mate. "I'll live but he won't unless he gets seen to fast."

Trudy nodded. "Priority case, lads," she shouted.

The bandaged man winked his thanks.

Trudy crawled towards the cockpit. The pilot saw her approach and unclipped himself. Trudy could only see the back of the head of his co-pilot.

The pilot blocked her passage. "Don't waste your time," he muttered, and jerked his head towards the prone form. "He's dead, and he's not looking his best." He grabbed her shoulders and gently pushed her back. "We need to get clear. This plane's full of kerosene fumes."

An exploding shell, close enough to make the aircraft rock, showered the plane with debris and provided an added incentive to evacuate.

Trudy ran to the water tank and knelt beside the soldier with the shattered right arm. Loss of blood rendered him unconscious. She opened the satchel and rooted about for a tourniquet. She felt a rising sense of panic. She was unfamiliar with the bag and its contents. To her dismay, it contained a leather strap, a few tubes of salve, and bandages made from ripped sheets that looked as if they'd been used before.

"Don't waste bandages on him."

She glanced up to see the man with the 'Russian scrap-iron' injury watching her. "His arm is beyond help. Use the tourniquet." He pointed to the strap.

She did as he directed and wrapped it around the top of the injured man's upper arm.

"Tie it tight. The arm's lost, but you might save his life."

"You done this before?"

"Too many times."

"This is my first."

"You're doing fine."

Although it seemed like hours, the off-loading took less than ten minutes, and Doctor Voight quickly arrived to take over. They escaped with all the wounded from the three planes just as the shellfire found one of the aircraft. It exploded in a sheet of orange flames.

Trudy watched the column of thick black smoke in the wing mirror. Despite the dangers, she felt pleased with herself. She hadn't flapped and, in her own small way, she felt certain she'd helped save at least one life and that felt good. There was plenty more to be done. For the rest of the day, she helped with basic nursing tasks: cleaning wounds, applying bandages, holding drip bottles. When not helping out the medics, she was pressed into making batches of cabbage and turnip soup that, along with hard stale black bread, she came to realise formed the diet of the hospital. The intensity of work helped take her mind off Dagmar's fate.

By late evening most casualties were stabilised. Only three succumbed to their wounds. That, according to Doctor Voight, represented a good result, given the severity of the injuries.

"You did well," he said, during a brief lull in activities.

Trudy smiled her thanks.

He appraised her out of the corner of his eye, then apparently made up his mind that she was no bother. "What's your usual job?"

"Searchlights."

"You're better off working here than wasting your time turning lights on and off. You'll work in the hospital from now on," he said curtly. "Don't worry, I'll sort everything out," he added, to forestall any discussion on the matter.

Trudy wasn't about to object. He was right. Manning searchlights was now a waste of time. All flak guns had been transferred to an anti-tank role and had moved east. There was no point lighting up enemy aircraft without the means to shoot them down.

He lit his cigarette. "You'd better find somewhere to sleep in the hospital. I'll need you to be available at short notice. Soldiers can be bloody selfish regarding getting shot-up. Any time of day or night suits them."

Trudy felt a wave of relief. She couldn't imagine returning to the Greber's house after what had happened.

Moving out of the Greber's was traumatic. The discovery of Dagmar's mutilated body broke her father's sanity. "You killed her," he screamed, pointing an accusing finger at Trudy, his wife, or anyone else his wild, mad eyes alighted upon. Trudy grabbed her belongings and fled, leaving behind a disintegrating household.

She made space in a storage room in the hospital basement and, with the help of Corporal Schultze, equipped it with an army camp-bed, blankets and a small dressing table and chair 'liberated' from an abandoned house. Having established her nest, she threw herself into becoming a nurse - soaking up knowledge and advice from the medical staff, doctors, and even some of the wounded who'd become adept at administering first aid and life-saving techniques through grim necessity.

The 'scrap-iron' soldier proved especially helpful. Doctor Voight managed to remove the shrapnel from his arm and stomach in a painful operation, undertaken with minimal anaesthetic that merely dulled the pain. He lay recovering on his camp-bed, watching her clean the bullet wound of a semi-conscious sergeant.

"You need a lot more boiled water," he said. "When you open the wound, make sure you get into every nook and cranny. I've seen soldiers have bullets removed, only for them to die from infection afterwards."

Trudy was grateful for his further advice on stitching the wound. "You should be a doctor yourself," she said, and sat back to admire her handiwork.

He chuckled and levered himself to a sitting position, wincing from the pain of his operation. "I just want to return home."

"You're making a good recovery. Hopefully, the war will end soon and your wish will be granted." She glanced at the soldier lying beside him. "Is he your friend?"

"My cousin and best mate. We've known each other since birth."

"He's doing quite well."

He turned his bandaged head towards his friend. "I'm hopeful. He opened his eyes and recognised me." He fell silent for a bit. "Each day brings progress."

"He's lucky to have you." She smiled at him. "I've seen you giving him water and trying to get him to eat."

He looked at her with laughing eyes. "Yeah, blown up by Ivan, only to be poisoned by cabbage soup!" He scratched his neck and looked thoughtful. "We made a pact when we joined. Leave together, and come home together."

She packed her equipment, got to her feet and stretched her legs that had grown numb from kneeling. "You'll both make it."

The distant sound of machine-gun fire broke into their conversation.

He looked rueful. "Providing the Russians don't get us first, eh?"

Outside Haldersdorf the fighting raged. After four weeks, it was obvious the counterattack had failed. Casualties mounted and the hospital buckled under the pressure. Disinfectants, morphine, saline drips and anaesthetics quickly ran out. Men lay crammed against one another, forcing the medical staff to step over bodies. The refugee columns that had clogged the roads heading to the west, and the evacuation of wounded soldiers to better-equipped hospitals, slowed to a trickle.

Shells landed in the town, and Russian aircraft deliberately flew low, further terrorising the inhabitants. The water supply was hit, forcing the closure of the hospital laundry. Buckets were deployed as the sewage system backed up. The stench in the hospital became overpowering: sewage combined with the all-pervasive smell of cabbage soup, men's sweat, and stale tobacco, as the men smoked continuously in an attempt to steady nerves and mask the stink. Parasites and infections spread rapidly. Constant itching and scratching added to the patients' misery. The medical staff weren't spared either. To her horror, Trudy woke one morning to find herself covered in angry, red bites.

"How long can we last before we have to evacuate?" Trudy asked, as she and Doctor Voight sat taking a break on the steps of the hospital, watching the refugee columns snake towards the bridge and safety.

He sighed wearily, rubbed his eyes, then lit his familiar cigarette. "The Wehrmacht Commander has assured me the town will be defended. If the bridge stays open, and we can continue to transfer the more serious cases west, we'll stay put." He gave Trudy a sideways look. "You'll be evacuated if the Russians advance any closer."

And that will force my decision, she thought. She'd already posted her intentions to Franz. She'd try to reach Austria as close as possible to the Swiss border. She'd register her name and location of wherever she ended up with the Red Cross, so he could find her.

"What will you do if the Russians break through?"

He shrugged and said nothing.

They watched a patrol of Nazi vigilantes pull young boys and old men from the refugee column. They lined them up, before marching them back down the road towards the trenches and tank traps. The doctor emerged from his musing. He pointed at the thugs using their batons to club women, while they physically tried to drag their husbands and sons away from enforced conscription, and said, "One thing is certain though, I've no intention of being part of this Nazi obscenity any longer than I have to."

MAY 1945 – DIOCESE OFFICE

Father Thomas consulted his notes from his meeting with the Bishop, then reread the letter. He was sure he hadn't left anything out. Nevertheless, if there was one thing he had learned from his former boss, it was the importance of being meticulous. He'd written several similar letters in the past two months, but the Bishop made it clear that this one was particularly important. The instructions needed to be precise. The recipient demanded nothing less. He traced the script with his finger and methodically ticked off each instruction from his notes.

The recipient was to make his way to Innsbruck. There he would find accommodation at… Thomas checked the date and address. He would be picked up the following day and transported by car to the monastery of the Teutonic Order in Merano, South Tyrol. He would stay there for two nights. He would be issued with a letter from the Church confirming his new identity and then be taken to Rome. Once there, he would present the letter to the Red Cross, who would issue the appropriate passports as a formality.

Thomas rechecked his notes. Passports were clearly stated. It would seem that his fugitive was meeting up with comrades or perhaps family. The recipient was then required to contact a shipping agent in Civitavecchia for onward transport. All fees to be agreed with the agent.

Satisfied he'd missed nothing out, Thomas placed the letter in the envelope and sealed it. He then sat back and gazed about the room. For the first time in months, he felt relaxed and content. The Bishop seemed to be pleased with him. Wherever Monsignor Wagner was, it was clear he wasn't coming back. The audit had revealed the extent of his corruption, and the Bishop seemed concerned that there should be no public scandal.

Better still, his eminence had assured him that not only was his job secure but, if he continued to serve the Church well, further promotion could be expected. Thomas found himself staring at the half-full decanter. He'd never indulged but now seemed the right time to treat himself. He poured a small glass, gave himself a silent toast and took a sip. His eye was drawn to the line of portraits. The Bishop had just commissioned his own to join the ranks of his predecessors. Thomas stared at the vacant space on the wall and allowed himself to dream.

MAY 1945 - HALDERSDORF - GERMANY

Trudy woke and immediately sensed something was wrong. Exhaustion meant she usually slept so deeply that nothing could disturb her. She glanced at her watch and groaned. It was two o'clock in the morning. She'd only had three hours sleep. She allowed her senses to work out what was happening. An approaching roar threw her into a panic. Outside, a tank passed at speed, followed immediately by another, until the basement shook with what sounded like a whole armoured column passing the hospital. She dressed quickly and sprinted up the stairs, only to bump into Corporal Schultze waving a torch.

He shone the light into her face. "I was coming to fetch you."

"Is it the Russians?"

"No. It's our lot. A tactical retreat. They're taking new positions on the far side of the river." He grabbed her arm and guided her through the prone bodies. "They've taken a lot of casualties. Doctor Voight says you can either come with me or stay here and help."

"What do you mean?"

"I've been ordered to head over the river to see if I can scavenge some supplies. If you come with me, you'll be safer. The Russians are less than five kilometres away, and north of the town they've already reached the river."

Trudy felt a sense of outrage wash through her. She felt she was part of the medical team. To abandon them didn't feel right at all. "I'll stay here. I'll leave when everyone else does."

In the semi-darkness Corporal Schultze squeezed her arm.

For the rest of the night and well into the morning, Trudy helped out with a seemingly endless series of brutal operations. Everyone blanked out the screams of men as arms and legs were amputated, bullets and shrapnel extracted and shattered bodies patched up, all without the use of any anaesthetics. Every medic sprang into action. The doctors worked fast. Treatment became like a conveyor belt. Once a casualty had been dealt with, he was off the operating table and immediately replaced by the next. Life and death decisions were made in seconds. Anyone with a serious abdominal wound was doomed. There was no point wasting time and scarce medical supplies on them. The theatre looked like an abattoir. Every now and then, an orderly sluiced the blood-soaked floor and casually threw any severed limbs into empty buckets for incineration in the hospital boiler room. By three in the afternoon, the medical team forced themselves to take a break. They'd been working for twelve hours non-stop.

Trudy joined Doctor Voight and the other drained medics, sitting or sprawled out on the steps of the hospital. In front of them, tanks, armoured cars and towed artillery cut a swathe through the refugee traffic that had been forced off the road into ditches or pressed up on the pavements. Nothing was allowed to impede the progress of the retreating soldiers. Exhausted, mud-spattered troops clung desperately to the turrets of the passing armour. Those unlucky not to have hitched a ride, trudged like automata through the town, their rifles dangling loosely from tired hands, heavy machine guns slung over hunched shoulders. They staggered along with glazed, expressionless faces as if they were already dead.

The approach of a three-ton truck, being driven at speed against the flow of the column, caught their attention.

The doctor cursed, stood and crushed the butt of his cigarette under his heel. "What the hell is this all about?"

The lorry skidded to a halt in a cloud of dust. Corporal Schultze leapt from the cab. "They're mining the bridge," he said breathlessly.

"Are you sure?"

"Engineers are strapping on dynamite. I've seen them."

"*Scheisse!*"

"That's not all, sir. They've opened the stores. It's a free for all."

"Bastards!"

Trudy looked confused. "What does it mean."

"It means our bloody Wehrmacht Commander lied. They're not defending the town. They intend to blow the bridge and, presumably, form a new defensive line on the other side of the river. Leaving us high and dry." He threw his hands to his forehead and forced himself to think. "Corporal, get yourselves to the stores. Grab as much stuff as you can. Get a rifle. Use force if you have to. Then get your arse back here."

"What are we doing that for?" Trudy tried to kick her wearied brain into gear.

"We need to evacuate the hospital as fast as we can. We'll need supplies." He suddenly looked at her. "You can drive, can't you?"

She nodded.

"Then drive the truck." He waved his arms angrily at them. "Go on, get moving."

Word had already got out that the town stores at the old school were no longer guarded. Civilians emerged like ants sensing a drop of spilt honey. By the time Trudy and Corporal Schultze arrived, the school was teeming. Dozens of men, women and children fled with loaves of hard bread, cheeses, tins of meats and anything else they could carry. They scurried out, desperate to get the booty back home quickly enough to allow a second or third journey before the store was stripped bare.

"Back up to the door as close as you can." Corporal Schultze leapt out the cab before the truck even halted. He sprinted off and disappeared inside.

Trudy hadn't even completed reversing when she heard the sound of items being thrown in the back. She leapt out and entered the free-for-all inside the building. In the thick of it, the corporal bullied and barged his way to the front, grabbing great armfuls of anything that came to hand.

"Grab what you can from over there," he shouted, jerking his head towards piles of cardboard and wooden boxes at the far end of the hall.

She dived in - pushing, shoving and elbowing anyone who got in her way. There was no order, good manners or deference to age or sex. This was a primaeval battle for survival. After years of rationing, people now had a chance to gorge themselves. Tempers frayed, fists flew, kicks were exchanged, and the air was filled with shouting and swearing. She caught sight of Corporal Schultze flattening a man who tried to clamber into the back of the truck. A small child disappeared under the feet of a crowd who'd discovered several wooden boxes containing real coffee. Trudy had no idea what she was collecting. She threw boxes, packets, tins, anything she could lay her hands on into the back of the truck as fast as she could. The knowledge spread like a wild-fire across the town and among the refugees. The melee threatened to turn into a riot.

"Grab the rifle and defend what we've got," the corporal shouted, as another hoard burst through the doors.

Trudy heaved herself over the tailboard. The sight of her wielding the weapon provided sufficient deterrent to anyone tempted to clamber on board.

In the store, fights broke out, and savage tugs of war were fought over boxes that neither protagonist knew the contents of. A shouting, screaming rage took hold. Some Feldgendarmarie appeared and drew their weapons. They were not there to instigate order but to grab their own share of the loot. The corporal managed three more sallies and decided they should withdraw before more shots were fired and the violence became even worse.

They arrived back at the hospital to the sight of four trucks parked-up and the more able-bodied patients being helped over the tailgates.

"Is that it?" Corporal Schultze put his hands on his hips and looked in disgust at the tiny convoy.

"It's all that could be spared." Doctor Voight looked equally unimpressed. "The Commandant's view is that the hospital should be allowed to fall into the hands of the Russians. He thinks they'll look after our boys. Geneva Convention and all that crap."

The corporal looked unconvinced. "I didn't know the Russians believed in that sort of stuff."

"They don't. It's bullshit." He pushed the corporal towards the hospital. "Make yourself useful. We need these trucks away as fast as possible. The bridge gets blown at three o'clock. Load as many as you can squeeze in. Nurse Trudy, stack the boxes and make as much room as possible in your truck."

"Where are we heading?" Trudy asked.

Doctor Voight looked at her for a second and shrugged. "Head for Leipzig. It's still in our hands, and there's a hospital there." He cast his eyes around the road as if suddenly becoming aware it had fallen eerily quiet.

311

The fleeing German troops had already crossed the river. Groups of refugees pulled themselves from the verges and moved towards the bridge. A small column of elderly Volkssturm, accompanied by several Hitler Youth, trudged in the opposite direction towards the Russians. Each boy carried a single shot Panzerfaust anti-tank weapon. Beyond them, the road out of Haldersdorf lay empty. "Last-ditch defence," he muttered. He glanced back at Trudy. "We need to move fast. The Russians could be here any moment."

Thirty minutes later, the four trucks departed with forty-two patients - less than a third of the hospital population.

"Corporal, load the last truck."

"Which patients, Doctor Voight?"

"No patients, the priority now is the staff. Anyone that wants to leave." He turned to Trudy. "You don't have a choice. You're going. You can drive."

Trudy opened her mouth to protest.

"Best do as he says," a muffled voice whispered in her ear.

It was the shrapnel soldier.

"What are you doing here?" She glanced at the truck convoy already weaving through the refugees towards the bridge. "You are supposed to be on that!"

"My mate needs to get to Leipzig. There was room for one stretcher. We've looked after each other for five years. I wasn't going to fail at the last eight hundred metres."

She opened the truck's passenger door. "If you want to make sure he makes it, you'd better make sure you do as well."

He heaved himself up.

Behind her, Doctor Voight yelled at the medics. "Don't hang about. Try and catch up with the other trucks."

The medics were still tumbling over the tailgate when Corporal Schultze threw open the passenger door, hurled in a large pile of blankets and screamed, "Get going, quick go, go, go." He craned his head out the window and looked back along the road. "Russian tank. For Christ's sake, Trudy, put your foot down."

Trudy didn't need any encouragement. The truck shot forward, leaving Corporal Schultze clinging on for dear life to the still open passenger door, and throwing the medics in the back to the floor. In the wing mirror she caught a glimpse of a dull grey tank, enveloped in dust, hurtling towards them. Hanging off its turret, like ants, were dozens of soviet soldiers.

She pressed the accelerator to the floor, urging every ounce of power from the motor. She crashed through the gears, swerving around the hapless refugees. The shrapnel soldier leaned over and pressed the horn. The bridge was less than six hundred metres away. Already, the German engineers were running back across the bridge. They were aware of the

312

Russians racing towards them. A series of shells exploded on the far bank. Another shell landed in the river, sending a column of water across the central span and bowling the sappers off their feet. The buildings along the whole of the far back rippled and collapsed as dozens of mortars landed.

Trudy gripped the wheel and almost stood on the throttle. She wasn't deviating now. In front of her, groups of terrified refugees scattered. If anyone got in their way it was their own fault. The truck engine screamed as she crashed through another gear. The bridge now lay less than two hundred metres ahead. Some mortars scored a direct hit on the central span, hurling an already injured sapper over the parapet and into the water. His comrades picked themselves up and sprinted. Their panic transmitted to the refugees who dropped their few meagre belongings and ran in a desperate race to cross the river. The far bank became obscured by a cloud of dust and debris as more shells and mortar bombs landed.

The shrapnel soldier furiously hit the horn. "Don't stop for anything," he yelled.

The distance dropped to less than fifty metres. The entire span became awash with fleeing men, women and children. They dived out of the way as the truck bore down on them. The air was suddenly ripped apart by the whoosh of a tank shell. It exploded in a building on the far bank, sending bricks crashing into the street.

They flew across the bridge. Trudy let out a silent sigh of relief.

"Don't stop," the soldier screamed again, as he sensed Trudy taking her foot off the accelerator. "We're not out of it yet." As if to prove his point another tank shell screamed past them. Trudy swerved the truck around the debris and peered through the thick dust coating the windscreen, trying to spot where the road was leading. Behind them, the sappers triggered the demolition charges. The bridge seemed to leap into the air before crashing into the water. The shock wave nearly burst their eardrums and rocked the truck violently on its suspension.

"Keep going," the soldier urged. He glanced in the wing mirror. The tank had come to a halt, and the infantry were already pouring down the banks, carrying rubber assault boats. Two further tanks hove into view, disgorging ever more shock troops.

"God help Doctor Voight and the others," Corporal Schultze muttered.

They drove headlong for five minutes past the remnants of the German army. Dozens of heavily camouflaged tanks, armoured troop carriers, half-tracks and tank destroyers were dug in on either side of the road. Everywhere, troops were digging trenches, foxholes and machine gun positions, filling sand-bags or cleaning weapons. The bridge and town of Haldersdorf might be lost, but there was still a will to resist.

They drove into the evening, accompanied all the way by the sound of a ferocious battle behind them. The entire eastern horizon glowed and flashed with continuous explosions. Flares lit the sky, and the searing white trails of rockets arched upwards before disappearing in a ghostly haze into the clouds. Occasionally, low flying aircraft screamed overhead. Whether they were Luftwaffe or Soviet it was impossible to determine. Eventually, they caught up with the tail of a refugee column.

"Pull over," the shrapnel soldier ordered. "It's getting too dark - we can't force our way through and we don't want to be showing lights. Best we grab some food and sleep while we can."

They broke open some of the looted rations and stretched themselves out in and around the truck. As a result of unspoken courtesy, Trudy found herself alone in the comparative comfort of the cab. She relaxed across the bench seat and pulled the blankets over her. The noise of battle and the constant biting lice ensured she got little sleep.

She woke to an aroma she hadn't smelt in a long time. Real coffee!

"I'm sure you wouldn't have thanked me if you'd missed out."

She peeped over the blanket to see the shrapnel soldier holding a steaming mug.

"We've got a stew on the go. Real tinned meat, potatoes and Sauerkraut. You want some?'

Suddenly she was ravenous.

The meal revived everyone's spirits. Corporal Schultze wiped his mouth and sat back contentedly. "I can't remember when I last ate so well. Beats bloody cabbage soup. Eh, Leutnant Breitner?"

Trudy found herself pleasantly surprised. She'd never had time to find out the names of any of the casualties. Each was just another injured soldier. Now shrapnel man had a name, making him seem more human. His rank also explained why he easily assumed command. She watched him as she ate. He served each man in turn, tipping healthy portions into their bowls. Only when everyone had been looked after did he feed himself. He squatted and gazed back towards the town from where the explosions continued unabated. "Sounds like they're holding the Bolsheviks up," he said.

"For how long though?"

"I don't think we should hang around to find out, Corporal. As soon as we've finished scoffing, we must move on and try and catch up with the others."

They set off twenty minutes later and made good progress. The groups of refugees were more spread out and quickly overtaken. Traffic coming in the other direction was sporadic. Only one convoy of supply trucks heading to the front held them up for a few minutes. Despite making headway, Trudy was aware the Leutnant was acting increasingly more

314

anxious. He kept looking out the windows as if he expected a Russian ambush. An hour later they entered a forest and ground to a halt. A long column of static refugee vehicles - tractors, trucks, carts, horses and cars stretched ahead.

"*Scheisse,*" Corporal Schultze swore. "Just when I thought the day was going so well. I'll find out what the problem is." He jumped out of the cab and slammed the door. He was back ten minutes later.

"What's the score, Corporal?"

"Overturned tractor and trailer, sir. No way around it."

"Can it be shifted?"

"Oh, yes. A bit of organisation and brute force. I'll take the men. We'll have it clear in no time."

The Leutnant moved to join them, earning a rebuke from the Corporal. "No, sir. You stay where you are. If you try and lift anything, you'll rip your stitches out. We'll sort it." He disappeared up the road, leading the medics.

The departure of the men made the Leutnant even more anxious. He jumped out the truck, scanned the surrounding forest and the sky before jumping back in the cab.

"What's the matter?" Trudy asked.

"A column like this makes a juicy target." He leant over her and gazed out into the forest. "Back the truck up a bit. About thirty metres."

Trudy did as he asked. "What was that all about?"

"A precaution. Keep your eyes peeled." He gazed at the sky.

"Leutnant Breitner, you're making me nervous."

"For good reason." His manner changed abruptly. "Get the truck off the road. Quick." There was no mistaking the urgency of the order.

For a second, Trudy floundered. "What?"

"Aircraft!" he said, pointing to the sky. Up ahead, four tiny black shapes rose slowly into the air. Another two joined them. They looked so graceful as they banked and dived towards them. "Get off the road," he shouted. "Down the track. Come on,"

Her reactions kicked in as she saw the fast-approaching danger. She fired up the engine and risked a quick glance through the windscreen. The first aircraft levelled out and began its attack. She crashed the engine into gear and heaved on the steering wheel. The truck lurched and bounced across the ditch. Above the noise of the approaching fighter and the truck's diesel engine, she could hear the refugees screaming as the realisation of what was about to happen struck home. The aircraft raked the entire length of the column with deadly cannon fire. It soared into the air like a triumphant bird of prey. Behind it was a sea of devastation. Vehicles were overturned, set ablaze, or smashed by the force of the shells. Bodies of horses and humans lay scattered; some were still alive, desperately crawling for cover in the ditches beside the road. There was no respite. The second aircraft was already spewing its lethal fusillade.

315

Trudy struggled to hold the steering wheel as the truck bucked and wallowed on the narrow forest track.

"Just get clear," the Leutnant yelled, as the third and fourth aeroplanes swooped in for the kill. The last two planes lined up for the coup de grace. Four bombs dropped. In seconds, the refugees were consumed by a ball of fire.

"Keep going, don't stop."

The track was rutted, and the truck slewed about. The steering wheel spun from her grip as the front wheels collided with a large tree root. Trudy wrenched the vehicle back on course. In front of her the track straightened up. She pressed hard on the accelerator, and they bounced their way deeper into the forest.

The Leutnant stuck his head out the window and scanned the sky, trying to spot the aircraft through the trees. Another aircraft appeared from nowhere and flew low, directly above them. He hauled himself back into the cab and slumped on the seat. "Keep going. They'll have difficulty seeing us."

Just as quickly as the aircraft appeared they left again; the roar of their engines replaced by the familiar sound of distant shellfire.

They drove on in silence - both imagining the horror and carnage behind.

"Should we go back?" Trudy asked after a while.

He shook his head. "It's a busy road. Help will already be on its way, assuming anyone survived."

"Do you know where we're going?"

He gazed out the window. "West. As long as the track takes us in that direction we're heading away from danger."

It became obvious the trail was little used. At times it was so overgrown it almost disappeared. They slowed to a crawl. The light faded and progress became impossible.

Trudy gazed around at the surrounding trees. Whichever way she looked it all seemed the same. "How do you know we are still heading west?" They'd stopped for the night and sat in the back of the truck, eating from cans of processed pork and Sauerkraut.

He pointed to the fast-fading light. "The sun sets in the west, and moss mostly grows on the north side of tree trunks." He spooned in another mouthful. "I reckon we have driven about twenty kilometres."

"Feels like a lot more. We've not got much fuel left."

He nodded, "No point worrying about it." He scooped the last morsel of food from the tin and gazed out over the tailgate. "It's clouding over. That will make flying more difficult for them." He unravelled the bandage that swathed his head.

"What are you doing?"

"Bloody lice are driving me mad. They've taken up residence."

She glanced around the truck. Somewhere she'd seen a first-aid kit left behind by one of the medics. She spotted it, reached over and dragged it towards her. "There'll be fresh bandages in here." When she looked up again he'd removed the dressing to reveal his face. He wasn't what she'd expected. Under the ragged beard he looked young, almost boyish. He gently rubbed his jaw, then cautiously opened and closed his mouth. He seemed pleased with the result. "I reckon that's set pretty well. How about the cut across my head?" He bent towards her, inviting an inspection. She knelt beside him and examined the long gash and the neat row of stitches. "I can't tell. It's too dark." She gently touched the wound with her fingers. "It doesn't seem to be weeping."

He laughed. "That's because the lice are feeding off it."

In the half-light she grimaced. "Don't be gruesome."

He chuckled. "All God's creatures have their uses." He jumped off the tailgate and strode off into the woods.

"Where are you going…oh," she said, as he stopped and gave her an *isn't it obvious* look.

They slept in the back of the truck. It was a night spent scratching as the parasites feasted. It seemed to Trudy, the more she thought about them the worse the irritation. She tried to block them from her mind. Beside her, the Leutnant slept soundly. It appeared he could grab rest at will. Perhaps it's a soldier thing, she thought, as she lay back, listening to his breathing and trying to distract herself from the feeding lice by guessing his name. He looks a bit like Franz. Wouldn't that be a coincidence if his first name actually was Franz! He's not a Lothar, I'm sure of that. Maybe Michael, or Gephardt? With that, she pulled up the blankets and fell asleep.

317

MAY 1945 – CZECH/GERMAN BORDER

They woke to the sound of gentle drizzle pattering on the tarpaulin cover of the truck. Trudy deliberately got up early to avoid the embarrassment of him seeing her 'visiting the woods' When she returned, he was wandering along the side of the track with an empty mess tin.

"What are you doing?"

"Looking for clean water. I feel disgusting. One thing I can't stand is not being able to clean my teeth in the morning." He grinned at her. "I've lost a few at the back thanks to the Russians. I fancy holding on to the remainder." He bent down and scooped some water up from the ditch.

"What's your name?" she asked.

He stood up abruptly and looked at her in bafflement. "What's that got to do with my teeth?"

She laughed. "Nothing. I was thinking last night that I don't know your name."

"Johan Breitner." He spread his arms out and gave a half-bow as if formally introducing himself.

"Trudy Heppel." She joined in his game by giving a brief curtsy.

"Pleased to make your acquaintance, Fraulein Trudy Heppel."

"The pleasure's all mine, Leutnant Johan Breitner."

He gestured towards the lorry. "Shall we dine?"

After breakfast, they resumed their journey to nowhere. The truck struggled on the increasingly wet ground. Twice, they had to reverse and take a run-up to stop themselves becoming bogged down.

"I'll be seriously miffed if this track runs into nothing now," Johan muttered, as once again the wheels spun, spewing out clods of wet earth and sinking the truck further into the ruts. Trudy backed the lorry out of trouble and picked a piece of more solid ground. The drizzle turned into a steady downpour.

Johan glanced at the fuel gauge and then through the windscreen, searching for any sign of civilisation. "I reckon we only have enough diesel for another ten or twelve kilometres."

"There's something ahead." Trudy pointed. "There, to the right, down the slope. It looks like a lake."

The track led them towards the water.

"There's a hut."

Trudy stopped the truck and killed the engine.

They studied the cabin for a while. "Stay here. I'll check it." Johan jumped from the cab, went to the rear and emerged with the rifle. Trudy watched him cautiously approach using the cover of the trees. She scanned the surrounding area. Apart from the constant rumble of the distant battle to the east, and the gentle patter of rain falling on leaves, the forest seemed peaceful. He reached the hut and creeping to a small window, crouched and peered in. Seemingly satisfied, he made his way around before trying the door. It was padlocked. He turned and beckoned Trudy to approach.

As soon as she pulled up, he unclipped the trenching tool from its mount on the side of the truck. In seconds, he forced the lock and disappeared inside. She followed him in.

"What is this place?" Trudy looked around in surprise. From the outside the hut looked a rough and ready log cabin. Inside, it was cosy and neatly furnished. It was divided into three. A large stone fireplace dominated the biggest room, which had the feel of a small Stube. A solid wooden table lay alongside a bench seat. A small dresser, containing a few plates, mugs and basic cutlery, occupied the wall opposite the fire, and a large paraffin lamp hung from the beam of the high, open ceiling. A second smaller room, directly overlooking the lake, contained a single bunk bed with a hard, straw mattress. A writing desk upon which an ancient typewriter sat, its keys covered by a thin coat of dust, was placed in front of the window. The third room was a store.

"I reckon it's some rich man's fishing retreat." Johan said, holding up a couple of fishing rods. He pushed the store-room door open. It was full of all sorts of items: fishing equipment, wet weather clothing, pairs of waders, cast iron pans, a large iron slipper bath, a can of paraffin, balls of string, ropes, some bottles, and various cleaning implements.

The place smelt of a mixture of pinewood, burnt ashes, paraffin and the stale mustiness of a building left unoccupied for a long time.

"It's not been used for months, if not years." He pointed to the fireplace. "The ash is damp and this has rust." He wiped his finger around the inside of a large cast-iron cauldron that hung on a swivel over the fireplace.

"Any food?"

"Doesn't look like it." He gazed around. "We should make the most of this." He glanced at his watch. "We should stop here tonight and let the rain pass through." He looked at her. "What do you think?"

"It would only be a matter of time before we became bogged down."

"Decision made. You fetch the food, I'll light a fire."

An hour later, they sat on the bench seat feeling sated, watching the fire take hold.

"This feels like my home," Johan said, as he stared into the dancing flames.

"How long have you been away?"

"Five years at least." He absently scratched his neck.

"You shouldn't do that?"

"What?"

"Scratch."

"Why? The bloody things irritate the hell out of me."

"Because it makes me want to scratch too. It's like when someone yawns, you want to yawn as well."

He stared at her and then the fire. "It's time we de-loused ourselves," he suddenly announced. "We'll never get a better chance." He slid off the seat and went into the store, re-emerging with a bucket in each hand. He jerked his head back at the store-room. "See if you can find some soap in there and a scrubbing brush." He barged through the door and made his way to the lake. After several trips, the large iron cauldron was full and swung over the now roaring fire.

"I found a bar of carbolic soap and a nail brush," Trudy called, as he disappeared outside again.

"Excellent." He went to the truck and hauled the blankets out, before walking to the lake and submerging them. He returned to the cabin, looking pleased with himself. "That will drown the bastards."

"What about the lice on us?"

He grinned at her before hauling the slipper bath from the store. Trudy looked horrified. "You are joking!?"

He laughed. "Your choice. It's either this, a dip in an ice-cold lake or modesty and lice." He started to undo his shirt. "I know which I prefer." He dipped his finger in the cauldron. "It's getting warm." He laughed again as he saw her appalled expression. "Don't worry, I'll turn my back." He threw a few more logs on the fire.

Trudy found herself almost panicking with indecision. She looked around to see how she could at least preserve some privacy. Short of banishing him outside, there didn't seem to be any options.

"Do you want to go first?"

Johan's question threw her. "What do you mean?"

"The bath. It won't take both of us." He grinned and seemed to enjoy her discomfort.

"I, er, don't know. Yes, I suppose so."

He dragged the bath over to the fire. He dipped his finger in the cauldron again and quickly withdrew it.

Trudy felt dread replace panic as the moment of inevitability approached.

He dipped the buckets in the cauldron and filled the bath. "Get in before the water gets cold." He laughed when he saw the relief on her face as he disappeared through the door to replenish the buckets.

When he returned, Trudy was sat in the bath with her arms clutched around her knees. Her face was beetroot red, and it wasn't because of the heat of the water. To her surprise, he acted as if seeing a naked girl in a bath was nothing out of the ordinary. He threw the soap into the water. "You need to scrub your hair and the folds of your skin. That's where the little bastards like to snuggle down." He looked around. "Where are your clothes?"

320

She pointed at a neat pile on the bench. He picked them up and threw them in a heap by the fire. "These need to be boiled."

Trudy opened her mouth to protest but thought better of it. She concentrated on bathing herself instead, warily watching him out of the corner of her eye, but Johan kept his back towards her. After a few minutes she relaxed. The sheer pleasure of having a bath overcame her self-consciousness. She covered herself in soap, working up a thick lather and massaging it into her hair and scalp.

"Want a top-up?"

She looked up and met his eyes.

He held her gaze. "More hot water?"

She nodded, not trusting herself to speak.

He poured another bucket in. The feeling of additional warm water swirling around her body felt luxurious.

"You need to scrape the eggs from your hair. Do you want me to help?" He took her silence as acquiescence. He knelt behind her and systematically ran the nail-brush through her hair from her scalp to the tip of her tresses, slowly and methodically. Her initial shock from his touch evaporated as she allowed the sensuous massage to ease her tension. She became aware that he was talking to her.

"We'll have to boil everything to be sure we kill them all. They're tough little bastards."

"How did you get rid of them at the Front?"

"We didn't. The best we could do was control them." He chuckled. "At times, we were like a pack of apes picking lice off each other. Or we used candle wax or squeezed them between our fingernails." He moved around, and she felt his fingers lift the locks of hair around the back of her ear. "Do you know how the Russians get rid of lice?"

She tried to ignore his touch and focus on the question. "I've no idea."

"They take their uniforms off and bury them, leaving a little corner, say a cuff or the corner of a collar, poking out of the dirt. Then they pack down the soil."

She frowned. "How's that supposed to work?"

"The lice under the soil are suffocating. They make their way to the protruding collar. The Russians douse them with petrol and burn them."

Trudy turned her head to see if he was serious.

He held his hand up. "I'm telling the truth. Now keep still, I'm nearly finished."

She smiled to herself as she realised his talk was designed to relax and reassure her. He continued with his lecture on the various techniques soldiers used to kill lice. The British apparently believed washing in paraffin would do the trick. Until the High Command put a stop to the practice because too many Tommys' smoked. The consequences were sometimes catastrophic.

"Don't expect me to believe that," she said, laughing.

The water in the cauldron began to steam. Johan eased himself to his feet, picked up her clothes and threw them into the boiling water. He stripped off and added his own clothes, then carefully unwound the bandages covering the shrapnel and bullet wounds in his arm, chest and abdomen.

Trudy suddenly felt slightly stupid. He didn't seem at all bothered about being naked in front of her, and there was she acting like a prudish schoolgirl. He unclipped one of the curtains and gave it a good shake outside the front door before handing it to her. "Wrap yourself in that." He turned around and occupied himself by stirring the clothes in the boiling water. "Let me know when you're decent."

She stepped out of the bath and wrapped the curtain around her. "It's all yours." Despite the butterflies in her stomach, she tried to sound casual and focused on drying herself as Johan eased himself gently into the water.

"Here's where I find out if I'm still waterproof.' He winced from the pressure on his wounds. Having settled himself, he let out a contented sigh. "Do you know, it's months since I had a proper bath."

She sniffed. "I didn't like to say, but…!"

"You didn't need to. There were times I could smell myself."

She moved to the bench, sat down and watched him.

Johan lathered himself and vigorously scrubbed his body with the nail brush. Finally, he took a deep breath and eased himself under the water. He stayed submerged for a full minute before breaking the surface. "That will finish-off the little sods." He held out his hand for her to throw him the other curtain. After discretely drying himself, he wrapped the curtain around his waist and stepped out of the bath. He stood directly in front of her, a broad grin across his face. "How good does that feel, eh?" He rubbed his hand through his beard. "Shame there isn't a razor."

Suddenly, the boiling cauldron overflowed, sending water cascading into the fire. He swung the cradle to remove it from the heat, then rummaged around in the storeroom, emerging with a length of rope. Between them, they lashed a clothes line to the roof beams and hung up the wet clothes. They worked in companionable silence. He began to hum; a folk song from his village, Trudy assumed. The fact that bathing in his presence hadn't resulted in anything worse than embarrassment eased her tension. He seemed a decent sort, she decided.

She noticed a thin trickle of blood seeping from one of his wounds as he stretched to throw his trousers over the rope, and felt a wave of concern. "Stop! You'll burst your stitches."

Johan glanced down and wiped the blood with his hand. "Damn it. I threw the old bandages in the cauldron to be boiled."

She made up a wad from the first aid kit. "Hold this against it."

He did as he was told, while she found the original dressing and hung it close to the flames to dry. "It won't take long."

"So, what shall we do in the meantime?"

"Are you hungry?"

He shook his head. "We ought to get to know one another better." He moved along the bench. "Sit down and tell me about your life."

She settled herself beside him at the table, rested her chin on her hands and gave him a sideways look. "Where do you want me to start?"

"Your earliest memory."

For the next two hours they exchanged their life stories. The more they talked the easier the conversation became. Mid-way through, he got up and retrieved one of the bottles from the store.

"No idea what it is." He held the bottle up to the light. "Could be wine or Schnapps or weedkiller. Shall we chance it?

"Why not?" She searched for a glass. "There's only one wine glass and one Schnapps glass. Whoever owns this hut clearly prefers his own company." She placed the glasses on the table and sat on the bench, drawing her legs underneath her so she faced Johan.

"It's some sort of wine," he said, as he sniffed the bottle. "Elderflower, I'd guess." He poured a drop in her glass and waited for her to sample it.

"It's okay," Trudy declared, and held her glass for it to be filled. "Prosit!" she said. They touched glasses. They held each other's gaze. "Tell me about your village," she said to get them back on track.

So began another hour's chat. The wine helped them further relax. It felt like they'd enjoyed a good Sunday meal and settled themselves for an afternoon's conversation. They laughed a lot. Things only turned serious when Trudy told him about the Hamburg raid, and he related the fate of the Rubensteins and his experiences on the Eastern Front. He lit the paraffin lamp as she turned the clothes round on the line and threw another couple of logs on the fire. It was dark by the time they'd finished the wine.

"You've had a tough life," Johan said.

"So have you."

He shook his head. "I've had a good life - just a tough war. I've been lucky. I survived."

"We both have." She leant back. "God knows what the future holds."

He was silent for a bit as if considering the matter. He opened his mouth as if about to say something, then thought better of it. "Take each day as it comes." He glanced at his watch. "We ought to get some sleep."

"You should bind your wounds." Trudy pulled a dried dressing from the line. "Stand up, I'll wrap it around you."

Johan did as she asked and was immediately conscious of her proximity as she wound the bandage around his stomach and across his shoulder and chest. His throat constricted and he struggled to catch his

323

breath as her fingers traced the edge of the gauze across his stomach, while she straightened the twists and creases. He felt her hair brush against his back, and the closeness of her face to his, as she replaced the dressings for his arm and head wounds.

Her eyes met his as she finished the task. "All done," she said.

He managed to keep his voice steady. "Thanks." He picked up the empty glasses and nodded towards the small bedroom. "You take the bed. I'll stretch out on the bench."

She appreciated the gesture. However, mid-way through the night, she woke feeling cold and shivery. The fire died, and the temperature in the bedroom dropped. She heaved the mattress off the bed and dragged it in front of the fire. She scraped the ashes with the poker, threw on a couple of logs and settled herself to resume her sleep. She found herself looking directly at his sleeping form, and the memory of the day came flooding back. It had been a wonderful day, she decided. He'd been great company. More than that, he was kind and considerate. She cringed as she recalled her coyness. She'd loved his touch. She closed her eyes and relived the feeling of his fingers running through her hair. The shock of seeing him naked, and the firmness of his body as she'd dressed his wounds, felt bizarre. She'd seen hundreds of men in all sorts of undress in the hospital, and yet there was no denying the thrill she felt with him. She felt the chilliness leave her body to be replaced by a warm feeling of contentment.

The rain abated by lunchtime the following day.

"When shall we leave?" Trudy gazed at the still overcast sky.

"Are you in a rush?" He smiled at her.

The truth was she was in no hurry at all. They'd ended up in an oasis of peace and tranquillity. She closed her eyes and soaked up the atmosphere of the forest. "Listen." She grabbed his arm and felt him tense.

"No, I mean just listen."

He looked at her in confusion. "I can't hear anything."

"That's the point." She gave his arm a squeeze and gazed at him, her eyes gleaming. "There's no noise, no sound of guns."

Johan cocked his head and concentrated. The forest was perfectly still.

"What do you think it means?'

He grimaced and pressed his lips together, as he considered this. "Could be anything - the Russians have withdrawn or there's a lull in the fighting. It might be that a change in the wind direction is taking the sound in another direction." He became aware of her arm entwined with his.

"I've never heard silence go on for this long."

He only half-listened to her. The warmth of her arm seeped into his senses. He stood stock-still, unwilling to risk any movement that might break the exquisite feel of her contact.

At that moment she too became aware of her spontaneous intimacy. She looked embarrassed. "Sorry," she muttered, and slipped her arm from his.

"Don't be." He smiled.

Trudy looked awkward. "Shall we leave?"

He took his time responding. "The ground is still saturated. If we left now, we'd only get bogged down. We should make the most of our good fortune. Fill ourselves with food, grab a good night's sleep and leave tomorrow, if it's dry." He studied her face for a reaction. " What do you think?"

She didn't hide her relief. "Makes sense. I like it here; I feel like I'm being recharged."

"In that case, let's recharge ourselves even more." He held his hand out. "Shall we dine?"

"Again?" she laughed. For some reason she felt extraordinarily happy.

They ate well and once again fell into easy conversation. This time they exchanged their likes and dislikes.

"I enjoy dancing, Café and Kuchen, a quality wine, getting dressed up for a party, a good book but dancing most of all." Trudy suppressed a smile. "Go on. Your turn."

"Ah! I'd love to say dancing, but I was told many times by almost everyone in my village that I was the worst dancer ever."

"That doesn't matter. If *you* enjoy it, that's what matters."

"I suppose I like dancing with someone who makes my efforts look good."

"What else?" She looked at him, her eyes dancing with delight. Each revelation peeled back another layer of his personality. And she found herself increasingly captivated.

"Men things, obviously - being with my mates, having a beer in the Gasthaus after a long, hard week. My mum's cooking, especially her Zwiebelrostbraten. Singing... oh, and pigs, or rather piglets!"

She arched her eyebrows. "Piglets!?"

He nodded enthusiastically. "Piglets are adorable; they are bright, intelligent little creatures, very affectionate, and they are quite clean. They'd make better pets than dogs."

"You're pulling my leg?"

"I'm not. Honestly, they are the most misunderstood of all animals. Added to that, they make great sausages."

She gave him a playful shove. "You don't mean that."

Later that night, Trudy replayed their conversation and Johan's mannerisms in her mind as she snuggled under the now lice-free blankets. He laughed easily. She ought to have guessed from the laughter lines on the edges of his eyes. She could picture his family and village from his vivid description. She envied him his childhood, so different from her own. She sneaked a look at him. He lay on his back on the bench with his arms stretched out above his head. He looked totally relaxed.

She didn't realise his apparently tranquil posture masked an inner turmoil. He couldn't get her out of his head. Throughout their conversation, despite all their shared laughter, it seemed to him she was a lost soul. At times he caught her unguarded moments, when an expression of melancholy briefly flashed across her face or she looked wistful. He tried to imagine what it must be like to be alone in the world, and failed. Most of all he was troubled by his own feelings when she had unconsciously linked her arm in his. To him, it felt like an electric shock. In fact, when he came to think about it, every time they made physical contact, he'd felt something undefinable. He struggled to explain it - a meeting of spirits or some kind of chemistry. Once again he thought about the afternoon, dwelling on small incidents, conversations, or her expressions that filled his heart. She was enchanting, that was for sure. With that thought, he turned over and tried to force his mind to leave her be.

"I'm sorry to be leaving that little hut," Johan said, as the truck heaved itself up the track.

"Yeah, it was our little haven." He caught a sad, wistful expression on Trudy's face that tugged at his heartstrings. For a second, he thought about suggesting they stay for another day or so. As the idea entered his head, an image of Russian infantry pouring through the trees snapped him back to reality.

"This section of the trail has been used more often. This must have been the main drive to the hut. Keep your eyes peeled, I'm guessing this leads to a main road."

After twenty minutes the truck engine spluttered and died. They looked at each other in dismay.

"We should have something to eat," Johan said.

"We've only just eaten!"

"Trudy, if there is one thing that has kept me alive over the past five years, it's that I ate and drank whenever the opportunity arose. We can't carry the food so the best thing to do is eat it while we have the chance."

They filled their stomachs before contemplating moving on.

"It's a waste." Trudy cast a forlorn glance at the tins of abandoned food.

"The whole bloody war has been a waste," Johan muttered. He eased himself into his backpack, wincing as the straps cut into his wound, then swung his rifle over his shoulder. "You ready?"

She picked up the two rolls of blankets and, despite her nervousness, gave him a smile of encouragement. "Let's go into the unknown."

They'd only walked for twenty minutes when he suddenly held his hand up and dropped to a crouch. She sank down beside him. "What is it?"

"Listen."

They strained their ears. Through the forest came the sound of engines and the distinctive clatter of tank tracks. Johan slipped off his pack.

"Stay here." He glanced around. "Get yourself under cover. Hide under that fallen tree and don't come out until you hear this." He gave a low two-note whistle. He helped her crawl under the trunk, then covered her with some broken branches and foliage.

Trudy lay still, hardly daring to breathe. The distant sound of tanks became obvious now she was aware of their presence. She pressed herself into the dark, damp soil, squeezed her eyes shut and prayed, "Please don't let it be Russians." She could feel her pulse thumping in her head. She kept glancing at her watch. He'd been gone twenty minutes, then thirty. After forty minutes she convinced herself he'd been captured. She imagined Russian soldiers creeping their way towards her through the trees. An image of Dagmar's fate caused her to break out in a cold sweat. Her heart froze as she heard the soft crunch of boots on the gravel track, then she felt overwhelming relief at the sound of his whistle. He dropped the rifle and held out his hands to help her to her feet.

"Is it the Russians?"

Johan shook his head. "There are a lot of refugees, and tanks I've not seen before. I think they are Americans."

"They can't be. They were at least a hundred kilometres to the west."

He rubbed his beard. "I know. Unless they've moved bloody fast. It makes no sense."

"What shall we do?"

He looked at her. "What do you want to do?"

"What do you mean?"

"If they get me, they will either shoot me or take me prisoner." He looked gravely at her. "If they take you…" He left the statement hanging in the air. "We could stay hidden in the woods and try and make it back to our lines."

"Go back to where we came from?"

He nodded.

She shook her head emphatically. "We know that's where the Russians are." She grabbed his hands in both of hers. "I'd prefer to take my chance with the Americans."

"Sure?"

"Yes, as long as we stay together."

"That might not happen."

"We'll have to chance it."

He stared into her face. "Let's get this over with." He picked up his rifle and they set off.

A few minutes later, they emerged from the edge of the forest to be confronted by an endless column of bedraggled refugees, who walked with grim-faced resignation, heads hung low, looking exhausted and beaten. The sight of Trudy and Johan hardly registered. On the opposite side of the road, a column of tanks suddenly appeared. Instinctively, Johan and Trudy ducked behind a tree and watched their approach. Half a dozen soldiers hung on the turrets. As they passed by, they threw items to the refugees. The children responded with shrieks of delight, making the soldiers laugh. In less than a minute, the last of the tanks had rumbled by in a cloud of dust.

Johan jumped down to the road and picked up a few items the children had missed. He held them up as Trudy joined him. "Chocolate." He held up another item. "Chewing gum." He threw them towards a couple of youngsters riding atop a farm cart piled high with pots, pans, bedding, battered trunks and an ancient sewing machine. "Must be Americans," he said, "Russians don't have this stuff." They stood to one side and watched the column pass. "We might as well join them. Safety in numbers."

A few minutes later, a couple of half-tracks sped past, followed by a dozen trucks crammed with infantry, their faces peering out the back. The troops appeared in good humour. They shouted and cheered as the children caught the gifts that emerged in showers from the back of each truck.

Despite the desperate circumstances of the refugees, the atmosphere felt relaxed.

"What's going on?" Trudy looked bemused.

Johan sounded perplexed. "I'd say we've accidentally crossed into enemy-occupied territory."

"I'll ask." Trudy turned to approach the refugee family behind them. As she did so, a Jeep hurtled past. It suddenly skidded to a halt and reversed at speed until it was level with Johan. Immediately, two soldiers in the back swung a heavy mounted machine gun towards him.

"Drop the weapon, now!" one screamed at him.

Johan didn't need any encouragement. His rifle clattered to the ground.

"Hit the deck." The soldier waved his palm to ensure Johan got the message. Immediately, the driver dismounted and roughly patted Johan's prone body.

"Turn over."

Johan winced as the soldier's hands thumped into his wounds.

"Stand up and put your hands on your head." The soldier looked mildly concerned as he watched Johan struggle to his feet. "You got a problem?"

"A few bullet and shrapnel wounds."

"Take off your shirt." He watched as Johan painfully removed his shirt. The soldier watched him warily. "Arms on your head." He scrutinised Johan's left armpit.

"I'm not a member of the SS, if you're looking for their tattoo."

The soldier continued with his inspection. "You speak English?"

Johan nodded. "I understand you perfectly."

The American looked confused. "You English?"

"No. I'm Austrian. My mother is English."

"How come you're in this column?"

"We were separated, following an air raid on our convoy. We travelled through the forest and came out on this road about a kilometre or so back. You can find our truck in the woods."

The soldier immediately looked suspicious. "We? How many of you are there?"

Johan glanced towards Trudy. "Just my wife and I."

"Your wife!?"

"She's a nurse." He gave a meaningful glance at his bandages. "She and I met in the hospital."

He glanced disbelievingly at Trudy, then back at Johan. "The dame's not in a nurse's uniform."

"Luftwaffe searchlight regiment, transferred to nursing duties."

"She looks nervous."

"So would you be if you were a woman and the Russians were in the neighbourhood."

"Bastards," the soldier muttered.

"That's an understatement."

"Your English is very good."

"Better than yours!" Johan met the GI's eye. "A Dame is a member of the British nobility," he said, grinning.

"Wise guy, eh?"

Johan thought it best not to say any more.

"Get in the Jeep."

"Not without my wife."

The soldier rolled his eyes. "Of course not without your wife. Jesus! You're one lippy Kraut."

They drove past the refugees for a couple of kilometres before arriving at a village, and a military roadblock set up beside what appeared to be the settlement's only Gasthaus The Jeep pulled up outside, and the soldier ushered Johan and Trudy inside.

"What's happening?" Trudy whispered.

"I don't know. By the way, you're Frau Breitner."

"What?!"

"You're my wife. We met and got married at the hospital, if they interrogate you." He shrugged and threw his hands out, indicating that was the best he could come up with.

She didn't get a chance to respond. The door opened and Johan was beckoned through. Trudy was offered a chair by the window. She sat there for over three hours, getting increasingly worried. She occupied her time by watching the scene outside. The Americans had set up a checkpoint. As the refugees arrived, they were forced to pass down one side of the road. Half a dozen soldiers on either side scrutinised every face. They occasionally pulled a vehicle over for a more thorough search. She saw a couple of men and a woman being led away, she assumed for a more thorough investigation. Later on, some unarmed Wehrmacht soldiers passed through. The Americans ordered all of them to strip off their shirts. Trudy was puzzled. The German troops were not under any armed guard. What intrigued her further was that having passed the inspection, the Americans were happy to share their cigarettes with their enemy.

Eventually, the door opened and Johan stepped through, accompanied by the soldier from the Jeep and an American officer who looked like a bank clerk. To Trudy's relief, Johan looked relaxed.

"Sorry to keep you waiting so long, Frau Breitner."

For a second, Trudy was thrown by his schoolboy German. She smiled her thanks. "What's happened?" she asked anxiously.

Johan smiled broadly. "Germany has surrendered, Hitler's dead and the war is over." He held open his arms.

Trudy took the cue and rushed to embrace him. It wasn't an act. She was relieved to see him and thrilled by the news. His kiss, however, startled her. That wasn't an act either – at least not on Johan's part. He'd endured an intense interrogation, and all the time his mind revolved around what was happening to her. His relief on seeing her released his pent-up emotions. Right at that moment, she was the only thing he wanted to see.

"So, what happened?" She adjusted and fiddled with her hair to mask her surprise.

"Captain Swann needed to be reassured I am who I say I am. My rank, regiment, where I served, who my commanders were, which front I served at, where I saw action."

"I'm sorry, Frau Breitner, but there are a lot of bad men that are trying to stop capture."

"You speak the language well," Trudy said politely.

"I do, Ma'am. But not as well as your husband speaks English."

"They want me to help them for a few days as an interpreter," Johan said.

"We're short on German speakers. I am the only one on this check-point." Captain Swann looked apologetic. "It's only for some days until better German speakers arrive. Then we'll help you with your trip back home, as a thank you."

"Where will we stay?"

"We'll fix you a room upstairs, Frau Breitner. You'll be well looked after. You have my word."

Behind the Captain's back, Johan raised his eyebrows and beamed at her.

Once they were alone in the room, they looked at each other for a second before falling into each other's arms in an excited celebration.

"No more war. Hitler dead. The Nazis gone. I can't believe it!"

"And you've got yourself a wife."

"Ah, yes. Well, that *is* a surprise!"

"That's an understatement."

He furrowed his brow. "I know it sounds drastic, but honestly, Trudy, what else could I do? The thought of being forced to abandon you terrified me. I had to think of something."

She stayed silent for a while, then reached up and kissed him on the nose.

"You don't mind?"

She looked to one side and shook her head, not trusting herself to speak in case she burst into tears. Nobody apart from Tante Bri and Katerina had demonstrated they cared that much about her. She felt overwhelmed. The truth was she'd been petrified when the Americans had pointed their guns at him.

A knock on the door startled them out of their embrace.

"Come in," Johan called.

A young American soldier stood holding a couple of kit bags. "Begging your pardon, sir, Ma'am, but Captain Swann ordered me to give you these."

Once he'd gone, they tipped the contents on the bed. A US Army issue wash bag and a pair of US Army pyjamas tumbled out.

"A razor, toothpaste and a proper toothbrush." Johan held each item up as if it was cast in solid gold. "Where's the bathroom?"

As soon as he disappeared, Trudy sat on the bed, burst into tears and let her emotions run unchecked. It felt good to let go. Initially, she didn't know why she wept but gradually reasons emerged. Partly it was sheer relief from all the horrors she'd endured. Between her sobs she recognised relief and joy. She was no longer alone in the world. She'd found Johan, and he had showed her he cared. As soon as the realisation entered her head, it was chased away by doubt. He had a family and a place he could call home, whereas she was heading where? To some unknown location in the hope of meeting up with Franz, who she assumed would want to meet her. It felt like she was taking two steps forward, knowing in all probability she'd be forced to take three back.

The sound of Johan's singing floated along the corridor. She found herself smiling - his good humour acted as a pick-me-up. She wiped away her tears and pulled herself together. They were in a situation, and she resolved to do her bit to make the best of it. She needed to toughen up.

He entered the room with a dramatic flourish. He threw his hands out as if presenting himself to an expectant audience. "The new, rejuvenated, improved, reborn Johan Breitner."

She laughed and gave him some applause.

"What do you think?" He bent down and admired himself in the dressing table mirror. "I'd forgotten what I looked like clean-shaven."

"You look very handsome," she said.

He looked back at her to see if she was serious.

"I mean it." She stood up and leant her face beside his. They stared at their reflection.

"Look at yourself though," he said softly. "That's real beauty."

Despite her resolve, she felt a lump in her throat and tears welled up. "Stop it, Johan," she murmured. "It'll go to my head."

"You can't stop me telling the truth." He grinned at her embarrassment. "We ought to eat now."

"Johan! Is food all you think about?"

"I do when it is being provided by the Americans for free."

"I'd like to freshen up first."

"I'll meet you downstairs."

Later, she surprised herself when they returned to their room. "What are you doing?" she asked, as he pulled the counterpane off the bed.

He looked puzzled. "Making up a bed. You're not hogging all the covers, are you?"

"No! Of course not."

"I'll stretch out here." He jerked his chin towards the floor beside the bed.

"You won't. You'll sleep in the bed." Trudy said firmly. "Whoever heard of a husband and wife in separate beds." She made light of it; however, her heart pounded. It seemed so scandalous. What she did next astounded her even more. She got undressed! - although she kept her back towards him. There was such a thing as decorum after all. She clambered into bed. Her bright red face peeped over bedclothes she'd drawn to her chin. "Don't try anything!" she said, as he slipped under the sheets beside her. "Not that you would," she added quickly, as she saw Johan's hurt expression.

He leant back on the headboard with his hands behind his head. "We've landed on our feet again."

"Maybe we're just lucky. We've both had near misses and come through okay."

"I can't believe how friendly the Americans are. It makes you wonder what the war was all about."

"What do they want you to do?"

"Help arrest Nazi leaders, members of the SS, concentration camp guards, anyone they think might be guilty of war crimes. They've caught a few hiding in amongst the refugees or disguising themselves as ordinary soldiers." He looked across at her. "I'm to help with interrogations."

She looked alarmed. "Not torture!"

He laughed. "No, just questioning to see if their stories check out."

They were quiet for a bit. "Funny things, wars," he said, breaking the silence.

"Why do you say that?"

"Good things happen in amongst all the bad."

"Like what?"

"Well, you and I wouldn't have met for a start."

She smiled under the covers. "Yeah."

The silence returned.

"You know that game we played in the fisherman's hut."

"What, the one where we listed our likes and dislikes?"

"Yeah."

"What about it?"

"Well, I reckon you make my list - of likes, I mean."

"Really?" She looked across at him.

"Yes, I reckon you come ahead of my Ma's Zwiebelrostbraten." He was quiet for a bit, then said, "But not as high as the piglets – obviously."

Trudy nudged him playfully in the ribs. "You're quite high on my list, you know."

"Hey, maybe we should get married." He leant over and kissed the top of her head. "Good night, Frau Breitner," he chuckled, before snuggling under the sheets.

She couldn't stop smiling.

"It takes a while to get used to them."

"The Americans or the refugees?"

"The Americans." The Gasthaus owner's wife bent her head towards Trudy and lowered her voice. "They are loud, always smoking, chewing gum, and they don't seem to be able to survive the day without having music blaring away."

"I like the music."

She pulled a sour face. "I suppose we'll have to tolerate them."

"Better than having to deal with Russians." Trudy looked through the window at the seemingly endless procession of tired, desperate-looking humanity. The two women gazed in silence, both wondering what tales of horror and despair lay behind the exhausted faces.

"This won't do," the landlady said abruptly, as if clearing her conscience. "I'll fetch that dress for you." She disappeared towards the back of the inn.

Outside, the American soldiers lounged about, smoking, chatting among themselves and casually observing the passing cavalcade. They only sprung to life when groups of their defeated enemy turned up. Officers, those in an SS uniform or anyone who looked suspicious, were immediately separated and led away for questioning. Ordinary Wehrmacht soldiers could expect cigarettes and some mild banter.

A civilian in a battered leather hat caught her eye. He sat with the rest of his family on a wagon, immediately behind a column of refugees. Something about his demeanour struck Trudy as odd. While everyone else focused on the children, who were running alongside the wagons, laughing, shouting and holding out their hands for the expected largesse of sweets, he sat looking morose. A GI swooped a child up in his arms and threw him into the air, before reaching into his pockets and producing several Hershey bars. A melee of over-excited youngsters quickly surrounded the soldier, begging for a similar treat. In an instant, soldiers were throwing youngsters over their shoulders, up in the air or swinging them around by their arms in a glorious merry-go-round.

Like everyone else, Trudy became absorbed by the spectacle of shrieking children. By chance, she glanced back at the man. He sat with his head bowed, his face turned away from the GI's but facing Trudy. She gasped in shock. A jagged scar ran from his forehead, over the bridge of his nose and across his left cheek.

"I think this will fit you."

Trudy swung around to see the landlady holding up a gingham dress and admiring it in the light. "It's hardly been worn." She held it up against Trudy. "You're very slim. It will need some taking in."

"I can do that and any other sewing or mending you want doing, if you like."

The landlady looked pleased. "I'll take you up on that. My fingers are getting too arthritic. I'll fetch you my sewing box."

Once she'd left, Trudy peered out the window. The cart had passed through the checkpoint, and only the top of a hat was visible above the pile of household items. She felt conflicted. She had no desire at all to have anything to do with Lothar, if indeed it was him. Already doubts started to creep into her mind. On the other hand, he was a link with her old Hamburg neighbourhood. He might know what had happened to Tante Bri. If she was quick, she could probably catch up with the wagon.

The approach of Captain Swann and Johan, in earnest conversation, interrupted her indecision. They entered the room, still debating something in English.

"Ah, Frau Breitner. I was telling your husband that hamburgers were invented in America. He insists they are named after the city of Hamburg. As a native of that city, you can settle the argument."

"I'm afraid my husband is correct, Captain. Although I think the Americans put the meat into a bun. So, I guess you are both right."

Johan picked up the dress. "For you?" he asked.

She nodded vaguely.

He noticed her distraction. "Something up?"

"I've just had the oddest experience. One of the refugees looked exactly like someone I used to know in Hamburg."

"A friend?"

Trudy grimaced. "Absolutely not! The man is a disgusting piece of work. He's a criminal. Everyone hated him."

"What's he doing this far east?"

She shook her head. "I've no idea. I might be mistaken. It might not be him. The man I knew joined the SS. This man was dressed as a civilian."

Captain Swann showed immediate interest. "He's SS?"

"Yes. I'm certain that's what my Aunt told me. He joined early in the war. Some special unit. The Einsatz I think it was called."

"The Einsatzkommando?" The Captain looked astounded. "Where is he? What does he look like?" He was already halfway out the door.

"He's on a cart, large leather hat," she shouted after him.

She and Johan moved to the window to see Captain Swann yelling at the GI's to chase after the cart, which was already out of sight.

"What time do we have to be ready?"

"Whenever you like. As far as Captain Swann is concerned, you're his heroine."

"I'd no idea Lothar was such a prize for them."

"He's on their most wanted list. Will you keep still!" He sat back on his haunches and glared at her in exasperation. "I can't put these pins in if you keep dancing about."

"Sorry." Trudy looked contrite. "What will happen to him?" she said, after a while.

"Put on trial and hanged, I guess." He stood up. "All done."

Without a second thought, she pulled the dress up over her head, being careful not to dislodge the pins. She'd grown so used to his company that she no longer felt bashful being in her underwear in front of him. She sat in front of the dressing table, threaded a needle and started to put the darts in.

Johan couldn't stop himself from casting surreptitious glances at this stunningly beautiful girl. He'd spent long glorious minutes studying every contour of her face as she slept. Now the rest of her body was partly uncovered, he found himself flustered. He stood up, walked to the window and stared out, to distract himself. For the first time, the road outside was free from refugee traffic.

"How far will they take us?"

"I didn't ask. So long as it takes us nearer to Austria, and not to a prisoner of war or refugee camp, I'm not fussed."

She fell silent.

He knew what she was thinking. He turned around and leant on the windowsill. "You need to think about what you want to do," he said gently.

She buried her head in her sewing. The speed of her stitching indicated her anxiety. "I'm not certain about anything. So far, I've landed on my feet. Maybe I'll stay lucky."

"That's not a plan."

"It's as good a plan as all those refugees have got."

"They've got nowhere to go."

"Neither do I." She turned the dress over in her lap and stared at it as if the enormity of the void of her future had suddenly opened up in front of her.

"That's not true."

She lifted her head and gave him a questioning look.

"You should come with me. You can stay with my family until you find your bearings."

"You're being kind. You'll have enough on your plate and I'm sure your family don't want to be burdened."

He held her gaze. "Let me put it another way, Trudy. I'd like you to come with me, and I'm not being kind, I'm being selfish." He grinned. "I can't see myself waving a handkerchief at you in some railway station."

"What are you saying?"

Johan's grin got broader. "Let's just say that the piglets no longer have top spot."

She smiled back at him. "You're in top place yourself, you know."

"Is that a yes, then?"

She nodded. It felt as if a massive weight had been lifted off her shoulders. At least she now had a destination. The feeling of relief was gradually replaced by something else. She stole a quick glance at him to find he was still grinning and staring at her. She felt a warm glow inside her and an overwhelming desire to drop the dress, get up and throw her arms around him. She'd never met a man like him. He was considerate, kind, amusing and physically attractive. There did seem to be a spark between them. The image he'd painted of waving goodbye to her was too horrible to contemplate. "What makes you think we won't be sent to a refugee camp?" she said, trying to sound casual.

He shrugged. "I can't be sure. But we represent no risk and can be easily repatriated, so there is little point sending us to a refugee or POW camp. And we've proved useful to them."

"What will we use for money?"

"Good question. I gave my Wehrmacht Reichsmarks to Captain Swann in exchange for American dollars."

"Why?"

"Dollars are always accepted, and Reichsmarks will become worthless. He wants them as a memento. He's collecting stuff to take back home. Apparently, an officer's Luger pistol is much sought after." He gave her a bemused look. "I know, it's crazy! In addition, he'll sort out some travel warrants. It's another reason to head for Austria. We'll not need money in my village."

Trudy stood up and examined the alterations, before throwing the dress over her head and pulling it down. "Can you do up the back."

Johan couldn't believe how distracting watching a girl putting on a dress could be. His eyes lingered on the smoothness of her skin, the curve of her back and the neatness of her waist. He slowly and reluctantly did up each button. The dress hugged her figure.

She stepped back and examined herself in the dressing table mirror, twisting and turning to check the fit. She turned and looked at her reflection over her shoulder. In that moment, she remembered doing exactly the same thing as a young girl in Tante Bri's apartment. She'd decided she was beautiful then. She smiled at the memory and glanced at Johan. "What do you think?"

He looked dazed. "I wish I could take a photograph."

She felt her throat constrict. He always found the right words. "You're a nice man, Johan Breitner."

"I'll feel a bit shabby next to you."

"You're handsome enough."

"You should see me without stitches."

"I can take them out if you want. They've been in for weeks." She rummaged around in the sewing box and waved a pair of scissors at him. "There're some tweezers in here as well. We really need some disinfectant."

Later that evening she waited for him to reappear from the bathroom. He arrived bare-chested and looking apprehensive. "You've done this before?"

She rolled her eyes and waved her hand dismissively. "You'll be fine."

He sat on the edge of the bed and steeled himself. "Let's get on with it."

"I'll take the ones in your head out first."

She slowly and methodically snipped her way along the neat line of stitches.

All the time, he was aware of her closeness as she bent over him: the clean scent of soap, her thigh pressing against his arm, a tantalising glimpse of her smooth stomach through a gap in her pyjamas. He could feel the warmth of her breath and the light brush of her hair against his face as she worked. He tried to focus on something else and failed. All that happened was the image of her sitting naked in the bath formed in his memory. He winced as she gently pulled a tough stitch out.

"Sorry," she whispered. "Last one." She stood back and looked concerned. "Are you all right?"

"Yes, why?"

"I could feel your hand shaking on my leg."

He had the irrational feeling that his inner thoughts had been exposed. "Just nervous tension."

She gave a half-smile. "Lie down, please."

He swung his legs up on the bed and lay flat on his back. Once again, Trudy got to work. Johan's torso was muscular and lean. She stole the occasional glance at his face as he lay still with his eyes closed. Despite his boyish looks, he had the physique of a man who was used to outdoor life and hard living.

The stitches came out easily. She carefully wiped the pink wounds with the handkerchief soaked in disinfectant. Once finished, she allowed her fingers to run through the hairs on his chest. She rested her hand on his heart. She could feel it pumping. She studied his face. He seemed peaceful and content. She couldn't decide whether she preferred him clean-shaven or with his beard. Her eyes were drawn to his lips, and she felt an urge to bend down and kiss him.

Johan opened his eyes. "All done?"

"They're healing up nicely. You'll always have the scars - something to show the grandchildren in your dotage." She put away the scissors and tweezers, then climbed into bed, looking thoughtful.

"You okay?"

She smiled at him. "Lots to think about."

"Like what?"

"Stepping into the unknown." She turned to face him. "When I was young, I yearned to travel - see other parts of Germany, big cities, the world. Now all I want is certainty and to feel safe."

"That's not surprising, given everything that's happened to you."

"Sometimes I feel like the stuffing's been knocked out of me."

He pulled the bedclothes to one side and eased himself in beside her. He lay on his back, put his hands behind his head and stared at the ceiling. "You're not alone feeling like that. Let's face it, almost every German, and Austrian for that matter, was told they were the master-race, all-powerful. For a few years, we regained our national self-respect. We pulled ourselves up by our bootstraps. Now look at us. Back to where we were after the Great War, only worse. Every German knows we were murdering the Jews. The Allies can do what they like with us."

"They can't put us all on trial. We're not all guilty."

He gave a cynical laugh. "I bet you'll have difficulty in finding anyone who'll admit they were a Nazi or voted for them. It will be their next-door neighbour, the man across the street, the woman in the top apartment." He sighed. "We're tarred by the same brush."

"I just want to disappear. Why couldn't we have stayed in that fisherman's hut?"

"That was our little bit of heaven."

She snuggled up to him as she relived the experience. "A small cosy hut, a big fire to keep us warm in the winter, and nobody bothering us."

"Yeah. Mind you, we'd have got sick of living out of tins."

"You could have caught some fish, shot a few deer."

His arm dropped around her shoulders as they reminisced. Neither noticed. It seemed natural. She instinctively made herself comfortable in the crook of his arm, her head resting on his chest.

"God, do you remember the lice?" She gave an involuntary shudder.

He laughed. "I've lived with them for years, and I can honestly say they are the most disgusting creatures on the planet. Worse than cockroaches."

"I wonder who owns the hut?"

"We've a mountain hut that's very similar."

She lifted her head and looked at him. "Really?"

He nodded. "I'll take you up there. You'll love it. It's almost exactly the same, except it's surrounded by meadows high up in the mountains. You can see all the surrounding mountain-tops. It's idyllic."

Their unconscious intimacy grew as their conversation developed. Her toes gently stroked his ankles; his fingers caressed her hair.

Gradually, a feeling of warm contentment and tiredness slowed their talk. She turned over, draped her arm across his chest and was soon asleep.

OCTOBER 1945 - BRANDT - AUSTRIA

"We're going to be too late." He looked again at his watch.

"There's no point worrying about it."

"I was hoping we could make it all the way."

She looked at him sitting in the seat opposite and shook her head. "I'm the one who's supposed to feel nervous. This is all new to me." She gestured at the foothills of the Alps that were sliding by outside the train carriage windows. "You're going home and yet the closer you get the more agitated you're becoming."

He groaned as again the train slowed to a halt. "What now?"

"Relax, Schatz. We'll get there."

It was just before ten when the train pulled into Brandt station.

"We've missed the last train, and also the last Postbus to Achbrugge." He threw their small kitbag on the ground in frustration. He glanced around, half expecting to see signs of the ravages of war. But even under the streetlights the town looked reassuringly familiar. If it wasn't for the presence of a group of French occupation troops lounging against their armoured car and nonchalantly smoking cigarettes, anyone could be forgiven for thinking that conflict had bypassed the town.

"We'll have to stay at a Gasthaus" He took her hand. "Fortunately, I know a decent one."

"Have we enough money?"

He dug in his pocket and retrieved the dollars. "If they don't accept these, I'm sure I can get credit. The landlord knows our family."

Ten minutes later, Johan had his first taste of a homecoming welcome.

"Johan Breitner! It's good to see you. Lotte, come and see who's here." Immediately, the landlord was joined by Frau Braun. "Mein Gott, you survived." Johan was engulfed in an enormous bear hug. "And who is this beautiful young lady?"

A look of panic seized Johan. In his haste to find accommodation, he hadn't thought through the consequences of introducing Trudy. "Er, um, this is… is…"

"I'm Trudy Breitner." Trudy held out her hand. "Pleased to meet you."

Frau Braun took a step back in astonishment. "Well, I never. I had no idea."

"So much has happened. Life is full of surprises," Trudy said smoothly.

"Yes, indeed." The landlady didn't bother to hide the fact that she could see neither an engagement nor wedding ring.

Trudy followed her gaze. Without batting an eyelid, she leant her head beside Lotte's and whispered, "Doesn't pay to wear anything valuable."

"Very sensible. These Rottkäppchen have been nothing but trouble since they arrived. You'll want a room?"

"With a bath, if you have one."

"Of course. Kitchen's closed, though." Frau Braun looked apologetic.

"No matter."

Herr Braun picked up the small suitcase and led the way up the stairs.

Johan waited until the sound of the landlord's footsteps faded. "I'm so sorry," he said.

"About what?"

"Putting you in that position. I didn't think."

She laughed "I recall you getting us married, but I don't believe we got divorced." She gave him a mischievous look. "Unless you're going to surprise me again."

"No, not at all." He sat on the bed, bent over and rubbed his head with his hands. "I guess I'm tired."

She peeled off her coat and smoothed her dress before sitting beside him. "You're not tired, you're stressed. Five years is a long time to be separated from your family. Things might have changed. Who wouldn't feel anxious?"

"Yeah, you're right. I kind of built myself up. And I should have anticipated problems with the trains."

"It's better this way. We'll wake up refreshed and tomorrow's a new day." She stroked his cheek with the back of her hand. "I need to take a bath. You should go and have a Pils, and relax."

Apart from a few locals and a group of off-duty French soldiers, the Gasthaus bar wasn't busy. Johan deliberately chose a quiet table in the back recesses of the room. Frau Braun was soon at his side to take his order. She returned quickly and placed a glass of clear, foaming Pils in front of him, before sitting opposite. "It's on the house." She reached over and rubbed his forearm. "A welcome back present."

Johan was surprised and pleased. The gesture instantly raised his spirits. "Thank you. It's much appreciated. Prosit!" He raised his glass.

"Heading for Doppelgau tomorrow?"

He nodded as he took his first sip. "My, that tastes so good." He wiped his lips. "Has much changed?"

She looked philosophical. "Nothing and everything." Her eyes flicked towards the French soldiers. "This lot turned up a few months ago."

"Doesn't seem to have been much damage caused."

"They just drove in. There wasn't any resistance, despite the views of a few Nazi fanatics." She threw open her arms to emphasise the obvious.

"The war was lost; most neighbourhoods hung white sheets from the windows. No point having more people killed."

"Got away lightly?"

"The first tanks drove straight through. They thought the fanatics might take to the mountains and continue fighting. The follow-up troops caused the problems." A look of disgust crossed her face. "They wanted revenge - their pound of flesh. For a couple of weeks, they strutted around the place, looting, beating people up they didn't like the look of or who gave them some lip. We had to barricade the doors to keep them out of here - otherwise, they'd have drunk the place dry."

"Seems quiet now." Johan looked around the bar.

"The Burgermeister had a go at the French commander. To be fair, he did act quickly. Confined troops to barracks and flooded the town with military police." She leant forward and lowered her voice. "Even so, I'd advise your wife not to go out alone – day or night." She glanced across at the French. "They're in charge now. We must hope for the best." She suddenly brightened. "Anyway, enough of them. It's good to have one of our boys back."

"Have many have returned?"

Her face fell. "Very few. It's early days. Rumour is it will take months, maybe years. Apparently, some are being held in camps in America and Canada. And God help any who were captured by the Russians, they probably got transported to Siberia."

Johan said nothing. He doubted the Russians packed any prisoner into transport. They'd make them walk, hoping most would perish on the journey.

"A few cases turned up in Brandt hospital." Lotte suddenly brightened. "Including someone you might know, as he comes from Doppelgau."

Johan felt his throat constrict. "Do you know who?"

Frau Braun beamed. "Young Jurgen Wachter." She cocked her head to one side. "I'm right in saying you know him?"

"Yes, I do." He managed to put his glass down without spilling it. "Do you know how he is?"

"Okay, according to his father." She softened her voice as she noticed Johan's reaction. "He lost an arm and has a bad head injury. But he'll recover in time, or so the doctors say." She patted his hand sympathetically.

Trudy was asleep when Johan returned to the room. For several minutes, he sat on the bed and gazed at her face. He gently brushed a wayward strand of hair from her eyes, then traced the curve of her nose with his finger. She had the relaxed breaths of someone in deep, contented sleep. He kissed the tips of his fingers before softly placing them on her lips, and climbed into bed, being careful not to disturb her.

He woke to the sight of her face pressed up to his own.

342

"Good morning, piglet," she whispered, smiling.

"Was I snoring?"

"Only a little."

"You should have given me a shove." He yawned and stretched his arms.

She snuggled up. "I slept like a baby. I feel so full of energy."

Despite her assertion, they were content to remain cuddled up in a blissful half-sleep.

"What time is it?" he said eventually.

"Seven forty. Did you have a good night?"

"I didn't stay long. Just the one glass." He cradled her against him.

"By yourself?"

"The landlady sat with me at first, but I was happy to be alone. Gave me time to think."

"About what?"

"You remember my friend?"

He felt her nod and tense up as if anticipating bad news.

"Well, he made it!"

She rolled over, her face wreathed in an enormous smile. "That's fantastic news." But she quickly turned serious. "Is he okay?"

"He has some bad injuries, but he's alive and strong. He's got a long battle in front of him."

"Oh, what fantastic news!" She spontaneously leant forward, kissed him on the lips, hugged him, then lay with her head nestling on his chest. A few seconds later, the realisation of her action sank in. Another line in their intimacy had been crossed. She lay perfectly still, wondering at herself and how he might react. She could hear his heart thumping, and feel the gentle stroke of his fingers as they caressed her hair and traced the nape of her neck. It felt so sensuous that she found herself wanting more. Her fingers began to gently stroke his skin.

"What else did you think about," she murmured.

"You, me – but mostly you."

She giggled. "That must have been nice."

"It was." His serious tone made her glance up at him.

"And?"

He stared at the ceiling and stayed silent.

She nudged him. "About what?" Her interest was piqued. She moved so she leant on his chest and could see his face.

"Us."

"Go on." A small frown appeared on her brow.

Johan paused for a bit as he gathered his thoughts. "I know it was a shock for you when I told that American you were Frau Breitner."

"You were being practical."

"Yeah, I know, but it was presumptuous."

Her frown increased. "What are you saying, Johan?" She sounded apprehensive.

"Well, I'd like to ask for your permission this time?" It was his turn to look anxious.

Trudy pulled herself up so she knelt beside him. "What exactly are you asking my permission for."

He looked nervous. "I'd like to be Herr Breitner."

"You already are!?" She looked confused.

He became flustered. "No, I mean I'd like to be Herr Breitner if you wouldn't mind being Frau Breitner – not for practical reasons this time, I mean... permanently."

"Is this your way of asking me to marry you?"

"I suppose it is."

"Well, why don't you come out and say it."

He looked confused. "I don't know really." He looked at her before making up his mind. "Frau... Trudy Heppel, would you please do me the honour of becoming my wife? – no, wait!" He clambered out of bed, took her hand and knelt in front of her. "Let me do it properly." He looked up at her. "Trudy Hep..."

"Yes."

"What?"

"I said, yes. I'd like us to be married."

"Oh! - Are you sure?"

She failed to stop herself laughing. "Yes, I'm sure. I'm very sure." She bent and kissed him gently on the lips. "You're an easy man to love, Johan."

"I made a bit of a mess of that, didn't I?" He looked sheepish.

She laughed. "It could have done with a rehearsal."

EXILE

He was Ferdinand Waldheim. He endlessly repeated the name in his head. Somehow, the past needed to be left behind as a new future beckoned. He glanced around at the other passengers leaning on the guardrail, craning their necks to get the first glimpse of the coast. He instinctively moved away. No one could be trusted. Throughout the two-week voyage, he'd rarely left the cabin. Now sanctuary was in sight. Just one more border to cross and then he could disappear. Argentina was a big country; he'd been tipped-off to head for the mountains of Patagonia and the remote town of San Carlos of Bariloche. Already a commune of the faithful had been established, and he and his family could expect a warm welcome. He dug in his pocket for his cigarettes and felt the letter. A bolt of shock passed through him. How could he have been so careless? Despite his caution, he couldn't resist one last look. It was the last link to the Fatherland. He read the neatly written instructions. A surge of rage ran through him as he read it. Fleeing like a common criminal, like a thief in the night. Spending two nights in a cold monastery cell as if he was a condemned soul. How had it come to this? He screwed up the letter and threw it overboard. Bloody Jews might think they've won, but he knew different: one day a new Reich would rise from the ashes.

He couldn't help wondering whether the mountains around San Carlos of Bariloche would remind him of Brandt.

HOMECOMINGS

"Are they expecting us?"

Johan grinned. "I've no idea. Last letter I sent went through the American military mail service. That was two weeks ago. Who knows what the postal system is like?"

"Oh my God, so they'll have no knowledge of me then?"

He stretched his arm around her shoulder and gave a squeeze. "I'll just say you're a penniless waif that I picked up."

She gave a half-laugh. "That's not far from the truth. Although I'm not completely destitute."

Don't tell me. You're really a Bavarian princess with three castles, and as an only child you'll inherit millions from a distant aunt."

"I wish!" She laughed, before turning serious. "I think I might have some money tucked away in a bank in Switzerland."

"In Switzerland!?" Johan looked astonished. "How much?"

She shrugged. "I've no idea. It was invested a long time ago."

"It doesn't matter. Let's assume that we're starting with nothing. That way, everything we do will be about building something."

The Postbus reached the top of the climb from Brandt, and the whole of the Brandtnerwald stretched out before them.

"They'll love you. And I can't think of a nicer surprise."

She gave a contented smile as her anxiety melted away. "It's so beautiful," she murmured.

"It gets better higher up the valley." He pointed to the distant mountains still capped by the remnants of snow.

She fell silent for a long time. Johan thought she was drinking in the passing scenery, until she suddenly spoke.

"Johan."

"What?"

She turned towards him. "I don't want to be an ordinary housewife."

"What do you mean?"

"I mean, I want to pay my way, so to speak. I don't think I'd be any good at this Kirche, Kuchen, Kinder business."

He gave her a puzzled look. "Why are you saying this?"

"It's just that we never talked about how we might live together, and I don't want us to get off on the wrong foot. I'm quite independent – always have been. I hate being in anyone's debt."

He studied her, and a half-smile played about his lips. "It's a new world, Trudy. If you think about it, we were a team right from when we first met. Every decision we made, we made together. I can't see any reason to change." He grinned. "Life will be tough for us to start off with – but in a good way. Then we'll build something fantastic, bit by bit, piece by piece, and we'll get closer each day – I just know it."

She hit him lightly on the arm to mask an overwhelming feeling of tenderness towards him. "Why is it that you always seem to know exactly what to say?"

He gave a dramatic sigh. "Genius, I suppose." He laughed before kissing her gently on the lips. "We'll work it out together," he said.

They dropped into a cosy embrace which lasted until they passed through Achbrugge. Then she felt his body tense as the excitement of anticipation grew within him. He craned his neck as familiar sights and landmarks flashed passed the windows. He was like a little boy on the way to a party. She tried to imagine what he was feeling and felt a pang of sadness that she wasn't able to share it. An image of Tante Bri and Katerina flashed across her memory. Her past was dead. But he was right. It was a new world, and she was determined to make a success of it.

Ten minutes later the Postbus swung into Doppelgau.

"My God! They're all here," Sep suddenly exclaimed. "My Pa and, oh my God, my Ma is here!" He swung around to face her, his face full of astonished delight. "My Ma's here. Can you believe it?" He was on his feet, leaning across her to wave at his family. "Jurgen's here as well, and, oh my God, that's my little niece. Look at her, Trudy. Isn't she just so cute? And there's my sister."

She found herself caught up in his excitement.

"There's Tante Josey and Stephan." He grabbed her hand and hauled her to her feet before the bus had come to a halt. "Come on, Trudy. Come and meet everyone."

She laughed. "Johan, our things!"

"What? Oh yes, quick!" He reached up and grabbed their coats and bag from the overhead shelf. "Come on." They stumbled and tripped their way out of the bus.

Trudy could hardly remember anything of the next five minutes. It seemed everyone was laughing, crying, throwing their arms around each other, shrieking and all talking at once. Her initial concern that she would be on the side-lines evaporated. Johan wouldn't let go of her hand, and she was dragged into the joyous melee. She knew she was being introduced, but it seemed the Breitner clan had simply made the assumption that, because she arrived with Johan, that was good enough. It was Harriet who suddenly realised the significance of Johan's revelation.

"Did you say Trudy is your wife?" she said loudly enough for everyone to realise that, in their excitement, they had missed something important. There was an expectant pause as Johan put his arm around Trudy's waist. "Ma, Pa, Harriet, everybody – this is Trudy Heppel, the most wonderful thing that has happened to me. She put me – and you too, Jurgen," he nodded towards his friend who stood leaning on his stick,

347

grinning from ear to ear, "back together again. And she did me the honour of agreeing to be my wife."

His announcement signalled another bout of euphoric crying and laughing. Trudy now found herself the centre of attention. She had no idea what was happening or who was who, until Harriet and Marie took it upon themselves to be her chaperones as the family made its way in a riotous cavalcade to the Breitner's farm.

They burst into the Stube to find a table already laid out for a feast.

"I've made all your favourites, my boy," Susan said, her face streaked with tears.

Johan found himself overcome. He stared around the room that in his eyes hadn't changed in the five years he'd been away. He could smell the Zwieblerostbraten, the pinewood smoke, the soup gurgling on the range, and a hint of sweet apples and pastry seeping from the oven. He embraced his Ma, partly to hide his tears. "It's so good to be home," he mumbled into her neck.

"Are we going to eat?' Gunter said, earning himself an exasperated look from Marie.

They settled themselves around the table. Amidst all the chatter, that washed across and around the table, little Simone sat on her Opi's lap, staring in wide-eyed wonder at Trudy.

Beneath his joy, Johan managed to hide a deep dismay. The stress of the war on the family was apparent in his parents' appearance. They'd both aged prematurely. His Ma attached herself to his arm and seemed unwilling to let go.

"How did you know we'd be on the Postbus?"

His mother smiled. "We got your last letter saying you were on your way, and we asked Frau Braun to keep an eye out. She phoned the Post Office."

"When did you come home?"

"Last week. I left England as soon as travel restrictions were lifted." She gazed fondly across the table at Trudy, who was in deep conversation with Harriet and Josey. "She's a beauty."

"You and her have a lot in common then."

His mother chuckled. "And you have your Pa's charm." She glanced up and gave a quizzical look. "Are you really married?"

"That's our intention. We just haven't got around to the technical bits."

"Oh, that's good. I wouldn't want to have missed out on a wedding."

"Apparently, the village has now got the perfect man for the job." Jurgen's slight slur indicated that he was still on the road to recovery.

"We should invite Father Haphold and Herman over," Sep said. "They ought to be part of our celebration."

Stephan was already rising from his chair. "I'll go and fetch them."

"Will we have enough food?"

Josey flapped her hand dismissively. "Relax, Susan. We can always use my stuff. I've got some torte, and we can always grab a chicken."

Stephan paused outside and smiled to himself as he listened to the laughter within. It had been a long time since the families had enjoyed such merriment. He lingered to soak up the feeling of well-being. He shook his head as Gunter's boisterous guffaw spurred him on his errand. As he walked briskly towards the village, the sight of a Jeep parked outside the Rubenstein's house caught his attention. A bewildered-looking naval officer leant on the steering wheel, staring at a group of excited youngsters chasing the chickens around the pen. Stephan concluded he must be lost. He'd help him out if he was still there when he returned, he decided.

Inside the Stube, Trudy was still the centre of attention.

"He made you get undressed!" Marie held up her hand to her mouth and shrieked with laughter.

"I didn't *make* her." Johan tried to explain. "The lice forced us to take drastic action."

"Well, I hope you had the decency to leave the room," Susan exclaimed.

"He was the perfect gentleman, Frau Breitner."

"Please, Trudy. You must call me Ma. You're family now."

"So, what happened next?" Harriet was eager to know the next stage in her brother's courtship.

Trudy looked across at Johan. "We fell in love. Well, at least I did at that point, I fell in love with him. He was so considerate."

The entire room erupted in a collective, "Aaaah."

"When did he propose? Did he get down on his knees?" Josey leant forward, rested her chin on her hands and looked expectant.

Trudy moved the tale on. Gales of laughter were interspersed with solemnity as she related the exposure of Lothar and the plight of the refugees.

The sound of the Stube door opening barely registered as the families became increasingly absorbed in Johan and Trudy's revelations.

"We would have arrived yesterday if…" Johan suddenly stopped and stared at the figure framed by the door.

"I hope I'm not interrupting." The man looked nervous. He swept off his officer's cap.

For a second there was absolute silence.

Harriet turned white and held her hands up to her head in shock. "Simon," she whispered and slowly got to her feet.

"I'd have written, but I was at sea and only returned from the Pacific last month. And the post is so unreliable." He twisted his cap in his hands in his anxiety. "I said I'd return, Harriet."

The room fell silent, disbelief etched on every face.

"I stopped by the house." He jerked his head towards the window. "It seems to be full of children. I suppose it's been taken."

He got no further as Harriet threw her arms around his neck and burst into sobs. "I was losing hope." The fierceness of her embrace startled him.

"I'm sorry, sweetheart. I couldn't write. I couldn't get any messages to you." He cradled her face and looked into her eyes. "Every day, I thought about you and what you must be going through."

"We had no news." Harriet's words came out in a strangled croak.

Everyone was now on their feet, looking stunned. "We thought you'd been caught, mate," Johan said.

"So did I." Simon didn't bother to try and wipe away his tears. "I was captured. Fortunately by Swiss Frontier troops." He paused to kiss Harriet on the lips. "I can't find words to describe my relief and happiness at that moment."

"Best moment in your life then?" Jurgen looked mischievous.

"No." Simon gazed into Harriet's eyes. "Second best moment."

"You sure?" Jurgen's grin couldn't get any broader.

"Jurgen, stop it!" Josey frowned at her son.

A look of confusion crept across Simon's face.

Harriet half turned out of her embrace and gently waved an encouraging hand for Simone to join them.

The youngster didn't need much persuading. She slipped off her Opi's lap and toddled to her mother, before burying herself in her skirt. "This is your daughter, Simon," she said softly.

"Oh my God!" He knelt down and grasped the tiny fist that gripped her mother's skirt with fierce determination.

The room was filled with an overwhelming spirit of joy. It coursed through everyone, seeping into every sinew and sense. The floodgates were opened as tears and laughter consumed the families.

Johan sought out Trudy, determined that they would share the bliss of the moment. For Trudy, it was as if she was experiencing a rebirth. The feeling of once more belonging within a loving household, that she felt had long been banished with the death of her beloved Tante Bri, rose up inside her. She felt lifted and ecstatic.

The war was over. The families were bruised, battered and scarred, but they had survived. Trudy shared a look with Johan. She could tell he was thinking the same as her. They belonged together, and nothing could stop their happiness.

FREEDOM

The first rays of sun kissed the great statue. It appeared everyone on board was on deck, eager to see the sight. For the thousands of GI's, it was the first glimpse of their homeland and their return to family and friends, baseball, the Superbowl, the Stanley Cup, Thanksgiving celebrations, and all that made the US of A the greatest country on Earth. For the hundreds of war-brides, it was the hope for rekindled passions and a new, more prosperous life. For the refugees, it represented hope and liberty.

For Franz Kaufmann, it was the promised land of blues, jazz and swing, and he couldn't wait to catch the Greyhound to Chicago to begin a life he'd always dreamed of.

OTHER PUBLICATIONS FROM G. L. VERNON

FALLEN HERO

G. L. Vernon

A TALE OF LOVE AGAINST THE ODDS, LOST INNOCENCE,
HUMOUR, TRAGEDY AND HUMANITY.

RETINA UK 50% of all royalties of this book will be donated to Retina UK, a
registered charity working to treat and cure sight loss

The acclaimed prequel to "RELUCTANT HEROES" is available on Amazon as Kindle, or paperback.

Search: www,amazon.co.uk/FALLEN HERO G L Vernon

"….so well written, I could see, hear and feel the atmosphere"

"…could not put the book down. This book should be 100% recommended."

"A Gripping Tale. "Fallen Hero" is a beautifully written debut novel that bounces seamlessly between the inconceivable horrors of WW1 and an idyllic childhood in the countryside."

"An enjoyable read from start to finish."

"Debut novel of outstanding warmth. Fallen Hero is an excellent story that lifts the spirits."

"A well written book that had me gripped from the moment I started reading. I hope this is the first of many."

"This book has hit every human emotion. It shows great humour that had me laughing out loud, also tragedy and love."

Visit www.vernonmedia.com to read further testimonials

The author welcomes all feedback. If you enjoyed this book, please leave a review either on the amazon website, Goodreads or via the contact page on www.vernonmedia.com, or e-mail the author on glvernon@vernonmedia.com.

Printed in Great Britain
by Amazon

59148831R00200